# A Touch mortal

LEAH CLIFFORD

Greenwillow Books
*An Imprint of* HarperCollins*Publishers*

This book is a work of fiction. References to real people, events, establishments, organizations, or locales are intended only to provide a sense of authenticity, and are used to advance the fictional narrative. All other characters, and all incidents and dialogue, are drawn from the author's imagination and are not to be construed as real.

 For information address HarperCollins Children's Books, a division of HarperCollins Publishers, 10 East 53rd Street, New York, NY 10022.
www.harperteen.com

The text of this book is set in 11-point Ehrhardt MT
Book design by Paul Zakris

Library of Congress Cataloging-in-Publication Data
Clifford, Leah.
A touch mortal / by Leah Clifford.
p. cm.
"Greenwillow Books."
Summary: Eden, once a lonely human who lost her heart to a fallen angel and now trapped between Heaven and Hell, discovers that her Touch can strip away the morals and logic of mortals, but may also be able to provide Siders like herself with release.
ISBN 978-0-06-200499-4 (trade bdg.) — ISBN 978-0-06-200500-7 (lib. bdg.)
[1. Future life—Fiction. 2. Angels—Fiction. 3. Demonology—Fiction.
4. Dead—Fiction.]
I. Title.
PZ7.C622148Tou 2011 [Fic]—dc22 2010011695

11 12 13 14 15 LP/RRDB 10 9 8 7 6 5 4 3 2 1
First Edition

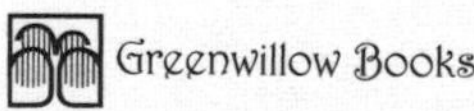

To Karen Prickett and Marie Ricotta,
my second- and fourth-grade teachers

*"For her house leads down to death*
*and her paths to the spirits of the dead."*
—PROVERBS 2:18

# CHAPTER 1

Eden dug her hand into the damp sand, black polish chipping off the tips of her fingernails. The sand was cold, the beach pockmarked by late afternoon raindrops. A gust of wind ruffled through her dark hair. Eden sighed.

Last month there had been a string of parties, out-of-control times. She checked her phone. No missed calls. She couldn't figure out what she'd done to get the cold shoulder from everyone the last few weeks. Even her mom no longer questioned where she was, if she was even alive.

*Screw them. I just have to hang on until graduation and I'm out*, she thought, trying to convince herself she'd make it that long. An entire year. But then she could hit the road, go somewhere else where every day wasn't bullshit. Start over.

Even in her head the words sounded like lies. It wasn't like she had a college fund, or could take off to some far-away campus. She didn't have the grades to get in anyway.

*So that's the extent of your brilliant plan?* Eden sifted her fingers through the sand, coming back to the same facts. No car. No money. No job. If she got lucky, she'd spend the next fifty years working the front desk at one of the hotels in this crappy tourist town.

Her mind went to her other option, the one she considered more every day. What was the difference between feeling dead, knowing her whole life would be that way, and actually being dead? It wasn't like anyone would miss her. They clearly didn't now.

This time she didn't push the idea away. She wanted the thought of death to hold some thrill, terror. Wrongness. Instead, it held an empty acceptance her body ached for.

She dug her fingers deeper, and something distinctly not sand hit her fingers.

"Sick." She yanked up her hand, taking a cluster of decayed scales with her. The wind changed direction, bringing the faint smell of salty dead fish. "Little late for the warning," she muttered, scanning the area for an abandoned towel, anything to wipe off the goo. She grabbed a soggy magazine page out of the sand and tried to scrape her fingers clean. "God, can *nothing* go right?"

As if in answer, Eden's skin prickled. She raised her head.

The beach had cleared out while the sun finished setting.

Only two couples remained, but she could barely make out their horizontal outlines in the darkness. Carnival sounds and the scents of popcorn and cotton candy floated down from the boardwalk. There were two guys walking close to the water's edge coming down the beach. They were still a good fifty feet away, but closing the distance. She watched them for a moment, wondering if she knew them. They seemed to be heading right for her.

Eden rolled her eyes once she realized she didn't recognize them, preparing herself. It was Jersey; getting hassled by guys was just another fact of summer. She normally put a few hours' effort into achieving her normal balance between the fashionable "leave me alone" and a more stylish "I'm not afraid to knee your groin." Lately though, even makeup seemed like too much work. She settled for a glare, hoping it would be enough.

The blond one was in a dark green polo, the color setting off his hazel eyes. With the short sleeves and his tattered-to-be-trendy jeans, he had to have been freezing. *Suffering just to pander to underage cheerleaders. Clearly a winner*, she thought, and then second-guessed herself. Something about him set her gaydar screaming. *Lovers' stroll?* She eyed the other one. Brown curls, dark sweater, paired with cargo pants. *Be gay. Be gay and keep walking.* He noticed her giving him the once-over and smiled in a way no gay boy in history had ever smiled at a girl. She shifted her eyes back to the water, but they stopped next to her. Perfect.

When she turned toward them, the one who had smiled at her brushed his hair back from his face.

"Your eyes are blue, like the ocean." She raised an eyebrow in annoyance, unable to believe he went with a line so pathetic. Slightly behind him, the other's mouth cocked an apologetic half smile. At least he knew his friend was an idiot. "I think I'm lost at sea," lover boy continued, his voice sincere. A snort of laughter burst from somewhere between her throat and nose.

"You can't be serious." She stood, brushing the sand from her black leggings.

"Damn. Gabriel, did you hear that? That was the sound of my heart shattering." His face twisted in mock pain. He gripped his sweater so tightly it left behind divots. Next to him, Gabriel rolled his eyes.

"Come on, Az."

"Fuck off," Eden enunciated each word, trying not to sound as amused as she was. "The water's not even blue, jackass."

She turned toward the stairs to the boardwalk and the guy grabbed her arm. Even through the material of her thermal top, his fingers were frigid. He offered up another smile and shrugged. "'Storm-tossed' seemed a bit cliché."

Her lips twitched before she could stop them.

"Was that a smile?" He dipped a bit, studying her face.

She fought the treasonous grin, managed to smother it away. "Are you kidding me with this?"

She met his eyes for the first time. He jerked forward suddenly, more of a stumble than a step, as if she'd yanked him closer by some invisible string. She should have shot off some comment about staying out of her personal space but the retorts vanished, her thoughts melting away like scorched snowflakes. It was almost too bad his pick-up lines weren't as pretty as his eyes. Their color like cooled anger. Blue sea glass.

"Wow," she whispered. He looked equally stunned, his smile bringing out dimples so subtle she hadn't noticed them until now. How could she not have noticed them?

"Az, stop." The voice was faraway. She didn't bother to really register it at all, just let it slide by as she sank deeper into those eyes. *Nothing's wrong*, she wanted to say. *Everything's perfect*.

"I'm not doing anything, Gabriel," he said slowly. She couldn't take her eyes off Az. A tingle started deep in her chest. She gasped as everything inside her seemed to come back to life, shift into place.

"Who *are* you?" Az asked, his words coming honey slow.

"No one," she managed. "Nothing." She hesitated before she ripped her gaze away, dizziness rolling in as the connection broke.

A pressure at her elbow held her upright as she slumped, unsteady. It was the blond one, Gabriel.

"I'm fine, it's just . . ." She pulled her arm away slowly, trying to get her bearings. What the hell had that been? Az reached out to her, concern in his eyes. She stepped back, unsure and off-kilter.

"You look kinda shaky," Gabriel said. He'd moved aside, but looked ready to step in if her legs gave out. Luckily, they seemed to be in working order again.

"Dinner," she said. "I haven't eaten yet." *Wasn't even hungry*, her brain spat out, *let alone starving enough to hallucinate some dreamy lost-in-his-eyes stare down with a stranger.* She pushed away any contradictions, forcing the excuse into reality. Just hungry. Which didn't do much to explain how different she'd felt.

How alive.

"Would you let me take you out to dinner, then?"

She glanced up at Az, expecting the same rush when their eyes met, not sure whether to be disappointed when it didn't come. "I don't think so."

"Why not?" He offered her a tentative smile. His hand hovered there between them, looking more orphaned as the seconds passed. But he didn't move, a picture of patience as he waited. "Tell you what. You *don't* smile, and dinner's off."

"Don't smile?" She stared at him in confusion. "Easy enough. Why the hell would I have dinner with you, anyway?"

"Because I'm an amusing young gentleman wooing you into a better mood. Because, with your high standard of pick-up lines, I think you'd be able to hold a decent conversation." He shrugged, his eyes dancing. "Because I'm paying?"

Eden crossed her arms, rubbing her lips together to crush his victory before it fully formed.

"Did I just see one?" He tilted his head, eyebrow raised. "Was that a yes?"

"Damn it," she said, giving up, letting the smile break loose.

His own grin brought back the dimples.

## CHAPTER 2

"I'll take whatever's most expensive, please." Eden handed the menu back to the waiter without opening it, waiting for Az's reaction.

"Actually, now that you mention it"—he didn't break her gaze as he returned his own menu—"expensive sounds wonderful. I'll have the same." When the waiter retreated, Az leaned over the table, lowering his voice. "Out of curiosity, what are we eating?"

Eden shifted forward. "I have no idea."

Az laughed, pulling back and draping his arm across the back of the booth. "So, awkward, but you haven't told me your name."

A list of fakes scrolled through her mind, but in the end she figured the least she could do was give him her real one.

"Your name is Eden?" The grin slid away. "You've got to be kidding me."

She rolled her eyes. "Yeah, go ahead and get the forbidden garden comment out of your system. And no matter what witty snake joke you're considering? Trust me, I've heard it."

"Gabriel's going to have a field day with this one," he muttered.

Eden startled as the waiter dropped a basket of bread onto the table. She waited for him to elaborate, but instead Az took a slice and buttered it as she peeled the wrapper from her straw, dunking it into her glass of ice water.

Eden eyed him over the bread basket and grabbed a roll. *What happened between us on the beach?* The question bobbled around her head, but she couldn't bring herself to voice it. Not yet, anyway. "So I assume you're on vacation? Couldn't afford to go somewhere good?" she asked. At least it would tell her what he was doing here, how long he'd be in town.

"Jersey's far enough away for us to relax, but I can get back to the city." Az unwrapped his silverware slowly. "We." He paused. "We can get back to the city if we need to." His fingers slid down the hem of the napkin, straightening it before he dropped it to his lap.

Eden stared at him, her knife dipping into the unwrapped pad of butter. "The 'we' would be you and Gabriel? So you go to school together?"

Az shifted. "Kind of."

"College?" He didn't answer. Maybe he'd dropped out. *Great*, she thought. *The guy's got one touchy subject and you zero right in on it.*

"Things have been crazy lately. We needed a vacation. So you live here?"

Subject change. Thank God. Eden sipped her drink before giving him a sarcastic smile. "Lucky enough to be stuck here year-round!"

Az looked surprised. "Are you kidding me? It's gorgeous here."

"Sweatshirts in August aren't gorgeous."

"True. But you can't let a little rain ruin your fun." He caught her eye across the table, smiling. "Besides, it cleared up just in time for things to get interesting." She felt a blush creep up her neck, her face growing hot. Az glanced over her shoulder. "Looks like our mystery dinner is coming," he said, sweeping his bread plate to the side. "I hope you're in the mood for . . ." He trailed off, pausing as the waiter set down the plate. "Lobster tails."

"You're not allergic to shellfish or anything, are you?" she asked.

"Nope."

"Good, because that would have been a deal breaker. Their lobster's pricey, but it's to die for," Eden said, taking up her own fork. Az cocked his head, his jaw dropping a bit.

"Here I thought we were on this grand adventure into spontaneity." His eyes danced. "You knew what we were having the whole time, didn't you?"

"I live here. You think I don't know what they serve?" Eden smiled.

Tinfoil swan of leftovers tucked under her arm, Eden stepped through the door Az held open. A thrill jolted through her when his hand touched her back, guiding her past him.

The temperature had dropped while they were in the restaurant, the cold air rousing her a bit from her food coma. When they reached the boardwalk, Az turned to her.

"I should get going," he said. "Gabriel's probably hungry." He held up the dinner he'd ordered to go, but didn't move, almost seemed to hesitate.

She nodded, shifting to lean against the railing, struggling to think of something to say, an excuse to keep him there. "Thank you, for convincing me to come," she said finally. "I was having kind of a shitty night."

"Me too." Az tapped the heel of his hand against the bag he held. "It's been a while since I had one this good." Something in his gaze stopped her from calling him out for how cheerful he'd been on the beach, made her take him at his word. She wondered how he managed to hide it so well. "You know, I'm gonna be in town for a while." He pulled his phone from his pocket. Eden took it from him, entered her number.

"There," she said handing it back. "Maybe sometime we can go for the least expensive thing on the menu."

He laughed, tucking the phone away. "You buying that round?" She rolled her eyes.

He reached for her, his hand cupping around the back of her neck, easing her toward him. Eden's heart jumped at the sudden touch of his fingers. She closed her eyes, her body rocking forward, anticipating the kiss.

It never came. She opened her eyes, and he pulled back another inch, face lit up with his smile. "I'll call you soon, okay?" he said, and turned away without another word.

Eden stepped back, the railing hitting her spine. She tried to find a snappy comeback but nothing came quick enough as he retreated into the crowd. *Who pays for dinner and then just bolts?* She couldn't figure it out. And then pulling out of a kiss *he* initiated? Who the hell was this guy?

Her cell phone rang. She yanked it from her pocket, taking a second to check the caller ID before she put it to her ear. The number wasn't one in her call list.

"Just wanted to make sure the number wasn't a fake," Az said.

She couldn't help her bitter laugh. "Well, you can go

ahead and erase it. A bit of advice? Either kiss a girl or don't. Never stop halfway through." She pulled the phone away, her finger already heading for the End button when his voice came through the speaker.

"Didn't want to risk it."

She lifted the phone again. "Risk kissing me? What the hell's that supposed to mean?"

"Had to leave you wanting more. That way you'll say yes when I ask you out again."

A thrill passed through her, the same she'd felt on the beach. But she kept a flicker of sarcasm in her voice. "You're kind of an asshole, you know that, right?"

He laughed before his voice grew serious. "You do something to me." She heard his pause as he struggled for words. "It kinda freaks me out a bit. But I like it."

Her breath seemed to stall before she found it again. "Me too."

"Plus, if you see me again? I can almost *guarantee* I'll kiss you," he added.

"If I let you," she teased.

"Hey now," he said, sounding hurt. "Be fair. I earned it. That was an expensive lobster."

She burst out laughing. "My kisses don't come cheap, lover boy, but they are very worth it." She snapped the phone shut. *Always leave them wanting more*, she thought smiling. She'd have to thank him for the advice.

# CHAPTER 3

He's *kissing a dead girl.* Gabriel dove again as a wave crashed against his back, letting the momentum carry him a few feet closer to the shore. On the beach, Eden and Az were on a blanket, tangled around each other. *You have to tell him*, Gabriel thought.

"But she's not dead yet," he grated out in a harsh whisper.

Even now her laughter mixed with the crash of the ocean. He twisted sideways as another swell pounded past and she waved at him as if she'd never been happier to be alive. Gabriel forced his hand up, rocked it once before letting it drop back to the water, and waded to shore.

*Where is she hiding it?* he thought. He wasn't sure what he was expecting. Would she fade into skin and bones, die from the inside first? He had no clue what a girl was supposed to look like before she killed herself. She was going to sooner or later, of that much Gabriel was certain.

He dropped onto the blanket and toweled off. He should have told Az the second he'd gotten back from Upstairs. He'd put off checking her path too long anyway. He couldn't remember the last time he'd seen Az so happy, not having to struggle against the Fall. He couldn't deny it had to do with Eden. And now it was all going to end.

Eden grinned. Her skin glistened with sunscreen, tan and healthier than she'd looked two weeks ago. Summer was almost gone.

"Gonna come with us?" she asked. "We're getting something to eat."

Gabriel shook his head.

She leaned toward him, her voice falling to a conspiratorial whisper. "We can check out the hot boys in the arcade?"

He couldn't meet her eyes. Scoping out boys on the boardwalk, after Az had fallen asleep, even the stupid judge shows they hated to love. Everything would eventually be labeled "the last time." He couldn't bring himself to start counting down yet. Telling Az would be terrible enough. "I'm suffering from a lack of awesome today. Think I'll sit out this time."

Eden groaned in mock frustration, scooting away. "Ugh! You're killing me, Gabe!" He startled before he could stop himself.

"Everything okay?" Az asked.

Gabriel forced himself to meet Az's eyes.

"Can you give us a minute? I'll text you when I'm on my way, okay?" He wasn't sure what Az saw, what he gave away, but it was enough.

Az reached for her hand, led her a few steps away. From behind him, Gabriel heard the soft sound of their kiss, broken fragments of her concern for him.

Gabriel kept his head hung when Az dropped onto the blanket next to him, face hidden behind his blond curls. For once he was glad he'd let them shag out, though he'd spent the last month bitching about the lack of New York–quality stylists.

"What's up?" Az asked, pulling up his knees, throwing an arm out behind him for balance.

Gabriel raised his head, staring off into the water, eyes focused far past the horizon. The knot of dread tightened in his stomach.

"I went Upstairs last night." He turned toward Az as he spoke, watching for the reaction. A shiver passed across Az's shoulders.

Az forced his face into a mask of nonchalance. "You didn't mention you were going Upstairs."

"Because it bothers you," Gabriel said quietly.

Az scoffed. "You're Bound. I'm not. I hardly think of that place at all." His voice stayed casual, but the rest of him failed miserably. He blinked hard, as if it would be enough to hide the rusted tinge to his irises, the anger turning their color. His shoulders were rigid, his hands clenched into fists.

Gabriel turned back to the water. "Az, it's about Eden."

"No!" Az jumped to his feet. "This time is different! I can feel it, Gabriel. I don't care what she was *supposed* to be doing." People were staring, Frisbees falling forgotten. Gabriel felt sick. Az had never shown up on a mortal's path. Every relationship he'd been in, he'd been crushed when the girl left him, going back to the path she was meant to be traveling. Only twice had they not. Luke had gotten to them first.

Gabriel bit his lip, hoping the pain would keep the tears unshed. He wouldn't let that happen. "Az, it's worse." His vision blurred. "She's . . ."

"What do you mean 'worse'?"

"She has no path." Gabriel said quietly. The words crackled in the air between them. Out on the water a gull screamed. The color drained from Az's face, his shoulders dropping.

"You made a mistake, then," Az said. "Just because she doesn't have a path doesn't mean—"

Gabriel cut him off with a shake of his head. "You know what it means." He stayed silent as anguish flooded Az's face.

"Eden's not one of them. She's not a Sider." Az glared, no longer repressing the red flare in his eyes.

"I'm sorry." It was all Gabriel could think of to say. He focused on the corner of the blanket, peeling it back. Underneath, the sand was cool and damp against his fingers.

"You knew," Az spat. Gabriel looked up in surprise.

"No, Az. I swear."

"So, what? We came all the way to fucking Jersey to get away from your obsession with the Suiciders and you just *happened* to stumble on her?" He drew a breath, choked the words out between clenched teeth. "You pointed her out to me. Did you set me up?"

"I didn't know. She was so sad. I thought you would cheer her up, but then . . ." His mouth dropped open as the realization hit him. "Oh, God. She was planning it out."

"What are you talking about?"

"The night we met her, I caught her thoughts." He swallowed hard. "It was like she was screaming for help. I figured she was just depressed but, Az, I think she was deciding to do it. To kill herself."

"Maybe we just changed what was supposed to happen? So she was suicidal. She's not now. We saved her."

"If she was killing herself she'd still have a path. That's a mortal death." Gabriel glanced up. "Without a path, there's nothing to change. Maybe we've delayed it, but it's her fate, Az."

Gabriel caught the change in Az's eyes even before his breathing went shallow, was on his feet when the color of his eyes shifted to bruised purple. Only half Fallen, Az struggled to keep from going full. The prospect of losing Eden had tipped him, darkened his thoughts.

"Did I do this? Did I mess up her path?" Az stopped dead, his sudden stillness disconcerting.

Gabriel softened his voice. "Of course not. This isn't your fault." Az knew a Bound angel couldn't lie, but when he looked up his eyes hadn't lightened.

"What if me being with her took her off?"

"You can't affect paths that way. It's impossible."

"A Sider." Gabriel heard the change in Az's voice. "She has no path." He paused. "So I'm not taking her away from anything. That's why she hasn't left me. Right?"

Gabriel winced.

"And when she becomes a Sider, we can be together."

Gabriel forced a deep breath, wishing the salty air would dry him out inside, make this hurt less. "This isn't a good thing, Az."

"Why not?" The ache in his voice was painful to hear. "I think I love her, Gabriel. I didn't mean to. I know it puts her in danger, but I can't lose her. She makes me happy."

Gabriel managed a smile. "I know." He hesitated, not wanting to set Az off again.

"Isn't this what *you've* wanted?" Az asked. "To find a

Sider that hadn't gone through the change yet?"

Gabriel followed his lead, changing the subject. "Well, yes. But not Eden. I don't want her to be a Sider at all." He yanked his hand through his hair, the blond curls springing back into place. "They're cursed."

"You're sure there's no way to stop it?" Az asked. He turned, searching the boardwalk above for Eden.

"I don't think so." Gabriel rubbed his temples. The throbbing there was getting worse by the second. "What are we gonna do? We can't do this by ourselves. The Bound don't know about the Siders, so I can't consult Upstairs."

"Kristen?"

Gabriel's mouth opened, a dozen protests clustering before he closed it. The idea wasn't entirely bad. Still, Az's reply had been more question than answer, and with good reason. Kristen was one of the first Suiciders. It wasn't that she wouldn't help; she owed him more favors than Az would ever know. The problem was, well, it was Kristen. Worse, she was the best option.

"I'll head to the Bronx tomorrow. See what she says."

# CHAPTER 4

Az opened the door to the hotel room. One glance at Eden as she entered and his expression shifted to sympathy.

"No license?"

"My mom forgot the fucking appointment." She caught his hand as she passed, both of them plopping down on the bed. "Then we finally got there and I didn't even get to take the test!" Eden's shoulders slumped. "My Social Security number wasn't in the system. They couldn't pull up my file."

*She's already disappearing*, he thought, trying to keep his emotions under control. So far it'd been easy to hide his eyes. He knew they'd be a paler blue today, but doubted she'd notice. He moved behind her on the bed just in case, rubbing her shoulders. "You can go back when they figure it out, right? That's not so bad."

She'd never get her license. It was such a small thing, yet meant so much to her. He leaned over her shoulder, kissing her neck. So many things she'd be missing out on. *But she'll have me*, he reminded himself. "And I'm within walking distance."

"True." She closed her eyes, leaning into him. "It's just, I know you and Gabe are only here for the summer. I wanna be able to come see you in New York."

He sensed her hesitation, draped his arms over her shoulders, and hugged her. They hadn't talked about what would happen when summer ended. He murmured her name, ran a hand down her cheek. "We'll get you to New York safe. I promise."

He pressed his lips together before he gave away too much, but she only nodded, breaking into a smile. How many more did she have before the depression took over, stripped them away from her? Would she be the same when she became a Sider?

Would she still love him?

"You're staring at me," she said. He didn't answer, pulling her with him as he leaned back on the bed. Everything about her felt numbered. He kissed her hard, his lips greedy. He wanted her, the need hitting him in a rush. Wanted her now, while she was mortal.

His lips wandered down her neck, across her collarbone, her breath coming faster as he followed the curve of her tank top down. Her fingers grabbed suddenly at the bottom of his shirt, lifting. He rolled onto his back, stifling a groan, knowing he'd killed the moment. Again.

"Tease." She smacked his chest. The playfulness dropped from her tone. "Why do you always pull away?" Eden asked.

He moved carefully, adjusting until he leaned against the headboard.

"You're right," he said. His fingers toyed with the hem of his shirt. He could tell her. Explain. "I do pull away."

"Are we going too fast?" she asked.

He shook his head. "It's not that at all, trust me." The bed creaked as she crawled closer, laying her head on his chest. His arm curled around her.

"Then what is it?" she whispered.

He tipped her head up, stole another kiss. "It's not you."

"Jesus, I hate it when you pull this shit." She made for the edge of the bed, but he grabbed her shoulder. She turned on him, her eyes blazing. "One minute you're feeding me lines about seeing you in New York, and the next you act like you don't even want me to touch you."

Part of him wondered if it was just the depression, if this would be the moment it shifted, took over. *You're going to lose her.* The thought dug in, even as he tried to push it away.

She yanked her hand away. "I need to know what's going to happen when summer ends. I need to know if this is just a temporary thing for you."

"Oh, God, Eden, no!" He reached for her hand again. This time she let him take it. "This isn't 'temporary' for me. It never has been."

Her eyes flicked away. "Because I love you," she said. She swallowed hard. It was the first time she'd been so blatant. The same quicksilver happiness coated his insides, whisking away the dark thought, but his smile was because of her alone.

"I love you, too, Eden." He wanted to say it again, loving the sound of her name paired with those words, knowing how true they were.

"Then what's wrong? Tell me." She squeezed his hand, leaning forward, tucking her head against his neck. He closed his eyes, knowing his fear would stain them yellow.

"Just . . . don't freak out, okay?" He raised her from his shoulder, caught her gaze for a split second before he lifted his shirt over his head.

"What's wrong with your eyes?" she asked quietly. He didn't answer, couldn't look at her as he began slowly unwinding the ace bandage around his chest. "Az?"

"So, usually I get one of two reactions," he said, his voice quaking. He pulled off all but the last loop of material and glanced up. "I blame the corsets for the fainters. They wore them so tight . . . couldn't breathe right. But they've been out of style for centuries, so I think we're good on that one."

"Centuries?" Her voice had gone up an octave. "What's wrong with your eyes?" she demanded.

"They turn yellow when I'm scared," he said, keeping his voice as calm as he could manage.

"Scared?" She was still talking. So far, so good. But he knew what he showed her next would be enough to send any mortal over the edge. *She's different*, he promised himself.

He dropped the last of the bandages. His cramped muscles begged to stretch but he did his best to hold them tight.

"Yeah, scared." He climbed off the bed, backing away to the middle of the room. "The screaming I can handle. Being called a devil, a witch, a freak. No big deal. But what will happen to me if you decide you don't love me anymore?"

"Az, you better tell me what you're talking about because you are freaking me out." She'd risen onto her knees, her hands held in front of her, eyes darting to the door and back. He didn't dare move. "Az?"

He heard the fear in her voice, knew every moment he drew this out would make it worse. His head dropped as he forced himself to roll his shoulders, the wings uncurling from their cavity behind his rib cage. When he flexed them out, all fourteen feet of the atrocious things spanned the room. Joints at odd angles, so they folded in like a pterodactyl, feathers layered across the skin. Nothing about them was beautiful. They were a punishment.

"I'm a fucking angel, Eden." A feathered tip brushed the TV stand, knocking an open can of soda to the carpet. Her silence was worse than any screaming.

He closed his eyes, trying to keep calm, keep under control. His cell phone was in his pocket. If things went bad, if he felt tempted to Fall, one phone call and Gabriel could get there in seconds.

An unsure giggle broke from the bed, building into a laugh. His eyes shot up, found her doubled over on the covers. His wings lifted, the feathers rustling quietly in his confusion.

"So lame!" She took a deep breath, wiping her eyes, trying to get her giggling under control. "And you owe me a Coke, too!" she said, pointing to the can, the liquid soaking into the carpet.

He opened his mouth, but when nothing came out she hopped off the bed, crossing the room to him. Az stared at her, not sure what to say.

"Did Gabe put you up to this?" she asked. She rolled her eyes as her fingers traced one of the feathers. "He's *that* pissed that I kicked his ass in skeeball? I never figured you two for pranking types. Though this is beyond awesome." She gave a joint of his left wing a hard squeeze. Az grimaced, knowing she felt the bones grinding.

"Jesus. These things are, like, movie prop worthy."

She rounded his shoulder for a better look at his back and he knew it was over.

She sucked in a sharp breath. "You have holes in your back!"

He nodded slowly. "The wings tuck in. Most times a sweatshirt is enough to hide them."

His anatomy had been rearranged, concave scoops on either side of a spine lined in muscles, where the wings attached inside. A thin layer of skin hid blood and bone along his rib cage.

"Wings?" She took a step away, her voice shaking. "You were hiding *wings*?"

"It's not exactly something that goes in a personal ad, Eden. Enjoys long walks on the beach and sarcastic girls. Bird fetish a plus. Can I put them away now?" he whispered, his head hung low. When she didn't answer, he contracted his shoulders, then folded the wings back in and grabbed for his shirt in a single motion. He put it on as he dropped onto the bed, and glanced up at her.

"This is seriously happening, isn't it?" Her eyes were wide, her head cocked as it finally hit her. Her face paled when he moved toward her. "Don't come any closer!" He froze, but she stepped back anyway.

"Eden, I'm not going to hurt you. I promise."

"Is that, like, an angel rule or something?" she asked, her breaths coming faster.

Az winced. "No, it's a boyfriend rule. Not all angels are good."

"Neither are all boyfriends."

"I used to be the good kind. Of angel," he clarified. "Bound, like Gabriel. I got in trouble. The wings, they're like probation." He forced himself to stop the ramble and met her eyes.

"Gabe too?" She took a shuddering breath, shaking her head. "No. No, I've seen Gabe with his shirt off. I've gone *swimming* with him."

Az nodded. "The Bound don't have wings. Neither do the Fallen." *So Fall. Lose the wings and you'll look normal enough for her to love you.* Az squeezed his eyes shut, trying to push the thoughts away, make them stop. *The Fallen aren't punished for love.*

He swallowed hard, lowering his hand to his pocket. "I understand. If you don't love me anymore." *Look how worthless you are.* He didn't want to call Gabriel, not while he was at Kristen's, but if it got any worse there would be no other choice.

"I didn't say that," she said. She hadn't left, hadn't lost it. He forced his eyes open, concentrated on Eden, trying to gauge her reaction. Her expression still hovered somewhere between panic and disbelief, but she was holding her own. It didn't guarantee she wouldn't leave, but it was enough to push the darkest thoughts away.

She stared at him for a long moment. "What's green mean?"

"Green?"

"They've always been blue." She lifted a finger to the corner of her eye. "If they go yellow when you're scared, what's green?"

"Blue and yellow?" He tried out a smile. "Happy fear? Hope?"

He watched as she struggled with herself before she slowly crossed the room. She sat on the bed with him, against the headboard, closer but still keeping her distance.

"Are you okay?" he asked.

"I don't know."

"Does this change things?"

She looked up at him, exasperated, drawing her knees to her chest. "Az, you're telling me you're an angel. This is either the most fucked-up day ever or I need to be locked in a psych ward. I'd say it changes things."

He scooted closer to her. "I meant . . . does it change us."

Her brow wrinkled. "You've had them the whole time, right?" He nodded, his heart in his throat as she seemed to consider. "Anything else you wanna get off your chest?"

Az dropped his hands to hers. *So much*, he thought.

"How are you okay with this?" he asked. It didn't feel real. Her still being there.

She pulled her hands away slowly. "I don't know." Her voice grew even quieter. "If I freak out and leave, I lose you. I don't want that." Her fingers found his again, entwining with them as their eyes met. "I want *you*. And if this is you, well . . ."

He pulled her into his arms, the tension in his shoulders releasing as her arms wrapped around him. "I love you so much."

# CHAPTER 5

Ivy grew thick across the back of the house, the broken path across the yard lost under green tendrils. Gabriel didn't bother hiding his presence, using his key to slip in the back door. It was an old servant's entrance that opened to a narrow staircase. He didn't turn on the light, his fingers finding the wall out of habit, using it to guide him.

There was no sound in the stairway, nothing from the hall. One fluid movement took him into Kristen's room. The door swung on well-oiled hinges, clicking quietly shut behind him.

She didn't look up when he entered, though he knew she was aware he'd arrived. He watched her for a moment, a long leg balanced on the edge of her vanity table as she painted her toenails a shade close to black. Finally, with a breath across the polish, she glanced up at the mirror, meeting his eyes through the reflection.

"You haven't been answering your phone," she said,

not turning to him. She capped the polish and dropped it into a drawer.

"I came as soon as I could."

Kristen swiveled the chair toward him finally, her face indifferent. The quiver in her lip was so slight, he almost missed it.

"Oh, Kristen," he said quietly. He didn't have to read her mind to guess her thoughts. "I should have called. Did you think I wasn't coming?" She seemed to give in suddenly, forgetting the pedicure and hurrying across the floor to throw herself into his arms. He hugged her tight.

"How's my little black rain cloud?" he asked, pulling her back. The dress she wore was dirty, the antique fabric tattered and torn, but that wasn't out of the ordinary for Kristen. He'd half hoped that she'd been holding her own, even with her appearance. The room gave her away.

On the top of the dresser were ten writing utensils. Lined up in a row, the pattern was simple enough, a pencil higher than the blue felt tip beside it, the marker after rising again, even with the pencil. Up, down, up, down across the polished wood. Iambic pentameter in pens. On her nightstand, the hair clips seemed random until he counted them. A row of five, of seven, of five again.

"Kristen, haikus?" He cupped her chin in his hand. She wouldn't meet his eyes. "You should have left a message! I would have come!" She started to speak but he shushed her, closing his eyes. He bowed his head, concentrating until he picked up her thoughts.

At first, he only heard her fears. *. . . came back this time but what if I'm too much of a burden and are the pencils straight think of something else so he doesn't see how bad . . .* A rush of poetry assaulted him, the lines and couplets screaming past his ears in stereo. He raised his hands to her shoulders, his eyes still shut tight.

"Kristen," he chided, then softened his tone. "You're not a burden. Now let me fix it, okay?" He squeezed her shoulders. Under his fingers, she relaxed a bit, giving in. Every few weeks since he and Az found her, he wiped her mind clear. Saned her back to herself. It never held long; the roots of the disease had dug deep while she had been human. The residue of her schizophrenia slowly reclaimed her brain if left alone. He could only clean so much.

A jumble of words and thoughts coated her brain like plaque, flaring knots of insanity wrapping tighter the longer he left the schizophrenia alone. He narrowed his focus, untangling the damaged threads of thought. He'd nearly finished when he came across the patch of static. They'd appeared suddenly last year, strands of white noise he couldn't get rid of, as if they were operating on a different frequency. He'd thought at first that she was getting worse and the disease was progressing anyway, but they never spread.

*I should have been here*, he thought. He swallowed, guilt tightening his throat, and pushed his own thoughts away. The volume skyrocketed, her mind opening to him, playing out like a song, the lines of static humming dully in the background.

Steam poured from the crack of the door, though the shower had been off for ten minutes. Gabriel flipped though a magazine, the glossy pages sliding past unread.

"You okay in there?" he called out. The door swung open in answer, the handle bouncing lightly against the wall. Kristen looked almost normal, save her sense of what passed for fashion. He eyed the black ball gown with distaste. "Look, I know you like to be different and all, but do you have to be so nineteen-forty-six debutante?"

She ignored him, opening one of the dresser drawers, sweeping away the pens and markers. "Silly, really," she said, turning to him. "Anyone with their wits about them would know Sharpies make for bad inspiration. No wonder I hardly wrote anything this week."

Gabriel tossed the magazine aside, pulling a pillow under his chin as he shifted to lie down on the bed. He ran the words through his head before saying them, trying to find the cadence to make them sound nonchalant. Of course, when he opened his mouth, they came out clipped and too quick. "I need to talk to you about where I was.

Why you couldn't get a hold of me." The pause after was long enough to be theatrical. Kristen set the hairbrush down.

She said his name, her voice unsure and faltering. Hidden between the syllables were the questions her pride wouldn't allow her to ask. When she answered, though, all insecurities had dropped away.

"Something serious?" The flash in her eyes dared him to attempt an excuse.

"Az has a girl." Kristen twisted to the mirror, pulling the brush through the tangled wreck of her hair.

"Huh," she mused to her reflection. "All this time I thought him celibate." Gabriel shot her an impatient glare. "I hardly see how this is relevant to me."

"She's Pathless," he finished. "She's one of your kind. Or will be."

She silently brushed blush over her cheekbones. "So Az thinks, what? She'll go Sider and they'll skip off into the sunset for fuck's sake?" Kristen's jaw tightened. She went back to the mirror, pulling her eyelid taut, smearing kohl liner with an expert hand.

"This girl, Eden, she's good for him. He's doing better than he has in centuries. He's hardly struggled against the Fall since he met her." Gabriel closed his eyes, blotting out the distraction of the room, the collection of top hats shelved above the mirror. "I want you to take her in after she changes. Keep her safe until we figure things out." He opened his eyes. A slow crescent chiseled its way onto Kristen's lips.

"We're nearly immortal, Gabriel. You know that." Her brown eyes already glittered from his unintentional slip. "Keep her safe from what, exactly?"

Gabriel glanced away. "Luke."

"I do recall you mentioning how he enjoys ripping apart Az's love life." She lined her other eye and tossed the pencil back into the drawer. "Last one was straight down the middle, right?"

"Really, Kristen?" Gabriel's eyes flashed maroon and Kristen dropped her gaze, rummaging through her makeup drawer. "When she does go Sider, I want her in the best hands. Ones on the right side. You are the best hands, Kristen."

"Of course I am." Kicking a foot up, she shoved off the vanity. The chair hurdled across the floor, past her wall of filing cabinets, carrying Kristen to where it collided against the bed. She leaned closer. "And the best," she said, her words humming against his ear, "do not babysit."

She pulled back, giving the chair a lazy spin. The black taffeta of her dress bloomed around her, made her look almost innocent until she opened her mouth. "Dump her in Queens."

"With *Madeline*?" Gabriel's jaw dropped. "Now you're just being cruel."

Kristen's hands plunged down into the folds of the dress, her head cocking incredulously. "And you're being selfish. You're asking me to put myself and every Sider in this house at risk in exchange for what, flattery?"

"What risk?" Gabriel argued. "It's not like he'll be searching her out. Luke won't even know she's a Sider. All I'm asking is that you give her a place to stay, teach her what she needs to know."

Kristen tapped her finger against her lips.

"Just as long as it takes for her to get a handle on how things work for your kind. Come on, Kristen. We both know Madeline's loyalties tend toward the Fallen. I don't know the others well enough to trust them with something this important to me. You're the *only* one I trust."

She sighed dramatically, but a glint of satisfaction found its way to her eyes.

Gabriel slid around her, standing, his head dipped in apology. "Maybe you're right. I was wrong to think you'd be up to the challenge, what with all your Bronx minions to keep watch over." It was all he could do to keep the smirk off his lips. Twisting the babysitting comment against her had her face nearly purple. "I know how much you hate doing things out of the kindness of your heart. . . ." He trailed off, waiting.

"It's not that I don't like to. It's just there's not much kindness in there. I save it for special occasions." She dropped her foot over one of the armrests, letting it swing for a moment. "And what if the Fallen figure out she's with Az? If they come after her here—"

"Luke doesn't know she's going to be a Sider. Hopefully, he never will. Right now, he's looking for a mortal, but Eden won't be one much longer."

Kristen dropped her head back, staring at the ceiling. "This would be *such* an inconvenience."

Gabriel held his breath.

Finally she lifted her head. "Well then, I suppose we have quite a bit of work ahead of us." She smiled at his confusion. "Special occasions require a party."

# CHAPTER 6

Being Bound had its advantages. First off, faster travel options. Sometimes he pitied Az, having to take the subway when he wanted to get around.

Gabriel materialized in the doorway of a closed shop he'd scouted out earlier, in a quiet neighborhood just down the street from the hotel he and Az had made home. The crowds had thinned. The prospect of a few minutes to himself was more than Gabriel could resist. He pulled his cell phone from his pocket. Az answered on the second ring.

"It's taken care of," Gabriel said.

"Already? You on your way back here?"

"No. Think I'm gonna head down to the beach."

Boots scraped against the asphalt behind him. Gabriel fell silent, concentrating. Someone was there, walking in the road, instead of on the sidewalk. The sound traveled well in the stillness.

"You there?" Az asked. Gabriel didn't answer. Luke

had worn the same style of boots, all zippers and buckles, long enough for Gabriel to recognize the distinctive sound.

"Is she with you?" Gabriel whispered, trying to keep the urgency from his voice, avoiding Eden's name in case he was overheard.

"No, I walked her home half an hour ago. Why?"

"Call her. Make sure she's there. Do not come outside." He snapped the phone shut without elaborating. "Spectacular," he muttered.

Luke made no effort to soften his steps. Gabriel did his part in return, slowing enough to allow him to catch up. It was best to get the little tête-à-tête over with.

For a long minute, neither of them spoke, walking side by side. Finally, just before the street merged into the main road, Gabriel gave in, flashing him a glare.

"Gabriel!" Luke cried, bursting into a grin so wide it gouged his cheekbones. "My my my! It's been ages, hasn't it? So tell me . . ." The grin fell away, his eyes reflecting maroon in the diffused glow of the streetlights. "What exactly brings you to the neighborhood?"

Gabriel gave him a once-over. "Vacation." In a dream world, Luke would have laughed and left it at that, the two of them just passing strangers in the night. Unfortunately, the Fallen were more nightmare than dream. From the look of him, Luke was still playing gigs in dingy bars.

Still partial to the cheesy Jim Morrison look he had when Gabriel had seen him last. He'd even grown his hair out for the part, long black curls dangling below his collar.

"And is this a working vacation?" Luke probed. He leaned against the railing of the boardwalk, his tight leather pants creaking as he adjusted his stance. They'd played the game hundreds of times. Luke would have his questions, knowing the Bound couldn't lie. He lifted his jaw in the direction of the hotel. "If you have some free time, maybe I'll stop by." Gabriel's heart sank at the satisfied smile. Luke never bluffed.

The question now was how long he'd been onto them. What he had seen.

"Are we done here?" Gabriel turned, heading back toward the hotel, not bothering to conceal his destination.

"I really have been bad about keeping in touch," Luke called after him. "I owe Az a visit, don't I?"

"Stay away from Az, Luke. I mean it."

"Still trying to save your lost little lamb?"

Gabriel paused, turning back toward him. "He might not be ready yet, but one day he will be. He'll use the wings. He'll come home."

"I beg to differ. Which reminds me, tell him I approve of this latest girl. She's quite pretty, don't you think?" Luke pushed off the railing, covering the ground Gabriel had put between them in a lazy stroll and moving past. Just before he turned onto the quiet side street, Luke spun back. "She looks like a fighter. And they're so much more fun to break."

Gabriel stumbled back to the hotel, the elevator ride passing in a blur. Az had been strong enough to keep from choosing a side so far, but if Luke got a hold of Eden, tortured her, it would be the catalyst to set off his Fall. Az opened the door before Gabriel could use his key.

"What's wrong," he demanded.

"Is she safe? Did you call her?" Gabriel collapsed on the bed.

"She's fine. What the hell happened?"

"Luke." His voice broke. "It's Luke. He knew we were here. Az, he knows about Eden."

Az's legs went out, dropping him onto the other bed. "How much?" he whispered.

Gabriel met his eyes. "I don't think he knows she'll be a Sider, but he's going to come after her. I'm sure of it. If he takes her . . ."

There was no reason to say it, to add details out loud. Az flinched as if he'd been slapped. Luke wouldn't kill her outright. He'd keep her in pain as long as possible.

Worse, she wouldn't be the first. Twice before. Violent, drawn out, and painful. Every day had been a battle against the Fall for Az, searching in vain, knowing Luke kept the girls alive. The search only ended when the packages started to arrive. A finger in a jar. A hand wrapped in newspaper.

Gabriel had barely gotten Az through the loss, through the guilt. For weeks after, he'd done his best to pull him out of the depression, didn't let him out of his sight.

Even now, Az's breaths came fast, his eyes darkening as thoughts of vengeance no doubt crossed his mind.

Az shook his head, his eyes still glazed. "I told her today. About what we are."

"You should have waited for me!" Gabriel tried not to look startled. They were going to tell Eden, but he hadn't expected Az to take it on himself. "You didn't tell her anything else, did you?"

Az shot him a look. "Of course not."

"Well, you didn't call, so I guess she took it well?" He tried not to feel left out.

Az nodded. "Gabriel, with Luke being around . . ." Gabriel heard the hesitation in his voice. "If he gets to her first, and does to her what he did to the others." He swallowed, unable to go on.

"We're not going to let that happen," Gabriel insisted.

"What happens if Luke cuts her." His shoulders shook. "Cuts her up," he went on.

Gabriel ran his fingers through his hair. "If he kills her, she'll come back when she's with him. He'll know what she is. Az, he won't stop."

"We can't let that happen," Az said.

"Well then, we can't wait much longer. Luke knows

Kristen's on our side. And as long as he doesn't know Eden's going to be a Sider, he won't come looking for her. She'll be safe there." He dropped his hands to his knees. "As long as she goes Sider before Luke can get to her. Az, we're running out of time."

Az rose to his feet, staying silent as he made his way to the balcony door and slid it open.

They hadn't exactly been looking for a grand view when they'd booked the room. Instead of facing the shore, the balcony provided an aerial glimpse of the homes behind the hotel. Twelve stories down the fog dimmed porch lights to the muted glow of a dozen fireflies. Az squeezed the rusty railing, his knuckles white, his back to Gabriel.

"She's happy. She's not going to do it in time." Az's voice broke. Gabriel moved to stand beside him, leaning his arms on the railing.

"She has to." He glanced at Az, met his worried eyes. He did have an idea. It was horrible to even think about, but he had to suggest it. "We could give her a nudge."

"What do you mean, nudge?"

"Losing you would break her." He pointed his finger at Az. "She's happy because she's with you, Az. If you took that away from her—"

"You're seriously suggesting this?" Az interrupted, his face full of disbelief. "That I what, dump her so she kills herself? That's fucked up."

But Gabriel couldn't get the image out of his head. What Luke would do if he got to her. "Once she's settled at Kristen's, you can explain."

He leaned over the railing next to Az. Far below, the parking lot was only half full, car hoods wet with moisture from the fog. Az followed his gaze.

"I can't do that to her. I love her. She knows I do. What am I supposed to do, tell her I changed my mind?"

Gabriel rolled his eyes. "Of course not. Tell her it's for her own good, that you're not good for her. It's a sacrifice you're going to have to make."

"A sacrifice," Az said quietly. His expression turned thoughtful. "Where is everyone? Shouldn't there be more people?"

"It's Sunday night. Most people are already headed home." Gabriel pulled back, leaning against the glass of the open door. "Why?"

Az didn't answer the question. "Think it'll be the same tomorrow? Empty like this? I don't see anyone around."

"Probably," Gabriel said. He was losing patience. "Az, breaking up with Eden is the best option. Let's just hope it's enough."

"We can't risk it." Az turned, heading back into the hotel room. "Whatever we do, we need to make sure it *is* enough. I have an idea."

# CHAPTER 7

Az reached forward and tucked a few strands of her hair behind her ear. Eden glanced up, smiling. The hotel comforter was scratchy, but she didn't mind as she stretched out on the bed. She reached up to pull him closer, her hand sliding over his back, feeling the shape of his wings under the fabric. They were real. Still there and not some figment of her imagination. Az really was an angel.

He flinched and she lowered her hand.

"What time is it?" she asked.

He pulled out his phone. "Almost midnight."

Eden groaned, taking out her own cell and dialing home. Her mom answered on the second ring. "Hey, it's me. I'm with Az. Just wanted to check in." There was silence on the line. "You there?"

"Who is this again?" Her mom sounded confused.

Eden sat up in bed. "It's your daughter? Eden? Firstborn?" She didn't know why she bothered anymore.

"What time do you want me home?" she asked, finally.

Instead of an answer, the call disconnected. "God, she can't even talk to me?" Eden snapped the phone shut, turning to Az. "I haven't done anything bad all summer and she just gets more and more pissed at me. She acts like I don't even exist." Eden forced her mom's weirdness out of her head. She winked at Az as she ran a finger across his chest, her voice coming out sultry. "I could just stay here all night."

He didn't smile like she expected. Instead, he clicked off the television, rolling over and off the bed.

"Where are you going?"

"I need air." He crossed the room to the balcony, not looking back. He raised his hand to the metal of the handle and left it there, his head drooping. The exit sign behind her buzzed a steady, angry hum.

"Seriously?" She felt her cheeks redden with humiliation, wondering why he'd pulled away.

He flung open the balcony door without an answer, rattling it down the track. Eden jumped as it slammed. When he was outside, he slid it almost closed, leaving only the last inch open. An invitation.

She sat, unbelieving, on the bed. *What the hell is wrong with everyone lately?* The blinds still swung wildly. Slowly she stood and made her way across the room and slid the door open.

"Are you okay?" she asked cautiously.

"No." He leaned, his hand hanging beyond the railing of the balcony. Her fingers grazed his arm, following down until she caught his hand. She squeezed. His head fell onto her shoulder. His fingers found one of her rings, slipping it gently against her knuckle before he dropped her hand and turned away.

"Az, if something's wrong you need to tell me." When he looked up, the sadness in his eyes caught her off guard. "I can handle it. You don't have to keep secrets from me."

"Everyone Upstairs gave up on me a long time ago. As long as I keep the wings I'm not technically Fallen, but Gabriel's the only one who sees it that way." A sarcastic snarl crept into his voice. "Of course, I'm welcome back the minute I repent for my horrible misdoings." His anger seemed to burn out as quickly as it came. His voice sounded shattered and small, breaking. "I never told you why I was cast out."

She'd never considered why he'd been kicked out. She stepped closer to him, her heart hammering as she steeled herself. *I'll love him no matter what*, she thought, knowing how naïve the promise was even as she made it. "What did you do?"

"I fell in love."

"Love?" She couldn't keep the disbelief from her voice. "*That's* why they kicked you out?" Her fears of something terrible, horrendous, melted away. "But that makes no sense. I thought Upstairs would be all about love."

"Exactly. We're welcome to love angels, but not mortals? It's delusional! When we were caught, they wanted me to admit I was wrong for loving her. I wouldn't do it. So they kicked me out." He pulled his cell phone from his pocket, checked the time before he shoved it back.

Eden moved behind him, closing her arms around his waist. Under his shirt she could feel the wings shift slightly. "Well, that's stupid."

"I was supposed to go back," he said quietly. "I was supposed to repent and run home with my tail between my legs. But I didn't. I wasn't wrong. I gave up everything for her."

She kissed his neck softly. "Romantic, though. A bit like Romeo and Juliet." Suddenly she stopped.

An awkward silence bloomed between them, the question obvious. She asked. "Az, where is she now?" He swallowed hard.

"Dead. She died a long time ago."

"Jesus," Eden whispered. "What happened?" she asked.

"I don't know what I'd do if I lost you." A dark shadow seemed to pass over him. He shuddered as if to shake it off. "I'm afraid for you."

"Afraid for me? Why?"

He swallowed hard. "As long as I'm not full Fallen, I could go back Upstairs. The Fallen will do whatever they can to get to me, make me one of them. They'll come after you, Eden. Hurt you." He pulled away from her, hopped up on the railing, his legs wrapped around the spindles for balance.

Panic twisted in her stomach but she forced it down, met his eyes. "Let them fucking try."

"She said the same thing." The raw pain seemed to radiate from him. "They're capable of cruelty you can't imagine."

She laid her hand on his knee. "Stop," she said gently. "Nothing is going to happen to me." She tried out a smile but Az shook his head. He let go of the railing, dropping his hands onto his knees.

When he looked at her, the sorrow in his eyes made her breath catch. "You're going to regret me."

"Regret you! What are you talking about?" She stepped toward him, confused. "You lost me, Az."

At her back a door slammed. Her stomach dropped as Az's eyes widened. *The Fallen*, she thought. She spun, ice running down her spine. Her hip smacked against Az as she turned. Gabriel stared at them blankly from the door he'd just closed.

She didn't have time to register her relief before she heard Az gasp, turned back toward him.

Tipped off balance, his hands flailed through the empty air. There was no sound in the moment before gravity took over, when time froze, when she looked at him, where their eyes met.

He fell.

# CHAPTER 8

One split second passed where she could have reacted, could have reached him in time.

Just enough time to grab his hand. Used up on locking eyes when she should have already been pulling him back. And then it was gone.

"Wait!" Az cried as he went over, and at the same time from behind her Gabe screamed, "Wings!"

She heard Az hit the pavement. Gabe crashed into her from behind, forcing Eden into the railing.

She saw him.

One of his legs bent back in the odd half-cocked angle overused in a thousand movies. His sweatshirt pulled up, like he'd struggled to get it off, to get the wings out in time. She shut her eyes but it was too late, the image burning behind her eyelids.

A keening ripped through her, up her throat as she yanked back, pushing Gabriel off her, dropping.

She thrust out a shaking hand, grabbing the railing above her, ignored Gabe's panic. "Is he moving? Is he . . . ?" Her voice shook, syllables broken by half-formed sobs.

She twisted away from Gabe, brushing off his hands as she rushed into the room, through the door, spilling down the emergency staircase.

Her sobs echoed through the stairwell, grief moaning back from the walls. Dead. The word leached into her, a chill she couldn't shake. No. It wasn't possible.

She heard Gabe shout her name. At the ground floor her legs went out from under her.

He caught up as she collapsed, catching her as they sunk to the floor.

"Tell me angels can't die. Tell me he's okay." She pulled back, desperate. "Gabe?" When he lifted his head, she caught the wet shine of his eyes.

His whole body shook. He looked away. "Don't make me answer."

"No," she whispered. "I have to get to him!"

She pulled herself up by the doorknob.

"Eden." The tone of Gabriel's voice stopped her. "You don't want to see him." His fingers found hers, trying to lift them from the knob, but she turned it anyway.

"What if he's not dead?" Even to her the words sounded hollow. "What if he's hurt?" she asked.

Gabriel pulled the door open, cupping a hand under

her chin. "I'll check for you, Eden. Would that help?"

She nodded numbly. There was no hope in his voice. Deep in her heart something broke loose, draining away everything inside. She walked through the doorway into the lobby in a daze, out the main entrance of the hotel.

*It's all over.* The damp night air curled around her like denial, cold and still and empty. She hugged her arms around herself, not caring where she went. Somehow she made it across the road, down the stairs to the beach, knowing Gabe would look for her there.

*I bumped his leg*, she thought, barely aware of walking. The lights from the boardwalk grew dim. *I just left him there.*

She dropped to the sand. Every hope. Every dream of their life together, gone. Her life over.

"Eden?" Her heart jumped at her name, but it wasn't him. Gabe. Only Gabe. He shook his head.

"Are you sure?" She glanced over to Gabe, barely able to make out his face in the darkness.

"You shouldn't be out here alone, Eden." Gabe's voice was soft, careful, as he squatted down next to her. She winced when he touched her hair, running his hand down to her back. He took her hand, pulled her to her feet.

"Why?" she asked. "He was worried the Fallen would kill me." He nodded in confirmation, and she turned. "I hope they do," she whispered, too low for him to hear.

"Eden?" Gabe released her hand when she pulled away. For a moment she thought he'd heard, would argue, but then he leaned forward and kissed her cheek. "I am so sorry," he whispered.

She blinked hard, staring into the open water. She walked into the surf, swaying as the waves broke against her knees. "Leave."

He hesitated, but only for a moment. She watched, stunned, as he made his way back to the stairs, climbed them without looking back.

The retreating water swirled as it rushed away, pulling at her ankles. Az was really gone. *I'm all alone.* The thought brought back her tears.

She kept her eyes on where the horizon should have been. There were no stars; it was impossible to find where the water ended and the sky began, only waves retreating into black.

A dark sea of nothingness.

# CHAPTER 9

Gabe's hands clutched the rock, his legs quaking, threatening to give out, tip him into the fresh puddle of sick beside him in his hiding spot. He pulled himself up, fingers cramping and sweaty against the stone he'd hunkered down behind.

Eden's body was facedown, far enough from the water's edge that only the most ambitious waves brushed her heels. The shadowed figure at her side had her by the wrist. Gabe swallowed hard. *Leave her, Luke. Walk away.* He sent the thought out, hoping the suggestion would be enough. *She's dead. She's nothing to you.*

There was no reason for him to take her now, mutilate her. No gain. But with Luke, anything was possible.

*Dead.* The word echoed through his head, louder each time. *She's dead. She's really dead.* He squeezed his eyes shut. *Stop. She's gonna be fine. Three hours from now, you'll have her at Kristen's.* He stifled a relieved moan when

Luke cast Eden's wrist loose, the arm falling, deadweight.

Gabe stayed hidden long after Luke made his way up the stairs and out of sight. Finally, he stumbled to Eden.

Her head was turned toward him, her eyes closed. The skin he could make out under the veil of her sopping hair was tinged blue.

All he had to do was get her to the parking lot, to the rental car.

"Come on, love," he whispered, scooping a hand under her knees, another under her back. "We caught some luck with Luke seeing you like this. He'll think you're dead." Her head lolled and he tightened his grip, pulling her against his chest. "Now we just gotta get you to Kristen's."

He straightened, stumbling in the sand.

There would be people on the boardwalk, but even if they suspected something was wrong, he doubted they'd get involved. If there was one thing to be counted on, it was how eagerly the mortals ignored what they didn't want to see. The truth passed right by, and never once did they open their eyes.

# CHAPTER 10

Eden nuzzled deeper into the covers, letting the warmth lull her, waiting for the new dream to take over. Already there was a soundtrack, the strange sound of violins mixed with a thumping bass beat. *Carnival music? The boardwalk?* The thought seemed to wander around her brain, bringing with it a dusty scent like dried roses. Her nose wrinkled. Eden opened her eyes just before a sneeze slammed them shut again. The smell was real.

"What the hell?" She fumbled in the dim light, her fingers clawing up the base of a lamp, clicking it on. The brightness made her wince. "Hello?" she called, forcing her eyes open. A glance was enough to tell her the room was empty. She wasn't in her bed, not in the hotel; the room wasn't one she recognized.

Somewhere in another part of the house, voices drifted, strange music, the sounds of a party.

The room wasn't large, only the bed and a dresser. A

mirror above it. She caught her reflection. Even the dark circles under her eyes were puffy, eyelids an angry swollen pink from crying. Az's face crashed through her thoughts, the desperation on it as he fell. She closed her eyes, but the image only intensified.

Her chest tightened. Everything inside her felt ripped out, raw. She tried to remember. Az. The hotel. She'd been on the beach, standing on the shore. Endless water. She forced her eyes open and threw off the covers. The air hit her clothes, the damp fabric already taking on a chill. Her hair hung in nearly dried clumps.

"Gabe?" No one answered. She dropped her bare feet to the floor, scanned for her shoes. On the back of the closet door hung a ball gown, the black fabric standing out several feet. Her own shoes were nowhere, but tucked against the wall beside the dress rested a pair of black heels. An envelope rested carefully across the ankle straps. Eden crossed the room.

Inside was a note, the words written in delicate calligraphy.

*Please join the festivities at your earliest convenience. Proper dress has been provided.*

It was unsigned.

The handwriting wasn't Gabe's, but he had to be

downstairs. Eden stared down at the shoes. They seemed to be her size, or at least close. She eyed the dress wearily. *Why did he bring me here?* she wondered. Maybe it was a memorial. *He must have thought I'd want to come.* Being around people was the last thing she wanted. She'd find him and force him to take her back to the hotel. She couldn't deal with going home.

Eden's feet slid perfectly into the shoes. Even with her own clothes damp and cold, she wasn't about to throw on the dress.

She ran her fingers through the tangles in her hair, suddenly overeager to be downstairs, to find Gabe.

When she opened the door, the hallway beyond was dark, just enough light to find her way down it, the sweet serenade drawing her on.

It was an old house; she could tell by the pinched walls, the way they seemed to close her in. Ahead, a swath of light cut around a corner. She drew her shoulders up, quickening her step.

The banister began long before the slow wind of the staircase. Through the spindles, she could see a sea of black tuxedos, coattails twirling when the music demanded. Dozens of guys danced in a pattern straight out of seventeenth-century France. They ducked suddenly, hands clapping out a rhythm.

The room below seemed to take up half of the first floor.

It looked like something out of a sideshow where a person paid a nickel to see dead babies in jars. Sure enough, surrounded by candles housed in blackened goblets, there was a jar on the mantle. A sunken lump of black rested at the bottom. Eden forced her eyes away.

The music swelled and she made out a swirl of color, then another. Gowns twirled through tunnels made of human arms. The song ended in the long draw of a bow against strings, holding the note until the dancers bowed and dispersed.

Idle chatter drowned out the final strains of the music as everyone made their way to folding chairs set up against the walls. Hundreds of candles dripped lazily onto whatever surface they had been placed on, complementing the soft light from a chandelier. One of the rare girls mingled, spending a few seconds with each group before making her way to the next, her crimson dress like a beacon in the crowd of black suits.

Eden watched, enraptured, until she managed to pull her eyes away, searching the crowd for Gabe. There were too many guys to find him, the masses blending together. She had no choice but to go down among them. She stood and made her way to the staircase.

At the first landing, a young blond boy leaned against the railing, his elbows cocked back. He pulled his hands in as she made her way down, the white gloved fingers wrapping around the banister.

She hesitated when she reached him, only because his mouth opened as if he were going to say something. She waited, neither of them moving.

"Um," she started.

She wracked her brain, but there didn't seem to be a protocol for waking up in a strange bedroom only to find fucking Versailles come to life downstairs. She wondered if perhaps it was a memorial for Az. She hadn't met any of his other friends. Maybe that was why Gabe had brought her? But hours after he died? A sudden feeling of disorientation overwhelmed her. Had it only been hours? How long had she slept? *And why the hell are they all wearing gloves?*

When she turned back to the kid to ask, he was holding his elbow out to her.

"Kristen's been delayed." He thrust the elbow out again. He couldn't have been more than twelve, thirteen tops. His eyes were unnerving. Desperate.

"Who?" Eden asked. She took a step back, but he only moved closer. "Thanks, but I'm looking for a friend."

He glanced behind her, eyes darting though his head barely moved. He hooked her arm, no longer waiting for her permission. His tone morphed into an urgent whisper. "Go! Before she sees that you're up."

"Cameron." The voice came from far beyond him,

somewhere in the darkness of the huge house. The boy's shoulders clenched up, his feet stopping dead. He didn't look back. "It is Cameron, right?" the voice asked sweetly. He squeezed his eyes shut, nodded his head. Eden spun, her arm still latched around his, pulling him with her. "Exactly what advice were you passing on to her, Cameron?"

A hand was wrapped around the ball of the newel post. Perfectly manicured nails scratched lightly against the wood. A ball gown swept around her feet as she rounded the post. The deep green of the gown matched eyes sparkling with malice. Her bun of red hair only set them off further.

"Look, I'm not sure . . ." *How I woke up here, if you are all in a cult, if the police will find pieces of me buried in the backyard.* Eden started again. "I'm looking for my friend."

The girl never turned to Eden, never even acknowledged she was there. Her attention stayed on Cameron. His arm clutched tighter around Eden's.

"Kristen told me to stop her before she got downstairs. . . ." Ball Gown held up a finger, silencing him. A sad smile dug into the corners of her mouth as she began to take the stairs, dropping step by step.

"You're avoiding the question, Cameron."

"I'm sorry, Madeline." His voice disintegrated into a terrified whine. "Please don't tell Kristen."

Eden stepped forward, between her and Cameron. At Eden's back, the kid shivered.

"Hey, listen. Madeline, is it? It's fine, really. I need to find—"

There was a yank at her arm, a thudding up the stairs as the boy broke into a run. Eden tried to watch where he went over Madeline's shoulder, but the glare called her attention back.

"I was speaking." Her face pinched, as if she couldn't quite believe Eden dared to address her. "And you interrupted me."

Eden was ready to spit out some form of "sorry" until she remembered the terrified look on the kid's face. Anticipation surged into Madeline's eyes. Clearly an apology wasn't the way to go. "I'm looking for a friend of mine. Excuse me." She tried to brush past, but Madeline blocked her path.

The girl finally smiled. "So you're Kristen's new recruit? You can follow me. I'm sure she'll be along shortly." She spun away, the heavy material of her dress swishing with her every step.

After a second of hesitation, Eden followed her down the stairs into the crowd, to the back of the room. Madeline, wearing a friendly grin, took a seat on an antique settee.

"Sit!" Madeline said, her finger twisting the flame-red

strands that had come loose from her bun. The gloves she wore matched her gown. *What the hell's with the gloves?* Eden wondered again as Madeline patted the empty space beside her. "So, how are you holding up? The first few days are awful, but it gets better."

Eden choked back a breath, unprepared. *He's really gone.* Her eyes welled up. So it was some kind of memorial. "I'm . . . it was unexpected." For some reason the comment brought an appreciative chuckle from the other girl.

"How could you have known?" Her smile faded before she caught it, pinned her cheeks back with renewed vigor. Her eyes jolted to the stairs and back, almost too quick to catch. "Well, you must be special. Kristen brought out the good china for your little shindig," she prodded, flicking a hand to the stenciled teacup beside her. She lifted it, took a slow sip as she gave Eden a once-over. "Though I have no idea how you got past her wearing that attire."

"This isn't my 'shindig.'" Eden didn't bother to dull the frustration from her voice. "Listen, I lost my boyfriend tonight, so I could honestly care less what you think about my—"

"Boyfriend?" The statement clearly caught Madeline off guard. "I can guarantee your boyfriend's not here."

Eden's stomach twisted. "Lost as in he's dead. Gabe must have brought me here after Az—"

"Az?" she interrupted. "And Gabriel?"

Eden hesitated. None of this made sense. "This is a memorial for Az, right? It's the only reason Gabe would—"

Madeline's face paled, the only color surviving in two perfect swipes of rouge across her cheeks. "Are you saying Az is dead?" The teacup sloshed in her shaking hand, splashing onto the floral material of the cushion between them.

Eden let out a slow breath. "There was an accident," she said quietly. Madeline hadn't known.

The gathering wasn't a memorial. Her eyes skirted the room for Gabe again, but didn't find him. *What if he* didn't *bring me?* She tried again to remember. She'd been on the beach, alone. Gabe had been worried about the Fallen. *You don't know what they look like.* Dread trickled into her as she turned back to Madeline. "Why am I here?" she asked.

In her peripheral vision she saw a figure break from the crowd. Her gaze shot up as a red-gowned girl barreled toward them, long brown hair streaming down her back, eyes brimming with madness.

"That piece of furniture you've just ruined is older than you could ever hope to become," she screeched, snatching the cup away. She slammed it down, the rest of the tea dripping off the end table onto the carpet.

"Kristen!" Madeline yelled. The room around them stopped. Eden turned, meeting dozens of eyes now locked on their corner. Madeline thrust a finger into Eden's face. She dropped her voice to an accusatory hiss too low to be heard by any but the three of them. "She seems to think Az is dead. Care to clarify why I wasn't told?"

"Possibly because you don't need to know everything." She spun on Eden. "Who told you to talk to Madeline? You were supposed to stay with Cameron to avoid this very thing." Kristen let loose a squeal of frustration, slamming her foot down. "You're ruining everything! And after the energy I've expended to make you feel welcome?"

"Welcome her?" Madeline sneered. "Kristen, there are more important things than one of your hideous debut parties! What happened to Az?"

Kristen's jaw dropped, brown eyes filling with rage. "My parties are *not* hideous!"

The crowd parted again to let a guy through. He stepped in front of Kristen, his face eerily calm as his eyes locked on Madeline, his hand clamping onto her shoulder.

"You're only scaring the poor girl, Madeline." His voice was a warning. "Kristen, perhaps we should call it a night?" It wasn't a command, the end lifted in a question. Kristen nodded.

"Gentlemen and ladies," he yelled, his voice booming. "The evening has come to an end." The effect was instant, the room splitting in two. Half the dancers retreated up the staircase, down the left wing, the opposite direction

Eden had come from earlier. The others stood frozen, as if awaiting command.

"Go home, Madeline," the guy said. She glared at him, shrugging off the hand at her shoulder.

"I think that's a fucking brilliant idea, Sebastian." Madeline flicked her hand toward the door and the dozen leftover teenagers trudged out silently.

"Madeline." Kristen's voice dropped, her eyes steely. "You will not whisper a word of this. Are we clear?"

"Az's girlfriend a Sider?" Madeline threw a hand on her hip. "Keeping that secret is going to cost you." Eden stared. Who the hell were these people?

Kristen sighed. "I am aware of that."

"I'll call you with my price." Madeline smiled with satisfaction and headed out the door.

"And now . . . ," Sebastian trailed off, his chin jutting Eden's way.

"I *know* that, Sebastian," Kristen ground out before turning to Eden. "Would you follow me?" She wandered across the floor, kicking a streamer out of the way. Eden took a few steps before she stopped, hesitating between the staircase and the front door. Sebastian leaned against it, his arms crossed over his chest. His stance didn't exactly scream "you're free to go."

"I'm not going up there. Where's Gabe?" Eden asked. "And what the hell is a Sider?"

Kristen had made it halfway up the staircase. She groaned when Eden spoke, throwing her head back in frustration. "Could you *please* just follow me?"

"I want to go home." The whole night had been one mind-fuck after another.

Kristen dropped back down half a dozen steps. When she spoke, her words were slow and short, patronizing. "It's been a disaster of an evening. I am using the very last of my patience to show you back to your room, after which I'll be tracking down Cameron to ensure his failure has a fitting consequence."

"My room?" Eden stepped back once, toward the door.

Kristen swept up the rest of the stairs, coming to a stop at the top. "Gabriel left you in my care. Perhaps you'll follow me for his sake?"

"Where is he?" She couldn't keep the shaking from her voice.

"He was concerned about your safety while he addressed some . . ." She met Eden's eye. "Issues that came up tonight."

"Then give me a phone. I'm not staying here. I need to call home for a ride." She knew it wasn't likely anyone would answer, didn't care. She'd fake the phone call and get the hell out. "My mom has to be freaking out," she added. "She's probably filed a missing person's report by now."

Kristen leaned against the banister, watching her in silence. "I doubt that very much."

Then she spun, heading down the hall, ending the conversation, leaving Eden little choice but to follow.

The first few doors on either side of the hall had been closed, light glowing from under the cracks beneath them. Beyond those few, though, they were all open and dark. Kristen finally reached into one, flipping the switch. Eden slowed her steps, leery. She watched Kristen for a moment from the threshold before she sat on the edge of the bed. Kristen closed the door, leaned against it.

"If I could just call Gabe," Eden started, but Kristen waved her into silence. She ignored her. "You're a friend of his?"

Kristen ran a finger down the door, tapping her nail against the knob. "One might say that." Her tone suggested something more.

Eden raised an eyebrow at the insinuation. "Then clearly you don't know him that well."

Kristen threw her head back as she laughed. "Really now? Isn't it possible that you don't know him as well as you thought?"

The air seemed to leave her lungs. Everything she'd known had been twisted around tonight.

Kristen rolled her eyes. "Honestly, Eden, you're such an open book. I can actually see you puzzling it out." Her voice rose an octave, mocking. "'This girl I've just met told me he was lying so he must be.'" Her face went hard. "Gabe is your friend. Try to show some fucking loyalty, hmm?"

Eden's mouth dropped open in shock. "Who *are* you?"

"Where were you tonight, Eden? Before you woke up here."

"After Az . . ." The words thickened in her throat with the memory of Az's face as he fell, his body lying broken on the pavement.

Kristen nodded, her face almost sympathetic. "Go on."

"I was on the beach," she stuttered.

"In the water or out?"

"In." Her brow furrowed. Why was it so fuzzy? "I was standing, in the water." She hesitated. "I was standing in the water and . . . then nothing. I woke up here." Kristen slid off one glove in a deliberate sweeping gesture before turning her attention back to Eden.

"All right, my little blank slate, let's just dive in, shall we?" The gloved hand shot forward suddenly, grabbing Eden's wrist.

"Let go!" Eden jerked, but Kristen held tight. "What are you doing?"

Kristen's grin spread. She dragged Eden's hand closer, until it hovered just above the ribbed corset of her dress.

"You're lying about the beach." Kristen sneered as

she yanked. "Everyone remembers their death."

Eden's fingertips hit Kristen's collarbone.

The skin slid loose from Kristen's face, down her cheeks. Eden couldn't tear her hand away. Couldn't move. One of Kristen's eye sockets went hollow, the bone behind yellowed. What was left of her lips ripped apart as her smile widened.

Eden wanted to scream, but nothing would come out.

"Not even a shriek?" The features slid back to where they belonged, the pert nose seeming to form out of nowhere. There was no blood, everything back to normal. "Do not puke on my rug," she said before releasing Eden's hand. It hung there in the air, shaking.

*I'm hallucinating*, she thought. It was the only explanation. Her mind clamped onto the idea, though her body hadn't caught up, her mouth opening and closing like a dying carp. *Stress. Grief. Or they drugged me.* The excuses explained everything away in a dainty little package.

"Would you like to know what happened on the beach, Eden?" Kristen snapped. She stepped closer even as Eden shrunk from her. "The idea of living a life without Az was just too much for your pretty little head. You stood in that water, and you couldn't stand the thought of going on. You gave up."

"No," Eden whispered.

"Whatever horrible existence you managed to carve out

for yourself died with you." Kristen went on, her words slow and careful. "You must have noticed them forgetting you. Family, your friends? It may have taken Az's death to give you that final push, but your suicide was already inevitable."

"I'm not dead, that's just . . ." She'd been on the beach, in the water, in shock. Eden shook her head, trying to rattle the sanity back into it.

"Your old life is over, Eden. You're a Sider now." Her bare feet padded across the floorboards. Just before she reached the door, she turned. "Gabe brought you here because he knew you needed to be with your own kind. I took you in as a favor to him. But I don't have time to coddle you. You're dead." A smile twitched her lips. "Live with it."

Eden checked the door after the sound of Kristen's footsteps faded. It didn't surprise her to find it locked, though her heart still sank. She scanned the room, searching for a phone, another way out. The window was second story.

Dead. The word echoed through her mind. If she were dead, there would be nothing, none of the grief cleaving her heart in two. Shaking, she sunk onto the bed. *Is that why I can't remember?* Her brain felt fried, overloaded.

She stared at the door, too numb to cry. There was nothing to do but wait for it to be opened.

# CHAPTER 11

The hesitant rapping on wood was enough to pull her out of the fugue state she'd passed the night in. Eden bolted upright just as the door clicked open.

A guy peered around the door, not bothering to hide his stare while he sized her up. Eden returned the favor. Shaggy brown hair, maybe a few years older than her. Jeans and a T-shirt for some band she'd never heard of. He looked normal enough. Maybe last night's costumes were just that. Costumes.

"Breakfast?" He moved his arm in past the door, revealing a covered silver tray. The smell of sausage and syrup drifted across the room. "Yeah?" He waggled the tray a bit, smiling.

"I'm not hungry." *The dead don't eat, anyway,* she thought. Fresh tears filled her eyes. She yanked her ponytail holder free, rubbing her face before she rebound the tangled mess of her hair.

Her stomach betrayed her, belting out a low protest.

"Not hungry, huh?" He crossed the room and plopped down on her bed uninvited. A puff of steam escaped as he lifted the lid. "I'm taking your bacon then."

"Where's Gabriel?"

"Don't know any Gabriels." True to his word, he tossed half a strip into his mouth.

"But you know Kristen?" she asked, eyeing him.

He laughed. "I definitely know Kristen. I live here."

"So, you're . . . dead." He nodded, nonplussed, and crunched another piece of bacon. "If you're dead, why are you eating?"

"Because bacon is awesome? You can eat or not, your call." He shrugged. "Oh!" he said, digging into his back pocket. "Mail call." He threw an oversized manila envelope at her. It spun through the air, one of the points catching her skin as it hit her chest.

"That fucking hurt, asshole!"

He stopped chewing. "Jesus, I hope you know better than to talk to *Kristen* like that." When he'd finished his mouthful, he added, "I'm Adam."

There was a chance, however slight, he was sane. For now, any semblance of a violent streak seemed placated by pillaging her abandoned pancakes.

"Eden." She held out her hand.

He let out a quiet chuckle, cocked a finger at her hand.

"We shake hands, it's gonna get ugly." He traded a smile for her blank stare. "Once you've been here awhile, you'll stop reacting to the other Siders."

She flashed back to the ball, the dozen guys in their formal wear, the girls in ball gowns. All of them had been Siders. Dead. "Yesterday you were all wearing gloves."

"Look, Kristen went all *Dawn of the Dead* on you, right?" he asked, gesturing to his face. "She wasn't rotting in real time. You haven't been around her, so your Touch dropped her glamour. We don't spend enough time with the other boroughs to grow immune, and yesterday Madeline's group came in from Queens. Hence the gloves."

*I'm in New York?* she thought. "Madeline. She's the one I talked to last night."

Adam froze. "You talked to Madeline?"

Something in the way Adam gaped at her told her she'd pulled off some kind of undead faux pas. "She seemed a lot less crazy than Kristen."

Adam dropped the fork slowly to the tray, pushing it away. "Crazy's not always the worst thing." He paused long enough for her to wonder if he would go on.

"So, you look . . ." She swallowed. "If I touch you, you'll look like Kristen did?"

"Not as rotty as she probably did. The more Touch you're storing, the worse you tend to look, and Kristen is always testing the limits. Probably has a lot to do with how come she's . . ." He trailed off, giving the door a quick glance before he twirled his hand around his temple. He lowered his hand. "Do you wanna see what I look like? I mean, I don't just go revealing my inner self to every girl I meet but . . ." Adam held out his arm, his fingers relaxing into a loose fist. "Go ahead."

She jiggled her knee, her finger flexing closer. "Will it hurt you?"

"Won't feel a thing."

She kept her eyes on his face as her finger brushed against his wrist. His skin sallowed, the cheeks hollowing out. His brown eyes clouded over, but didn't burst the way Kristen's had. Clusters of blackened capillaries bruised a thick ring around his neck. And then it was over. His features shimmered back into place as the glamour took hold again.

"Not so bad, right?" Adam dropped his hand to his lap. Eden let out an awkward laugh, but shook her head. "A few more days here and nothing will happen when you touch me. Do you wanna see what you look like? Because I can show you." He pointed to the mirror above the dresser.

"Will it be bad?"

"Nah, you can't have built up much Touch. You're like, what? One day in? You'll still be pretty." A blush burst across his face.

"Here," she said quickly, offering him her own arm.

She felt the shift, a subtle tingle racing across her hairline, down her spine. Adam yanked back.

"What? What is it?" She twisted to the mirror, caught the fading dull cream of cheekbones under stripped flesh before her skin knitted over again.

"Holy shit," he whispered.

"I'm not supposed to look like that, am I?" She tore her eyes from the mirror. "You said it wouldn't be like that!"

"How the hell?" He sounded out each word. "Has Kristen touched you?" She shook her head, her eyes wide. "Eden, you cannot let Kristen see you without your glamour. Do you understand?"

"Why? Why did I look like that?"

"No one builds up Touch that fast. No one can *store* that much."

"Adam, please. What's going on?"

He slid off the bed, putting distance between them. His tone shifted, coming out strained, formal. "Kristen has requested the pleasure of your company in the foyer once you've finished breakfast. There's a shower across the hall." His voice dropped to a whisper. "Obviously you're not new, and I have no idea how you're storing that much and still functioning, but you are *far* too potent. She'll make you a Screamer."

"What the fuck is that?"

"She locks them in their rooms. Doesn't let them pass

Touch. We don't see them again. But we hear them."

"What's Touch?"

"If you just needed somewhere to crash for the night, fine, but I'd get out while you can. Kristen's worse than any rumor you've heard." He opened the door and slipped out without answering her question.

She stared after him. After a minute her eyes fell to the large envelope waiting beside her, her name splayed across the front.

She ripped at the sealed flap, swiping the inside. At first she thought it was empty, but then the edge of a photograph slipped under her nail. She pulled it out.

"Oh," she whispered. The sudden image of him caught her off guard, tears blurring his face. She blinked hard until he cleared.

Her eyes were closed in the shot; her head in Az's lap as he'd leaned down to kiss her forehead. They looked deliriously happy. She ran her fingers reverently over its surface.

"Az," she murmured. She hadn't known Gabe had snapped the picture. Never seen it before now.

She slid the picture back into the envelope, glancing around the room for a safe place to keep it. There wouldn't be enough words to tell him how much it meant to her when she saw him again. If she saw him again.

# CHAPTER 12

Eden descended the stairs, scoping out the room below, but there was no sign of a trap. No sign of Sebastian or Adam waiting to ambush her. Only Kristen, flopped across an overstuffed armchair. One of her legs swung idly over an armrest, her hand draped across her forehead.

She wore a different dress, this one a dark blue vintage circa 1950. Nothing as garish as last night's ball gown. Judging by how Kristen had stocked the closet in Eden's room, dresses were apparently her thing. Eden hadn't managed to find much that was passable in the dresser. A black skirt and a few layered tank tops had gotten the job done.

Kristen sat up at the creaking stairs. "Dear Lord, child. Does it always take you so long to shower?"

Eden didn't answer. She'd held her shit together last night and through breakfast, but once she stepped under the faucet head, the water streaming over her, it was over. She'd given in to her grief, clamped a hand over her mouth to muffle her cry, while the spray stripped tears from her eyes before they had a chance to fall. Now she felt nothing but hollow.

"You're not afraid of me after last night, are you?" Kristen leaned forward, raising an eyebrow in amusement. She took Eden's silence for a no and catapulted herself out of the chair. "Wonderful! I thought perhaps you'd like to go somewhere with me."

Eden's brow wrinkled. "What, outside?"

"This isn't a prison, Eden." With a glance up the stairs, Kristen cupped the side of her hand around her mouth and stage-whispered, "At least not to you," her over-theatrical wink laced with sarcasm.

"Which is why you locked me in last night?"

"Oh, Eden. Let's not be bitter about last night. I'd like you to feel at home during your stay here."

"And how long will that be?"

"Long enough," Kristen offered as a non-answer.

"Where's Gabe?" Eden asked, knowing there wouldn't be an answer. If he had left her here, he didn't seem to be in a hurry to get back. Maybe it was because of what happened to Az. "Is he Upstairs?"

Kristen raised an eyebrow. "You mean a lot to Gabriel. He cares about you."

Eden nodded, unsure where Kristen planned to go with the conversation. "He's my friend. I want to make sure he's okay. We just lost Az." She hesitated, forced herself to stop. "You keep saying you know him, but you don't seem to know anything about him."

Kristen's stare was piercing. "I don't give away his secrets to those I don't trust. Knowledge is power, Eden, and Gabriel is important to me. You'll forgive me if I'm not as loose with sensitive information as you."

"What's that supposed to mean?" Eden couldn't keep the frustration from her voice. She felt like she was in some nightmare. That she'd wake up curled next to Az in the bed at the hotel. But dreams were painless. The ache in her chest drummed reality against her rib cage with every beat. She'd never wake up next to Az.

"Last night you told Madeline you were with Az. His girlfriend," Kristen said.

"So? I—" Eden cut off, not sure what tense to use. Am his girlfriend? Was his girlfriend?

"Did you even stop to wonder if *Madeline* might be loyal to the Fallen before you babbled away?" Kristen shook her head, disappointment in her eyes. It seemed directed at herself rather than Eden.

"She told the Fallen about me?" Eden managed. Her heart hammered. "Gabe trusted you and you gave me right to Madeline?"

Kristen's eyes flashed anger. "Luckily the girl can be bought, so she's keeping your secret for now. Cameron should never have allowed you to talk to her. It's important that the Fallen believe you died on that beach. It was important that she see you. Important that she thought you were just another Sider. But you went and spoiled it. You don't understand what they will do to you, just to hurt him."

"If Az is dead, what does it matter?"

Kristen's look was even. "You're a liability, Eden. I don't particularly adore you being here. Not until I see you can be trusted."

"So this is that whole 'welcoming' thing you keep talking about?" Eden snipped. "Because I can go."

"Where? I don't know what he sees in you, but I promised Gabriel I'd keep you in one piece." Kristen smirked, walking toward the front door. "We're going to start over with some girl bonding. Bonding builds trust. I've had quite the exhausting morning. I thought we'd unwind with some window-shopping."

Now it was Eden's turn to stare. "You want me to go shopping with you?"

"We won't be bringing anything home today, just looking. But it'll grant me the opportunity to kill two birds."

Eden shadowed her down the steps, following the path to the sidewalk. When she glanced back, she caught her first view of the house from outside. It offered no hint to what went on behind the closed door.

"Come, come," Kristen hummed, snapping her fingers.

"I must admit, I thought I'd have to revisit last night's little show at least once to convince you that you hadn't lost your mind." She slowed her pace to match Eden's, scooting over to make room so they could walk side by side. "The tenacity does earn you a point or two."

"Does it?" Eden's voice was flat. She eyed the street warily. The neighborhood looked normal enough. Her muscles tensed as she debated making a run for it. Quiet neighborhood, no transportation. Sure, she could take off. But Kristen was right. Where would she go?

They walked by the arched walkway of an estate, rose bushes climbing the trellis. Kristen snagged a bloom, caressed it as they walked.

"I'd rather Gabriel and Az not be mentioned by name under my roof." She ripped a petal free of the flower, casting it aside. "No one really knows much about the Siders. Gabriel's trying to figure things out, but until then, it's best his association with us is kept quiet. To answer your question, he had some loose ends to tie up. I'm sure he'll be in contact soon."

"And so I just wait, no questions?" Eden sighed hard. "I wake up in some random house, I'm told all kinds of crazy, and now I'm supposed to what? Stay here?"

Kristen stopped dead. "Let's get something straight. With Az and Gabriel in your past, you're nearly guaranteed to be trouble to anyone you come in contact with. You were damn lucky to have me take you in. No Sider wants the Fallen to come knocking on her door. You're here to learn. Not to pontificate the cruelties of fate. Those you surround yourself with should fall into one of two categories. The used, or the amusing." She gripped the rose high up on the stem, snapped off the bloom with her thumb. The break wasn't clean. The head dangled, damaged beyond repair. "You'd be wise to pick a category, Eden, because anyone else is a burden."

"So which one is Gabe?"

Kristen froze. A plastic grin swept her lips up. "Lesson two. Everyone has a weakness. Loyalty happens to be mine." She let the flower fall, careful to step around it. "Tenacious and maybe even a bit clever. See! Our bonding is working! I like you a little more already."

Kristen dug into the cleavage of her dress and pulled out a dainty silver case. She snapped it open, palming a piece of paper before she offered Eden one of the clove cigarettes lining the inside. Even before Eden shook her head, Kristen had lit one for herself and tucked the case away.

"Quite a pleasant surprise. When I found Az was with a mortal, I assumed he was just slumming."

Eden winced at his name, but Kristen didn't seem to notice. "Slumming?"

"The Fallen have their little digressions. Mortals are shiny to angels, but they don't belong with them. Those silly girls never manage to sink their claws in for very long." Kristen's lips pressed together as if she realized she'd said too much.

"It wasn't like that with us." Eden stared off down the street, searching for a question, anything to camouflage the empty heaviness every time she thought of him, heard his name.

Kristen took a long drag and made a weak attempt at blowing a smoke ring. The circle wobbled and broke apart as it left her lips. "Sebastian doesn't approve of me smoking. Says it sets a bad example. But it's the one vice I could never quite shake." For a girl who claimed knowledge was power, she sure seemed to be doling it out.

Eden rolled her eyes. "It's not like it's gonna kill you. You're dead. Or undead." A guy across the street caught Eden's eye. She watched him walk, tuning Kristen out.

Eden couldn't take her eyes off the guy. His hair wasn't curly enough, not quite the right shade of brown. She shifted her eyes to the house beyond him, let him fall further out of focus. *Better*, she thought.

"If I'm dead, where's Az?" she asked. The guy must have felt her staring and turned toward her. Eden's stomach dropped, but from the front there wasn't even a passing resemblance. From the corner of her eye, Eden caught the shake of Kristen's head, spun back just in time to catch her gaze flash to the guy and back.

"You may have killed yourself thinking you'd get to be with him, but this isn't the afterlife, sweet pea. It's the Bronx." Kristen flicked the cigarette and hit it again. "You won't find him here."

Kristen dropped what was left of the cigarette, crushing it underfoot with her last step before she came to a stop. She handed over the piece of newspaper she'd been holding.

It was an obituary. The picture showed a woman in her twenties. Eden scanned the article. Car accident. Fashion student. "What's this?"

"Passing knowledge of the deceased. Proper funeral-crashing etiquette dictates at least knowing her name." Kristen tipped her head to the side.

The parlor looked like a normal house, designed to blend from the white siding down to the choice of flowers in the mulched beds. Only the wooden sign staked down in the middle of the lawn betrayed its purpose. That and the well-dressed mourners plodding up the walkway. Cars lined either side of the street.

"It's packed in there already and we're fifteen minutes early. My theory, proven once again," Kristen said, climbing the stairs.

"What theory would that be?"

"Everyone adores a tragedy." The door opened before them, the suited usher nodding, his expression serious until he actually looked at them.

"Hey, Paul." Kristen raised a hand, giving him a slight wiggle of her fingers. She gasped, gripping the sides of her dress in excitement. "You've redecorated! And such a wonderful eye for color! Cheers to the death of that dreadful wallpaper," she exclaimed, taking in the hallway beyond. "Eden, meet Paul. His dad owns this place."

"And he told you you're not allowed to be here. Why don't you just hang out at Starbucks like a normal girl?"

As if a switch flipped, Kristen's delight faded. "This one I know, Paul."

Eden stared between the two of them. Paul wasn't sold. Not even with Kristen's pained expression, the dramatic sigh before she went on. "Amanda was my babysitter when I was little, our neighbor. I hadn't seen her since we moved, but my mother requested that I make an appearance since she's unable to attend." She added a sad shake of her head, lowering her voice. "I don't want to get you into trouble, Paul. I only need a few minutes."

He nodded, blushing with embarrassment.

When they were safely out of his earshot and into the main viewing room, Kristen murmured, "That'll teach him to call me out."

"You're sick. You know that, right?"

Kristen snorted a laugh, twisted it into a sob, covering her mouth with her hand. She grabbed a tissue and dabbed at her eyes. "I'm skilled. What you just witnessed?

Beginner's manipulation. And also a classic example of why research pays." She sniffed, tossing the tissue into the trash.

"Look." Eden glanced around. The room was filling up, family and *actual* friends occupying the rows of chairs. "Why are we even here?"

Kristen had led them to the receiving line. She tilted her head toward the man standing five feet to the side of the coffin, greeting each of the mourners after they paid their last respects. "Frank Watson. In seventeen days he'll celebrate the big five-oh. He's a CEO, but an honest one. Old money—the family has a crypt in the cemetery down the street. Usually upbeat, a nearly unbearable brand of cheerful. If I had spread Touch to him last week, chances are the Touch wouldn't have killed him."

There it was again, the same word Adam had used. "What is that? Touch?"

"Am I not explaining that now, Eden? Really, try to show some patience." Kristen crossed her arms, taking a few steps to keep up with the line, but staying far enough from the mortals that they wouldn't be overheard. "How are you feeling this morning?"

Eden rolled her eyes. "I'm feeling annoyed that you never answer any questions."

"A bit uneasy, maybe? Like you've had too much caffeine? That's usually what it feels like when Touch isn't spread, at least the first day."

"Currently I have a headache from *lack* of coffee. No jitters."

"Nothing?" Kristen took her in for a moment, as if waiting for her to break down. "Well, it's still early, I suppose. Touch is, unfortunately, our burden to bear." She glanced down at Eden's hands. "And the reason you should be wearing gloves in public. Each day, starting tomorrow, you'll be passing it to a different mortal. This needs to be done every day, Eden. If you let it build, it becomes lethal."

"So if I don't touch people, it'll kill me?"

"No. Immortality is one of the rare upsides to being a Sider." Kristen lowered her voice. "If you let it build, it will feel like being eviscerated. But Touch won't kill you." Her eyes darted to the coffin and back. "It'll kill them. It's a virus, and we're the host."

"We make them sick?" Eden whispered.

Kristen looked thoughtful. "It feeds off their feelings, strips away the ability to see right and wrong, to know when to stop. A mortal on Touch sees no consequences. I guess in that way it's more like a drug than a virus. If they're happy, satisfied, they come through with a few crazy stories."

Kristen swept her bangs out of her eyes, her fingers lingering on her brow. "Not every Sider takes it to a good place. Take Madeline, for example. She seeks out the suicidal. She enjoys it, Eden," she said, enunciating each word. "Fancies herself some kind of reaper. Nothing gets that girl off more than using Touch to give them that final push."

"And what about you? What do you do?"

"Not that."

"You don't seem like the type to care. I mean, you gave her too much Touch and it made her crash." Kristen's head snapped up, the movement so sudden that Eden jumped.

"I did nothing of the sort. I didn't lay a finger on her."

"So what happened to her?" Eden asked. The line in front of them had run through. Kristen closed the gap, kneeling down in front of the coffin. Eden copied her, glancing around uncomfortably.

"Obituary said car accident." Kristen fell silent, her lips moving in prayer.

Eden stared at the girl, found herself feeling sad for all the plans she'd put off for "maybe someday" that had died with her. There was a makeup line just below her ear, the hideous purple of a bruise showing through.

Kristen rose from her knees. Eden followed when she backtracked past the people lined up behind them and toward the front door. Paul opened it for them. Kristen shot him a wink before traipsing down the stairs at the end of the walk, heading back toward her home.

"What was the point? Paying your last respects?"

Kristen dug for the silver case again, lighting another clove.

"If we're going to spend our day with these little girl chats, Eden, do learn to pay more attention. Her family has a crypt. Yes, they're usually easy to get into, but I still like to check out the merchandise before I expend the energy." She exhaled another cloud of smoke. It drifted into Eden's path. "Jewelry was costume. Dress was hardly noteworthy. Black cocktail is so cliché. I just saved myself the trouble of finding out the hard way. As I said, research pays."

Eden's head twisted as she reassessed Kristen's dress, the antique rings adorning her fingers. "You're telling me you rob graves?"

"Nine times out of ten, the dead wear designer, and I'm on a budget." She rolled her eyes at Eden's hanging jaw. "Oh, honestly. I wash them."

"You're insane!"

"And you're boring. You sounded much more interesting when Gabe was begging for my help."

Eden shifted out of the path of the smoke blowing in her direction, didn't give Kristen the satisfaction of a cough.

"How is Gabe even friends with you? How do you know him?"

"You really want to know?" Kristen kept her eyes

ahead, threading her fingers through her hair. She hesitated. "I guess I can bore you with a history lesson. There were no others when I became a Sider, at least not that I knew." Kristen toyed with one of her rings. "Unlike you, I woke up on a park bench, not in a bed. Vodka and pills. I assumed it hadn't been enough, figured it would be best to head home and face my father's wrath." Kristen's gaze had gone far off. "It was an office, my room. It hadn't been an office when I'd left a few hours before. None of my notebooks, no school portraits. Like I never existed. I thought he was trying to scare me for breaking curfew. For a long time, I thought it was just an amazingly creative way of kicking me out. Truth was, I don't exist to them. They have no memory of me." Her fingers trailed along the shrubs lining the sidewalk, separating the manicured yards from the street. "Now you understand why I wasn't willing to show you to a phone last night."

Eden's voice came out a whisper. "Did Gabe forget about me? Is that why he hasn't come?"

"Mortals forget us because we're not part of their path. We don't have one. Neither do angels. He remembers you just fine." Kristen dropped the clove, crushed it with her next step. "I found a cemetery, slept on a pew in its chapel. I had to figure out for myself that I felt better when I touched people. I wasn't doing so well in those days. Reality and I had a bit of a tiff. I ended up living in that chapel for two years." A wistful smile hinted at her lips. "Two years of utter hell, ended, when they walked through the door."

"They? I thought you said it was Gabe?"

"Your little deviant was with him, of course." She glanced down at her hand as if wishing for the cigarette to still be there. "I tried to hit them up with Touch." Eden's jaw dropped. "Oh, relax. Angels are immune to fingertips." She swallowed hard. "Gabe told me he knew of others, though I was the first of our kind he spoke to. He fixed things for me."

They turned up the walkway to Kristen's house. Kristen jangled her keys as she walked through the door and Sebastian appeared like Pavlov's dog. "I don't do well with debt. I've owed Gabriel too much for too long, but he broke the bank with you, sweet pea."

Eden tried to keep the pleading from her voice. "I don't understand what I'm doing here."

"I gave him my word that I would teach you what I know, as little as it is. You will have a roof over your head, food, anything you need. I'll do what I can to keep you safe."

"And then what?" Eden asked.

Kristen smiled. "Why, Eden. If I told you, it'd spoil the surprise."

# CHAPTER 13

Eden wiggled her fingers, the gloves on her hands too tight, the material sticky with sweat. She hadn't wanted to wear them, but Kristen insisted. The subway was packed. Kristen hadn't said where they were going. She sat silent next to Eden, her eyes closed, hands gloved and folded in her lap. *Another day, another dress*, Eden thought.

The train lurched around a curve and Kristen's eyes snapped open.

"Next stop, we get off."

Eden spun one of the rings she wore. "So, what will it feel like? Passing Touch?"

Kristen turned toward her. "Intensely painful. Think root canal with no anesthesia." Eden's eyes widened. Kristen snorted. "Relax. You'll feel a release. It's quite pleasurable. Then a bit of relief from the tension you're feeling."

"But I don't feel any—"

Kristen stood, cutting her off as the train screeched into the station. "Don't leave my side. Madeline gave me her word she wouldn't tell the Fallen you exist, but we're not as close as we once were. I don't trust her. She might decide spilling a secret as large as yours would be worth the damage I'd inflict."

Eden hurried alongside her, trying to keep pace. For not wanting to lose her, Kristen sure as hell seemed on a mission to do just that. "You used to be friends with her? What, were you two fighting over boys?" Eden asked sarcastically, trying not to show Kristen how winded she was from the run up the stairs.

Kristen slowed as they reached street level, turning to stare at her. "Who said that?"

Eden smirked at her unintentional strike. "No one. You used to be friends with her. You're not anymore. That usually means there's a guy involved, unless you were after Madeline herself."

A sudden laugh burst out of Kristen. She skirted around a vendor on the sidewalk. The smell of relish hung in the air, mixing with exhaust. "Madeline! God, I could never date her, even if I went that way. She'd drive me insane. And yes." Kristen stopped at the corner, waiting for the crosswalk. "There was a guy, though not how you'd suspect."

"What happened?" Eden asked, glad for the chance to

finally catch her breath. The light changed. They followed the stream of pedestrians, crossing the street.

Kristen held up her hand, the fingers splayed. "Five of us, originally. Gabe told me where to find them. I introduced myself, suggested we'd do better if we pooled our resources, compared notes on what we knew. Only Madeline and Erin agreed. Watch your step," Kristen said, leaping over a pothole full of slimy water and cigarette butts.

"So you lived together?" Eden skirted around the hole.

"As you saw yesterday, suffering brings people together. We'd each thought we were the only Sider. You'll never know what that's like." Kristen gave her a once-over as they turned a corner, passing a bookstore. "Then, suddenly, we were a triad. We learned quickly to trust each other. I was naïve enough to believe our bond was unbreakable. I was wrong."

Kristen fell silent, leading them across another street.

It took a few minutes before Eden realized their wandering wasn't random. They were following someone. A guy, his yellow shirt standing out enough that she noticed it.

"Remove your gloves," Kristen said. Eden's heart quickened. She slipped the gloves off, stuffing them into her pocket. They stayed directly behind him, Kristen creeping closer when he brought a cell phone to his ear.

As his conversation ended, she dropped back a few paces, turning to Eden.

"Are you ready?" Kristen asked. *This is it*, Eden thought. "Were you listening to him?" Eden shook her head. Kristen didn't hide her disappointment. "He told whoever he was talking to that he got it, that things were looking up."

"It what?"

Kristen gave her head a slight shake. "Doesn't matter. From the tone of his voice, things are going his way. This is how we chose our mark, Eden. Observations like these. It's not fail-safe, but we do what we can. When you dose him, it's likely he'll take the Touch well. Perhaps we're helping him celebrate. I want you to speed up. As you pass him, make sure your fingers make skin contact. Understood?" Eden swallowed the sudden knot in her throat, nodding. They turned a corner, heading down a side street. "Now," Kristen whispered.

Eden forced her feet faster, kept her eyes on the guy's hand, swinging at his side. She drew up alongside him, counting down in her head. Her hand drifted away from her side. She felt his knuckles graze hers, turned her hand. Her heart hammered as her fingers slid across his.

A current surged through her, a glow marking where her fingertips made contact. Eden gasped, her breath catching at the pleasure as the Touch left her. The guy sidestepped, looked down, and then glanced up at her in confusion. Eden smiled an apology.

"I thought you were someone else." He nodded, speeding up again.

Eden slowed.

"Well? How was it?" Kristen asked.

"It . . . it felt good."

"Of course it did," Kristen scoffed. "You saw the glow, right? And your anxiety dropped when it passed?"

*Anxiety?* Eden thought. *Maybe I missed that.* She nodded, unsure. That couldn't be all there was to passing Touch. No way.

Kristen ducked into a deli, sending a jangle from the bell on the door. The counter was busy, a long line of people snaking through a smattering of occupied tables. At one a couple stood, gathering their wrappers and empty cups as they prepared to leave. Kristen smiled at them.

"We'll get rid of that for you if you'll bequeath us your table." Behind Kristen, Eden tensed. *She's going to do it*, she thought as Kristen slipped off her gloves. Instead, Kristen sunk into a chair. "Thank you!" she called sweetly as the couple abandoned their table and trash to her.

Eden caught a snickered, "Freak" as the guy threw an arm around his companion, before he leaned in to add, "What the fuck does 'bequeath' mean?"

At the table, Kristen's eyes shot skyward. She blew out

an angry breath, her bangs lifting in its wake. “Sit, Eden,” she demanded.

Eden picked up a clean-looking napkin from the mess and swiped a splotch of ketchup from the tabletop. “You couldn’t even let them take their garbage? I thought you were going to hit them with the stuff,” she said. She plopped down opposite Kristen.

“One, I have reasons behind my behavior, always, and questioning them makes you look foolish,” Kristen said, her voice quietly dangerous. “If we were sitting at a clean table, we’d be bothered. Two, I barely spoke to them. I didn’t pick up enough to be sure they could handle”—she paused to smirk, raising her fingers in air quotes—“the stuff, as you so eloquently put it. Passing Touch shouldn’t be done without consideration for the victim. Their life is in your hands, Eden. Quite literally.”

Eden’s eyes flashed up to the door as the couple exited, the gravity of Touch hitting her. “I don’t want to kill anyone.”

Kristen smiled. “I’m glad to hear it. Madeline disagrees with me on that point.”

“She *wants* to kill people? Why?”

The smile faded from Kristen’s lips. “Madeline feels if she crosses paths with a mortal, their destiny is to die if she wills it.”

Kristen played with an empty straw wrapper, crunching

it into a tight ball. "I knew Gabriel's secret, and that he was watching us. He'd warned me of the Fallen. All I wanted was for us to stay off their radar. But Madeline had grown accustomed to playing God." Kristen's attention shifted for a moment, her head tilting as she listened to a passing conversation between two girls. Eden tuned in. She could only catch snippets over the drone of the deli: "thought I'd marry him," and "ten days before," and "what am I going to do."

Kristen frowned, lowered her voice to a whisper. "Girl A just got broken up with. A dose of Touch would easily be enough to send her over the edge. Maddy would have been all over that one." She straightened, meeting Eden's gaze. "You said a guy came between Madeline and me. That guy was Gabriel. I do my best to spare the mortals, not affect their paths, the way he taught me. Madeline . . ." She hesitated, her brow wrinkling. "She chose other alliances. Erin didn't want to split up the group, but Madeline laid down an ultimatum. Me or her. Bound or Fallen. Erin refused to pick sides. I've hardly spoken to her since."

"I don't get it," Eden said. "She wouldn't pick, so you stopped being her friend?"

"Madeline made a decision, albeit a bad one. She weighed her options and she chose. I respect that. And she respects me for the same reasons. Occasionally, we still count on each other for favors, as I did when you failed secret keeping one-oh-one. Though lately I've begun to wonder just how much to trust her." Kristen dropped her eyes as if losing focus.

"What about Erin?" Eden asked.

Kristen raised her gaze, shrugged. "She and Madeline grew close again. Madeline's standards for friendship aren't as high as mine. To me, Erin faltered. I can't abide by someone who hovers in the middle ground." Eden shifted in her seat, Az's face drifting into her head. "We'd already found a few other Siders by then. We were determined they'd be taught, kept in a group, not alone like we were. Without rules, discipline, everything falls apart. When we split, we let the new Siders choose who to go with. Sebastian left with me to the Bronx. Madeline to Queens. Erin to Manhattan," Kristen finished.

Eden studied Kristen for a moment, gauging her mood before she asked her question. Finally, she dared. "You said there were five originals. What did you three do to the others?"

"Nothing." Kristen looked confused. "They formed their groups on their own. The boroughs are natural territory lines to which we've all agreed. They'd moved into the empty spots in Brooklyn and Staten Island. They're no threat, so I don't bother with them." Kristen let out a laugh. "What, did you think we locked them up or something? Siders are immortal, Eden. Sure, there's torture, but without a purpose, it gets tiring rather quickly."

*Screamers*, Eden thought. "But you said 'they're no threat,' which implies Madeline and Erin are."

"Brilliant deduction." Kristen smacked the table with her hand, amusement dancing across her eyes as she pointed at Eden. "Madeline and Erin know my secrets," she said with a smile. "Fortunately, I know theirs." Kristen stood. "That's enough for today."

Eden shadowed her back to the stairs and down to the subway platform, lost in her thoughts. Her existence would be spent gloved up, every morning spent trailing a mortal, her Touch changing their life.

She hadn't been paying attention, startled as she tripped over the last stair. The smell of urine-soaked clothes retched a gag from her, hands clawing at her while she tried to catch her balance, pull away. Her fingers hit skin.

"You killed my baby!"

Eden jerked out of the woman's grasp as the release hit, her brain fighting the pleasure with horror. She heard Kristen's gasp. Managed to pull away. *I spread Touch to a baby!* her brain screamed. *I killed a baby?* The crowd pushed around the scene, a few eyes straying in their direction. She stepped back, her foot catching on something hard on the ground, sliding as it rolled beneath her shoe. She fell, her tailbone striking the stained floor, a pang shooting up her spine. Tears sprung to her eyes. *What have I done?*

She ignored the pain, getting to her feet, her twisted ankle throbbing as she took off up the stairs. Behind her, Kristen's fading voice called her back. The woman's scream kept her running.

*I'm not going to kill people. This can't be my life.* Panic froze her at the top of the stairs. *Just run*, she thought. *Get back to the hotel. Gabe could still be there. He'll fix this.* She whipped her head back and forth, trying to decide on a direction.

Before she could, Kristen grabbed her wrist. "Gloves, Eden! Did I not tell you to wear your fucking gloves?"

Eden yanked away. "I kill a baby and you yell at me about gloves?"

Kristen stared at her. "Baby? What baby?"

Eden faltered. "She said I killed her baby. I felt the Touch pass, Kristen."

"Eden," Kristen said gently. "Touch takes time to have any effect. How could you have killed *anyone* yet? Did you forget?"

"But." She paused. "The baby . . ."

"You didn't see?" Eden shook her head. "It was a doll, Eden. The arm broke off when she dropped it. That's what you tripped over." Kristen's jaw went hard at the relief in Eden's face. "Oh, so her life is worth less because she's unwell?"

"No," Eden argued, the rage in Kristen's eyes catching her off guard.

"Nice to know your standards, Eden," Kristen snarled. "You passed her Touch, as if her mind weren't tortured enough! You've doomed her, Eden."

"I don't want this!" Eden screamed into Kristen's face, her hands rigid at her sides. "I never asked for *any* of this!"

"You're a spoiled brat, Eden." Kristen stared her down. "You wanted Az and happiness and fairy tales and forevers. You're handed your forever and what do you do? You spit on it!"

"I wanted to *die*! I would never choose this!"

Kristen's look was level. "No one gets to choose, Eden. We spread Touch because we must. The best we can do is choose *who* we pass it to, bend Touch to our will. Take what little control we can." Kristen spun away, heading back down the stairs to the train. "And put on your goddamned gloves."

# CHAPTER 14

Every morning they'd climbed onto the train, she and Kristen, and sat across from each other. Outside, the brick buildings were a mess of taupe patches of painted-over graffiti. Eden had stopped paying attention after the second week. Every morning a duplicate of the last. No choice, no variation. Leave early, ride the train to a random stop, a nod from Kristen to point out the mortal she'd chosen, and Eden's fingers swiping skin. Then back home.

They'd talked at first, on the ride home, when they'd both woken up enough to be civil. Lately, though, Kristen's eyes skated across the crowd the entire ride, glaring at random strangers. Today, she'd lost the shifty eyes. Gone to staring into space.

"So," Eden tried. "I was kinda thinking it would be warmer out."

Kristen didn't answer. Her glassy stare set Eden on

edge, the empty insistence in its focus, stuck in middle distance between them.

Eden dropped the small talk, went for something she knew would get a reaction. "That dress is hideous."

Silence.

The chill running down her spine had nothing to do with the changing weather. She couldn't shake the feeling something really was there, something only Kristen could see.

"Are you okay?" Eden asked. When she didn't get an answer, she raised her voice. "Kristen! What are you staring at?"

"Oh," she said quietly, the word drawn out. "Nothing really. Just listening."

"To what?" she dared.

"Things under things under things." Her eyelids dropped in long blinks. "'Locations and times—what is it in me that meets them all, whenever and wherever, and makes me at home?'"

Eden stared, not sure what to say. The train rounded a curve, the brakes shrieking. Kristen blinked hard, the fugue seeming to end as her smile evaporated. Her eyes focused on Eden. "What?" she snapped, breaking contact, smoothing out the folds of her dress. "It's a *poem*, Eden. You don't have to look at me like I escaped an asylum. Get some fucking culture."

Eden sighed, too tired to deal with Kristen's attitude. "I would think if you were going to quote Whitman you'd go for something not taken from *Leaves of Grass*. Especially if you're going to pull the fancy cultured bitch card."

Kristen stayed silent, watching her. "Touché," she said finally as she stood and made her way to the door. "Speaking of locations, I heard from Gabriel."

Eden didn't bother to hide her surprise as they pushed through the commuters. Not once had Kristen given her a straight answer about Gabe.

"He apologized for his absence. He needs a few more days. The Fallen. He doesn't know where they are. He wanted to be sure they don't track him to you, so he's keeping his distance for a bit longer. Nothing for us to do but make the best of it, right?"

"But he is coming, right?" She'd given up hope, wondered if they hadn't been as close as she'd thought. If he'd only been her friend because of Az.

"You're only here to learn, Eden. Your stay was never meant to be long-term. Gabriel apparently considers you his responsibility," Kristen said. "With our time coming to an end soon, I have a new lesson for you tonight."

"On what?" Eden asked cautiously.

"Dosing." Kristen stepped out of the crowd streaming from the train before they reached the turnstiles. "Friendship comes with a price, and Gabriel's price is peril. It's the reason I'm cautious about telling others how close Gabriel and I are, why I'm sure to keep a number of Siders storing Touch at all times. Because he cares for you, the Fallen will do whatever they can to get their hands on you. Dosing is a skill you'll need, a way to speed up healing if you're injured by them. That is, if you manage to get away." Kristen rejoined the crowd, Eden following. "I'll come for you after dinner," Kristen said.

The knock came at dusk. Eden swung open the door.

Kristen stepped back into the hall. "Would you follow me, please?" She didn't wait for an answer, led the way past the stairs, into the opposite wing. Midway down the hall she whisked into a room.

The boy inside jumped off the bed as they came in.

"Oh, how rude of me," Kristen said, nudging the boy. "Eden, this is Marcus. He's going to sacrifice his evening plans to help you with tonight's lesson." She leaned over the kid's shoulder, grinning.

Eden switched her attention to Marcus. His eyes were locked on her, unbearably long eyelashes fluttering with his spastic blinks. He looked near tears.

She hadn't spent more than a few minutes with any of the other Siders in the time she'd been there. Her meals were set outside her room, announced with a knock and a scurry of departing footsteps. When she left, she traveled with Kristen. The fear in Marcus's eyes caught her off guard. How different did Kristen act around them to make them so terrified of her?

"Shall we begin?" Kristen's eyes danced as she dropped her hands to his shoulders. Marcus shuddered.

Kristen positioned the two of them sitting cross-legged on the floor, facing each other.

"Like a virus, Touch needs to be spread, and it can't do so without an able host. We're immortal, but injuries do occur, and Touch doubles as our own brand of Neosporin. Your body will use it to heal faster."

As she spoke, she circled around them, each one tighter than the last.

"If you're injured, and someone can pass you a dose of Touch, it can get you back on your feet in half the time." She dropped down beside them, turning to Eden. "I'm going to demonstrate on Marcus, and then you two will practice on each other."

Kristen swayed forward before Marcus had a chance to react. Her mouth slammed against his, her hand curling around the back of his head, pulling him to her. Eden balked. Kissing? A second later Kristen pulled away, wiping the back of her hand across her lips. Marcus's lashes fluttered in shock.

"Hold out your arm," she commanded. She shot Eden a pointed glance. "Drop his glamour."

A cold sweat broke across Eden's skin. Kristen had never seen her without her glamour before the immunity had kicked in. A trickle of unease wormed into Eden's stomach. "Won't he be immune to me?"

Kristen scoffed. "Not unless you've been making secret friends behind my back." She raised an eyebrow. Eden caught the subtle shift, the way Kristen zeroed in on her hesitation. "Certainly that's not the case."

Eden sucked in a breath, leaning forward, swiping him with a finger and pulling away before the kid touched her back. His cheeks sunk, dark patches of rot breaking out across his neck, the tendons underneath tight over bone.

Kristen smiled, satisfied. "Of course, Marcus isn't injured, so if I leave him this way the Touch inside him will begin to settle. It will feel the same as it would had it built up. Only there will be no slow adjustment. Every moment worse than the last." She put a hand to his cheek, pulling down to get a better glimpse of his terrified eyes. "Which is why I'll be taking my dose back."

He tipped forward, brushing his lips against hers. When he pulled away again, he kept his eyes down. Only Eden witnessed the quiet victory in Kristen's smile, how she relished manipulation.

"See? Easy as pie," Kristen said. "There's a small window of time before your own body begins to react to the

Touch inside you, when there is no pain, none of the normal effects of letting it build."

Kristen stood, striding to the door. "Now practice," she commanded, closing it behind her.

"That was a little messed up," Eden said, hoping to kill some of the tension. Marcus gave her a ghost of a grin. "What'd it feel like?"

"The power of it . . . It's crazy." His smile faltered. "If I pass to you, you'll give it back, right?"

"Trust me, if it's as much of a pain in the ass to store as Kristen says, I want no part of it." Eden held her breath in anticipation as he scooted closer.

"Here we go," he whispered. His lips barely touched hers before he pulled away.

Eden's lips tingled. "That's it?"

"That's *it*?" He stared at her in disbelief. "You don't feel it?"

"Maybe you did it too fast. Should we try it again?"

"Again? But I gave you everything I had. You don't feel anything?" Marcus dropped his hands into his lap, straining toward her. "That's impossible. You're lying."

The venom in his words caught her off guard.

"I'm not a liar. Do you want your dose back or not?" She reached down, grabbed his shirt to yank him forward. Her lips were suddenly only a few inches from his.

"Hurry up." His breathing was almost frantic.

Eden sighed hard as she leaned forward. "I *am*."

Before she could pass the dose back, Marcus tipped to the side. She didn't have time to react, to catch him before his face collided with the floor. A stab of pain shot up her arms from wrists to elbows.

Eden froze. "Hey. You okay?" Marcus wasn't moving. Eden leaned closer. His eyes were half open, rolled back into his head. "Kristen!" she screamed, scooting away. She sat in shock as footsteps pounded down the hall, her arms throbbing, the feeling spreading to her shoulders.

"What happened?" Kristen asked before she'd even made it into the room. She grabbed Eden by the arm and hauled her up.

"I don't know," Eden stuttered, trying to get her feet under her. "He passed me the dose and I was going to pass it back and . . ."

"He's not . . ." Kristen stared at Marcus, the anger in her face fading into shock. "No, that's impossible." She stepped back from Eden, yanking her hands away. "You killed him. How?" she demanded. Her attention traveled to the open door.

Adam peeked around the threshold, confusion in his eyes as he took in the scene—Marcus on the floor, Kristen moving away from the body. Eden opened her mouth, the plea for help barely formed and not yet spoken when Kristen cut her off.

"Close the door. Tell no one," she said to Adam.

Without so much as a glance at Eden, he pulled it shut. The sudden swing sent a draft across the floor. As the air rushed past, the body burst into ash.

Eden choked in a breath before she could stop herself. Grit caught in her teeth, gagging her as she tried not to swallow. Kristen's shoes scratched across the wooden floor as she backpedaled. Gray flakes settled onto her toes when she stopped. Their mouths hung open in silent horror.

Kristen's paralysis broke first. She went for the knob, her hand digging into the pocket sewn into her dress.

"No!" Eden realized what was happening too late. Kristen had already opened the door, slammed it shut again behind her, sending the ashes airborne. Eden's hand covered her mouth, keeping them out even as it held her scream in. She heard the lock click.

# CHAPTER 15

All she needed was one loose screw. Eden slipped her fingernail into the groove in the metal and wrenched it with a sharp twist. *You killed him.* Her nail snapped. She ripped it off with her teeth and went back to the doorknob, lining up the next finger. *You killed that boy.* One loose screw and the other screws would give a bit and she'd be able to take the whole fucking doorknob off, lock and all. *He's dead.* Snap.

She searched the room again, emptying the dresser onto the floor, tossing the drawers aside. What she wouldn't give for a goddamned screwdriver. Anything with an edge thin enough or sturdy enough to help.

"Fuck!" Eden screamed, kicking the door. Her throat was dry, the words breaking out strangled. Eden heard a voice booming down the hall outside the locked door. She pressed herself against the door, as far from the drift of ashes as she could get, sliding around the perimeter of the room before she sunk to the floor. "Oh God, I killed him," she whispered, rocking, her arms wrapped around her head.

She couldn't move, didn't lift her head when she heard the key turn and the door open.

A rush of footsteps shuddered to a stop just inside the room. Only one set kept running. She flinched, even as the arm encircled her.

"Damn it, Kristen. What happened?" The arm around her tightened.

Her brain stalled out at the voice, the gears grinding to a halt. Her head snapped up.

"Gabe!" He pulled back to look at her, using his sleeve to wipe the tears from her cheeks.

"I'm here, sweetheart." He sounded calm, gentle, but his eyes gave him away, the irises a rusty crimson.

"Kristen, what happened?" he asked without turning around.

"You tell me, Gabe," Kristen demanded, her voice a quiet threat. "I bought your whole 'best hands' speech, and how the Fallen would be after her if they knew, because of Az. But clearly, there's more to this story than you're telling."

Gabe picked up Eden and pushed past Kristen, giving the ashy outline on the floor a wide berth. She followed them down the hall. "She killed one of mine. Killed him!"

She shook her head, as if not quite believing it herself.

"I didn't mean it," Eden started to say again, but he raised a gentle hand to her cheek, silencing her.

"Kristen," Gabe whispered. "Give me a few more days."

"Not a chance."

Eden dared a glance. Kristen was shaking. *She's scared of me.* The thought bounced around her head, refusing to settle into logic. Kristen's unflappable exterior had cracked wide open.

"Where is her room?" he asked. "I need to get her settled." He emphasized the last word. Kristen huffed, storming down the hall. Eden heard her boots clamoring down the stairs. Aside from the sound, the house seemed empty. Every door along the corridor was shut. Eden wondered if the others hid behind them, if they knew. Were they cowering from her the way they cowered from Kristen?

"Sweetheart? Can you tell me where your room is?"

"Past the stairs. The door is open." She pulled her head off his shoulder, staring at him. "Where have you been?" Her voice came out stronger than she thought it would.

Gabe didn't answer until he'd rounded the corner, set her down on the bed.

"Eden, what happened in there?"

"I don't know." Her heart hammered as she trembled against the pillows.

From Kristen's room down the hall drifted the scent of cloves. Close on its heels came the sound of a hushed argument, a male voice. From the way his jaw tightened, Gabe seemed to hear more than she could. He crossed the room, closed the door. His hand hovered near the knob as if he were looking for a way to lock it from the inside, before he gave up.

"What're they saying?" Gabe didn't answer. The words built up, clustered against her tongue before they escaped in a rush. "What are they gonna do? Gabe?"

"Are you comfortable?" His forced smile unsettled her even further.

"Comfortable? No, I'm not comfortable!" Her eyes darted to the door, to the window. Maybe there was a way to climb down, to get out. "She's gonna make me a Screamer!"

"Eden?" He put his finger under her chin, tipping up her head. She met his eyes.

Az had told her about the trick, how Gabe could use his gaze to calm people. It struck her as a stupid ability, useless. Especially since it only worked if the person it was being used on was open to being calmed down. But as the connection took hold, suddenly everything seemed distant, silly. A smile wound across her lips. Even as it happened, she knew it was out of place, that it was the wrong reaction, but it just felt like it needed to be there.

"Better?" He pulled back, watching her.

She nodded, her head full of cotton.

"Eden, can you close your eyes for me?" She let them slip shut, the outside world falling away. The dark was nice. "What happened down the hall? Can you walk me through it?"

She bit her lip. She couldn't form the words, hadn't realized she'd held her own hands out until Gabe's slipped into hers. "Don't touch me!" Her voice came out slow and lethargic, didn't have the panic she felt as she forced her eyes open.

"No, it's fine, I promise. Touch doesn't work on me. See?" He reached forward, grabbing her hand again. There was no glow, no passing of Touch. She was shaking, the effect of his eyes, thc calmness, wearing thin as she closed her eyes again.

"He fell apart," she choked out.

Someone slammed against the door. Eden jumped, coming out of her stupor enough to hear Kristen's protest, Gabe's whispered curse. The door opened.

Impossible.

So impossible, but he smiled and it was his smile. Not someone who looked like him, not a mistake. His smile. Him. Alive.

"Az?" she whispered.

# CHAPTER 16

"Eden," Az sighed. He tried to hide what was left of the limp as he stepped forward. Another week and the leg would be healed, but for now it still twinged when he put his full weight on it. Kristen mumbled something to Gabriel about trying to stop him, but Az wasn't listening.

Eden's eyes flicked to Gabe, Kristen, back to him. She looked different. Fragile and hopeless and pale. Her eyes were swollen, tears staining her blotchy cheeks. He took another step forward, but she didn't jump into his arms the way he'd pictured, looked more shell-shocked than happy. "You're . . . How are you here?"

He turned to Kristen. She'd thrown an indignant hand on her hip, buried her fingers in the nasty fabric of her dress. "I told you this was not a good time. *You* chose to ignore me."

"Oh, for fuck's sake, Kristen," he mumbled, turning back to Eden.

"I saw you fall." She started to shake, the quiver spreading through her as he watched.

"I know. But look!" He held out a hand, flipped it over. "See, good as new!"

Her head fell to her hands, palms pressing against her temples. A sob exploded from her as she leaped off the bed, into his arms. Az caught her, pulling her against his shoulder.

"I'm so sorry," he whispered. "If there was another way, I would have taken it."

Her arms loosened, her voice muffled by his shoulder. "What do you mean 'another way'?"

"For you to turn into a Sider." Her hands slipped from his shoulders. He reached for them on their way down, but she pulled away.

"Wait." She raised her hand, her gaze fierce as it searched his. "You know what I am?"

He nodded. "Once I knew you had no path. . . ."

"You knew I was going to kill myself?" She stepped back. "Why didn't you stop me?" This was not going how he pictured. Not by a long shot. Her face paled as she connected the thoughts. "You tricked me into thinking you were dead? What the fuck is wrong with you? I thought you loved me!"

"I *do* love you! I was trying to keep you safe!" he said as she backed away from him.

"Safe?" she spat. "I *killed* myself!"

"I have enemies, Eden! Enemies who would have come for you, done horrible things. Things you can't even imagine. They knew about you! At least as a Sider they can't kill you. Can't take you away." *Selfish.*

His vision blurred, the skin on his back tightening as his wings curled in on themselves. *I destroyed her life.*

"If I would have done it anyway, why did you make me think you were dead?" She spun on Gabriel. "And you. Did you know?" Her face fell when he hesitated.

"No," Az whispered, Eden's hatred ringing in his ears. "Not now." But already it was starting, the swirl of black behind his eyes, the words like ribbons trailing through his head. *All I do is hurt others. She doesn't love me. Never will. She'll leave me. Never look back. I will always be alone.*

*Fall.*

"Az?" It was Gabe. "Kristen, get him." A hand grasped his shoulder, another around his waist.

He stumbled, Kristen holding him up. It would be so easy to give in, to Fall. To let go.

"What in God's name is wrong with him?" Kristen gasped.

"He's only half Fallen. Part of him wants nothing more than to finish what he's started." Gabe's voice lowered to a whisper, though Az still caught it. "I've gotta get him out of here before he gets worse."

"Az!" Eden shouted. He fought his eyes open, found her. She'd backed against the wall, her hand held out in front of her, palm up. For just a second, he thought it was there for him to reach for, a lifeline, as Kristen and Gabe dragged him into the hall.

And then he saw her eyes, heard the broken moan in her voice. "How could you do this?"

The door slammed shut, cutting her off, a key twisting in the lock. He collapsed, her frantic pleas to open the door shattering him.

"Take him, Gabriel. I'll take care of her."

"Kristen . . ." Az gritted his teeth, felt her hand on his back as she crouched next to him. "Don't hurt her. Please."

"I won't hurt her," Kristen said. "As long as you don't Fall."

# CHAPTER 17

*Az is alive.* Every time Eden thought it, her heart jump-started. *Liar.* Over and over and over the word ticked through her mind. *He lied. He did this to me. But he's alive.* She sunk to the floor. Maybe someone would come. Gabe. Gabe wouldn't just leave her there. Not again.

Eden slid closer to the door, eyeing the keyhole, pushing Az out of her head. The sun set.

The first time she heard the sound, it was close to noon. She barely registered it, the sound or the time, until it came again, the soft pat of an open palm.

"Who's there?" Her voice cracked, sore and unsteady. She swallowed hard, pressing her ear against the wood, straining.

From the other side came three whispered words. "You killed Marcus."

Eden jerked away, slamming her hand against the

door. "I didn't mean to! That wasn't my fault!"

A hiss silenced her. "They're going to hear you!" Eden waited through a long pause before the voice came again. "I don't care if it was." On the other side of the door, fingernails clawed a trail upward, Eden's wide eyes following the tiny scritches from floorboards to knob. "I have a key," the voice said.

"Then open the door." Eden's calm command surprised her.

"Only if you agree." Desperation twisted the last word into a question.

Eden stepped back from the door. "Agree to what?"

"Marcus was an accident. Do it on purpose."

She rocked back from the wood, shocked into silence.

"I heard Sebastian talking to Kristen. He said you're dangerous, that she needs to get rid of you." The tone shifted to panic. "There's not much time. . . ."

Another voice cut in. "Give me the key." Someone slammed against the door, a shoulder hitting the wood. "I said, give me the key, Jacinda." A second later the knob twisted. Eden backpedaled, sliding away across the floor as the door opened.

Adam smiled. "Hey there, stranger. I've come to spring you. You game for a daring escape?"

Eden jumped to her feet as Adam tossed her the empty backpack he'd been holding.

"Pack."

She didn't hesitate, scooping what she could from the drawers, cramming tank tops and a pair of jeans into the bag. Underwear and a sweatshirt filled the rest of the space. A bit of yellow peaked out from under the abandoned clothing. The envelope, the picture of Az. She shoved it in, knowing it would be wrinkled by the time they got out of there, not sure why it bothered her or why she was bringing it at all.

"Done." She turned to face Adam. Behind him stood a girl, dark circles under haunted eyes, her shoulder drooping against the doorframe. Her skin was pale enough to show every thin vein lining her arms. Eden had never seen anyone look so worn through, so completely exhausted.

"Help me." The plea seemed to emanate from her every pore.

"Go back to your room, Jacinda." Adam snagged the bag from Eden, throwing it over his shoulder. "You ready?" he asked. Eden didn't answer. She'd locked eyes with the girl.

"Adam, wait." Hope flared in her eyes when Eden spoke, her fingers tightening against the doorframe. "I can't leave her."

"Fine, she can follow out the front. But we've gotta move. Kristen's been gone all morning. And there's nothing she loves more than the dramatic entrance."

Eden stared at the girl. "That's not what she wants. Leaving here won't change anything for her." *You can't do this*, her mind screamed. *You can't just kill her.* But it wasn't like that at all. "You really want me to do this?" she asked.

Jacinda's nod was immediate. "I wasn't some messed-up kid having a bad day. I made my choice. I didn't hurt anyone, because no one remembers me. And instead of death, I got this. It's worse."

Eden reached for her hand.

"What are you doing?" Adam asked, but he seemed so far away.

"I've only done this once. It might not work."

Jacinda nodded, her eyes brimming with determination. "There are others. Screamers. They're still in their rooms."

"I'll find them," Eden promised. "You have my word."

Eden shut her eyes, forcing herself to remember the night before. She'd been nervous last night. She'd leaned forward. Sighed.

"Hands," she whispered. Jacinda's fingers found hers.

"Ready?" Jacinda squeezed. Eden took a deep breath, let it out. She couldn't open her eyes, didn't want to see what was happening, if it worked.

A burning current tingled up her arms. Her bones felt electrified.

"Jesus Christ!" Adam whispered.

Eden opened her eyes. In front of her, ashes lined the floor in the shape of the girl. All that was left.

She snatched the key out from Adam's hand, heading down the hall, into the left wing. The doors there were closed, everything silent and still. She was pretty sure the key was a skeleton by the shape of it. Sure enough, when she tried it in the first door, it clicked open.

The boy on the bed jumped, his eyes wild when he caught sight of her.

"Jacinda found you!"

"We don't have much time." A sudden bolt of pain shot up her arm. "What the fuck," she hissed through clenched teeth, shaking it out. It disappeared as suddenly as it had come. She turned her attention back to the boy. "You know what I can do?" He hopped off the bed, nodding. "Still in?"

"If I wanted torture, I would've stayed alive. High school was better than this shit." She couldn't help but return his smile.

Footsteps sounded in the hallway, stopped. For a panicked moment she thought she was caught, but it was only Adam.

"Eden, we gotta *go*." He glanced over his shoulder. "We do not want to be here when she gets back." She ignored him.

"Sit." The boy did as he was told. Eden followed him

down. "Hands," she commanded, not hesitating. She counted backward from three, closing her eyes at one and sucking in a deep breath. When she let it out, opened her eyes, he was still there, staring at her.

"When's it gonna happen? Do I have to wait?"

Unease crept into her stomach. What if that was it? What if she'd only been able to do it a few times and whatever was different about her had burned out? She pushed the questions away. *No, think. You can do this.*

"Adam, you were watching when it happened." She pointed to the boy. "What did he do different?"

"Um." Adam's eyes jumped between the two of them. "He . . . she breathed in. She was taking a breath and his mouth was closed?" He looked at her like he expected her to give him a cookie and a pat on the head for a right answer. Like she had any idea what it was.

"Okay, we'll give that a try," she whispered, her voice giving away the trembling inside of her. "Take two. When I breathe out, you breathe it in, got it?" He nodded.

She grabbed his hands, inhaled. "Now," she said as she breathed out. This time she kept her eyes open.

He leaned forward, his lips pursed, pulling in air hard enough to whistle. It took. Her fingers tingled, the sensation spreading up her arms slowly but growing stronger. A muscle wrenched in her neck, quivering spasms through her back.

"It didn't work. He's still here."

"No," she said. "It worked." His body lay on its side, eyes rolled up just enough to be unnerving.

She scooted back across the floor. One of her shoes grazed the body.

The effect was instant. A dozen comparisons crackled in her brain, none of them quite right. Sand castle hit by a wave. Needle piercing a balloon.

"Holy fuck," Adam whispered.

*Yeah*, Eden thought. *That about covers it*. She winced as her hand cramped into a claw.

"You all right?" he asked. She looked up, ready to tell him sure, everything was fine, but his head cocked before she could get the words out. "You look . . ."

"What?"

She winced as another pang shot up her arm. He held his hand up close to her cheek, but stopped before touching her. "Are you hurt? Is it because of what just happened? What you did?"

"I'm not exactly an expert, Adam." She got to her feet, made her way to the next room. Before she could get the key in the lock, he dropped his hand to the knob.

"You don't look so hot. Maybe we should call it good." He shot a glance toward the stairs. Kristen could come home any second. Leaving was one thing. Taking out Kristen's Siders would have consequences. What they were, Eden couldn't imagine, but the bridge was already lit. Might as well burn it down.

"Few more." Eden fought the urge to brush his hand away. When he pulled back, she opened the door to an empty room. She didn't bother shutting it, went on to the next. Empty.

"Where are they all? Shouldn't there be more?"

"Kristen took the strongest ones with her this morning. She left me to watch the rest."

Eden stopped, the key stuck in the next lock. Behind it, she heard whispers but ignored them. She kept her eyes on Adam. "Why you?"

He shrugged. "Because I was the only one in the kitchen when she walked in? Kristen doesn't really plan things out, in case you hadn't noticed."

*Adam's watched your every move,* she thought. *Trap?* Maybe that was why he was so eager to get her to the door. To stop her. He only needed one, maybe two deaths to figure out her technique, how she'd dispatched of Marcus. She considered him. The idea of Adam doing Kristen's bidding didn't sit right with her. "Why not Sebastian, though? Wouldn't she have left him in charge?"

He shrugged. "Those two were all hush-hush before they took off which usually means something's up. And when something's up, Sebastian's on that chick like glue." Eden had seen him that way at the ball the first night. She turned the key, opened the door to three sets of eager eyes.

She leaned against the wall on her way back to her room. *Something's wrong*, she thought. *You're fine*, her brain commanded. *Just keep walking. Get the backpack and get out.* She pushed off the wallpaper, forced herself to keep going though the hallway shimmered in front of her.

Adam called her name from somewhere behind, but she didn't dare turn. If she did, she was pretty sure she'd go down. She grabbed the threshold for balance as she passed through.

"Just gonna grab the bag and . . ."

Burning laced across her clavicles, corseted the bones of her ribs. She gasped. The feeling wrapped around her hips, sliding into her gut. Her whole body clenched, her legs giving out.

"Whoa, you all right?" Adam's hand was on her shoulder.

"Don't touch me," she hissed, though the words came out pain-slurred. She slammed her hand against the floor. Everything inside her felt like it was ripping apart, rearranging.

"Eden, look at me." Adam moved in front of her and

crouched down to her level. She forced her eyes up, blinking hard. "What's going on?"

"I don't know. Hurts."

"You look like the Screamers when she's left them too long. Like you have way too much Touch. Haven't you been passing?"

She nodded, her jaw clenched. The pain was diminishing, her vision clearing. She got her hands under her, staggered to her feet. "Kristen took me yesterday."

"Jesus, did you get it *from* them? Is that even possible?" His voice changed, filling with wonder. "You took in their Touch."

"Adam, please!" She took a tentative deep breath, expecting another wave of hell from her entrails. When none came, she straightened. "Can we not do this now? I've got to get out of here before . . ."

The front door closed. Eden and Adam snapped toward the sound. She heard Sebastian, the sound of footsteps on the stairs. In seconds, Kristen would be aware something was off, if she wasn't already. No time to make a run for it.

"Fuck." Eden wiped any trace of fear from her face. "She's coming. You want out? There's still time for me to . . ."

"I want out, but not like that." Adam moved a step closer, still keeping his distance. "I want to come with you."

Her eyelashes fluttered, sharp needles of pain digging a trail across her shoulders. The rush of the last bits of Touch left her shaking. She felt it inside her, each particle wrestling for space. Adam watched her, waiting. "No. You can't come with me, but I can take one more." She wasn't sure how much more she could handle, if she'd offered Adam an empty promise.

"Hear me out." His eyes darted toward the door. Confident footsteps that could only have belonged to Kristen glided up the stairway. "I have a few hundred bucks. . . ."

"Then go. You can handle yourself. Besides," Eden added, "I'll be lucky to make it out of here."

From beside her, Adam started to say her name, cut off as Kristen rounded the doorframe. He slid back further into the room. Eden flexed her fingers at her sides, squaring off.

Kristen stopped in the doorframe, her face the perfect blank canvas Eden strived for herself. One look at Kristen and she knew she'd never master it. Not like that.

"You look quite . . . guilty," Kristen said. She made no move to come closer. It wasn't exactly a hesitation, but the best Eden could hope for.

"Guilty? Depends on the point of view, I guess."

Sebastian slid in next to Kristen. His hand on her shoulder, he moved to get around, in front of her, breathless from his rush down the hallway. "They're gone."

"Who's gone?"

"The doors are unlocked." He didn't take his eyes off Eden, though he spoke to Kristen. "All of them."

Kristen's jaw dropped, uncertainty creeping into her eyes. "That is unacceptable," she said, turning to Eden, noticing Adam behind her for the first time. She snapped her fingers at him. "You. Where are they?"

Sebastian answered. "Ashes," he said quietly. "On the floor."

Eden dropped her hands as he spoke, her fingers uncurling.

"What have you done?" Kristen pushed around Sebastian.

"I'm leaving," Eden said quickly, trying to keep her voice even. "If you try to stop me, I'll do what I have to." She'd lost some of the hard edge, had to press her hands against her sides to stop them from shaking. The backpack sat in the corner, near the door. She wondered if she'd make it that far if she took off running. If Sebastian would take her down. Kristen would lock her up, make her a Screamer. Or worse, turn her over to the Fallen.

"You can't be *serious*." Kristen's expression shifted, the annoyed squint of her brow unraveling into amusement. She stepped out of the doorway with a sweeping gesture. "You're free to go if you choose."

Now it was Eden's turn to falter, all the words she'd

planned, the different scenarios she'd played out and . . . "You can't trick me, Kristen." That had to be it. Leaving couldn't possibly go down so easily.

"It's nothing of the sort. I kept you here to protect you while you learned enough to survive on your own. Clearly, you can. I consider my promise fulfilled." Her eyes shot to Adam and back. "Frankly, if you'd spoken to me instead of acting like a rash child, we could have avoided this unpleasantness." Kristen shook her head.

Eden circled closer to the door, to her bag. "So you mean to tell me I take out half your crew and you're just gonna let me walk out the front door?"

Kristen's eyes sparkled, a half smile etching into her cheek. "'Do not go gentle into that good night. Rage, rage against the dying of the light.'" She smoothed the folds of her dress. "They did not rage. I have no use for the weak. One might say I owe you for using your talents to my advantage." Her lips turned downward, eyes falling as she tapped with her finger. "I'm not one for gathering debt. Let's pay it off now, shall we? In advice."

Kristen leaned to the side, slipped her wrist into one of the backpack straps, and lifted it off the floor. "First, anger should never affect your loyalties. Going to Madeline for help might seem like your best option, but I would discourage this. When she finds out you're playing house in Manhattan, she will not be happy."

“Manhattan? What about Erin?” Adam flinched when Kristen met his eyes.

“Erin and her brood are on vacation.” She turned back to Eden, shot her a wink. “I’ve had a busy morning.”

“What did you do, Kristen?” Adam shifted behind her, moving closer as he spoke. “A dozen Siders don’t just go missing.”

“Really?” Kristen mused. “Because it seems to be quite the popular phenomenon as of late. They did clear out quite quickly.” She tossed her hair over her shoulder with a dismissive flourish. “Perhaps they went south for the winter. Erin’s always been fickle.”

“You think Madeline’s just gonna accept that? Erin is her best friend. They have an alliance, Kristen.”

“Had. The past tense of which will drive Madeline into a fury.” Kristen fell silent, tapping her free hand against the doorframe. “You should already know the logical move. You need to start thinking like a leader. Thoughts?”

“They kept you in check, didn’t they?” Eden asked. “Madeline and Erin. They were in an alliance. Against you.” Kristen raised an eyebrow, waiting. “So you’d need to break that, but you’d need backup after, to make sure Madeline doesn’t come after you herself.” The last puzzle piece slipped into place. “You want an alliance with me.”

“Bravo.” Kristen dropped the backpack, clapping softly. “My terms. A truce between you and I, uncontestable as of this moment. If Madeline makes a move against mine, you will come to my aid. You're the only threat to their eternity. Plus," Kristen said with a smile, "you're on my side! Oh, I can't wait to see how this all plays out."

"So you're just gonna blame Eden, then? For Erin?" There was a protective edge to Adam's voice that hadn't been there before. Kristen snorted.

"If I know my dear Maddy, she'll pull her spoiled-brat pout for a bit and move on to a new BFF. Eden here has more pressing threats than Madeline." She turned to Eden. "Don't you?" Kristen's face went solemn. "In exchange, I give you my guarantee Madeline will not be a problem for you, regarding said pressing threats. Your talent is not something *They* will find amusing."

"If I agree to this alliance thing, you'll just let us go?" She heard Adam suck in a breath.

"Us?" Kristen asked.

"Adam comes with me, or the deal is off."

"Agreed. With a talent like yours, you'll be found eventually. You're going to need backup."

"And another thing. You don't tell . . ." Eden glanced toward Adam as she reached forward, took the backpack from Kristen. *He doesn't know about the Bound or the Fallen*, she thought. "You tell no one where I've gone, should anyone ask."

"The city is large enough to get lost in. Keep a low

profile and stay off the radar." She held out a gloved hand. "Are we agreed?"

Eden shook her hand, throwing the backpack over her shoulder. "Where do I go? Once I get to Manhattan?"

"Not my problem." Kristen shook her head, smiling. "And not something you should want me to know." She spun on her heel. "You're nothing but a rumor now."

# CHAPTER 18

*(Two Months Later)*

Eden reached blindly for her phone and shut off her alarm as she crawled out of bed. The curtains covering the window blocked the morning light, but she crossed to the door without turning on the lamp. She'd memorized her room enough to make her way.

The apartment was quiet. Adam slouched on the couch. He glanced up as she entered and nodded hello before lowering the monitor of the laptop balanced on his legs.

"Scoot," Eden mumbled, still half asleep. He threw himself over a few feet on the beat-up couch, pulling the blanket with him, not even offering a corner. Apparently, mornings weren't for sharing.

"Asshole." She ran the zipper up on her hooded sweatshirt and plopped down. "Anybody else up?" she asked, combing the tangles out of her hair with her fingers. The door to the boys' room was closed. A two-bedroom apartment had been more than enough for just her and Adam.

Then Jarrod and Adam had shared. No one had objected when she'd pulled the girl card and insisted on her own space. Two weeks ago, when they'd added James to the mix, things had moved from crowded to crash pad. The whole hallway smelled like a dorm room.

"You know Jarrod. He's either up by seven or comatose till noon. James wasn't moving around yet when I came out here."

She rolled her eyes. "Well, obviously, he needs the sleep. Hissy fits burn up a lot of energy."

"Don't do that."

Eden yanked at a chunk of her bangs, separating one of the hot pink highlights. She still wasn't used to the cut, the strands tapering off near her ears.

"What do you want me to do, just stand by and watch him suffer? He looks like a fucking zombie half the time." James had passed the easy stage, where Touch only had to be passed once or twice a day. By now, he should have been hitting up at least five. Instead he was being a child. Refusing.

"Look, he's rough. No denying that. I'm surprised he's been able to resist spreading it this long. But he's a kid, Eden. Eventually, he's gonna break. He'll start passing, get used to it. He'll be fine. Besides, it's not like you can force him."

Eden yanked herself up off the couch and headed for

the door. *What to do with James?* The question plaguing them all week.

"I'll be back in half an hour. Wake him up and tell him to get his ass ready. He's passing today."

She shrugged on her black peacoat as she took the stairs. Peering through the little window beside the security door, she kept herself just out of view. On the stairs of the apartment building, five Siders were already waiting for her, gloved up and a cautious distance apart. To the morning rush of pedestrians, they would have been chalked up as street kids. Eden knew better. A swipe of her fingertips on their skin would drop their façade and show the truth.

Five today. It had never been so many.

"Time to greet the fan club." Eden sighed as she twisted the knob.

The security door clicked shut behind her. She tucked the key into the pocket of her coat and turned to face them. Their whispers, snippets of "has to be the one" and "right where she was supposed to be," intensified as they caught sight of her. The Siders began showing up a few days after she and Adam had taken off from Kristen's, even before they'd managed to scrounge up enough money to get an apartment.

"Where who said I'd be?" she demanded. "Who sent you?" She knew they wouldn't answer. No one ever did.

"It's true, isn't it?" The one who spoke up couldn't have been more than twelve. "That you breathe death?" He stared at her, taking her in like some kind of urban legend come to life. She didn't need Touch to tell they were new, all of them.

"Please? You can, right?" His body shook with need. Eden's anger melted, the last of her resolve faltering as it always did. She could never turn them away. Not when she was the only one who could end their suffering.

"The least you could do is show up *post* coffee," she suggested. The boy tilted his head. Eden gave up on the sarcasm, holding out a resigned hand. "Do you have it?" she asked, knowing they would. The tattooed one dropped a ball of crumpled bills into her palm. "This for all of you?" He nodded. She didn't bother to count it. All two hundred and fifty would be there. She hadn't set the price, though they'd always offered the same amount.

The Siders fell in behind her, following blindly as she led them into the alley. Some mornings she was tempted to do a little sidestep shuffle, a jig maybe, just to see if they'd copy. Today wasn't one. She wasn't smiling as she turned to face them.

The youngest led the pack. Perspiration beaded on his forehead. Even in the cold, he reeked of desperation. She focused on him, letting the others fade into the background. Her hand hovered near his cheek. She brushed the sweaty hair from his temples with a black-polished fingernail. Reaching down, she took his hands in hers.

"Stay still, okay?" She meant to reassure him, adding a measure of kindness to her voice, but when he moved to speak, she lowered her red tinted lips to within a millimeter of his mouth, completing the circuit. Her timing was well practiced and perfect.

A sharp exhale propelled her breath into him. Her hands tightened their grip on his. For a span of two heartbeats, she thought it wouldn't take, that she was free, no longer their only out. But then his eyes spiraled back into his head as her breath did its work. Her palms blazed and itched as his Touch became hers. She closed her eyes and clamped down on her lip as the burning spread up her arms, tingling flames across her collarbones.

One by one, she emptied them of Touch. The bodies fell as empty shells, their power now hers.

A breeze from the next passing taxi, even the vibration from its tires on the asphalt, would scatter what was left of them into nothing.

Eden looked up, shading her eyes from the sunlight. She'd never been able to make anything out after the act, no light, no choir of angels. No hellfire either. If they were really dying, they went in silence without so much as a clue. Though it would have been nice to know what happened to them, being pathless, she knew it wasn't an answer likely to come from above. Still, the glance had become habit.

"Yeah, you're welcome," she sighed, pulling a twenty from the roll of bills. She pocketed the rest and headed through the alley, around the corner to Milton's.

Even if there were no answers, just once she wished one of them would stick around long enough to say thanks.

# CHAPTER 19

The bell on the coffee shop's door sounded when she walked through, but the guy behind the counter didn't look at her. He looked at the clock.

Pulling a tray out from some shelf she couldn't see, he set it next to the register and handed her a bag. She already knew what it would contain—two dozen packets of Equal, creamers, and a few stir sticks thrown in for good measure. "You're late today."

Eden looked up at the clock. Two minutes past eleven.

"I had something," she said, not bothering to elaborate. "How goes it, Zach?" she asked, squinting as she dropped the bill onto the counter. She rubbed her wrist absently, pain lingering in the joints.

Behind the counter, Zach shrugged. "It goes," he said. He swiped the money from the counter, entering the numbers into the cash register. As always, his hands were gloved, the latex enough to keep him from spreading Touch to customers.

"Money tight?" she asked pointedly. She'd offered to put Zach up, have him join them and let her worry about the bills. So far he hadn't taken her up on the offer.

As usual, he only smiled, replied with the same lines he always did. "I'll consider it, Eden. No promises, though."

Other Siders lived in the area too, though they feared her enough to maintain some distance. They'd heard the rumor. If a Sider sought Eden out, it was for one reason. She didn't mind their nearness, did her best to stay just another face in the crowd.

She sighed. "It's tight, but we could upgrade to a bigger apartment if you moved in."

"So you've mentioned," he said, amused.

She'd kept her group small to stay under the radar. Clearly *that* plan was failing. If she needed backup, there was only Jarrod and Adam. The fact was, she needed to start building her numbers. Just because word of her hadn't gotten to the Fallen didn't mean it wouldn't. She'd taken in James out of pity. The kid had been scared and alone. Living on the streets. Zack, however, would be able to handle it if she needed to pass him Touch to get rid of what she took from the other Siders. She slipped an extra ten into the tip jar. Half full of coins and bills, the chipped cup had a new sign taped around it.

Eden angled it away from her as she read. "'Thanks a latte'? Are you fucking serious?"

Behind the counter, Zach only laughed.

"No way am I claiming that one. New guy. He's taking over the opening shift on Monday and Thursday. I trained him, so he knows the routine. Told him you were VIP . . . that Carol-Anne chick's dark, twisty sister." He grinned at Eden's confusion. "Theeeeyyy're hhhheeeeeeeeeere." She groaned, trying to kill her smile. "*Poltergeist*!" Zach laughed. "Come on, that's classic!"

Eden shook her head, balancing the to-go tray in one hand and opening the door with the other, the bag of extras tucked between the cups. "Thanks, Zach. See you tomorrow."

James wasn't waiting for her. She didn't bother taking off her coat as she made her way across the living room.

"One of those for me?" Jarrod didn't give her enough time to answer before jumping up to take the tray. "Adam! Coffee's here!" he called toward the kitchen, before fully turning his attention her way. "How many were out there today?"

"Just two," she lied. Both he and Adam had been worried, wondering how much Touch she could take in before it became too much. So far, aside from the brief pain after, she'd managed. She'd also gotten better at hiding it when she didn't.

"Thanks for the coffee." His face held no expression, his voice monotone.

"If there's a problem, I'll let you know." She'd been dosing Adam and Jarrod, sure she was too potent to pass to the mortals with any chance of them making it through. She held his gaze as she crossed the room, gave the door of the boys' room a cursory knock.

"He's in the bathroom," Jarrod said.

James didn't notice when the door opened. Eden watched him, crumpled against the tub and drawing a razor blade down the length of his left wrist. Brow furrowed in concentration and pain, his trembling hands only managed to gash a few weak lines down the right. The doorframe creaked when she leaned against it, loud enough that James finally looked up, his expression guilty.

"We're back to the wrists again?" she asked. A long moment stretched out before he bowed his head, the blade falling from his hand.

"It helps sometimes," he whispered, his voice breaking. Eden had never heard him sound so tired.

"You can't kill yourself. It doesn't work." She reached into the medicine cabinet, moved aside a few random bottles, and pulled out a roll of gauze.

"I know that. I'm not stupid," he whispered, defeat in his voice. "But the dark thoughts, they just build, Eden. This makes them stop. It gives me a few hours of feeling okay." She looked beyond him, to the dozen spots of plaster standing out from the yellow paint.

"Why can't you just pass, James?" He hid his eyes. She took his hand and turned it over to study the gaping wound, the starburst of scars he'd cut through to open his veins. "This is Touch." A fresh ribbon of red slid from his wrist and fell to lance an accusatory path across her own. "You can't not spread it, understand? I'm done playing around."

James leaned back against the edge of the tub, a pool of red spreading across the tiles as he met her eyes. "I'm not killing them. I can't do it."

"If you'd spread it out, you wouldn't be lethal. And you wouldn't be bleeding on the fucking tiles."

She wanted to reach out to him, shake some sense into him. If she could just convince him to pass the Touch, she was sure he'd even out. When he'd moved in with them, he'd been half frozen, near delusional from not passing but too new to be harmful. He'd gotten better, but the last week he'd been apathetic, hardly getting out of bed. She wasn't sure if it just was the buildup.

"James, if you want me to—"

"No. I don't want to die. I won't kill them and I'm

not gonna make you kill me," he said, his voice full of determination.

Her eyes fell to the dark maroon stain around the base of the sink as she gently wrapped the wounds; the blood from the past cuts had slipped into the crack in the tile there. She'd scrubbed a dozen times, just part of the ordinary regimen of cleaning now, but it hadn't so much as faded. Eden stayed silent for a moment, watching the gore seeping into his jeans.

"You're not solving anything, James." Taping the gauze down, she dropped his hand. He'd stored enough that the wound would heal quickly.

"Clean up," she added, trying for that cold edge she knew she couldn't muster. She couldn't tear her eyes from the blood. "You're not getting out of going with me."

Eden shut the door behind her, padding across the tan carpet. She notched the thermostat up another few degrees, lifting her face to the vent as the heater kicked on. Jarrod was still on the couch.

"He's not cut out for this," he said, keeping his voice low.

"He'll be fine. What am I supposed to do? Kick him out? Send him to Kristen? Because he's too young to survive on his own. He needs us."

"Eden, he's had time. The kid's suffering. Maybe it's time you put him out of his misery." She stopped. From the kitchen, the sound of dishes clanking as

Adam made breakfast fell silent as he, too, waited on her response.

"He doesn't want that," she said, quickly, tucking a pink lock behind the multiple studs piercing her ear. Beside them, James slammed the bedroom door, cutting off their conversation.

"Let's get this over with," he grumbled, grabbing his coat off the hook and yanking it on. His blond hair was still tangled with sleep, a rat's nest of a snarl poking out from the crown. He untied his shoes instead of yanking them on, his wrists barely strong enough to handle the movement.

She headed out the door, satisfied he would follow.

On the sidewalk, she turned toward the cluster of shops down the street, James trailing behind. She was buttoning her coat up the last few inches in a desperate attempt to keep out the cold when he spoke.

"It's not fair. They're people, Eden." When she turned, he stared at her; unmoving. "I'm going home." He spun back toward the apartment.

She called his bluff, waiting him out. Sure enough, he hesitated, not quite brave enough to act on his words.

He made an effort to meet her gaze. His pale hair lusterless, the skin under his eyes a clouded violet, he looked more than just tired. He looked dead. Or at least not *alive.* Whatever category Siders fell into, today, James looked the part.

"You have to spread Touch." A rough wind rippled her skirt, whipping it against her legs. She could see the effects of the buildup in his facial expressions, permeating his body language. From how Jarrod and Adam explained, it was horrible—desperation and broken thoughts spinning out of control. Of course, Eden knew little of the feeling, a rare perk of whatever was messed up with her. Not that she'd gotten completely off the hook.

Eden checked her watch. Despite their late start, they were still right on time, coming closer to the corner where they would run into her gift to James.

And then there he was.

Brighton Daniels. Twenty-four years old. No children. Single. Some kind of corporate something or other. Eden shifted their course, following as Brighton took a left, his briefcase swinging by his side.

She'd found the details out easily enough, following him on his commute from work the past three days, listening in on his phone conversations. It was amazing what one could overhear if they only paid attention.

James hadn't noticed they were shadowing anyone yet.

"See *him*," she said, giving her chin a jerk in the man's direction. Ahead of them, Brighton paused at a crosswalk, idly glancing at his watch, waiting for the stick figure to grant him permission to move. *Sheep*, Eden thought, knowing he couldn't be blamed.

Even as he nodded, James was tucking his hands into his pockets.

"He's your mark." She pulled her gloves tighter, straining her fingertips against the fabric. "He got promoted yesterday. Big raise. He's happy about it, James. Ecstatic."

Slightly ahead of them, the crosswalk sign cycled from orange to white and Brighton Daniels strode on with confidence. James, on the other hand, didn't look so good.

"What?" Eden groaned. "I did all the work for you. He'll probably just go on some kind of celebratory bender. Sure, he'll be out of control for a bit, but he'll live through it. Even with a dose your size."

"You don't know that," he said.

"Trust me." She started walking again, determined not to let Brighton get away. Another gust of winter air rushed past. She'd given James enough time to make the right choice. "Do it," she said.

He frowned and she knew he'd gotten the message, the shift from request to order. James swore under his breath. He jogged a few steps, tapped Brighton's wrist with his fingertip.

"Time?" he asked innocently.

Eden watched the bare skin James had swiped. In the daylight it was hard to make out, but there was no denying the brief glow. Oblivious as he yanked his arm up, Brighton smiled. It was a good sign, though it would be a few hours before the Touch took hold. Before they knew for sure. "Almost noon."

"Thanks." James stopped in the middle of the sidewalk, thrusting his hands back into his pockets, ignoring the glares of the other pedestrians. Brighton Daniels, whose future held either a blissed-out night without fear of consequences, or a spiral into his darkest thoughts, turned the corner and vanished from sight.

"Happy?" James mumbled as he pivoted, heading back in the direction of the apartment.

"Nope." Eden stepped in front of him to block his path. "You need to get rid of more." James rolled his eyes.

"I'll deal with the buildup."

"Because that's gone so great for you, right?" she said. The sooner they got this over with, the better. It was freezing out. Winters in New York weren't pleasant. Her leggings weren't enough to keep her warm under her skirt.

"*You* don't have to do this. You take it from the Siders, and then instead of spreading yourself, you get to dose Adam and Jarrod!"

She couldn't help her bitter smile. "I have to dose Adam and Jarrod. With all the Touch I take in, they have better odds than the mortals of making it through. Would you rather I spread it myself? Kill them?" She yanked her hands into her sleeves. "And I'm genociding our kind. I deal with enough death."

He fell silent as a group of teenagers burst out of a corner drugstore, ripping open a pack of Oreos while they laughed. James watched them as they stumbled off down the street, one girl yanking the cookies above her head, taunting the others.

"I miss that," James said, staring after them.

Eden snorted. "Oreos?"

"No. Fun. Normalcy. None of *this* bullshit."

"You killed yourself, James." Eden shivered, giving up and leading the way back to the apartment. "Doesn't seem like you were exactly striving for fun. Now all you do is bitch about having a second chance."

She'd only gone a half a block before she realized he wasn't following, stopped so he could catch up. He hesitated, before slowly making his way to her. As he drew closer, she could make out a deep hurt radiating from his eyes.

"I'm sorry, James. I'm tired and pissy and I shouldn't be taking it out on you."

"No," he said, keeping his eyes on the ground. "Maybe you're right. Maybe I screwed up the first time around."

"I just want you to try." She tucked her hands into her pockets, waiting. He didn't answer. "For me?" she added.

He glanced up. "I'll give it a chance."

Her phone rang, interrupting them. Eden pulled it from her pocket. She hit Ignore and shoved it back.

"Who was that?"

"No one," she answered, trying to keep her voice even. If Az left a message, she would delete it without listening. Just like she had all the others.

# CHAPTER 20

Gabe stalked past the corrugated metal covering the storefronts, his finger tracing vibrant bubble-lettered graffiti. He gauged the honey sky, the smog already fading to amber. The sun would set soon.

Jamming his hands into his pockets, he slowed his pace. He'd cut out of the apartment early, but even the long walk hadn't done much to rebound his mood. Az's snippy little comments had damaged his usual cheer. Sure, Az had reason to be all angst and issues, but the constant drama was getting to be a bit much. He seemed to forget, he wasn't the only one who missed Eden.

A memory from summer flared. All he'd asked was for her to rub sunscreen on his back. Of course, she feigned innocence when the "missed" spots formed a perfect smiley face. It took him a week to get her back, polka dotting her arm after she fell asleep in the sun.

Gabe sighed, pulling the heavy coat around him. Now everything was a mess. All because of him.

He dropped onto a set of concrete stairs, pulling the hood of the parka over his golden curls. Heat filled every crevice, steaming into the sleeves. A drop of sweat trickled between the last curls near his hairline before it slipped down his neck. But instead of taking the jacket off, he yanked the cords on either side of the hood, drawing the fur lining closer.

He wondered again if he should tell Az about the other guy in Eden's life. He didn't know if she'd noticed the way the brown-haired boy looked at her yet. Kristen had said she'd kept Eden away from the others as much as possible, but he'd left with her.

From where Gabe sat, he could make out just enough of the steps of her apartment complex to know if she left. The city was lighting up, even here in the interesting part, before the ghetto really took hold.

He tucked his head down, playing the part of just another loitering degenerate, albeit one with a damn nice coat, and took in a few breaths of frigid air. The hood masked his eyes, but still let him see out. He focused on the steps across the way and down the street, ignoring the cars that fractured his view every few seconds.

Stilettos clicked behind him, someone leaving the building at the top of the steps he'd hunkered down on.

He kept his eyes low, staring down the street until a voice spoke.

"You got a cig?"

He peered sideways. The red stilettos were connected to a pair of legs in torn fishnets. "Don't smoke," he said, going back to his watch.

"A light then?"

"Why would I have a lighter if I don't smoke?" he asked, distracted. A figure had turned the corner. On the stairs, Gabe tensed. In the deepening twilight, he couldn't see the face. Every few feet the figure stopped, head cocked as if listening at every alcove and alley.

One of the shoes kicked lightly at his side. "You cute under that shit? You sound cute."

Gabe didn't answer, distractedly slipping the hood off to get a better look down the street. Next to him, he heard the girl take a surprised gasp.

"Damn. Looking for some company, angel?"

Gabe startled, turning to give her a good once-over. She was painfully mortal. It hadn't been an observation. Only a pet name, probably something she whispered to a dozen guys a night.

"We don't play for the same team, sweetheart," he said, keeping an eye on the trench coat making its way closer.

The hooker dug through her purse, probably looking for the misplaced lighter. "Ain't that just my fucking luck," she mumbled. He heard the swish of leather against nylon; the swinging of her purse back onto her shoulder. On the sidewalk, the shadowy figure was almost in front of him. Close enough to see the shoes.

The hooker finally noticed the newcomer. "How 'bout you, gorgeous? You up for some company?" The face turned toward the catcall, enough light catching for Gabe to get an eyeful. Luke's shoulders pulled up in surprise, long dark curls bunching and falling into place again as he relaxed.

"Gabriel," Luke tsked, recovering. "And what would the Upstairs say if they knew their golden boy was consorting with a lady of the night? I believe they'd be crest*fallen*."

Gabe didn't miss the emphasis. Luke knew damn well the prostitute was of no interest, slipped in the comment just to be obnoxious. He stood slowly, keeping his face calm.

"Luke." What Gabe wanted to follow up with was *I hadn't heard you were back into town*. It sounded so much cooler, so much more collected; but the lie fizzled, leaving the taste of sulfur on his tongue. He knew better than to voice the untruth, even without the not-so-subtle reminder.

"Where's the girl, Gabriel?" Luke asked.

Next to Gabe, the woman scoffed angrily. As she

clunked down the stairs in her too-high heels she snapped, "If you weren't interested you coulda just said so," behind her.

Luke leaned against the railing of the stairs. "The rogue must be close if you're out here playing watchdog." His black curls swung as he swiveled to take in the empty street. "Care to share who you're protecting her from?"

Gabe glared silence.

"You're not protecting her from me, are you?" Luke's jaw dropped in a false show of shock. He chuckled softly, his breath darting out in sharp clusters with each chuff. "We could always share her. Half for me, half for you?"

"Fuck you," Gabe spat, the anger boiling over. It felt good, the heat of it bubbling inside of him. His hands curled into fists, but he pulled them up into the sleeves of the parka. *Now isn't the time*, he cautioned himself.

Luke smiled. "Look at you! Using big-boy words." When he spoke again, his voice had gone hard. "We all know about her existence, Gabriel. Siders can't be killed, anyway. There's no reason to be so secretive."

"I'm just here tonight to watch," Gabe said.

"Does He know you prefer it down here?" He paused. "You tell me what you know about the Siders, and I can arrange for a permanent vacation from that stuffy Attic."

Gabe's face twisted into a sour mask. "It'll never happen, Luke."

"All the trips you've taken down here to gather information for Them and you expect me to believe you've never once had a tryst, told a lie? We both know there has to be something in that past of yours worth a Fall. All you have to do is say it aloud. We'll play confession." Luke lowered his voice, moving closer. "Whisper me your wickedness, Gabriel, and pretend all it will cost is a few Our Fathers like the mortals."

"Never," Gabe snapped. Nothing would've cemented the cocky sneer more permanently onto Luke's lips than Gabriel falling out of favor Upstairs. Let alone being the cause for it. He hadn't told the Upstairs about the Siders. It was technically an omission, not enough for a full Fall, but enough to get him wings. Secrets rose up in his throat, bubbled against the back of his closed lips. He focused his attention on the stairs beneath him, the cold. Anything to distract his mind, keep it from latching on to what he hid. The thoughts faded. Az had taught him well.

Eventually, he'd have to confess. He was Bound. But first he had to find a reason why the Upstairs shouldn't wipe the Siders out. He'd promised Kristen he'd wait until he found it.

"Let's not rule it out with a 'never' just yet," Luke mused. Gabe felt the hairs on his arms prickle.

Gabe snorted, unzipping the parka. He couldn't watch

for Eden now, not so much look in that direction. Luke wouldn't miss it.

Instead, he started talking. "You still have the same little fantasy of one of the Bound giving in to a Fallen? That's precious."

Luke reached into his pocket for a pack of cigarettes. He cupped a hand to block the wind and lit one, raising a finger to cut Gabe off.

"Don't try to pull that high-and-mighty shit on me."

He had to get Luke away. The best option seemed to be to just walk, and hope he would follow. As he stepped down the bottom two stairs, starting a slow saunter, Gabe swallowed hard.

"We're not here to catch up, Gabriel. The rogue . . ." Luke started, unsmiling.

"I'm watching her, just like the rest of the Siders. When we figure out their purpose, we'll decide what needs to be done with her specifically. From what little is out there, the only thing that's obvious is she's killing others of her kind." Gabe turned, his shoulders squaring with authority. "It's not the Basement's concern."

Luke sighed. "The girl is fair game. We both know that."

Gabe cocked his head. "Why so interested in her?"

"Just because I don't know how to work a toy, doesn't mean I don't want it in my toy box. She's shiny." He took a few steps, putting some distance between them. "And I want her."

Gabe watched him leave. Alone on the sidewalk, he closed his eyes, listening until the footsteps faded. He knew he had to go. Luke could turn around, backtrack. He slid the zipper of the parka back up. Turning down the nearest street, he dared a quick glance over his shoulder. Eden would be on her own tonight.

# CHAPTER 21

A quartet of police cars broke around the corner, lining up along the curb. Next to Eden, James shifted from foot to foot, pulling his shabby jacket closed. If anyone but James had spotted the growing crowd, she would have still been down the block, tucked away in her room and out of the wind. But it had been James, and so of course she'd said yes.

"Pigs are here. Should we go?" he asked, wide eyes looking past Jarrod and Adam to her. She offered James a twitch of a smile and he relaxed.

"They're not our concern." She glanced around at the crowd. It was easily large enough to keep them anonymous. No one seemed to be paying them any special attention. Of course, whenever the Fallen had been mentioned, no one had bothered to tell her helpful things like what the hell they *looked* like. The Siders knew how to find her, though. She knew it was only a matter of time.

"You didn't do anything wrong," she said, her attention drifting to the reason for the crowd, for the cops. The shadowy outline of a solitary figure paced the ledge twenty stories above.

"And we wouldn't wanna miss the grand finale," Jarrod added, gesturing upward dismissively.

Next to her, Adam chuckled. "Sometimes you're damn scary, you know that?" His long brown bangs obscured his eyes, but she'd caught the horrified amusement in them.

"Only sometimes?" she asked. She caught Jarrod in a sidelong glance. "Clearly, you're slipping."

Jarrod chuffed a laugh and Adam looked past the awning of the old hotel, past empty window after empty window.

"Think it's him?" James asked her.

"Too far up. I can't tell." She squinted, absently spiraling one of her pink highlights around her finger.

"If he jumps we'll get a closer look." Jarrod snickered.

Eden shot him an icy glare, the eclectic mix of bracelets on her wrist jingling as she threw a hand on her hip. "Well, he is taking his time up there." With her thumb, she toyed with one of the three silver rings adorning her pinkie finger. "I think our friend just might make it."

"Bet on that?" Jarrod asked, jumping onto a dented mailbox. He kicked his shoes against the side, met Adam's glare with casual indifference. "Look, either she thinks he really is gonna make it, or she's lying to the kid." He looked down to Eden. "Which is it?" he asked, his eyes sparkling.

She knew she shouldn't give in, that she was only encouraging the bullshit attitude he'd had lately, but bastard or not, he knew her. She glanced at James, making sure his attention was elsewhere, that he didn't see her hesitation.

"Screw it," she said suddenly. "You're on. When I win, you're on laundry for three weeks." She extended her hand, black fingernails absorbing the lights.

"And if I win you're gonna let us figure out how to help you with the buildup from clearing the Siders from our stairs in the morning. Something more than the dosing." She looked up at him, caught off guard. Apparently she hadn't been hiding it as well as she thought. Jarrod studied the businessman above for a quick moment, and then shook her hand. "Three weeks."

The man on the ledge teetered. The crowd hushed. The police stirred and Eden cupped her hands around her mouth.

"Don't do it!" she screamed.

"I'm fucking cold! Shit or get off the pot!" Jarrod's voice bellowed out louder than Eden's, drowning her out. A disgusted shriek sounded and he swiveled toward a girl glaring at him, her eyes a mixture of hatred and pity. *Murderer,* Eden read on her lips.

Jarrod's mouth fell open. Eden could almost taste his bitter retort. It was…right…there. After another second of silence, Eden glanced up at him. Jarrod looked from Eden to the girl, his eyes unreadable before he dipped his head, giving the mailbox a weak kick.

The girl spun away. Eden didn't miss the satisfied "so much better than you" mask plastered across her face, the superior air. *Bitch, please*, Eden fumed silently. *You're here too.*

"No one fucks with my boys," she whispered. Anger sent her ungloved finger forward, headed for the cliché flower tramp stamp. *No*, she thought, but the need was too strong, the draw of her fingers to the bare skin like a magnet. James caught Eden's wrist just before she made contact. She blinked in surprise.

"What are you doing? You'll kill her!" James stared at her in disbelief, disappointment in his voice. Already her anger was dissipating to guilt. She forced a deep breath, trying to calm herself as the girl walked off through the crowd.

A sudden scream ripped her eyes upward.

The ledge was empty. A whoosh of air sent Eden stumbling backward as the body hit the ground at her feet. Az, the balcony, the bent leg. The mental snapshot superimposed itself over the body. Inside her, a wail built. *It's not Az. That never happened.* She turned away, swallowing down her retch in silence, grief and embarrassment swirling through her. *I can't mourn him anymore. He's not dead.*

"Skin and concrete. Do . . . not . . . mix," Jarrod said, a look of amazement on his face that didn't reach his eyes. He slid off the mailbox, the soles of his feet hitting the ground just as the screams started. From beside her, she heard James groan, some mixture of devastation and acceptance. He took a step to the left, leaning closer to the mostly undamaged face of the jumper. He backed away suddenly, looking to Eden, his eyes full of surprise.

"James, I'm sorry he took it bad, but . . ."

"No! Eden, look at him!" His hands shook. "That's not my guy! I promise!"

She leaned in to the pile of limbs on the concrete. James was right. Somewhere in the city, Brighton Daniels was still alive. In theory.

They left the chaos behind, the sidewalk traffic thinning down to the normal New York rush of strangers. Eden tossed a glance back over her shoulder, taking in a panoramic of the shattered crowd.

"So I won the bet." Jarrod didn't seem particularly thrilled to bring it up, more like mentioning it was a necessary evil. Eden let another block pass beneath their feet before she answered.

"What exactly do you expect me to . . . ?" She trailed off. Jarrod stared, waiting for her to finish the thought.

Instead, she tucked the tips of her fingers into the back of the waist of her skirt, turning to cross the street. The boys followed without comment.

"What are you thinking?" Jarrod asked after a full minute had passed.

She swept him with her icy blue eyes. "I'm thinking you're not paying attention. Getting sidetracked by something meaningless." Eden whirled to the busy sidewalk behind them.

Only steps away, too close, was a blond girl. Her ponytail held the strands high, a delicate swoop of curls decorating the last few inches. She looked every bit the all-American cheerleader type. Not the kind of girl that would have descended from her pedestal to talk to them had they been alive and in the halls of some suburban high school. The girl froze, staring.

Eden pointed a jeweled finger into the startled face. "She's been following us for two blocks," she said, keeping her eyes on the boys. "You didn't even notice her, did you?"

Adam and Jarrod didn't dare speak, unsure of the next move. But James was still new enough to let out an attempt at an apology before she silenced him with a glare.

Eden brushed a finger across the girl's shoulder.

James gasped, but just as Eden suspected, there was no glow. Instead, the glamour fell away, dark circles smudging the eyes. The first signs of grave rot blushed the girl's cheeks as oblivious pedestrians cut around them.

*Great*, she thought. Now it wasn't Siders just on the stairs in the morning. They were following her around like paparazzi. Disgusted, Eden spun toward the neon OPEN sign of Milton's, the girl gasping in shock behind her.

"I am off fucking duty," Eden said over her shoulder, her voice cold. "Macchiatos and mercy kills don't go well together. Come back in the morning."

No more threat should have been needed, but the girl didn't take the hint. She twisted her hands into her coat sleeves, chewing her lip, but didn't move.

"Run along," Eden added, flicking her fingers through the air.

"So you *are* her?" the girl whispered in awe. "The Sider they're all talking about." Eden's hand paused on the handle. The girl stepped back. "Everyone said to stay out of the other boroughs. People say Manhattan is safe. Well, except for you, of course." She hesitated, unsure. "But unless they ask, you don't . . ."

Jarrod's mouth twitched. "Kill them?"

"You'd only heard I was in Manhattan and you managed to find me?" Eden stared, waiting for the girl to break, but she stayed silent. "Someone told you where I was. Someone told you how to find me."

"Black hair, pink in it. Small group. One of them a cocky skater punk type?" She gave Jarrod a once-over.

"Everyone's heard the rumors. The details are pretty consistent, but the location's never the same. When I saw you guys tonight, it wasn't exactly rocket science." The new girl raised an eyebrow, shot him a half smile. Her glamour had slipped back into place. Once again she looked like any other typical homecoming queen type; the only thing missing was the tiara.

Eden stepped closer, only a breath away. "What do you want," Eden prodded.

"I don't really know where to start." She lost her nerve, looked away. "I've been following leads, hoping I'd bump into you." She let out a nervous laugh. "I guess I just did."

"That guy on the ledge. Was he yours?" James asked. His voice wavered, as if his life depended on knowing the answer. As if it was important.

"He held the door for me this morning," she said. "I followed him. I normally don't go for ones who look like they'll take it bad. Do you guys normally watch after? Make sure they're okay?"

As Eden watched from the corner of her eye, James's gaze traveled to the girl's face. He seemed bewitched, his eyes glassy. It was almost cute until she noticed Jarrod too had given in, their little crushes evident on their faces. Though he would never admit it, even Adam looked to be giving her a bit more consideration than normal.

The new girl didn't seem to notice, keeping her eyes

on Eden. "Could I maybe buy you a cup of coffee? I was wondering if we could talk."

The chance, even so slight, that the girl had been told about her by whoever kept her stairs popular nagged at the back of Eden's mind. Too many Siders. Too many rumors. She didn't want to stop. Would never deny the Siders the choice of opting out. Just had to figure out how to control the rumors before the Fallen got wind.

"Someone's gotta death wish," Adam said under his breath.

She stared at him for a second before taking a slow step toward Milton's. "Actually, it's the opposite," she said, throwing the heavy wood open. "I need a place to live."

Eden's bracelets jangled as she settled into a wooden booth. She swirled her fingers through the steam rising from her cup. She caught Jarrod's eye from where he stood at the counter with James before turning back to the girl across from her.

"Okay, you have my attention." Eden took a sip of her coffee, not bothering to cool it with a breath first. "Make it quick."

"Here's the deal. I spent the last of my serious cash on a hotel for tonight. I've got two weeks until my phone gets shut off, and I can't get a job because I don't have an address." The girl wrapped her now ungloved hands around the warmth of her paper cup.

Eden shrugged. "So beg. I'll even lend you some markers. You can make yourself a real nice sign."

"Look, in the other boroughs, they have big groups. But you just got started. I learn fast. I could help you."

"We're fine how we are." Eden kept her face stoic as she shrugged her shoulders back into her coat, turning to climb out of the booth. She poked Adam, who'd slid in next to her.

"Wait!" the girl yelled, holding her hand across the table to stop her. "Hear me out!"

Eden looked down at the splayed fingers, waiting for Adam to move. Fortunately, in the months they'd been teamed up, he'd honed his talent for knowing when she counted on him to not obey. Eden feigned impatience just long enough to make the girl nervous before dropping back into her seat. She twirled her hand in the air.

"From the look of it, I have two choices. End up raped in some alley or join up with a group. The other Siders I've found . . ." She dropped her gaze, seemed to force herself to raise it again. "I ended up in Manhattan because I was told you didn't bother Siders here too much. But crashing under a bridge is not my idea of 'safe.' And I'm out of money."

"I am not a bank."

"I stand by my death wish statement," Adam laughed.

This time, he didn't need any prodding. He drained the last of his coffee and slid from the booth.

"Thanks for the coffee." Reaching back automatically, Adam took Eden's hand. She let him help her up, his fingers wrapping around hers. Neither of their glamours so much as flickered. They'd long since grown immune to each other. Jarrod glanced over, saw them standing, and tapped James on the shoulder. They crossed the room to her.

"Wait. Where are you going?" Trailing behind, the girl followed to the door, but Jarrod pulled it shut behind him, leaving her inside.

The streets glistened with nighttime city shine, brought to life by the drizzle that had started while they'd been inside. Eden wasn't surprised to see her breath. A few degrees colder and the discarded cigarette butts and straw wrappers would be frozen to the curb. Already the air smelled of snow under the exhaust fumes.

She led them past a seedy cabaret, ignoring the heroin eyes near the entrance. Turning down the alley that separated them from home, Jarrod's steps faltered.

"Eden! Stop."

She turned to him.

"Why'd you leave?"

"Because we don't need another mouth to feed, Jarrod."

Jarrod threw his hands in the air. "Oh, come on. You've been after Zach to join us for weeks now. Why not her?"

"Zach can take care of himself. That girl's looking for a handout."

"Are you kidding me? She needs a place to stay, and you need someone besides me and Adam to dose. Sounds like a fair trade to me."

"I also need someone I can depend on and trust." Footsteps echoed off the walls, cutting her short. "Great," Eden whispered.

The girl caught up, her attention focused on Eden.

"I wasn't finished!" Her defiant voice shattered against the brick buildings towering over them. Eden swiveled to face her, but Adam had already moved between the two.

"Whoa," he said, shielding Eden behind him. "Ease up on the attitude . . . girl."

"Libby," she spat. Her jaw tightened, a wave of determination cresting over her perfectly rouged cheekbones. "Will you at least think about it? At least give me that much."

Eden rolled her eyes, walking again. "I'll make you a deal, Libby. I'll think about it while you go get your money's worth out of that hotel room," she said as she rounded the corner.

She was letting her annoyance get the better of her. They were almost to the apartment, but Libby seemed satisfied enough to back off.

"Are you really gonna think about it?" Jarrod asked.

Eden smirked. "Any chance you'll let it go?" Jarrod let out an exasperated sigh. "Didn't think so," she said, climbing the stairs.

# CHAPTER 22

First it had been a car alarm; that had been easy enough to laugh off. But after jumping at the sound of the toaster, a blush colored Gabe's cheeks.

Transferring from Upstairs never got any easier. It didn't take any physical effort, just a pure thought of home was enough to get him there, but the New York tension, millions of tightly wound mortal coils, always seemed worse when he returned.

To top it off, on this trip there'd been an agenda. Most of his time Upstairs had been spent scouring through the record room, checking and double-checking. Tedious research on the dozen names Kristen had given him.

But he'd found what he was looking for.

Az shot him a sidelong gaze while he scraped butter onto his toast. "You're edgy. . . ."

A glob of butter melted off the knife, slopping onto the dish's daisy chain border. Gabe sighed, long and harder than he'd intended. "Nnnn..." His voice strained on the first letter. He couldn't finish the word.

Az dropped the blade onto the plate next to it, watching Gabe stifle a gag.

"No? You sure?" Az reached behind, opening the refrigerator. He groped the top shelf and handed Gabe a can of soda. "For the sulfur," he added.

Gabe cracked the pull tab, took a long swig. Az shoved a piece of toast into his mouth. He chewed slowly, his elbows cocked behind him, leaning on the counter.

The straight inky hair didn't look right on him. Gabe still hadn't grown used to the new look, the way the black of the dye set off Az's eyes. There were dark circles under them—yesterday's eyeliner had apparently given in to wanderlust while he'd slept.

The harsh light from the bare bulb glared against his shirtless chest, shadowing his abs. He'd lost weight when things had gotten offtrack with Eden. Now, from the look of things, he was losing more. His collarbone jutted as he took another bite of the toast. *Well?* he asked with his eyes.

"I was near her apartment. Near. Not *at*, right?" Gabe hesitated. "Because I don't want you to freak out at this next part."

Az lowered his hand. Gabe looked away. "I saw Luke."

He heard the wet kiss of the toast landing butter side

down, waited for the panicked yelling to start. Or worse.

For a change, Az seemed to be keeping his cool. "Is she all right?" he asked quietly. "Tell me that first." When Gabe looked up, he saw Az had closed his eyes. His hands were shaking.

"She's fine, Az. I would have told you if . . ."

"Okay," he said. "Tell me what happened." The quaking had spread to Az's legs. Gabe wasn't sure if it was in rage or fear. Either way it wasn't good. It had been weeks since he'd been overwhelmed with a temptation to Fall. His hips rattled against the countertop, yesterday's low-slung jeans offering no protection.

"The Basement knows there's a rogue, what she can do. Luke's getting close. I don't think he knows it's Eden," Gabe added, knowing it wouldn't matter.

Az scooped the toast from the floor, tossing it into the trash. He grasped the edge of the counter as he leaned back against it. "Yet. Like that won't change the second he sees her."

"Az, we knew he'd be after her as soon as he figured out she was different."

"But we were supposed to *be there*."

"And just how do you expect to be there?"

"She'll answer the phone." He stopped when he saw Gabe's shoulders shrugging up and down with soft laughter. "What?"

"You're delusional." Gabe ran his thumb across his lips, as if to brush away the smile.

"Prick," Az mumbled.

"Hey, I would be very nice to me were I you. Are we even talking about the same girl, because Eden is far too stubborn to randomly pick up the phone. You've been trying almost every day for how long?" Az's eyes flared, the blue ring rusting to a sour maroon, betraying his anger. "I think it'd be better if you left talking to her up to me."

"So what?" He pushed away from the counter. "You want me to stop trying?"

"Az," Gabe said softly. "Look how upset you are. Maybe it'd be better if you let her go. Use the wings," he said, hating the pleading arc that crept into his voice at the end. He opened his mouth, but already knew the answer when he saw the look in Az's eyes. "You could come home," he finished anyway. "I'd make sure she's kept safe."

"Not a fucking chance." Az pushed off the counter, striding to the front door. He'd slid on one of his shoes before Gabe caught up. "You know what 'upsets' me," Az ground out, tightening the laces in a double knot. He grabbed for his coat with one hand, yanking his other shoe on with a hooked finger. "That you think she's dispensable."

Gabe's jaw dropped. "When did I ever say *that*?"

"What'd you just ask me to do? Use the wings, come home," he mocked. "They'd never let me back down here," Az said. "I'd never see her again."

Gabe slammed a fist against the door.

"Okay, lover boy. I've had it with this," he said, tossing his hand in an angry flair. "This whole 'poor Az' thing. What are you gonna do? You think you can just say you're sorry and she's gonna let it all go? Let you waltz in there and play knight in shining armor? How'd that work out for you at Kristen's?"

"Fuck you, Gabriel." Az stopped suddenly, his coat in his hand, staring. "What's with you lately? You're all over the place."

Gabe glanced away, hiding his eyes.

"You know I love Eden. Now you want me to throw that away and go back Upstairs? I'm worried about her and you're *laughing* about it?" Az leaned against the door. "You're having trouble, aren't you?"

Gabe winced. "Not confessing goes against everything inside me. It gets harder every day." He lifted his head, let Az see the shame in his eyes. "I don't know if I can hold out much longer, Az."

"You can do this, Gabe." Az took a breath, let it out slowly. "You have to. Once the Bound find out about the Siders, things will only get worse. I need to get through to Eden before then. It's been two months. I gave her space, gave her time to cool off. I'm just gonna have to talk to her face-to-face."

"You do what you have to do, but give me a chance to talk to her first. I found something out when I was Upstairs. I don't want her to be all pissed off when I tell her. Turns out she's more different than we thought."

Az thought about it for a second before he nodded. "In the meantime, I think you need to stay away from Upstairs. The more you go up there, the worse you seem to get."

Gabe turned away. "I know," he whispered.

# CHAPTER 23

It was just after one in the morning when they left the apartment. Adam barely made it out the door before he froze. Jarrod pushed past him, got his own view of what had stopped Adam, and glanced back at her.

On the stairs sat two teenagers, staring at Eden. The one closest to her held out a handful of money.

"Little late, aren't you?" Eden asked, forcing the surprise from her face. She turned back to Adam and Jarrod. "Wait here."

The two Siders who'd been on the stairs followed around the corner. There was no denying that word about her was spreading.

A minute later, back at the base of the stairs, the boys fell into step behind her. She pulled the leftover cash from earlier out of her pocket, added the new bills to the stash, and handed it to Adam.

"That makes rent, right?" A steady ache throbbed

deep inside the bones of her arms, the Touch she'd taken in winding its way past her elbows, across her shoulders, and up her neck. She draped her hand against the wall to keep her balance. The fingers burned, but it had nothing to do with the way her knuckles scraped across the brick. Eden blinked hard, trying to clear the sudden blur to her vision.

"Already?" He counted. "With this we're only a hundred short," he said. "Plus what we spend tonight."

Jarrod sped up, pacing her. "How many have you taken since you last dosed us?"

Eden shrugged. The motion knocked her off kilter. She teetered for a split second before she steadied, focusing on the subway entrance only a couple dozen steps away. As she stepped off the curb, Jarrod grabbed her arm, spinning her around. The twirl seemed to keep going after her body stopped. She swallowed a wave of nausea.

"Eden, how many?" he growled.

"A lot, all right!" she yelled. "I don't need a lecture, Jarrod."

His grip tightened. "You can't keep going like this."

"We could move," Adam offered up. Just that he was suggesting it made Eden wince. They already knew how it would turn out. The Siders would be there before they'd even had a chance to get settled. It'd been that way when they'd gone from the hotel to the apartment. They'd found her.

Her stomach churned, the taste of warm bile rising into her throat. She fought it back down.

"They're showing up at night now, and you don't think we need to talk about this? Figure something out?" Jarrod demanded.

"Isn't that the point of what we're doing tonight? We'll see if it helps. You won the bet, so I'm sticking to my part of it. What else do you want from me?" she asked wearily.

As she made her way down the stairs to the platform, she glanced up to the apartment window where James watched from above. The blinds lowered.

"We'll figure it out, Jarrod," she promised. "Ready?" She handed him the key, her platforms clanking down the metal stairs, ending the conversation.

Two trains and a four-block walk later they could hear the thumping. Deep bass beats drew them through empty streets lined with warehouses. A smattering of mortal teens wandered in from the alleys, gathering into a stream funneled toward the same goal. Eden watched them, amused as she followed the crowd. Decked out in Day-Glo and wigs, a few had streamers hanging from their wrists and ankles, turning them into tornados of color when they spun happily. Two in the morning and the rave was just starting to gain strength.

Eden ran two fingers over her perfectly gelled hair, sliding the black waves dancing across her cheeks back into place near her temple. The pin curls had taken forever to get perfect, delicate enough to balance out the punk Goth mix of her outfit with a Suicide Girl edge. Back at the apartment, she'd been careful to separate the pink highlights out, give them their own curls. When it was done, there had been a kick-ass version of a twenties-style movie starlet staring back at her from the mirror.

Jarrod pulled a flyer from his low-slung cargo pants—their official invitation—and handed it to the man at the door. Adam doled out the entrance fees as they strode past, through an enormous metal door into the shadows cast by strobe lights inside.

Eden watched the crowd for a moment, her stomach knotting. Every part of tonight had "bad idea" written all over it. She thought about turning around, heading home, figuring out some other way.

The deep bass pounded its rhythm into her chest, spreading roots that tingled down through her legs and into the floor. The techno beats pulsed with a life of their own, the crowd jumping, spinning under the colored strobes. For just half a second she lost herself in the chaos. When she pulled out of the trance, Adam and Jarrod were there on either side of her, ready. Waiting. It was time to spread the virus.

She tried not to pass herself if she could help it. Her potency meant the difference between shooting sprees and midnight joyrides, stolen lives and stolen kisses. For any hope of survival it had to be diluted through the boys. Especially tonight. Seven. Seven today, but there had been nearly as many yesterday. It was an invitation for disaster.

Jarrod and Adam could handle the extra burst of Touch as long as they dispersed it quick, before it had a chance to settle in them. They were the only ones she trusted her lips around. "It's gonna be a bigger dose than normal. Ready?"

She shook her fingers out, stalling. Jarrod had already leaned closer. She pressed her mouth against his quickly, careful not to breathe. The sudden buzz that electrified her had nothing to do with the music. They shared a beat before Jarrod pulled away and the song went on. Eyes shimmering, he bit his lip.

She turned to Adam. He slid a hand around the back of her neck and pulled her close in a sudden rush.

The kiss lasted a second too long, the static thrumming through her as the throbbing from the turntables climbed to a crescendo. In the glow of the swirling reds and purples of the lights, Adam didn't blink, didn't leave her. A steady single pulse matched the sound of her heart as the DJ spun another record. Eden raised a shaking hand, pointing out into the crowd.

*Go.* She didn't bother to say the word, any hope of him hearing her voice above the music lost as the volume shook her. He turned, slipping behind a veil of gyrating bodies. The tremors didn't stop. *He only wanted the extra Touch.* She didn't let herself consider any other possibility.

Alone with the crowd, she had no one to distract her from the fingers, arms, and elbows all around her. Eden's legs shook with the need to get rid of more. She fought her way toward the middle of the warehouse, tucking her arms across her chest, concentrating on keeping the rhythm outside her head. Adam and Jarrod needed to hurry.

And then someone grabbed her arm and dipped her low before setting her on her feet again. Her hand brushed against bare skin. Her breath caught as the dose of Touch left her. A beautiful rush of endorphins coursed through her, left her lighter. Eden's hand moved on its own, searching out the next victim. *Just a few.* The thought was there, disorganized but demanding.

The spin started slow, a delicate twirling as she gave in to the spell the song cast. The beats wound their way into her, hands flying from her sides. As she spun, her fingers danced across a trio of shoulders, exposed collarbones that seemed to lean closer. *They want it*, she thought, her head pounding, rattling and lost. Every bit of skin she touched glowed, a wide wake of fireflies spreading out behind her as she danced.

The room crushed in, spiraling around her in a blur. The crowd as a whole didn't matter, only the parts. Her fingers caught cheeks, foreheads, exposed midriffs. Too many. Dozens. Hundreds. Limbs twisting, touching, brushing. Her eyes closed as she let go, lost in the ecstasy, the release of so much poison built up inside. The power ebbed from her, the pure joy of silence as Touch left her. Hair brushed her cheek and a hand cupped Eden's ear to yell words lost to the decibels. But the contact was there and gone so quickly and then there was only her, dizzy and buried somewhere in the mad mob. The music, the lights; nothing stopped.

She tried to lift a hand, find something to hold onto, steady herself. The awful queasy movement doubled, a feeling of emptiness, holes inside her where the Touch had been.

Words leaped off her tongue and into the silence as the song ended and then she was falling, lost in darkness beyond the strobe lights' reach. *I gave too much*, she thought desperately, trying to get an elbow under her, to get up again. Her hand slipped against the concrete, skinning her palm as she sank onto her back.

Her stomach heaved. She barely had time to turn her head before the rush of vomit spilled across the floor. The strobe lights flickered twice in her long blinks before going black.

# CHAPTER 24

"I think she's coming around." The voice floated out of still, dark space. Her ears hummed. A palm slapped her cheek lightly. From far away, someone called her name.

"Too much," she moaned. "Pass back." It was all she could muster before her head lolled back. Fingers pressed against the back of her neck. The strange feeling of floating, and then someone set her down and she realized she'd been carried. Smell of dirty leather and sweat. Backseat of a cab. She forced her eyes open.

Three dark shapes sat silhouetted against the lights of the city shining through the backseat windows. Her head leaned against a shoulder, the rest of her pulled onto the lap.

"She better not be OD'ing." She could barely make out the words through the thick accent. Cab driver.

"She's fine." Jarrod was there.

"Eden?" It came from whoever had her. Adam. His

fingers ran down her cheek and she shivered, leaning into the palm that followed.

"What happened?" Eden thought he was talking to her, but someone else answered.

"I don't know. I saw her and tried to talk to her. She looked so awful I thought something was wrong. And then she fell . . . after the whole screaming thing." Eden lifted an inch from Adam's shoulder, squinting to make out the outline of whoever had spoken. A pony-tailed head was squeezed in next to Jarrod's shape. The girl from Milton's last night.

Eden groaned and Adam pressed her head back down against him again. She let him; taking in sips of buildings and sky through the back window the few times she bothered to open her eyes.

Just when she began to wonder if the ride would ever end, the car stopped. Adam slid out from under her, but he was back a second later, lifting her from the backseat. She felt the bounce of each of the stairs.

"Are they waiting for me?" she whispered. "I need some."

"Key?" he asked Jarrod, ignoring her.

Jarrod swung the door open, led them up the four flights of stairs to their apartment. Someone closed the door behind them.

"Eden!" she heard James shriek, felt him pawing at

her, trying to get a look. "Who did this to her?"

"Move," Adam said, brushing past the boy. He set her gently on the couch, then settled himself with her head on his lap, sliding a hand across her eyes when she tried to open them.

"I'm almost empty," she croaked, trying to push his hand away. "Touch . . ."

"She did it to herself," Adam said, finally answering James. The boy was there when she opened her eyes for a second. She hated his look of worry and tried to smile for him, but it felt all wrong on her face, almost a grimace.

"Herself? How?" James asked.

"Is she gonna be all right?" *She* was there, plopped in the recliner like she belonged in their apartment.

"Adam. Please." Eden couldn't get the words to come. She swallowed and tried again, opening her eyes to focus on Adam's face above hers. "I got rid of too much. I need you to pass some back."

Adam held her gaze for a minute then lowered his lips, the peck passing her a bit of Touch. Her vision cleared a bit, the throb in her head settling into a dull ache.

"Better?" Adam said.

She nodded, her attention settling on Libby. "What are you doing here?"

"She's the one who found you. Eden, what the fuck happened?" Jarrod asked.

"I don't know," she mumbled, closing her eyes to blot out Adam's face. She felt color rush to her face. It was no less embarrassing, even though she couldn't see them. She'd totally lost control.

"You're lucky Libby got to you right before you fell. This could have been a lot worse." Adam's fingers gently probed the back of her head as he turned to James. "She's gonna need some ice. She's too drained to heal fast enough."

"This is why we need to do things different. More than just dosing us." Jarrod paced the length of the room before he turned on Adam. "Why aren't you backing me up on this?"

"Jarrod, not tonight." Eden tried to sound commanding, give them some illusion that she still had control of the group. Of herself.

"You wanna self-destruct, fine," Jarrod spat, pointing an accusing finger in her face. "But what happens to us when you do? This isn't just about you, Eden! You're paying the rent. Buying the food. You won't let us help. You realize if something happens to you, we're all screwed?"

"She said not now, Jarrod," Adam hissed. James handed Adam a bag of ice wrapped in a kitchen towel. He pressed the compress against the knot rising on her scalp. She flinched.

He slid out from underneath Eden, beckoning Jarrod to

the room the boys shared. She heard them arguing through the closed door, their voices muted. She made out Adam's "No, you're right. Tomorrow we'll tell her . . ." before the voices dropped too low to hear.

"Do you need anything?" Libby asked, trying to fill the awkwardness in the living room. "Water, maybe?"

Eden nodded absently, draping an arm across her forehead. James rushed to the sink, handing the water to Libby as if he was afraid of getting too close to Eden. The cool glass was lifted to her lips. She snatched it from Libby before the girl could tip it like a sippy cup.

"I got it," Eden said, taking a deep gulp to prove her point. She wasn't an invalid. Still, the crestfallen look on Libby's face made her feel a little guilty. "Thank you," she added, and handed her back the glass. Eden leaned into the cushions and closed her eyes, but it did no good. She could still feel Libby's persistent staring.

"What?" she asked finally. She heard Libby shift.

"So you killed them? All of them?"

"I don't know," she answered, surprised by the exhaustion in her voice. "Not all. But probably some."

"But—"

Eden cut her off with a flick of her hand. "Listen, I can't do this right now, okay? Tomorrow." Libby had been there. Adam and Jarrod hadn't. Eden owed her now. There was no getting around it. *Stupid*, she chided herself, letting her head sink deep into the cushion, relishing the numbness of the ice pack.

She heard the click of the bedroom door opening and Jarrod asking Libby if she wanted to stay, if there was anyone waiting for her.

"I don't have anyone," Libby replied. "I'm not like you guys." And for just a moment before sleep stole over her, Eden almost felt sorry for the girl.

Eden jolted upright. For a second she wasn't sure where she was; not in her bed. A blanket had been tucked around her like a shroud sometime during the night. Now it made her claustrophobic, but the warmth kept her from ripping it off.

Wet hair clung to the nape of her neck. *Am I bleeding*, she wondered, but the fingers she pressed there came back clean. A soaked washcloth lay on the pillow.

"Hey! You're awake!" The chipper tone came from the kitchen, then Libby stepped out smiling with the wattage turned up far too high. Even the room itself seemed too bright, the window shades pulled to let in the morning sun.

This morning, everything seemed . . . *too* something. Libby held out a cup.

"Coffee. Black. Adam told me you like it that way. Is it okay?"

"Yeah, perfect. Thanks." Eden took a small sip and set it down on the coffee table.

She looked around the room, stiffening. "Where's Adam?" she asked. "Jarrod? James?" Her voice shook as she called the names, the vulnerable feeling catching her off guard.

"Relax," Libby said. "They went out for a few. Jarrod said to tell you he was taking James out. He said you'd understand. It's okay, though, they left me to watch you."

"Watch me?" Eden asked. "And they just left?" Libby either didn't catch her snide tone or was ignoring it.

She smiled again, plopping next to Eden on the couch.

"Don't touch me!" Eden shifted uncomfortably, turned to the bright light coming in through the windows. The angle of the sun sent the wrong patterns of shadow across the floor. "What time is it?" she asked.

"Um, about twelve thirty?"

"Shit." Eden threw off the blanket. "I'm late." She stood, was half a stride from the couch before her body caught up with her brain. Her legs wobbled and gave out. Libby grabbed her around the waist. Already following commands, she was careful to only touch her shirt, not reach for her hand.

"What the hell are you doing? You're going to hurt yourself!"

Eden couldn't help but laugh at the thought of a slight bruise sidelining her. Her palms were already starting to heal from where she'd skinned them last night, but the bump was still a tender goose egg. Libby let out an unsure twitter. Eden leaned against her until she dropped back onto the couch. She felt better, but Adam's dose last night hadn't been enough. Touch built in the boys when they didn't spread, but Eden's came mostly from the Siders.

Eden considered Libby for a moment. Clearly the boys trusted her, which said a lot.

"Go to the window for me. Tell me how many kids are out there." Eden jutted her chin at one of the windows facing the street. Libby shot her an inquisitive look, but did as she said.

"Eight that I can see," she started. Eden wanted to sob. The number nearly doubled yesterday's morning group. "Four across the street at the bus stop, two over on the . . ."

Eden let out her breath. "How many on the *stairs*, Libby!"

She stood on her tiptoes, trying to get the best angle. "I can't really see . . . like maybe two? One for sure, but there's some feet."

Eden sighed in relief. Two would be perfect. Their Touch might even nix the last of her headache. And she'd already kept them waiting so long.

"You're going to help me get downstairs." Eden didn't bother making it a question. But Libby was already shaking her head.

"Jarrod said he needs to talk to you. He told me I was *not* to let you go downstairs no matter what you tried to bribe me with." *Bribe, eh?* Eden thought.

"Those are Siders down there," Eden said, choosing her words carefully. "And they're here for me. For what I can do." Libby twisted her hands. She had said at Milton's that she'd heard what Eden did. "I won't tell the boys, either," Eden added, hating the desperation leaking out. But she had to convince her. They were waiting.

"No, he said you'd try to . . ." Libby started. "What *do* you do to them anyway?" Libby's eyes gleamed, hungry for information. Eden met them.

"If you help me," she said, "I'll let you watch."

# CHAPTER 25

Libby was first out the door. Over her shoulder, Eden watched the hopeful look in the two sets of eyes glaze over before she stepped out from behind her.

"It's her!" the guy on the stairs yelped.

"Don't be stupid." The girl sitting beside him tossed a small rock down to the sidewalk. "That's not even close to what she's supposed to look like." Her head rose as she spoke, catching sight of Eden. "It's true," she whispered in reverence.

"Take me around the corner," Eden told Libby, a new wave of dizziness rolling over her. "They'll follow." The moment Libby moved, the other two were on their feet, poised to run if need be. *Not likely*, Eden thought.

In the alley, Libby leaned her against the wall and took an unsure step back.

"Stand there," she told Libby, pointing to the bricks opposite. The girl did what she was told. "Don't come any closer." Eden paused before adding, "No matter what happens."

She took the boy first.

At the exhale, her eyes caught Libby's. They blazed, taking notes on every detail, memorizing the way her hands gripped his, the way she kept her lips an inch away. As her breath did its work, his Touch passed into her, an electric current running up through her hands. Around her, the world steadied.

The other one barely waited for her partner to fall before she stepped in to take his place. When it was over, the leftovers lay, still, on the cold asphalt.

"They're *really* dead now, aren't they? You killed them." Libby said slowly.

"I freed them." Eden hesitated. "It's not fair that we're stuck like this. We should be able to choose."

A long moment passed before Libby spoke. "What are we gonna do with the bodies? Do you need me to . . . ?" She trailed off as Eden turned to the boy's shell and blew. The remains scattered into a million pieces, dust glistening in the sunlight before it settled.

A startled "Oh" drifted from Libby's lips. Eden waved a hand over the girl's body. In its wake was only stained asphalt.

Eden pulled away from the wall and turned to walk from the alley. Libby was instantly at her side, but Eden traipsed around the corner, no longer needing help. She vaulted up the stairs two at a time and slipped the key into the dead bolt, not even out of breath.

"You took their Touch, didn't you?" Libby said as Eden opened the door and walked across the room, dropping onto the couch. "But it doesn't affect you the way it does the rest of us."

Eden grabbed for the cup on the coffee table. She grimaced at the tepid swallow and then set it back down. Damn, the girl was clever. She knew just about as much as any of them did, now. *So let her stay,* Eden thought. Jarrod had been right. Something had to give if she wanted to keep doing her thing. And after last night, letting Libby move in might even be enough of a peace offering.

"So, I mean, if you still need a place to crash, I owe you for yesterday."

"Really?" Libby looked shaken by the offer, but held herself in check.

"Well, there's a catch. We're kind of low on space, so you'd be on the couch. At least until we figure something else out."

"No, that'd be fine." Libby hesitated. "Why the sudden change of heart?"

"Because we could use another Sider in our crew. And yesterday you proved to be an asset. Consider it a trial period."

"Oh, totally. And I'll do whatever you need. Really." Libby blushed, though her smile stayed. "Sorry, it's just . . . I haven't had a good day in a long time."

"Yeah, I kind of figured, you being a Sider and all. Why'd you do it?" Eden asked.

Libby sucked in a hiss of air, her smile vanishing as she dropped her eyes.

Finally she whispered, "Love."

Eden rolled her eyes. "What, the quarterback didn't ask you to prom even though you got hot and heavy under the bleachers?"

"You don't have to be so bitchy about it. It wasn't like that." But Libby's glare faltered, faded. "We did it so we could be together forever."

"Suicide pact?" Eden sat up a little, taking stock of the girl in front of her. "How'd that work out for you?"

Libby turned away, hiding her face. "He's not a Sider."

"Jesus." Eden shook her head.

Suddenly the room seemed too small. She could almost smell Az, crisp, like new snow. Her neck tingled, remembering the feel of his lips, the way his breath hit her skin. She closed her eyes and she was back there—the hotel, the sheets pulled loose and tossed aside, her heart pounding, hands pulling him closer, *needing* him closer. She forced her eyes open, shattering the memory.

Yesterday, she realized, for the first day in weeks, he

hadn't called. He'd probably given up. What was there to say, anyway?

"Oh, that's interesting," Libby said, studying Eden's face.

"What?" Eden asked.

"Who was he?"

She felt her face flush. "No one. He doesn't matter." Her phone hadn't rung. Part of her wondered if he'd Fallen, if she'd never get the chance to answer. She swallowed hard, willing up the familiar feeling of betrayal. Rage slid scabs over the wounds.

"He really never mattered that much at all," she found herself whispering.

Both girls jumped at the sound of the slamming door.

Jarrod stopped when he saw Eden sitting up straight, all traces of last night's escapade reversed.

"You let her downstairs?" He glared at Libby.

Eden waved away his words. "Don't be too hard on her. You know she didn't stand a chance."

"Told you she wasn't strong enough to prevail against the will of our mighty Eden." Adam sighed as he and James pushed around Jarrod. He set a tray on the coffee table before he graced Libby with a smile to show her everything was forgiven. "Java Boy asked about you," he added, turning to Eden.

Jarrod tossed a newspaper at her, the pages rustling

through the air before it landed with a heavy slap next to the cups.

"Ecstasy-fueled Rave Leaves Twenty Dead After 'Bad Trip'" screamed the headline. Eden's breath caught.

"Twenty?" she whispered. *I should have listened to Jarrod*, she thought. *I shouldn't have let it build.*

"I'm really sorry." James's hand squeezed her shoulder, an offer of comfort she couldn't bring herself to take.

"Eden, we need to talk," Jarrod said.

Adam fished two twenties out of his pocket and handed them to Libby. "You mind going down to Milton's? Through the alley, right, and a block down on the left. One caramel latte, two black, all tall? Grab something for yourself." Libby reached out to take the money, looking down at the tray of steaming cups on the table, then back to the bills in her hand. Adam blushed. "Yeah, I'm not so good with the whole 'subtle' thing. But can you just . . . ?"

"Yeah, sure," Libby said.

Adam snapped his fingers at James. "You're going with her," he said. The boy turned to Eden, who nodded. Pulling her coat around her, Libby went for the door, James at her heels. It barely shut behind them before Jarrod started in on Eden.

"Can you please just admit that it needs to end? We've tried talking to you, yelling. Nothing gets through to you, Eden! You were out of control last night!"

"Hey," Adam cautioned, taking a step closer to Jarrod. "She didn't do it on purpose."

"Yeah, well, she doesn't seem to be too eager to cast aside all that power, either, now does she?" Jarrod pointed out. "And it's pretty fucking obvious from last night that she can't handle it after all. Not as much as she takes."

"Any power I take is for *our* benefit. You do know that's why no one bothers us. Why Madeline doesn't come after us? They're afraid. They haven't even *thought* of challenging." *Challenging me*, she wanted to say.

"Look at you," Jarrod spat. "This isn't about you 'saving' the Siders anymore. You can't stop. You're addicted." He looked her dead in the eyes. "You're a junkie, Eden."

Eden felt her face grow hot.

"Jarrod, you're blowing this out of proportion," Adam said.

"You agreed with me." Jarrod's eyes flashed bitter sparks as he took a step closer. Mere inches separated the two. "She's losing control."

"Maybe you're just jealous you can't do what she can," Adam growled back. It was almost as if they'd forgotten Eden was there at all.

"Don't go getting all weak in the knees now that your little girlfriend is here," Jarrod pushed.

Adam's punch cracked against Jarrod's eye.

"Stop it!" Eden screamed, throwing herself between

them, pressing her hand against Adam's heaving chest. "You have no idea what it's like! They look at me like I'm the answer to their prayers."

"You're obsessed with them, Eden!" Jarrod said, his hand cupped over his eye. He didn't even pause, the built-up anger coming out in a rush. "What about us! What if Madeline had picked last night to kick you out of Manhattan and take over? You think you could have stopped her? You couldn't even *stand*."

With each word from him she flinched, her hands clenched across her chest. "What happens when they wear you down to nothing?" he whispered, his forehead knocking against hers. "And what happens to us when they do? Don't you care?"

She moved her head until his fell onto her shoulder. "I'm supposed to turn them away because I'm having a hard time? I can't just stop, Jarrod." *Why can't he see this is important*, she thought. "They need me."

His sharp, sudden push sent her sprawling, sliding across the wood floor. Her mouth dropped open in shock as she came to a stop against the wall.

Adam was on him before she could react, fisting the neck of Jarrod's sweatshirt into a knot and lifting him off the floor.

"Don't you *ever* lay a hand on her!" he yelled.

Neither of them even noticed when Eden slunk to her

bedroom, quietly locking herself in. She didn't bother to climb into the bed, just curled into a ball on the floor next to the door. So she could hear what Adam said after, even though he'd lowered his voice to a whisper.

"She knows how fucked up she was last night. If that doesn't get through to her, nothing will."

It wasn't until then that the tears came.

# CHAPTER 26

Hours passed before anyone dared knock, but finally a soft rap sounded against the wood.

"Eden?" Libby said through the door. "James bet me a twenty you wouldn't open the door and I only have Adam's change left which isn't even technically mine so I was hoping . . ."

Eden half smiled, wiping her hand across the mascara and eyeliner smearing down her cheeks. Unburying herself from the pile of blankets, she went to the door. Her hand was already twisting the knob when she heard a quiet, "I'll split it with you."

Libby's mouth dropped open as she caught sight of Eden's tear-swollen eyes, the black streaks. "Oh my God! What the hell did they say to you?" she asked, turning toward the living room. Eden grabbed her arm and pulled her inside, slamming the door before anyone else had a chance to invade her sanctuary.

"Wow." Libby stared around the room, taking it in, and Eden felt a trickle of pride. Draped from the ceiling around the bed and down the wall behind it a layer of rippled white lace hung in a makeshift canopy. The walls themselves were a dark maroon, decorated with a dozen crosses. Some black and sparkling with jewels, others a tarnished silver marking them almost archaic. While Libby was distracted, Eden crawled back underneath the covers.

Libby plopped down on the puffy white comforter. "Your room is . . . it's like heaven."

Eden cringed at the word. "Trust me, it's not. It's just somewhere to get away."

"What happened?"

Eden yanked at a stray thread on the bedspread. The fabric bunched. "Same argument, different set of extenuating circumstances."

"I told Jarrod you said I could stay. He seemed okay with it." She looked confused for a moment. "Actually, he seemed kinda relieved or something."

"Yeah, I bet," Eden answered, though she didn't elaborate.

"So James said Jarrod was mad about the ones on the stairs?"

Eden nodded.

"Why can't they just let you do your own thing? I mean, it's not a big deal, is it?"

Eden lifted her head. "You do know I'm the only one, right?"

"I'm sure you're not. There have to be others who can . . ."

"Trust me, there's not. It's why everyone stays away unless they want death. Not everyone's happy I changed that. They're afraid of me. We're supposed to be immortal."

"What's different about you?" Libby asked gently. When Eden didn't answer, she went on. "Instead of making you crazy, holding in all that Touch just makes you more lethal, right? You could use that, Eden. Take over everything."

"I wouldn't want to," Eden said, unconsciously bringing a hand to her neck. Her fingers laced around the delicate loops of silver that made up the necklace she wore. Her dozen bracelets slid down the cuff of her thermal top, clacking together at her elbow. Libby's eyes flicked up at the noise. "Even I have my limits. We learned that last night."

"That's really beautiful," Libby said, scooting closer. Eden flattened her hand over the necklace, the links pressing into her skin through the fabric. "Where'd you get it?" Libby asked.

Eden hesitated. "It was a gift."

"From who?" Libby asked. Then she managed to

catch Eden's eyes. "It was from him, wasn't it? The one you were going to tell me about before Adam and Jarrod came in."

"I wasn't going to tell you about him," Eden snapped.

"Can I see it?" She reached, her pinky tangling in the delicate chain as Eden leaned from her grasp. The links dug into the back of Eden's neck, straining until the necklace broke with a pop.

Eden watched in horror as the dozens of tiny ovals slid from the strand of silver weaving them together and scattered across the bed. A few tumbled off, twinkling as they bounced across the wood.

Eden's hands flew to catch them, scrambling for the few pieces she could feel against the softness of the blanket. She jumped from the bed, in front of Libby before she had a chance to move.

"I told you before not to touch me! You broke it!" She threw the handful of links into her face.

"I'm sorry," Libby cried, making a mad dash for the door. Her hair streamed behind her, almost catching in the jamb as she slammed the door shut.

"What did you do?" Eden heard Adam yell, the pounding of his feet as he rounded the corner, the bang of Libby's back hitting the wall as she moved out of his way.

Eden's shoulders heaved as she scraped up the chain and a few links from the floor. Her nails bit into her palm as she tightened her shaking hand, the knuckles going white.

The door flung open and Adam bounded in. Eden saw relief cross his face when he spotted her, vanishing at the rage in her eyes.

"You okay? What'd she do?"

"She . . . she." Her words wouldn't come together, her fingers burning. She held her fist out, the chain dangling from one side.

"What, did she break your necklace?" he asked. "That's why you're so mad?" He glanced up, unsure before his eyes fell again. "Jesus Christ, are you bleeding?" He grabbed her hand, pried open her fingers. "Eden, look at me. Breathe."

"Everything is so fucked!" she cried, the sudden tears catching her off guard. She leaned into Adam's arms, wondering if he would move, send her cascading to the floor to break apart with the pieces scattered there. But Adam caught her, held her.

"You and Jarrod hate me. If I stop taking the Siders, we're not going to have any money, Adam!" she said, her voice cracking.

"We'll figure it out." He tightened his grip around her, rubbing her back. "It's going to be okay, I promise."

"No, it's not! Everything's falling apart! Even Az gave up on me." The words escaped in hyperventilated gasps.

Adam pulled back. "Who's Az?"

Eden rubbed her hand on her pants, wincing as she opened the nightstand. She pulled the picture from the drawer, wrapping her arms around the frame and holding it close. Finally, she turned it to face Adam.

"Is this him?" he said, gently taking the frame from her hands to get a closer look.

She'd stared at the image so often it didn't register anymore, only the smell of the ocean, a lingering taste of happiness that was easier to push away than recall.

She could never quite get over the look on her face. The pure bliss in her stupid, trusting smile. The girl caught there was too much of a contrast to what she saw in the mirror to be real.

"Old boyfriend?" She couldn't answer, dropping her head in a half nod.

Her hair was longer in the picture. A flash of Az, her long strands dancing across his chest as she leaned down. *I love your hair.* She'd cut it the first night in the apartment. Anything to shed the last of her old life. A pink fingerprint still stained the porcelain from the dye. After, she'd held the picture over the toilet, a lighter hovering near the corner. She hadn't been able to burn it.

"You were serious about him?" Adam asked. She heard the longing in his voice for the answer, needing her to let him in, give him a glimpse inside. "What happened?"

She let out a bitter laugh. "He hit me up with some terrible pick-up line and I told him to fuck off." The words came easier than she'd thought they would, each one a little weight falling away. "And then I fell in love with him." Her smile faltered. "And then he lied to me. Made me believe horrible things. He's why I killed myself. And everything since has been shit."

"Hey, now." Adam tucked a short lock of her hair behind her ear, and put two fingers under her chin, lifting her head. "It hasn't all been bad. Has it?"

Eden's vision tunneled, focused on the nervous flick of his tongue. The air in the room thickened, every second drawn out into a thousand parts. *You've known this was coming,* her mind whispered. *Az stopped calling.*

For a moment, she leaned forward, the urge to feel wanted again overwhelming. She could close her eyes, pretend it was . . . Eden broke his gaze, turning from him.

Adam pulled away, his hand lingering on her cheek.

"I can't do this. . . ." she whispered.

"I'm not asking you to. I just wanted you to know," he said, taking a step back, giving her space. He dropped the picture onto the mattress. "That you have someone," he finished, his eyes downcast.

"Did you have anyone? Before?" she asked, following his lead into the subject change, not quite ready for him to leave.

"No. Nothing, you know, important. I was never really big on friends, girl or otherwise." He shrugged.

"Is that why you did it?" she asked, not bothering to clarify the "it" to which she referred.

"Honestly, I don't really remember why. I was in the woods. I had the rope there, I remember . . . wanting to stop, but . . . after there was nothing. I ever tell you that?"

"No," Eden admitted.

For a long moment neither of them spoke. "What about you?" he asked.

Eden paused. "I don't remember."

"If you don't want to tell me . . ." He stood there awkwardly, waiting.

She shrugged. "I was at the beach. Drowned, probably. Same result."

His fingers hovered near the knob, hesitating. "So, about the rave . . ."

She sighed hard. "Adam, please. Not today."

"Eden. We're worried about you. Something's gotta give. You can't keep this up forever."

"Then I'll keep it up as long as I can. Without me they're just stuck. It's not fair."

He was silent for a long moment. "What Jarrod said, about you being addicted," he started carefully.

She looked up. "Adam, come on. You know it's not like that. I'm the only one that can help them." She sat down on the bed, pulling her knees up to her chest. "I don't know what to do."

"We'll come up with something, okay?" he said, reaching for the doorknob. "Well, I'm gonna . . ." His fingers drummed a nervous rhythm against the trim. "Eden, about us."

Her stomach twisted as the ball of stress in her gut coiled tighter. She ran a hand through her hair, unsure what to say. Adam was the only person she could really talk to, who seemed to get things, get *her*. But she owed him the truth. "I don't know if I can handle an 'us' right now," she said quietly.

Turning the knob, Adam was halfway out before he spoke. "Just . . . think about it, okay?"

She nodded, though he was already closing the door. She stared at the picture, hating how much she still missed Az. Missed his touch.

"I hate you," she whispered.

*Maybe I should try to call Gabe*, she thought. *Ask for help.* She could call Kristen, get his number. But talking to Az or Gabe would mean forgiving them, letting it all go. *What would I even say to them?* She picked up the phone, running her thumb down the screen. *I miss you. I'm scared.* The display lit up as she scrolled slowly through the few numbers in her contacts list. *How could you let me become this?* She stopped on Kristen's name, but didn't hit the Send button.

*No.* She closed her eyes, trying to ignore the tremor in her fingers. *I don't need them*, she thought. *What would he be able to do to help anyway?*

She set the phone back down on the nightstand.

# CHAPTER 27

Eden pressed her ear against her bedroom door, listening. She heard the shake of cereal, a spoon hitting the side of a bowl, which meant Adam was in the kitchen. She heard footsteps as he moved to the living room. The springs on the couch. James was probably in his room, wouldn't stop her anyway. But where was Jarrod?

*Just go*, she thought. *Maybe he's still asleep.* She cringed as her door creaked open, her coat tucked under her arm, tiptoeing behind the couch. Adam didn't notice her.

She almost made it to the door.

"Where are you going?" Jarrod asked, keeping his tone genial as he rounded the corner from the kitchen. He slid between her and the exit to the apartment and tossed a casual hand against the wood, ready to hold the door shut if Eden tried to open it.

"It's eleven o'clock. You know where I'm going," Eden said, slipping into her coat. "Move." She stared him down. He wavered, but only for a moment.

"No," Jarrod said. Adam looked up from the couch, the page of his magazine mid-turn.

"Move your hand, Jarrod." She stepped closer, jaw set. James opened the door to the boys' room, drawn out by the tone of their voices.

"No," Jarrod said again.

"Get the *fuck* out of my way!" Eden yelled.

Adam slid between them, taking Eden's hand as he turned to face Jarrod.

"I'm going with her," he said quickly, cutting Eden off before she had a chance to defend herself. "No more than two. She promised me we'll try to come up with something different. We'll all sit down and talk about it when we get back, okay? James, come on," he added. He shot a glare toward Jarrod. "I think Jarrod needs some time by himself to calm down."

Eden slammed out the door. Stomping down the stairs, she covered two flights before Adam and James caught up.

"You're welcome," Adam said.

Eden whirled to face him. "And what exactly should I be thanking you for again?"

James edged around them. "I'm gonna wait outside."

"I got you out of the apartment, didn't I?" Adam yelled as the door closed behind James. His voice bounced through the stairwell.

"I don't need your help, and I really don't need you putting words in my mouth. Jarrod doesn't get to tell me what to do."

His face fell. "Eden, come on. What's the big deal? Take a couple days off." He reached for her hand.

"I said I'd *think* about cutting down. I never agreed to anything else."

"Just one day off, then. What can it hurt?"

"It hurts them," she spat, yanking her hand back to point to the door. "It hurts me because every day they're alive, they're spreading the word about me. More will show up the next day."

"I think it's safe to say the rumor's out." He frowned. "Jarrod was right, wasn't he? You can't stop."

She closed her eyes, forcing herself to take a breath. "I don't want to," she said a minute later. "You think I'm happy about this? Freeing the Siders sucks. I hurt, all the time. But it's important to me, Adam. It's important that they have a choice."

Eden threw the door open, half of her wanting to see a small army amassed out there. She would take every last one, Adam be damned.

Instead, she froze, Adam bumping into her from behind.

Libby sat alone on the stairs.

"Hey," she mumbled, wiping a tear from a blotchy

cheek. Strands of her hair had come loose from her ponytail in the breeze. The dark circles under her eyes set off the fierce blue.

"Hey," Adam said when Eden stayed silent. "Where's James?"

"He said you guys were yelling. He headed for the alley, I think." She turned back to Eden. "I'm really sorry about your necklace. It was an accident."

"Have you been out here all night?" Adam asked.

"I never said it wasn't," Eden said, not giving her a chance to answer Adam's question. "Listen." She hesitated, unprepared for the huge apology she knew Libby deserved. "I'm under a lot of stress right now. I overreacted."

"You told me not to touch you," Libby said, standing. "So it's my fault."

"Still . . ." Eden's gaze swept the stairs. "Where are they?" she asked, distracted. "The Siders. Did you send them away or something?"

"There weren't any," Libby answered. "I was hoping there'd be someone here to talk to, but no one came."

"No." Eden took the stairs slowly, anxiety filling her when it should have been Touch. "They're always here." Libby and Adam were at her heels as she headed for the alley.

She peeked behind the Dumpster, sure she would find

them huddled up and bitter over the wait. "I don't understand it. There's always been at least one, and that was in the beginning."

She turned to Adam, perplexed. He shrugged, hooking his thumbs into the waistband of his jeans. "Nothing better than an unexpected vacation," he offered.

"That's not what she wants, though." Eden and Adam both turned, surprised when Libby spoke. "She just wants to do her job. She likes it when things stay simple. It's kind of her thing in case you hadn't noticed."

Adam stared at her for a long second.

"Of course I noticed," he said.

"I mean, we're talking about a girl who won't even add sugar or creamer to her coffee. She likes things uncomplicated."

Eden's mouth dropped open.

Libby blushed. "Sorry. I'm observant like that, I guess."

"Okay," Eden said slowly.

"Speaking of coffee . . . Are you guys going to Milton's?" Libby asked.

An awkward moment passed before Adam nodded.

"James!" Eden yelled, spinning to the entrance of the alley. She gave him a second. He wouldn't wander. Hell, he barely left visual contact in public, let alone went far enough that he wouldn't hear her call. She raised her voice, calling his name again.

Adam took a tentative step forward, and glanced at Libby. “You said he came this way, right?”

“I wasn’t really watching,” she said.

Eden made her way back to the street. A few pedestrians straggled down the sidewalk, nonplussed. “Think he went back upstairs?”

“James.” She turned at Adam’s voice, following his line of vision to a storefront. Eden sighed.

“Are you coming with us?” She stepped toward the legs, crossed and splayed out from the doorway where James sat, the bandaged wrist resting cocked on the stoop. “What are you—” Her breath caught.

She didn’t dare to touch him. Instead, she dropped, her knees screaming as they cracked against the ground. Light shone through him, like tiny bricks suddenly missing the mortar. She saw it every morning in the alley.

“James?” she whispered, and looked up at Adam. His eyes squinted as if he could focus the picture until it made sense. Eden’s hair stirred, strands sliding against her cheek. The body burst into grains of ash; stinging eyes she slammed tight a second too late.

When she opened them, James was gone.

## CHAPTER 28

The windows and doors were locked, the shades drawn long before the sun had set. That had been hours ago. Eden curled her whole body into the armchair, her legs numb beneath her.

Every minute or so, Adam stood and walked to the window, twisting his fingers between the blinds, staring out into the blackness. Jarrod hadn't said much at all. None of them had.

Eden hadn't unclenched her fists, whispers of James caught in her palms. Smears dulled her cheeks. She shifted in the chair, dimly aware of the ashes grinding into her clothes.

"What happened to him?" Libby sat on the floor, leaning against the couch, her shoulder almost brushing Jarrod's leg. Eden jumped at her voice, suddenly there and blasphemous in what had been silence.

"We can't die," Jarrod said, almost to himself.

Adam's breath condensed on the glass through the crack his fingers spread in the blinds. He withdrew from the window and wandered back to his spot near Eden's chair.

Adam brushed aside his long brown bangs. "Do you have any ideas, anything?" His eyes burned into her, fear laced with resolve. Her mind went to the Fallen. Could an angel kill a Sider? If it had been only Adam and Jarrod, she might have told them everything, but even from across the room she felt Libby's eyes on her.

Reaching into her lap, Adam uncurled her hands, taking them in his. She didn't know why she let him. Her fingers actually creaked, stiff and sore from thc relentless clenching.

Jarrod spoke up. "Eden, we need to be careful until we can figure out what's going on, what happened. Just in case." She shook her head, already knowing what was about to come, but he didn't stop. "That means no more Milton's. No more gathering Touch." He paused. "We should stay low key."

Eden stood, dropping her hands.

"Fuck you."

"Eden . . ." Adam started.

"First it was you with your little protective thing." She turned to concentrate her rage on Jarrod. "Now you're using James's death to get your way? That's fucking sick,

Jarrod." She saw a flicker cross his face, words he'd thought better of and swallowed.

She stood before he could change his mind, closing the door behind her once she was in her room. She climbed into her bed without turning on the light. A moment later the door opened again.

"I brought your phone," Adam said, closing the door behind him and casting them into darkness.

She sighed, reaching out. Instead, he fumbled in the low light, setting her phone down on the nightstand, sinking into her bedspread as he sat.

"We're not against you, you know."

"No?" she challenged, crossing her arms. "Apparently you know what's best for me."

"Eden," he said gently. "I just want you safe."

Under the blanket, she moved her legs aside, giving him room as she pulled herself up against the headboard.

"I don't know what I'd do if something happened to you."

Eden was silent for a moment, remembering what Az had said on the balcony. *I don't know what I'd do if I lost you.* "You need to stop this, Adam."

"No," he said resolutely. "I know you've been hurt before."

"Az has nothing to do with this," she lied.

His fingers traced a tentative line up her arm, up her shoulder.

"Adam . . . stop," she whispered, her muscles tensing. But he didn't stop, and when he reached her neck she tilted her head, leaning into the cup of his hand, drawing comfort from the warmth.

"Hold your breath. I'm going to kiss you," he whispered. Her breath did stall, frozen in her throat as his lips found hers in the darkness. Her lips tingled as a bit of her Touch passed to him. Then he moved to her cheek, back down her neck, and away from the danger her mouth held.

"Adam. Please." She tried to say it without emotion, but it didn't come out as a thwart. It came out as a plea to keep going.

"Try to say it now," he said, his lips at her ear. "Tell me there's nothing here."

Eden shivered, hesitating. His chest pressed against her as he took a breath, released it against her cheek, waiting for any sign to continue. *Turn*, she told herself. *Just turn your head toward him.* She almost did, fighting her desire, before she reached across him. Her fingers fumbled for the lamp.

He pulled back from her in the light; only the darkness was strong enough to kill consequences.

"I'm going to see Kristen," she said, the words suddenly there.

"Kristen?" Adam stared at her, dumbfounded. Whatever had been between them was lost. "But why?"

"Something's going on. If there's any gossip out there, she'll know it."

He nodded once, as if trying to compose himself. "Okay. When are we going?"

"There is no 'we,'" she said. "I'm going tonight, so I'm gonna need you to cover for me. Distract Jarrod. I don't want him to know I'm leaving. He'll be dead set against it, and I want to talk to Kristen alone."

He leaned back, uncertain.

"Kristen's smart. She'll know something's up if I'm coming to her. We need to figure out what's going on, right?" Eden cocked her head.

"A night of Kristen's creepy shit. That should be fun for you." His words were sarcastic, though she heard the worry buried underneath. He stood, heading for the door.

"Adam," she said, halting him. "This goes in the vault. Not a word. To anyone." She hesitated. "Not just the Kristen thing." She didn't need to say Jarrod's name.

"Understood." He closed the door behind him.

Reaching across to her nightstand, she picked up her phone. A dull light illuminated the screen as she scrolled down the contact list. It was after midnight, but the hour worked in her favor. Kristen was practically nocturnal. On the second ring, the call connected.

"Well, if it isn't the badass raver from the West," said a voice dripping with honey. *Fuck*, Eden thought. Of course, Kristen would have caught the headline on her way to the obituaries. "Quite an interesting approach to keeping a low profile."

"How's my favorite wicked witch?" Eden replied, a mirror of condescending sweetness.

"Rather confused, actually." Kristen paused. "Is there something you need? Aside from common sense."

"A powwow," Eden said. "Just us. Leave your little shadow at home."

"Eden, honestly. If you're going to name call, at least give Sebastian the dignity of something slightly more evil than 'shadow.'"

"You'll have to forgive me if I'm a bit off. I lost one of mine today."

Kristen sighed, instantly losing interest. "If you're calling to ask me to keep a lookout for one of your missing flock . . ."

"Not as in missing, lost as in 'got himself perished,'" she said, quoting *The Crow*. Kristen would see the movie reference as a gift. "And it wasn't me. Little more inclined to accept my invitation?"

"When did you want to meet?" Kristen asked.

"Tonight. As soon as possible."

"I was supposed to go shopping tonight." The silence spun out as Eden held her breath, waiting. "I don't see why you can't meet me there," Kristen said finally. "Webster

Avenue and East Two Hundred Thirty-third Street. Bronx. Two hours."

"How will I find you?" Eden asked.

"Wander," she replied before the call terminated.

# CHAPTER 29

"She has *got* to be kidding." Eden shook her head. Spikes of black metal formed a gate before her.

Wedging a boot into the horizontal bar welded halfway up the spears, she threw her leg over and cast a quick glance around as she scaled down the other side. Still alone.

The grounds of the cemetery sprawled farther than Eden could see. Plots, mausoleums, great statues of angels reaching for the heavens alongside those fallen in mourning. For a moment, a vision of Az and Gabe came to mind, carving a hollow ache before she could banish it. She concentrated on finding Kristen.

Eden considered her options. Kristen called her "raver from the West" on the phone. That made Kristen East by default.

Eden started walking.

The frigid air smelled almost metallic, but underneath

she caught the scent of pressed flowers and clove, more memory than an actual fragrance. The smell of Kristen's house. She'd know it anywhere.

She jumped at the sudden scrape of metal against stone. *Get it together, Eden. You're losing it.* She cocked her ear, catching it again, and followed the sound to a mausoleum. The shattered lock dangled by its shackle. A yellow glow seeped from the edge of the partially open door. The carved marble above read WANDIR.

Four hundred acres and she'd only had to cover a quarter of a mile to find her. Kristen was playing nice tonight, the barb of curiosity hooked tight.

A candle sputtered as she entered the crypt, a plume of smoke wafting in her wake.

"'And each separate dying ember wrought its ghost upon the floor . . .'" Kristen pulled a lighter from her boot, flicked it to life, and relit the candle.

"Poe. How . . . melodramatic of you," Eden said. "It's good to see you, Kristen."

The dress she wore had been longer at some point, the seam ragged where she'd sheared it off. Threads skittered across the pale skin above Kristen's knees. It hung several sizes too big on her thin frame, but still managed to look right in all the places it should have been wrong. An antique belt of silver hugged her hips.

"Oh, Eden. Must we do the silly small talk? It's not

good for you to see me. It means you're in some deep shit." At her feet, the black silk that had shrouded the coffin lay crumpled on the cement. "Help me lift the lid," Kristen commanded.

Eden tucked herself under the lip of the coffin, the wood drilling into her shoulder. "Shopping going well?" she grunted. With an added thrust from Kristen, the lid slammed open against ancient hinges. The fatigued metal cracked, and the lid banged against the floor. Eden cringed, glancing toward the door.

"Quite well, actually," Kristen said, pushing up the velvet sleeves of her dress. "No one will bother us here. I've made sure of it."

"What do you mean you've made sure of it?"

"Oh, don't look so surprised." Kristen took up the pillar candle, illuminating the contents of the casket. "I know full well you don't travel without your sad excuse for an entourage." She turned when Eden stayed silent, studying her. "You *are* alone. How naïve of you."

"You think so?" Eden asked, leaning against the crumbling mortar of the wall, hoping to look unfazed. "Maybe I'm just one for keeping my word."

"Look at you! All business and attitude. Well done." Kristen laughed, the sound echoing wickedly through the small chamber. "May I?" she asked, curtseying dramatically. As she dipped, she lifted the frayed fabric of her dress, kicking up a leg like a burlesque dancer. She balanced the heel of her black boot on the edge of the coffin's platform. Above where the leather ended mid-calf, an exposed knee peeked out.

Eden pulled at the neckline of her thermal hoodie, revealing her collarbone. Both girls reached forward, sliding a finger across the other's bare skin. Their glamours faded.

Eden held her fingers out, marveling at the pale gray-green patches of rot, the skin puckering, holes open to the bone. Maybe the rave had helped. Another few days, though, and her levels would be right back up.

Strips of flesh hung from Kristen's arm as she pulled it back, the bone underneath still white.

"You've been storing," Eden observed. "Or stealing. Gearing up to torture some Screamers, Kristen?"

She shook her head, tsking. "Don't judge. It makes your face all twisty. Not a good look for you."

"Your sick idea of punishment is none of my concern," Eden said, her voice cold. "Besides, it's not like I have anything to fear."

"And aren't you just a little ball of contradictions tonight?" Kristen shook her head, a wave of dark hair swooping behind her shoulders as her glamour slipped back into place. "You have nothing to fear, yet you're here. There must be a reason. Ready to spill it, Eden? Or are we going to babble quips back and forth all night? Were your boys simply not satisfying your need for intelligent conversation?"

"Nothing to fear *from you*," Eden corrected. "But . . ." She paused, watching in morbid fascination as Kristen leaned into the coffin, pulling a half dozen rings from the skeleton's fingers. Trying them on her own, she tossed aside the ones that hadn't struck her fancy. The castoffs clattered into the shadows. "James," Eden said.

"The little blond one?" Kristen leaned into the coffin again as if it was a bargain bin. The old bones rattled as she shook the dress free of its previous owner. Her face lit up. "Purple!" she sang triumphantly, handing the dress to Eden. "I was *so* over the black thing this week too! How fortuitous!" She dove again, legs kicking up behind her as she dug deeper. Vaulting back onto the floor, her hands held up the prize, a flapper-style skullcap. *How appropriate*, Eden thought.

Dust dulled the strands swooping out from below the beaded fabric as Kristen adjusted the hat. She held her hand in front of the candle again, admiring her new rings for a moment before stripping one away and tossing it to Eden. Rubies glittered in the air.

Eden caught the jewelry, faintly repulsed as she slipped it over her knuckle. It clanked against the trio of silver bands already there, settling just below the joint of her middle finger. She held the hand up for Kristen to see.

"Approved," Kristen said, nodding. "Death looks good on you."

"Yeah," Eden mumbled, the memory of James's scattering ashes a fresh wound, slicing through the weak scab the day had formed. "Enough dress up," she said, tucking her hand into her pocket. "We have business to attend to."

"About the boy? You're just angry you didn't get to use your voodoo breath on him."

Eden clenched her jaw. She tossed the dress over her shoulder, freeing her hands.

Kristen only smiled. "Quell the rage, lovey. Tell me what happened to James."

Eden gave her an abridged version of how they'd found him. "Last I heard, I was the only one killing Siders. That is, unless you have news you conveniently forgot to pass along?" she finished.

"Eden," Kristen chided, sounding hurt. "Do you know how rare it is for me to find someone I consider an equal? In another life we might have been at the mall together, glaring at those bitches who take up all the tables in the food court and never fucking eat. As it is, you seem to have enough on your plate."

"You know something," Eden accused.

"There've been rumblings lately with your name in them. Not the territories. I think everyone's pretty well settled for now. But you have an enemy." Kristen stared at her for a long moment.

"The Fallen?" Eden asked, losing patience. She yanked the dress from where it hung over her shoulder, balling the material.

Finally Kristen spoke, her voice solemn. "'And devils also came out of many, crying out—'"

"Don't have time for this, Kristen," Eden interrupted, giving away her frustration. "Was it the Fallen or not?" Tapping a finger against her cheek, Kristen waited for Eden's response over the wood she leaned her elbows on. "Who? Tennyson? Yeats? I have no clue."

Kristen twirled a lock of brown around her finger, her gems dancing in the candlelight. "Actually, it's from the Bible."

"Who's the enemy, Kristen?"

"Of course it's the Fallen. Who else would it be?" She reached into her boot and slid out a clove cigarette as she got to her feet. Sauntering across the room, she lit it on the candle flame before returning to Eden. She slid down the wall, sitting cross-legged on the floor. "You and I have our alliance. We share information, help each other when necessary. Such things aren't just arranged between Siders," she said slowly. "You know how close I am to Gabriel. Rumor is, Madeline has chosen *not* to follow my shining example after all. And Madeline was tiring of lost numbers due to your . . . gift. Perhaps she finally grew frustrated enough to tattle on you."

Eden's eyes widened. "Madeline told the Fallen where to find me." Kristen nodded. "You never told me the Fallen can kill Siders."

Kristen shrugged, but Eden caught the uneasiness in her eyes. "It's news to me if they can. Have you spoken to *him* about what's going on?" she asked, not needing to say the name.

Eden winced. "Why would I?"

"I saw him," Kristen said carefully, gauging Eden's reaction. "This would be a few weeks ago. Shall I continue?" Eden nodded, her head feeling full and slow. Even a passing mention of Az and her whole world seemed to shift off its axis. "At first I thought he was one of the living, huddled down in a doorway against the cold the way he was. I was going to give him Touch. But then he lifted his head and I saw those eyes." Kristen took a hit, exhaling a cloud.

"Go on," Eden whispered.

"He looks like shit, Eden. I didn't even recognize him. He's going through some sort of Goth phase. All those beautiful curls straightened and dyed black." She paused, ashing into a silver vase that might once have held flowers.

Eden couldn't picture this new version of him, so far

from the soft brown curls and clear blue eyes. The Az she had known.

"And how's Gabe?" Eden tried to keep her voice neutral, but it came out strained, cracking.

"He's checking in on you," Kristen said. "They both are."

Eden looked up in surprise. "You're wrong," she said.

Kristen nodded slowly, drawing out the details in that excruciating way she had of speaking, her flair for the dramatic coloring her speech. "I could be. But I was standing there, looking into those crystal blues of his, and there was a sudden urge to update Az on the latest gossip. And most of what popped into my head was Eden-centric. Not exactly my favorite topic. You can imagine my shock." She snubbed out what was left of the clove, the sweet smoke drifting, lingering. "Listen, I understand your burning hatred of all things angelic, but I'm not who you should have come to. You know that."

Kristen snatched the purple atrocity from Eden as she passed, heading for the exit.

"Can I count on our alliance?" Eden asked, following her out through the door. "If it's needed, of course."

Kristen spun on her with a snort of disbelief. "Against the Fallen? Not a chance. Our agreement concerned only Sider issues. You understand."

Before them, the path forked. "If you hear anything . . ."

"You'll be the first to know," Kristen said. "Eden, were I you, I'd make sure my crew was ready. Blame Madeline, blame me if need be, but have them store Touch. They'll need it to heal. Most likely, they'll need it to help *you* heal, because if Downstairs gets a hold of you . . ." Kristen trailed off, staring up into the cloudless sky, the stars, as if hoping to catch sight of something beyond them. "If the Fallen are sniffing around, this is bound to be more than a passing storm."

# CHAPTER 30

Eden rubbed her eyes, trying to concentrate. She hadn't slept, waited until morning to talk to the rest of the group.

Adam, Jarrod, and Libby sat in nearly the same spots they'd been in yesterday. The same silence hung over the group. This time it was Eden at the window. Standing. Even that was part of her presentation. Putting herself above them, hoping the subtle act would keep them quiet.

The temperature had dropped as the sun rose. She closed her eyes, listening to the ping of the flakes as they struck the glass, gathering as much confidence as she could muster. She could feel their stares, the tension in the room building as she stared out the window, trying to decide what to tell them. None of them knew anything about angels. What would they do if they knew the danger she'd put them in?

Finally she spun to face them.

"I went to see Kristen," she said, standing at the end of the couch.

She stared at only Jarrod while the words came out. As expected, his mouth dropped open, a wide circle of surprise.

Libby spoke up from behind him. "Kristen? As in the one everyone warned me about? The *crazy* one?"

"Why?" Adam answered on cue, feigning surprise at Eden's admission, moving the conversation along.

He'd kept Jarrod busy while she'd crept out the front door, texted to let her know when he went to bed. Waited up for her in the kitchen. She'd almost told him everything.

Almost. Instead, she'd decided on Kristen's suggestion to get them to store in case there was a fight and they needed to heal. He'd agreed. Adam used his prior knowledge to steer the conversation today and blame things on Madeline.

"Why didn't you tell us you were going?" He must have practiced. The hurt in his question made her pause; it seemed so genuine.

And if she told him about the Fallen, the truth about Az, it would be.

"I did what I had to do," she said with absolute authority. To her relief, Jarrod stayed silent for once. "And it was the right thing. She heard some rumors."

"What kind of rumors?" Adam asked. His scripted

line slid into the conversation flawlessly.

"Madeline's apparently taken offense to what I do," Eden lied, keeping their attention on her. "She might try something. What, I can't imagine. It might be as stupid as a fight, but she could try to take hostages."

"What are we going to do about it?" Adam asked, filling the moment of empty space before anyone else could.

"She can't do much. I'm not even sure she'll try, but if she does, she'll have numbers. Having some extra Touch will help, in case we need to heal after." Eden turned her attention to Libby, the girl's eyes darting back and forth between her and Adam. "Without James, we're going to need you, Libby."

"You're going to *dose* her?!" Jarrod's jaw dropped, putting the pieces together.

"Eden, you didn't say anything about dosing." Adam's surprise was genuine.

"Libby, yes, but because of the rave, I don't have enough to dose you all. You both are going to stop passing."

Adam shook his head. "But that's like making her a Screamer."

"What's dosing?" Libby asked, uncertain.

"I'm going to give you some of my Touch, but instead of passing it to the mortals, you're going to hold it in. Store it."

"Eden, she's not ready for something like that!" Eden

couldn't look at Jarrod, kept her eyes on Libby.

"James wasn't passing, right?" Libby asked. She turned to Jarrod. "If he could handle it, I'm sure I can."

Eden could feel his rage building even before he spoke. "James was storing," he said. "Not dosed. There's a fucking difference."

Eden didn't acknowledge Jarrod, kept her voice calm. "You're new, so you're only used to having to pass to one or two mortals a day. Adam and Jarrod have gotten used to dealing with higher levels, so they'll be depressed but they'll be able to handle it for a few days. Dosing isn't the same. If you don't spread the extra right away, the Touch hits you all at once. It's ugly. But Jarrod's going to help you. If you can make it through, you level out, and then it's just a matter of holding those levels without letting more build." Another piece of the plan fell into place, this one Adam's suggestion. Jarrod needed Libby, something to keep him busy and occupied. "Jarrod is going to help you," she said, suddenly forgetting her place, repeating herself.

Libby waited, her face expectant then puzzled. Eden's eyes widened as she silently willed Adam to say something, anything. But it was Libby who spoke.

"Something's . . . off," she said, slowly. "With you two." She pointed to Adam. "He opens his mouth before you finish talking, like he knows the next question."

"He's good at what we do. He knows the questions that need to be asked to cut out the bullshit," Eden said quickly, trying to salvage what was left of the ruse.

"This is bullshit," Jarrod said suddenly, their heads swiveling to him. "Fuck Madeline. She couldn't have killed James. What about *that*, Eden?"

"I haven't figured it out yet," she said quietly. "But we need to be prepared for both. This is why Libby is even more important, why you are. We'll see how she handles it and go from there." She turned back to Libby.

"I'm in," Libby said, her voice confident. "Are you going to keep taking the Siders, then?" She seemed to be gauging Jarrod's reaction, though her eyes stayed focused on Eden.

"Saving Touch doesn't affect me much, but I want to get as much as I can. Your body will use up the extra Touch if any of you get hurt."

Adam's shoe tapped out a nervous rhythm against the floor. "Eden, I don't know about this. With Libby."

"If she gets too bad, we can always stop."

"How bad could it be?" Libby asked.

Jarrod stood, crossed the room, and slammed his door without a word.

# CHAPTER 31

The sound stole into her room through the keyhole. She'd shoved an old T-shirt under the door, trying to block it out, but still Eden could hear the moaning. It seemed to come from everywhere.

The groan crescendoed into a scream. She turned up her stereo, pumping Dresden Dolls at top volume.

Eden had forgotten the look on Adam's face when he'd told her about the Screamers. At Kristen's she'd been kept separated from the rest of the Siders. She hadn't seen a Screamer until the day she'd left, and then, only for the few moments it took to free them with her breath. Now she understood why Adam had been so unnerved. Libby was in agony.

The lyrics flooded Eden's ears, her eyes closed, fingers tightening into fists on the bedspread. But behind her eyelids, all she could imagine was Jarrod, there by Libby's side. He hadn't left her for a moment the last three days.

She could picture his face; hearing the music pounding through her wall and hating her for it, for trying to block out what she'd chosen to put the three of them through.

Eden snapped the song off mid-chorus. Libby's scream picked up where it'd been drowned out, wavering before the room beside hers went silent again.

Sighing, Eden opened her bedroom door. Adam lay on the couch, a pillow pressed around his head.

Things had gotten strange between them the last few days. She'd caught herself noticing the shadow that brought out the angles of his normally shaved jaw.

She plopped down on his stomach, felt the muscles tightening, his breath escaping in a sharp *oof*. He sat up, lifting his head over the edge of the couch to make sure the door to Jarrod's room was still closed. Satisfied the coast was clear, he curled an arm around her. Whatever was happening, he'd stuck to their agreement that it wasn't common knowledge. For that, Eden was grateful.

"How are you holding up?" she asked. Adam shrugged. Studying his face, she saw lines in his brow that hadn't been there even the day before.

"Rough," Adam whispered, not bothering to sugar-coat. At least that was one thing she could count on. "This helps," he added, tightening his arm around her. She leaned against his chest, telling herself it was only in the interest of helping.

"You're not affected at all?" he asked, some wistful tone behind the words. His voice strained. She looked up at him, and he put a finger to the corner of her eyelid, lifting it. "They're so blue, Eden," he whispered, leaning closer. "And cold . . ." She felt the shift as the Touch took hold, saw his own eyes glaze over. "Heartless . . . nothing for me in them."

She tried to sit up, but his arm tightened, pinning her to him like a strap.

"Nothing there. There's nothing," he whispered to himself.

"Adam, no."

He started to rock, his finger still holding her eyelid open. "We're all going to die. They're coming for you and we're all going to die. But not with you. Alone. We're all alone." She felt a shiver deep inside as she twisted her head, squeezing her eyes shut, breaking the connection.

"Kristen. The night I called Kristen," she said suddenly, leaning up to whisper in his ear, pressing her cheek against his. The clammy chill made her nauseous. "Remember it?" she asked, feeling a flutter of eyelashes as he closed his eyes, concentrating. "You said, 'Try to say it now.' Can you see it, Adam? Do you remember?" She felt him nod, the stubble of his cheek prickling. "You said, 'Try to say it now.' You said, 'Tell me there's nothing here.' What did I say, Adam?" she asked, pulling away when his arm went limp. She took his face in her hands, watching his eyes, the deep burning brown.

"I can't . . ." he mumbled.

"What did I say, Adam?" He blinked, a tear slipping from each eye, racing for his jaw.

"You didn't say anything." He opened his eyes again, focusing on her. "You didn't say anything because you couldn't." The realization hit him, the Touch fading back into the background. "You couldn't," he repeated, the words coming out a heavy sigh as he leaned against her shivering. She pulled the blanket off the back of the couch, wrapping it around both of them.

She tried to keep herself from going rigid, the confession that she hadn't been able to face before now leaving her vulnerable. There *was* something there. Something between them.

"Better?" she asked. He nodded, holding her close, his embrace tender again.

"I want to check on Jarrod and Libby. Will you be okay?" she asked, trying to shake away the image of violence. He nodded and she stood, helping him lie back down and tucking the blanket around him.

Walking across the room, she cast one last glance to Adam. What she felt wasn't the raging fire it had been with Az. More of a slow burn, growing larger with each day that passed. Enough to warm her insides, but not consume her. *Maybe that's what love is* supposed *to be like?* she thought. Her stomach fluttered as she knocked quietly on the door. There was a grunt from inside and she opened it slowly, preparing herself.

Jarrod was on the bed. Libby's head was in his lap, her eyes closed. Her hair was free for the first time since Eden had known her, draped around her in a greasy tangled halo. Around her face, the strands clung to her wet skin.

Jarrod dipped a washcloth in a pot of water next to him, running it slowly across her forehead. Libby grimaced as the cloth slid down her cheek, across her neck.

"She looks better than I expected," Eden said quietly, careful not to break the thin hold sleep had claimed.

"The first time is always the worst. But she's strong. She's holding her own." He looked up at Eden and she saw the shadows there, darkness behind his gaze. He closed his eyes, wincing.

Eden moved to sit beside him but he held up a hand. "Just give me a minute," he whispered. A tremor passed through him, Libby's hair shuddering across the sweat-dampened pillow under her. Jarrod took two impossibly deep breaths, and whatever had threatened to take over was gone.

"I didn't know how hard it would be for me to resist. My head's all messed up. I don't know what to believe. Adam told me what he heard through the walls when he lived at Kristen's, but I wasn't expecting it to be like this."

"It's been a few days. Shouldn't be much longer. If you need to stop, I'll understand," she said, but he shook his head.

"I got this." And there it was in his voice. That reassurance she'd been dying to hear from either of them.

Reaching over, he took up the washcloth again.

"You're doing good, Jarrod," she said, hoping the praise would help him, but meaning it just the same. He was coming through for her.

"Hey!" he said, stopping her at the door. "I'm sorry. About pushing you. Maybe we could talk about it, make things cool again?"

She wanted to say it back, but it would only lead to them talking about the Siders on the stairs again. Now wasn't the time to be calling attention to anything that volatile. Eden nodded.

Adam was sitting up when she returned to him, what happened five minutes ago forgotten.

She reached over to the chair, picking up her coat from where she'd left it yesterday for the brief minutes she'd left the apartment.

"That time again?"

Eden pulled the jacket around her. "I need to get all I can."

* * *

It was over in seconds. Eden rolled her shoulders, snapping a crick from her neck. Despite the uncomfortable ache in her bones from the Touch she'd absorbed from the four Siders on the stairs, she was determined to savor her few minutes away from the apartment.

She kept a cautious lookout as she made her way through the alley, exited, and crossed the street. The strong coffee smell greeted her as she entered Milton's. Behind the counter, Zach leaned down to get her tray.

"Just for me today," she said, stopping him.

He separated her cup from the others and set it on the counter. As he slid the tray off into the garbage, she heard a crackle of papers, a rush of liquid set free, the lids popping off when they hit. "Sorry for the waste."

"No prob." He shrugged and pointedly shifted his attention past her, off to where the booths were. "Not with the coffee."

"What's up?" she asked, stiffening. She hadn't been paying attention. Now that she was, Zach looked damn near skittish.

"Two o'clock. Middle booth," he said, his voice low as he picked up the bills she'd laid on the counter. He avoided her eyes, avoided looking at her at all as he punched buttons on the register. "Been waiting for you about an hour."

Eden fought the urge to turn. Dark hair, a dress in

anything but black, would be Kristen. Madeline would be easy enough with her fiery bun of red hair.

"Description?" she asked. She let out a fake laugh, pretending it was just a genial exchange of pleasantries with the local barista.

"Dude," he said, and Eden mentally crossed off most of the list in surprise. "Early twenties. Knew what I was right away."

"Sider?" she asked. Slowly Zach shook his head. Her heart hammered. She had no idea what any of the Fallen looked like. She risked a glance. "Jesus," she gasped.

"You okay?" On the other side of the counter, Zach slipped off his latex gloves. "You need backup?"

"No, just . . . I wasn't expecting him," she said, not bothering with the change on the counter when she turned. She made her way down the aisle to Gabe's table. Forcing a breath, she slowed her steps.

"I'm guessing this isn't a social visit," she said, crossing her arms when she got to the booth.

He twisted a rope of napkin around his fingers, the paper fuzzy and broken down. On the table were half a dozen others, already shredded.

He raised his head. The look in his eyes sapped her sarcasm.

"Gabe? What's wrong?" Her heart quickened, a thought of Az in trouble worming into her mind unbidden.

She jerked toward the window, searching the street before she could stop herself.

"He's not here," Gabe said. "Sit. We need to talk."

"Is . . . did he Fall? That's why you're here." The strength ran out of her legs. She dropped into the booth. "You came to tell me."

His shook his head. "Az isn't Fallen."

"Damn it, Gabe. I thought something had happened." She flopped against the back of the booth. She glanced away, not wanting Gabe to see the relief overwhelm her. The strength of the feeling unnerved her.

"I didn't mean . . ." Deep lines furrowed his brow as he started over. "It upsets me that you blame Az for all of this. He's upset you don't answer his calls. He's lost without you."

Her worry had tempered her anger, but now she gave in, her voice oozing malice. "Oh, he's lost? He's upset? Gee, Gabe. Maybe that's how I felt after finding out I was *dead*. You know? After you abandoned me at Goths R Us. Then again, I'm not really open to an apology."

"Sorry wouldn't be enough, anyway. It wouldn't even be a start," he said, each word pained and slow. "It wasn't supposed to be like this."

Eden set her coffee down. "How exactly did you expect it to go? I take my time killing myself instead of being pushed into it and ignore the fact that you did nothing to stop it?"

"You're right," he murmured, as if in a trance. "I should have warned you. Not—" He jerked his head up suddenly, sucking a deep breath. "I can't say . . . please understand. It's fine as long as it's never spoken."

"As long as *what* is never spoken?!" She shot him eyes full of hate. "I don't remember the beach after you left. What happened on the beach, Gabe?" she insisted.

He reached across the table, taking her hand in his, playing with the dozen rings on her fingers. "You happened. Everything changed the night we met you."

"Yeah," she snapped. "Things are a bit different for me, too."

"Az isn't meant to be with mortals. No angel is. Every girl finds her way back to her path. They leave him."

"I wouldn't have left him," she said defensively.

"It'd been so long since he'd been happy. And he loved you, Eden. Really loved you. I had to know when you'd leave, have a plan to get him through without a Fall. I tried to check your path. We thought the Siders were pathless only after they died. If you hadn't been with him, if he hadn't fallen in love with you, we never would have known they were pathless as mortals."

She drummed her nails on the tabletop. "Wonderful.

Glad to be of service. Why are you here, Gabriel? What do you want?"

He glanced up. "Kristen sent a few of her Screamers your way. She gave me their names first. After they . . . had contact with you, I took a trip Upstairs." She tilted her head, waiting for him to finish, her anger arrested. "They were there, Eden."

"What do you mean they were there? Upstairs?" She scoffed. "Don't be stupid, Gabe. They're suicides. They can't . . ."

He glanced around, lowering his voice. "Eden, sins or not, Siders shouldn't be there at *all*. Mortals follow a path for a reason. We thought Siders were immortal because there's nowhere for them to go. You put them back on the grid, Eden." He raised his head, staring at her for a long second.

Her fingers stilled. A rebellious smile twitched at the corners of her lips. "So I give them a path?"

"This isn't a good thing." Gabe sounded exasperated. He reached across the table to entwine his hands in hers, squeezing them tight before she pulled away. "You're putting souls where they don't belong. There'll be consequences when Upstairs finds out."

"You haven't told them yet?"

He glanced back out the window. "I didn't count on being so . . . involved."

"Are you going to get in trouble?" Somehow she didn't see Gabe coming out of this with a slap on the wrist. She tensed. "You said it out loud. Don't they know now?"

"Luckily for the Bound, Upstairs is on a 'pics or it didn't happen' kind of system. For us, sins need to be spoken. Punishment for lesser infractions needs proof. But every secret seems to burn its way out eventually." He crossed his arms, drawing into himself as something about the thought exhausted him. "You've gotta be careful. You're already being watched, sought out. And not just by us."

"It's a little late for a warning, isn't it?" Her voice had taken on a hard edge. "Pretty fucking unsubtle. But if killing James—"

"What do you mean killing James? When?" Gabe's face paled. "How?"

"Yesterday," she said, caught off guard. "The Fallen." She paused. "Right?"

"It's important that you listen to me, Eden, even if you hate me, just listen, okay?" She nodded, his panic seeping into her. "The Fallen can't kill Siders. Even if the Bound did know about the Siders, they shouldn't be able to either. You need to stop drawing attention until I figure out what *can*." He shifted, climbing out of the booth. Eden followed his lead.

"You have to call Az," he said. "You know how he feels about you. He'll protect you better than anyone else could.

And if something happens to me, he'll need you to get him through without a Fall."

Her head started a slow shake, building until she finally met his eyes. "No. He's not my responsibility. I'm over him."

"You've always been a terrible liar." He pulled her into a tight hug. "Don't be so stubborn! This is your excuse to call him. Use those feminine wiles to get back what you need"—he cast a quick glance at the door and stepped away from her—"instead of luring in boys who will never measure up. I trust you, and I trust you're smart enough to swallow your pride and do what's best. They'll protect you for now, but soon I'm afraid it won't be enough." He was looking over her shoulder.

Eden turned, following his gaze. Adam stood near the door, kicking the snow off his boots as he scanned the room, searching for her.

Gabe grabbed her close again. "If you need anything, don't hesitate. I'll be in touch, okay?" He made his way through the maze of low tables and couches. Adam watched him cross the room. Gabe kept his eyes down as he passed. Walking out the door and down the sidewalk, he didn't look back.

"Who was that?" Adam asked, jerking his chin toward the door.

"No one you need to worry about," she answered,

spinning around to throw an arm around his neck. Pulling him close, she kissed him deep and hard. He groaned as a bit of her Touch passed into him, but she only pressed harder, stealing it back. *Fuck Gabe*, she thought. *Az had his chance.*

# CHAPTER 32

She heard the screams through the door. Bloodcurdling, murderous screams, and for a second her hand froze and she couldn't turn the knob. But then some part of her brain snapped back into place and she was inside, throwing open Jarrod's door, Adam at her back.

Libby's back was arched, Jarrod pushing down on each of her shoulders and still she was bucking off the mattress.

"Eden! Help me!" he screamed.

She ran, swinging herself around the edge of the bed by the post on the footboard and grabbed hold of the handcuffs already snapped around the strong metal rungs of the headboard. Jarrod grunted as he forced Libby's arm up. Eden snapped the cuff around Libby's wrist.

"You bitch!" Libby screamed, her hair streaming loose, flying as she thrashed back and forth. Eden ignored her, climbed over to help Adam force the second wrist up to where she could hook Libby's other arm.

Eden yelped as the cuff locked, a jolt of pain bursting from her thigh. Libby's teeth sunk deeper as Jarrod reached down, squeezing the sides of her clamped jaw until it was forced open.

"Fuck," Eden groaned, limping to the doorway, rubbing the skin. The leather of her pants held a perfect dented impression of Libby's teeth around the hole they'd torn clean through.

Adam backed slowly from the writhing prisoner, as if he expected her to rip the cuffs off and come at them.

"Let me see," Adam said, dropping to get a better look at the wound. An angry tear settled into the corner of Eden's eye. "She got you good," he said, gingerly laying his fingertips against the edges of the hole in her ruined pants.

"Leave it. It's nothing. When did she get like this?" Eden asked in disbelief.

"Ten minutes ago," Jarrod said from the other side of the room, hovering close but out of range of Libby's kicks. "Came out of nowhere."

"I'll fucking kill all of you!" Libby screamed, wrenching her head back and forth, slamming her shoulder into the headboard, trying to break the bed apart. Jarrod picked a pillow up off the floor and slid it in, buffering her attack on the bed. Suddenly the evilness dropped out of her voice as her eyes found Eden. "Please let me go," she sobbed. "I have to get rid of it! Don't you understand how much it hurts?" The last few words were almost unrecognizable, her voice breaking into heaving gasps.

Jarrod's eyes widened as her focus switched to him. "You're just going to stand there and do nothing? They're killing me, Jarrod. They're killing us both, the two of them," she cried, locking eyes on him. Jarrod's face crumbled as he looked up at Eden, unsure.

"If it doesn't get better in an hour, she's gonna have to pass," Eden said, hating herself just the same.

"Jarrod . . . ," Libby's singsong call sounded out. She batted her eyelashes, streaks of mascara running down her blotchy face. "They're against you, you know. Look at them, Jarrod. Don't her lips look a little red? Like she's been *kissing* him?" Libby threw her head back, cackling. With her hands in the cuffs, pulled up on either side of her, she looked like some demonic marionette. Suddenly her head snapped up and she froze, whispering, eyes lolling up to Jarrod. "If she blushes, you know I'm right!" She kicked her heels into the mattress with glee. Jarrod could do nothing but stare, mouth agape like the rest of them. "Fucking look at *her*, Jarrod!" she commanded.

And he did. As he turned, Eden felt the heat start, trace up her neck and then deepen as Libby let out another round of kicks and gibberish. Jarrod's head cocked, watching Eden. Her head slowly started to shake a denial, but then she felt Adam's hand on her shoulder.

"I tooooold you!" Libby shrieked.

"Shut up, Libby," Jarrod said, his voice monotone. He pushed past them, not bothering to close the door. "Adam's been after her forever. She was bound to give in sometime."

On the bed, Libby's head dropped as if someone had suddenly switched her off.

"Watch out for the green vomit," Adam whispered. "Was I the only one waiting for her head to spin?"

"Not funny," Eden said, pushing past him.

She came up behind Jarrod where he stood at the window. "We were going to tell you. This just happened. Like, minutes ago." He sighed hard, turning on her.

"Would you fucking get over yourself? You think I care what you and him do? I'm worried about her, Eden!"

"Oh," she said, taking a step back. She watched him carefully, not sure if he'd given in to Touch or just gotten upset at Libby's outburst. If the difference mattered.

"James wasn't like this when he stopped spreading. Ever. I didn't expect . . ." He paused as they both turned at the sound of footsteps. Adam slunk into Eden's room, closing the door behind him to give them some privacy. "I just didn't expect that," Jarrod finished. "That was fucked . . . up."

"Yeah," Eden said, but couldn't find any follow-up words. No encouragement to offer. *Maybe I should end this*, she thought. *Take off on my own.* The Fallen would have to track her down, leave the others alone.

"She just turned on us," he said, confusion in his voice. "It was like she wanted us fighting."

"No, that wasn't her, Jarrod."

"It was some part of her," he whispered.

"No. She probably picked up on me and Adam, and the Touch just twisted it," she said. "That's all it was. You can't hold it against her. It's only going to make it worse for *you* if you're upset."

He turned back to the window. She put a hand on his shoulder, giving it a squeeze. "Let it go, Jarrod."

He nodded. She gave him a second, but when he didn't say anything, she crossed the room to her own door, opening it.

Adam was on the bed. His eyes opened when he heard the door, finding her shadow in the darkness the covered windows cast.

"So you think you can just wander into my room whenever you feel like it now?" she asked, crawling onto the bed.

He smiled, letting his eyes drift closed again, as she straddled him. "You kissed me. I figured I had some power."

"I took it back," she reminded him. For just a moment—half—there was that image, long hair gliding across Az's strong chest and then it was gone. She ran her fingers across the bare nape of her neck, the short strands tickling across her pinky.

"That's not the kind of power I was talking about," Adam said. He reached up, pulling her down into his arms. His lips wandered a broken trail down her neck to her collarbone. It almost felt treasonous, how easily her head leaned back in welcome, when Jarrod was probably still at the window, worried Libby wouldn't get better. But she couldn't help the butterflies, the way her fingers curled against Adam's back.

"Your phone," he whispered. Light blinked into the room as the display lit up.

"Ignore it," she mumbled, wishing she'd turned the damn thing off, but Adam had already glanced at the flashing glow as her cell rattled against the nightstand.

Pulling back to pick it up and hand it to her he said, "Can't. It's Kristen."

Eden sat up, flipping the phone open. "Yeah?" she asked, trying to concentrate, her brain not doing so well with the sudden topic change.

Adam wasn't helping. He leaned in, tucking a lock of her hair behind her ear and kissing the line of her jaw.

"'Never again would birds' song be the same. And to

do that to birds was why she came.'" Kristen's voice was full of wonder.

"Frost," Eden said. For a long time, they were both silent. Eden pulled the phone from her ear, sure the call had been dropped, but the counter on its face ticked off each second. "It's Robert Frost, right?"

"You're sending Siders Upstairs? Do you have any idea of the damage this will cause?" Kristen started.

Eden drew a breath, held it as she tried to think of some snappy comeback. Anything. "Gabe told you."

"Actually, no. I talked to your boy." For a moment Eden wasn't sure who she was talking about as Adam's hand wound its way down her leg.

"Az?" she said, bolting up. On her thigh, Adam's hand froze.

"Yes, Az!" Kristen yelled, for once agitated enough to skip the games. "He's worried about you, Eden. You're playing a dangerous game, and I won't be a pawn. You need to talk to him."

"Really, Kristen? You've demoted yourself to being a secretary?" And there it was; the sarcasm coming easy, but too late. She could hear the pause as Kristen rolled her eyes.

"I prefer the term 'administrative assistant,' if you must know. And if that's what it takes, then yes."

Eden pushed a fist into the mattress, adjusting to slide

her legs underneath her. Pain shot through her leg, the fabric of her pants pressing down on the bite. Adam sat up, crossing his legs, his eyes downcast.

"I'm not interested in anything he has to offer, least of all protection," she said through gritted teeth.

"No, Eden. He . . ." There was a rustle on the other end of the line, a murmur of another voice. "He says Gabe wasn't going to tell you everything . . ."—a scratch as Kristen slid the phone into her palm. Eden pressed until her ear stung, trying to catch the exchange in the background. "He says he has to tell you about . . ."

She barely made out the whisper of an argument and then, "Eden?"

His voice there, and hesitant, and full of remorse. Everything stopped. Her heart stalled in the silence as he waited for her to answer.

She tossed the phone away. It fell to the bedspread, propped up against Adam's knee.

"Eden? Are you there?" Az's voice was distorted, drifting unwelcome into her room, just enough to hear the confusion when he said, "I think she hung up?" before the screen went dark.

"The boy from the picture," Adam said, taking his hand from her leg. Eden nodded slowly, unable to look away from the blackened screen, the V shape of her phone. When Adam shifted, it flopped over.

"I hung up on him," she said, as if it had been a test of loyalty. But there was a nagging behind it. She hadn't. Az had hung up on her when she hadn't answered.

"I don't understand," Adam said. "I thought he was from before?"

"He is," Eden whispered.

"No." Adam hesitated, trying to put the pieces together. "You said he was the reason you . . ."

"He is," Eden repeated. "And he was." She tore her eyes from the phone, focused on Adam.

"He knows you're a Sider? Eden, but he's a mortal!" Confusion and horror fought for control of his features. "How does he even remember you?"

"No." Eden's shoulders fell. She shouldn't have listened to Adam, should have never answered the phone. "He's not human." When Adam didn't say anything, she went on. "He's not a Sider, either." Suddenly she wanted to spill it all, to tell Adam everything. "He's an angel."

"Angel," Adam said, his voice going deadpan. "You meant . . . like what, Eden? Like literally? Wings and halos?"

A sad sound somewhere between laughing and crying surged out of her. "No halo," she said. "Not anymore."

She watched his face. The first twitches across his forehead when he realized she wasn't joking. A half breath as if he was going to speak and stopped himself.

"You don't believe me," she said finally.

"No." He hesitated. "Angels don't exist. It's impossible. There is no God." His hand twisted into the cuff of his jeans.

"Why would you think that? We exist. It's not exactly a far stretch."

He shook his head, his face full of uncertainty. "There should have been answers. Instead there's just bullshit. There is no Heaven. There's no Hell unless this is it. And if it is, no one bothered to tell me, which is fucked up."

She held his gaze. "Is that why you killed yourself, Adam? To find answers?"

For a long time Adam said nothing, only stared at her. His eyes shone in the dim light. "So what? You think that's a stupid reason?" She didn't expect the anger in his voice. "You killed yourself over a guy, which is even stupider." She winced. Adam closed his eyes. "Sorry. I'm just . . . That's so . . . not you," he said, changing the subject. "And then the angel thing? You can't expect me to believe you."

Finally she whispered, "Just go, Adam." She couldn't keep the defeat out of her voice. Telling him anything had been stupid. "Get out."

Somewhere in the darkness between the bed and the door she heard him breathe deep, once. Twice. *Go*, she thought.

"If he's an angel, prove it." He found his way back to

her, sat down, and reached over to turn on the light. Eden cringed, the sudden brightness stinging her eyes.

"Why?" She knew she could. Gabe didn't have wings, but he had other ways of convincing. Gabe might be pissed at first, but having Adam's trust would be worth it. Hell, maybe Gabe's anger, the changing color of his eyes, would be enough.

"Because I want you to be telling the truth," he said.

"And you don't think I am." She sat up, putting her elbows on her knees, her chin dropping into her palms.

"Yeah, and that part kinda makes me an asshole, doesn't it?" He laughed, a ghost of his normal self creeping in.

She gave him a small smile. "A bit."

"So, you gonna get me a feather or something? Maybe a bell off Santa's sleigh while you're at it?"

"You've already seen one," she said.

"An angel? The Az guy? When?"

"Not him. The guy I was talking to in Milton's. Gabriel's one of them." She laughed at the incredulous look he gave her as he remembered. "He blends, doesn't he? He was best friends with Az. Best friends with me. Before . . ." Adam waited, watching her, but she couldn't bring herself to go on.

"Is there some deal with you and him?" he asked carefully. Eden kept the smile.

"Trust me, you have nothing to worry about from

Gabe. I'll see if I can arrange a meeting," she said. Her eyes wandered to the phone. She wouldn't call Kristen now, not while she knew Az was there, but in a few hours it should be safe. Gabe owed her this much. Kristen might know where Eden could surprise him with a visit of her own.

# CHAPTER 33

It was snowing as they made their way across the street. A flashing half-burnt-out marquee proclaimed the place "Aerie." Below the name of the club, black letters spelled out:

**7:30 PM SIX FOOT SHOVEL**

**9 PM DAWN'S SUPERNOVA ALL AGES SHOW**

"Kristen said Gabe would be at that second one." Eden grabbed Adam's hand as they neared the club and the crowd thickened. She left out the part where Kristen had told her it was a bad idea, that Gabe would find her if he needed her.

Outside Aerie, the sidewalk was a clustered mass of black clothes and skin paled by makeup. Next to Eden, a Goth girl squealed and clomped her eight-inch striped platforms past Adam to join a group of near clones,

Manic Panic purple hair trailing behind her.

"OMG!" the girl cried, pronouncing each letter. "Can you actually believe we're going to see DS? Singer is *hot*."

Eden heard Adam scoff. She turned toward him, her eyes playful as she surveyed his light blue sweater and jeans. "Now you see what I meant by 'restricted palette'?"

"Clearly."

Eden laughed, tugging at the pleats of her black skirt. Her legs were covered by her usual knee-high boots, this pair laced up the side with a white ribbon. A few hot pink clips in her hair and a matching tank top hidden under her peacoat completed her outfit. No one gave her a second look, but there were more than a few whispers behind glittery black nails as Adam led the way to the double doors.

A muscled thug sat on a stool at the door, the word "Staff" ironed onto his too tight T-shirt. Even he was wearing eyeliner.

"What's the cover?" Eden asked.

"No cover. Need tickets," he growled, barring their way with his trunk of an arm.

"How much?"

"Sold out. Next!" Eden tilted her chin, glaring at him in frustration.

"Well, fuck." She spun to face the crowd, zeroing in on the first person she saw wearing gloves. "You." She pointed her finger, stopping him. "You have tickets for this?" she asked. The kid nodded. "Two?" Another nod. "Good. I want them," she said, digging in her pocket. "Hundred for both?"

The kid laughed. "Not a fucking chance."

"You're serious?" Eden snorted. "Fine. Make it two."

"Just forget it, Eden. We'll do it another time." Adam grabbed her arm as she went for her pocket again. "Jarrod . . ."

"Is a phone call away if he needs us," she said, digging out the rest of the cash she carried, not bothering to keep anything for the cab ride home. "This is important, Adam." She looked up, meeting his eyes. "I don't want you to pass in here. If it gets to be too much, we can go. You ready?"

"Yes, but . . ."

She turned back to the boy, dropping a tightly wound tube of bills into his hand and snapping up the tickets. She handed one to Adam. "Your proof is in there. And you're going to get it." She smiled sweetly as she handed hers to the bouncer.

They both held out their wrists for the neon yellow wristbands reserved for the underage crowd. She swung open the heavy door, holding it for Adam to follow.

Heavy bass lines throbbed through the floor and wound up her legs. Each relentless note rattled into her lungs, ready to break her apart a particle at a time. The lights cut on and off, pulsing in time to the heartbeat of the bass drum, highlighting hundreds of arms raised and waving like tentacles. A guitar screamed chords over a techno beat so fast Eden's heart sped up in a struggle to compete.

The lights died.

Eden froze, disoriented. Without her sight, the only sensations left offered up the scent of sweat and a collective gasp from the crowd. In that moment, when the gasp stuttered into silence, before they had time to breathe again, a voice sliced across the room. The deep baritone fell from the air around her, the guitar crying out again as the singer moaned into the microphone. No words, just an escape of pleasure.

A single spotlight shone down, but the singer crouched low. Eden rose onto her toes, trying to catch even a glimpse of him.

He stood suddenly and stepped forward to the edge of the stage, giving her a clear view as he searched the crowd, his gaze hunting prey.

Leather pants clung to his legs. Even though the stage lights had to have been searing heat down on him, he wore a long-sleeved black shirt so tight it was a second skin. His head bobbed as he flashed a grin at the drummer. Sweat flew from the drenched inky curls hanging to his shoulders. His boot counted off the beat, and he swung an arm down, silencing the drums on cue.

"Without your hideous . . . beautiful . . ." he purred, searching the crowd. With a whispered breath, he moaned, "Love." It rolled from his lips like a promise, echoed layer after layer. Deep inside her, something shivered. "Can you love me?" he asked the crowd, prowling the stage. "Do you DARE?" The room surged forward. Screams drowned out his laughter. He held his arms out, head bowed, reveling in their reaction.

In front of Eden, a girl fainted. Two massive bouncers struggled to her. Each of them took an arm and pulled her away as if they'd been expecting it.

"Pretty good, isn't he?"

Eden jumped at the voice, a guy next to her clapping wildly as he screamed into her ear to be heard.

"Who is he?" she asked, unable to take her eyes off the stage.

"*That*," he said, "is Dawn's Supernova."

## CHAPTER 34

NO, Gabe thought, watching the pink clips bobbing in and out of sight through the crowd. He covered the distance quickly, slamming past shoulders, and grabbed Eden's arm.

Whipping her away from the Goth kid at her ear, he yelled, "What are you doing here?" into a face as shocked as his own must have been. The guy who lived at her apartment tried to claw his hand away, but Gabe ignored it.

Eden raised an eyebrow. "Didn't you say that if I needed anything . . . ?" She was trying to give off an air of amusement, but her blue eyes were strained, the teasing smile a mask.

"You're not in trouble, are you?" he asked. Gabe maneuvered her by her elbow, turning her so that her back was to the stage. "How did you find me here?"

"I have my ways," she laughed, twiddling her fingers in

his face, but her laugh was false. Gabe cringed.

"What do you *need*, Eden?" he prodded, unsmiling, tensing as the music stopped. He eased when the band dove full throttle into the next song. Eden's face grew serious.

"I need you to tell Adam what you are," she said, seeming like she wasn't quite sure she wanted to ask at all. "I tried to, but he didn't believe me. I need you to prove it."

"Eden . . ." *Damn it*, he thought. They'd risked showing up to corner Luke. Try to find out if he knew anything about the dead Sider. But he couldn't let him see Eden.

She threw a hand on her hip. "You owe me, Gabe. He's my second in command. He deserves . . ."

"Second in command? Is that what they're calling it these days?"

Eden blushed.

"Sorry, bad form." *You're sure about this?* he mouthed. She nodded. He would have done anything to get her out of the club.

He turned to Adam. "You must be the nonbeliever." The guy glanced to Eden. Gabe followed his lead.

She nodded in time to the music. Though the stage was no more than forty feet away, her eyes were concentrated much further and glassy. Gabe snapped his fingers. "That's your cue, sweets. We need introductions or something. It's getting awkward."

"Gabe, Adam. Adam, Gabe . . ." she said, turning away from the stage with a series of long blinks.

"Goth rule number one. No pastels," Gabe said, grimacing at Adam's light blue sweater. "Please tell me she at least hassled you a bit. If not, I'd seriously rethink the whole friendship." Gabe offered his hand. When Adam hesitated, he reached forward and pumped it once. "Doesn't affect me," he said. Adam watched as his fingers pulled away, waiting for the glow.

"So Eden wants you let in on a few secrets," he said, leaning in as if passing along a juicy piece of gossip.

"Gabriel!" The shriek came from their left, cutting off the conversation. A petite girl, hair done up in curled twists of pigtails, threw herself into Gabe's arms. When she pulled away, a trace of excess glitter from her cheek sparkled against his black shirt.

"Valerie!" he lilted, kissing the air on either side of her wide grin.

"Can you even stand to look at him?" she asked, pulling away. "That voice! I'm putty!"

Gabe looked to the stage, where Dawn's Supernova had just launched into the next song.

"He's *so* not my type. You know the bad boy thing just doesn't do it for me."

Gabe caught the wrinkling of Adam's brow at his words, but the look was there and gone.

"Oh! I'm sorry. You're here with someone!" Valerie gasped, turning to Adam. She raised her arms, leaning in to throw them around him in a hug. Adam's eyes went wide. Gabe stepped between them before she could complete the move and twirled her away from Adam.

"Not quite." Valerie stared up at him, confused. "Friend of a friend," he explained.

She winked at Gabe, no doubt thinking it was some sort of blind date. "Well then, I'll let you two get to know each other."

Gabe watched her wander into the crowd. From the corner of his eye he saw Adam leaning down to Eden's ear.

"Eden. Seriously?"

Gabe caught the remark, raising an eyebrow. "Is there a problem?" he asked.

"An angel . . . who's gay," Adam said, as if the contradiction should have been obvious.

"You seem like a smart guy, Adam." Gabe threw a hand on his hip. "God creates a race of beings, whose *sole* purpose is to love. Think He would do that and not expect them to love each other? That's just daft, especially when you mortals are off-limits."

"But her and . . ."

Gabe tsked, cutting him off and turned to Eden. "Someone has been a bit chatty, hasn't she?"

"He needed some backstory. It's important that he

knows what he's up against." She balked. "Believe me, I don't talk about Az unless I have to," she added quickly.

"Nice of you to clarify." Gabe turned back to Adam.

"What do I need to know?" Adam asked. "She apparently thinks you have all the answers, being as you're all knowing and whatnot." At his side, Eden was tense.

"What's he been told?" Gabe asked as he scanned the room looking for the space thickest with people, where she would be least likely to be spotted.

"Not much."

He palmed a bill to Eden, but never took his eyes off Adam.

"Your boy will have a Coke, with a shot of cherry juice. His mom used to make it for him that way. One of his favorite childhood memories. Three cherries, right?" he asked Adam. The question was rhetorical.

Adam swiveled between him and Eden, his face unsure. "I haven't told anyone that. Not since I became a Sider."

"I did some checking," Gabe said, waving it away. "You'll forgive my intrusion; I'm a little . . . protective of my friends," Gabe said, turning back to him. "This one especially," he added, sliding an arm around Eden's shoulder. He looked pointedly into her eyes. "I only do what's best for her."

"But, there's nothing to check on with me," Adam said.

"No one remembers me." He shook his head. "No, it was just a lucky guess."

Gabe checked the stage, annoyed. On it, Luke pranced across it like an idiot, winking at girls in the audience. If he didn't get Eden out soon, there would be a whole new set of problems. Of course, Eden was too stubborn to leave without Adam being convinced. *Time to turn things up a notch*, he thought. "Not checking on you, my friend, but your little brother. Barrett was easy enough to look up. I took a chance that you had the same taste. You should know he's doing really well, Adam. So is your sister."

There was an awkward pause as Adam choked back a shocked breath. Gabe turned to the stage, his head bobbing to the music as he gave Adam a moment to compose himself.

"So you tracked down my family? That doesn't prove anything."

Gabe sighed hard as he spun toward Eden. "You always go for the hardheads." Pecking her on the forehead, he added, "How about those drinks? Grab me a bottle of water. I need a few minutes with Adam here."

# CHAPTER 35

Eden pushed her way through the dancing bodies to the front of the bar, but the crowd was still too thick to get any service. She moved with the flow, winding her way around the edge until the people thinned out near the corner. Her hands she kept close to her sides. She cast a glance onto the dance floor while she waited, but Adam and Gabe were lost behind a curtain of colored strobes and flesh.

Eden tried not to notice the skin. Everywhere, it danced in creams and darker hues, shades of ivory. She dug her fingernails into her palms, hoping Adam was managing to cope. Finally, the bartender took her order.

She slid Gabe's cash over as the drinks were set down, picking up the glass. Before she could twist her fingers around the necks of the bottles, an arm slid around her waist, a man's voice yelling over the lead singer's syrupy wail.

"I've got hers."

A hand covered her own bill after slapping down two twenties. Eden jerked her fingers away. If she passed Touch once, opened the floodgates, she wasn't sure she'd be able to stop. She plastered a fake smile on her lips. Swiveling in the embrace to glance over her shoulder, she caught sight of him.

In her hand, the glass slid, condensation puddling against her fingers as they grasped too late, catching just enough of the lip to send it in a lazy spiral. It crashed against the floor, splinters slicing into the skewered cherries. A sneaker smeared the dirty pond of reddened cola, tracking bits of it away. Eden's hand froze, empty.

"Oh, fuck me," she said.

"That happy to see me, huh?" Az tightened the arms already snug around her waist from behind. His hair against her neck, his head nestling onto her shoulder the way he had always done broke the spell. She ripped away, twisting to face him.

Her first thought was that Kristen had been right about the Emo phase. His dark brown curls were gone, dyed black and practically ironed. The hair drifted over one of his blue eyes; the one she could see was lined in kohl. He was sinewy, the tight black thermal clinging to him, defined muscles strange on arms she remembered far less skinny than they were now. Her second thought was that

Kristen had been wrong about him looking like shit. He looked incredible.

"Seriously?" she asked, thrusting him away, ignoring the shiver that passed through her when her hands met his chest. For once, the feeling had nothing to do with Touch.

"You're pretty pissed, huh?" He offered her a weak half smile of apology, one of his shoulders rising as he cringed.

"You can't think that wounded puppy shit is gonna work on me?" Anger dislodged the words she'd wanted to say for so long. "Not after what you did."

He raised an eyebrow. "You're not gonna cut me *any* slack? I mean, I died for you."

"Yeah, and I died because of you. Only for me it wasn't an act." She stepped back, glass crackling under her boots. Az reached for her wrist. "Don't touch me," she seethed.

He pulled his hands away, lifting them to show he meant no harm. "I just don't want you to get cut."

Looking down, she realized her hands were empty. Behind her, the bottles were gone from the bar, stolen while her back was turned. Az took a step back. She hesitated before filling the space, stepping out of the puddle.

"What do you *want*, Az?" she asked, wondering if he heard the tremble in the words.

"Just to talk." He hesitated, just enough to let her know he was moving, and then brushed his hand across her cheek and back to her neck. "You cut your hair," he said, twirling a bit between his fingers. "I like it." He caught her gaze before she thought to turn away. His eyes, they pulled her deeper into them, drifting into cold blue whispers of comfort. *Remember us, Eden*, they begged. *Remember how we were.* She forced hers shut, breaking the hold while she could, surprised by the effort it took.

"You try to pull that shit on me again and I swear to God, Az." She didn't fill in a threat, couldn't think.

"I can make this right," he said, but without her sight she heard the uncertainty. She wasn't the only one he was trying to convince. "Just talk to me. We can grab a cup of coffee or something? Anything. Please."

"You'll never be able to make this right. I really don't need to hear this bullshit." She opened her eyes, searching for a break in the crowd, an escape. It had been so much easier when he was on the phone; she'd just tossed it away.

"I know," he mouthed, too quiet to be heard over the guitar riffs. He swayed closer, his lips now only a breath away. "Give me a chance and I can tell you why. Let's get out of here. Name a place and we'll go. Me and you."

He dropped his head forward, brushing his forehead against her cheek. Eden froze. Lips finding her neck, he kissed her once, a tentative brush against her skin. When she didn't move away, he wrapped an arm around her back, the fingers begging her closer.

She surprised herself, let her head roll back, the feel of

his hand against her hair rushing goose bumps down her arms. His mouth pressed harder this time and she drew a breath, her body remembering the familiar pleasure of it whether her brain agreed or not. Dizziness stole over her the way it had earlier, with Adam.

Adam.

"Az, stop." She lifted a leaden hand to his shoulder, turning her head in a faint attempt at breaking away. "Wait." Opening her eyes, she glanced over his shoulder toward the dance floor.

A spiral of twisting strobes pounded across the only face she caught, the only one staring back at her.

"Adam!" she yelled, charging past Az. She felt the hand slide down her arm as Az tried to catch her, watched as Adam's shoulder butted against Gabe's while he headed for the exit. "No!" She swatted the fingers away, trying to keep track of Adam's back bobbing through the sea of people.

Gabe caught her around the waist as she tried to pass, holding her back. "He's gone, Eden. Let him go. I'll call you a cab." He ushered her toward the front doors.

"You sold me out!" she screamed, turning on Gabe. Her hand cracked across his face, nails raking his cheek. "You set me up!" Her eyes blazed as pinpricks of blood wept into the welts.

Gabe's jaw hung slack. His eyes burst a morbid rainbow

from amber to maroon, the angry red so deep it was almost brown. He swiped his palm across his split lip.

"Is that what you meant by doing what's best for me?" she yelled. "You knew I didn't want to see him! You did this on purpose? Answer me, damn it!"

His body seemed to swell, rippling with unchecked anger. She flinched, taking a step back, shocked by the rage on Gabe's face. It left just enough room for Az to slide between them. Reaching behind his back, he took Eden's hand in his. She was too startled to pull away.

"You found *me*, Eden." Gabe rocked forward. "I sent you to the bar, hoping he wouldn't see you."

"Gabe, you need to calm down, right now," Az said. "I'm sure she didn't mean it. She's upset." He laid his other hand on Gabe's shoulder, but the dark eyes never faltered from her face.

"Maybe you should ask her why," Gabe spat. Az turned back over his shoulder, eyes catching on Eden.

"Who was that guy?" he asked, confused. Eden hesitated.

"Tell him, Eden," Gabe prodded. "*You* wanted answers. *You* wanted honesty. He's been pining for you like some brokenhearted schoolboy, and what were you doing?"

Az tugged her hand, pulling her next to him, not letting go. "Gabe, stop it! What's wrong with you?"

Gabe finally broke the gaze, eyes shifting to the stage.

The last chords of a song drifted across the crowd as the band announced a fifteen-minute break. “Forget it.” His anger had flashed and gone, but a weight hung on his words. “She needs to leave. Now. The last thing we need is for you two to be seen together.”

“Gabe. It’s too late.” Az squeezed her hand tighter, rings digging painfully into her fingers. “He’s looking.”

Eden whirled around to the space where their stares intersected. There were a dozen people milling about, but nothing obvious jumped out at her. She turned back just in time to see fear register on Gabe’s face.

“What’s going on?” Eden demanded. She stepped away from Az, toward the bar.

“We need to get you the fuck out of here.” Az flicked his gaze over her shoulder.

“Move, now.”

Az wrenched her through the crowd. She stumbled behind, a dozen sets of shoulders and hips slamming into her as he plowed through the masses. With each look back, he pulled her faster toward the door. She dared a quick scan over her shoulder toward the stage, but Gabe stepped into her line of vision.

“He’s seen enough, Eden. Don’t look back.”

They burst out of Aerie and onto the street, greeted by a cacophony of cab horns and throngs of club goers gathered on the sidewalk. The sky, lost above the glow of the city lights, hemorrhaged quarter-sized snowflakes. Already the sidewalks were covered, the awning paled under a cover of pure white.

The air froze the sweat on Eden's bare arms. Somewhere inside was her jacket, abandoned at the coat check. The snow melted as it hit her skin. Cold droplets trickled down her shoulders, pooling at her collarbones.

The flakes were less slow to collapse on her fingers; they'd already gone pale blue with Az's touch. The numb sensation spread up her arm.

Instead of taking her to one of the yellow cars waiting at the curb, Az pulled her past the ice-etched windows of shops. Car horns blared as they rushed through a crosswalk. Behind her Gabe's boots slapped against the concrete, nearly running to keep up.

Her chattering teeth clacked echoes off the walls of the alley Az led them down. A few dozen feet in, a high chain-link fence blocked the way, a fortress of cardboard boxes and trash bags lining the walls on either side.

"I need to go home. I need to find Adam." Her words jerked apart with her shivers. "Az? Please! What's going on?"

"She's going to freeze out here, Az." Gabe ran an agitated hand through his curls.

Az ignored her question, sliding his hands up and down her arms in an effort to generate heat. His icy fingers only made it worse. He tried to dust the flakes from her hair, but she brushed him away.

"I'm fine. Don't touch me," she said, backing away from him until her shoulders hit the bricks of the wall.

"Take her," Az said to Gabe, his attention on the sounds from the street. The snow was heavy enough that they couldn't see the opening to the alley, which meant no one could see them.

"Come here," Gabe said, wrapping his arms around her. He unzipped his jacket, but instead of offering it to her, he wrapped her in with him, trapping her in with his heat. "Az, we've gotta get her out of here. She's not safe."

Az's gaze flicked away. "I know."

There was an exchange between them without words. Az cocked his head, insistence in his eyes. Gabe shook his head. "No. That's insane. What if you can't hold her?"

"You know I can hold her," he said fiercely. "You can meet us there."

"Damn it, Az," he mumbled. She watched as Gabe shrugged off his jacket and held it out to her. "Put it on, Eden," he said, his voice defeated.

"Wait," Eden said. "I'm not going anywhere with you! Gabe?"

Az ignored her, throwing an arm back and catching the bottom of his long-sleeved shirt with a hook of his hand.

In a single motion he pulled the shirt over his head, tossing it away. A frigid gust of air spiraled empty cups and cigarette butts in a whirlwind at his feet.

His wings unfurled in a rush of feathers, swooping out to their full fourteen-foot span. He pumped them twice, stretching out the kinks. His shoulder muscles rippled. She could see the concave hollows where the back of his rib cage should have been, where his wings had been tucked tight. He turned back to Eden.

"Ready?" he asked, holding out a hand. Her eyes widened.

"Wait, those actually work?" She pressed herself harder against the wall, unsure. "How come you never . . ."

"I'm only supposed to use them to get back."

"Get back?" Eden practically yelled.

"The wings are an invitation to head home. So we're gonna use them for that. Kinda." He flicked his fingers, trying to catch her hand, but Eden moved it behind her back.

"What about you?" she asked, turning to Gabe.

He winked at her. Eden guessed he meant it to be reassuring. "One of the perks of staying out of trouble. Faster travel options," he said, taking her hand in his.

"Azazel!" a voice snarled from the head of the alley.

"Keep him busy," Az whispered to Gabe.

Gabe held a finger to his lips, and Eden's eyes went

wide as she nodded. He shoved her with both hands, sending her sprawling toward Az.

Az pushed off the second her arms hit his shoulders. She squeezed herself tight to him in reflex, her eyes closed as wind and windows rushed past, left below. Az's hands caught around her waist, her hair lashing against her cheeks as he strained, each pump sending them higher. She didn't dare open her eyes.

# CHAPTER 36

"Bend your knees," Az said as their speed slowed. Eden unclenched her eyelids, startled to find the ground a few feet below.

Az was already running when they hit, catching Eden when she stumbled and forcing her up the stairs to her security door.

He turned to her expectantly.

"I wasn't the one with the key," she said with a flippant shrug of her shoulders.

"Fuck." Az looked up, studying what he could see of the building through the blinding snow. Flakes caught in his lashes. "You the one with the lights?" he asked.

Her anger blazed back now that her feet were on solid ground. "What? Your little spies didn't keep you informed?"

Az rolled his eyes. "Save it, Eden. We don't have time for couples therapy this second. Who's in your apartment right now?" he asked, surveying the empty street around them.

"Jarrod. I don't know if Adam would have time—"

"He wouldn't," Az interrupted.

"To get here yet," she finished. "If he's even coming."

"Anyone else?" he asked, ignoring her comment.

"Libby. Libby's there too."

"Who's that?" he asked, backing down the stairs and looking up as if judging the distance to their window.

"She found us. I owed her a favor. She's been crashing with us the past couple days."

He shot her a look. "Can she be trusted?"

"What do you care?" she asked. A second later she rolled her eyes. "She's fine, Az."

"We don't really have a choice." Once again he pulled her to him, and before she had time to scream they were hovering at the window. Az rapped his knuckles against the glass. Two silhouettes cast shadows on the plastic slats of the shade.

*He uncuffed her*, Eden thought, surprised.

"Is there a code or something?" Az asked. Eden almost laughed.

"Yeah. If an angel flies me home and is hovering outside a window that also happens to be sans balcony, I rap four times." The sarcasm felt comforting, like some part of her she'd been missing the last half hour had come back.

The shade slowly rose. In the backlighting it was hard to make out the look on Jarrod's face, but Eden could see Libby clearly, her mouth open in shock.

"Open the window, Jarrod," she lipped, knowing he couldn't hear her through the heavy glass. His shadowy hand undid the latch, and she felt one of Az's wings flutter against her leg as they curled, drifting them back to give the window room to swing out.

"What the hell . . ." Jarrod cried as Az pushed Eden in through the window. Tucking his wings tight against his back once his feet were on the sill, Az followed, swiveling his naked shoulders to slide through the frame.

Jarrod and Libby stood back. Eden sunk to the floor, her quick breaths the only sound. One by one, each set of eyes turned to the wings of the figure crouched near the living-room window.

"She lost her key," Az said finally, shrugging. He stood, pointing left. "I need water. Kitchen?" Libby nodded blankly, her eyes still wide.

"Hey!" Eden called. He turned around just in time to catch the jacket she'd shrugged off and tossed to him. He slipped the leather coat on, covering his wings, and winked at her.

When he was gone, Libby turned to her.

"He's a . . ."

"Pain in the ass," Eden said, standing up on shaky legs,

hoping the tone of her voice would be enough to end the conversation.

"Where's Adam?" Jarrod asked, glancing at the open window. Turning away from him to close it, Eden kept her face hidden as she slid the hooked lock back into place.

"He's fine," Az said from where he leaned against the doorframe of the kitchen. He took a draught from the giant plastic cup in his hand. The ice clinked as he drained the last of it. "He needed to blow off some steam."

Jarrod took him in with suspicious eyes.

They jumped as the call box for the front door buzzed. Jarrod was the first to rush to the intercom.

"Adam?" he yelled into the box.

Static popped and hissed for two long seconds before they heard Eden's name whispered through the crackle.

"Who is this?" Jarrod demanded.

"Eden? Can someone come?" Each word strained through the speaker.

"Gabe!" Eden went for the doorknob, but Az grabbed her wrist, his other hand on her cheek, forcing her to look at him.

"You have to stay here, Eden. I need to make sure he's alone."

"No!"

"Don't let her leave here, understood?" Az said over her shoulder. Jarrod's arms encircled her before she had a chance to react, pinning her arms at her sides. Her feet swung furiously, and she bucked in his arms until he lifted her off the ground, twisting her out of the way. Az slipped out the door, closing it behind him.

"Stop it, Eden. Let him check it out!"

She settled with a last jerk of her shoulder.

A long minute passed before there was a kick at the door. Libby opened it.

Az had his arm around Gabe. One of his eyes was swollen, a shallow cut running from his eyebrow to his cheek, bleeding onto his chin. He hissed a breath through clenched teeth as he tried to put weight down on his foot.

"Oh my God," Libby gasped, not daring to look again. "That is *so* broken." At the ankle, his left boot was twisted almost backward.

"He just needs to sit down." Az helped Gabe to the couch, moving the table so he could stretch out his leg.

"Are you sure? It looks awful. Do you need, like . . . something?" Libby asked, unsure of what to offer.

Gabe reached down, gritting his teeth. With a swift twist, he ripped the foot back around, a shout squeezing past his lips. Everyone squirmed at the crunch of shifting bones.

"He'll be good as new by morning," Az whispered, his voice hoarse. "But thank you." He looked up at Libby again. "Actually, can I get another glass of water?"

Eden stood off to the side, where Jarrod had finally set her down. Her attention flicked to the door as it opened.

Adam stepped inside, his face unreadable as his eyes skipped across the scene, stalling on Eden.

"Adam," Eden sighed, covering the steps between them. She hesitated, but he held out an arm to her, pulling her into an embrace. He glanced at Gabe's bleeding cheek. "Are you okay? What happened?" he asked him.

Libby came back into the room, looking guilty as she handed Az the cup. Adam's jaw went hard. He squared his shoulders as he took a step closer to Az. "If you touch her again, I'll kill you."

Gabe raised an eyebrow at Eden. "Bit protective?" Adam turned to him, but Gabe lifted a hand. "Easy there, tiger. I didn't mean anything by it."

Az turned back to Eden. "They all get like this about you?" he asked, fascinated.

"Well, you didn't exactly make a sparkling first impression," she said. She met Az's eyes as she put an arm around Adam and his fingers found hers, squeezing tight. Az broke her stare without a word, his face stoic.

"You did good, girl. You'll need them." Gabe lifted his leg, tried to wiggle the ankle but winced and lowered it gingerly.

Az drained the glass of water in a single gulp, setting down the cup on the coffee table. He chewed an ice cube with a crunch and Eden cringed, thinking of the sound Gabe's ankle had made.

"It was the Fallen, wasn't it?" Eden asked.

Gabe leaned back with a nod, closing his eyes as his head hit the cushion of the couch. "He'll need a day to recover," he said. "That was too close, Az."

"So you're him?" Adam said, his voice icy. "She's with me now. And you need to get the hell out of our apartment."

She thought she saw a flash of something cross Az's face.

"Adam," Eden said. He jumped at her voice. "Stop it. You don't know anything about the Fallen. These two saved my ass tonight while you were off—" She cut herself short. "*Both* of them did. They're staying here tonight."

"This is ridiculous," he grumbled.

"Jarrod, set Az up on the floor. Gabe gets the couch." If Adam hadn't come out all defensive she wouldn't have opened her mouth. Now she was stuck with Az. Though Gabe did look spent. She crossed the living room and squatted down next to him, her hand balancing her on the armrest. "We're safe here? You'll be able to heal?"

He considered it and then nodded.

"Good," she continued, standing. "Party's over." She surveyed the faces. "Sleep if you can. We'll sort this out in the morning."

Her eyes darted to Az.

"Adam and I will be in my room if you need us," she said quietly, taking Adam's hand. Az only stared, the longing clear on his face. His fingers twitched as if he wanted to reach out for her, but he kept the hand at his side. She led Adam to her room, not looking back, sure she still knew Az well enough to hit below the belt.

Eden turned away as Adam closed the door, slipping her tank top over her head, too tired to worry about modesty. She yanked a long T-shirt on as he snapped on the light. His eyes floated across the pale skin of her midriff, before skimming to concentrate on the sneakers he untied and stepped out of. She unfastened her skirt, pulling it off, the fabric of the shirt drifting above her knees.

Climbing into the bed, she lifted the covers off the empty side next to her, watching his fingers fumble with the button of his jeans. He folded them too slowly, set them on the floor. His shirt dropped from his fingers.

Eden waited, her hand tucked under the pillow. Adam stood silent in his boxers, his head bowed.

Looking up, he licked his lips, parted them, but no words came. He moved then, only a hand, drifting out to tap a finger against the mattress.

Eden reached. She didn't take his hand in hers, just brushed his thumb with the tips of her fingers.

Her words came out slow, each one forced.

"I watched him sleep, once. The last night, before I . . ." She cut off, forced herself to go on. "I was so tired but I wouldn't let my eyes close because I was afraid he wouldn't be there when I woke up, that I just dreamed him. And then . . . and then everything changed," she said. "I thought I would die without him."

"Why would you say that to me?" he asked quietly, his eyes full of heartache.

Her fingers slipped under his palm. She spread them, but he didn't take her hand. "Because I did die. Because a few months later, it hurts me to even look at him, and I don't know what that means."

"Do you still want to be with him?" he asked.

"I don't know," she said.

He picked up her hand, moving it closer to her, and dropped it onto the sheets. He clicked off the light as he climbed into bed next to her. His hand found her back, pulled her closer so her head rested on his bare chest. In the silence, she heard his heartbeat, strong and steady and calm.

"What happened after I left?"

Eden closed her eyes. "I'm in some deeper shit than I let on. Not all angels are good."

Adam snorted. "Living room occupants excluded?"

"I didn't say that," Eden managed. He stroked her

hair and kissed the top of her head. His breath hit her cheek as she kissed his neck once.

"Don't," he whispered, tucking her head back against his shoulder gently. "I don't want that."

Eden felt her face flush. "I thought . . ."

"I want you to close your eyes. I want you to fall asleep first."

"Why?" she asked, suddenly afraid he would slip out of the room as soon as she did.

"Because I'll be here in the morning."

# CHAPTER 37

Next to her, Adam was curled tight into the blankets. She blinked again. The shock of the dream that awoke her was already fading into a low tide of unease. Something about Kristen. The night with Marcus. Something burning? *No*, she thought, *something really is burning.* Eden closed her eyes and sniffed as she ran her hand down her neck. The muscles there were stiff from sleeping half cocked over Adam's arm. He didn't stir when she crawled out of the bed.

Eden followed the fumes to the kitchen, a thin haze of smoke coming from the skillet on the burner. She climbed across a chair and slid open the window next to the table.

Az turned at the scrape, a look of apology on his face. He wore the same tight black pants he'd had on last night, but she recognized the dark blue T-shirt as one of Jarrod's. Some of the curl had come back into his hair. With it came a memory, their breath coming hot and fast, her fingers tangling in those curls, the sand shifting beneath them under the blanket.

"Did I wake you?" he asked, breaking her thought. The memory shattered.

"I didn't sleep well." The back of the chair dug into her stomach as she leaned against it. She pushed away, circling to sit down. Self-consciously, she yanked the hem of the shirt she wore down past her knees.

"Yeah, me either. Figured I'd try to make breakfast." He cracked an egg, tossing the shells into the garbage can. "Thought maybe you'd want some." He smiled then, and the motion sent her off kilter as if two worlds had overlapped, the perfect untouched glow of their weeks together wrapping around her unease, trying to smother it.

She dragged her attention away, her eyes roaming until they settled on the blue garbage can next to him. She heard the crack as he broke another egg, the white shells landing on top of old coffee filters and empty soda cans. Under the shells, a burnt pile of scrambled eggs still steamed lightly.

Eden shifted in the chair, dropping her feet to the cold tile. "They need milk," she said.

"Thanks." Opening the refrigerator, he scanned the shelves until he found the carton, adding a splash to the pan of yolks and white goo. He glanced up at Eden's sigh.

"Typically you add the milk before you start cooking the eggs."

A blush colored his cheeks. "Yeah, I haven't cooked in a while," he said, going back to his scrambling with renewed vigor. The milk sloshed across the nearly cooked eggs.

"I had a nightmare," she said. He half turned toward her, the spatula still clanking against the pan. "That's what woke me up," she added awkwardly, not sure where the need to tell him came from.

"What about?"

The details were long gone, just a trace of wrongness curled in her stomach. "I don't remember."

He nodded. "Happens like that sometimes." He watched the eggs, concentrating as though they'd become the whole universe. He flipped them, cutting chunks away and mixing the last of the uncooked parts. Milk steamed at the bottom of the pan. "Your brain shuts out the bad stuff." He held the handle of the utensil so tight his fingers went white.

She scratched a nail against the wood of the chair, the dream pushed far back. They were alone. She could ask him all the questions she'd spent months agonizing over.

Unfortunately, the fact that he was standing in her kitchen was more than a little unsettling. She'd run through every scenario of them meeting. Honed bits of dialogue, sharpened her wit to a razor-edge, ready to slice him as deep as she'd been cut, no matter the situation. Waking up to Az cooking eggs in her kitchen had never made the list.

"It's throwing me off," she said, breaking the silence.

He finally looked up, turning the heat down on the burner before he leaned against the back wall. "Are we still talking about the dream?"

"No. We're talking about *you*, Az. I don't want you here."

He crossed his arms. "And here it comes," he mumbled.

"Here what comes?" she asked, her voice clipped.

"Yesterday . . . maybe even last night, I would have gone all apologetic. You could have played the jaded card for however long it took me to win you back. But not anymore." His voice was controlled; each word thought out and delivered for maximum impact. Clearly she hadn't been the only one plotting this moment. "You don't love him," he said quietly. "You know that, right? He's a replacement, Eden." He almost managed to hide the quaver in his voice.

*Who are you trying to convince, Az?* She opened her mouth to say the words, go for the kill. But when her voice came she said, "Why did you make me think you were dead?"

The way he paused, she knew he'd expected her to fight him about Adam and what he meant to her, maybe even counted on it. She watched him run a hand through his hair, heard the frustrated "fuck" he whispered.

"Why?" He slammed a hand on the counter, lowered his voice. "Because I'm flawed. Selfish." He set the spatula down, bowing his head. She watched the emotions struggle across his face. Part of her wanted to reach out to him, touch him.

"Do you need me to get Gabe?"

"No! You need to hear this." He shuddered, gripping the countertop. "We just wanted to get away, Eden. Gabe and I, take a vacation. And then I met you. I thought it was safe." He glanced up. "But we were found. The Fallen."

"So you faked your death to get away?" she asked, exasperated.

"The Fallen don't like me happy, Eden. They saw me with you. I knew what they would do if they got a hold of you." He swallowed hard. "See, they don't come after me. They come after anyone I love. Torture, kill, with the hope that I'll give in and Fall. Do you know what that's like for me?"

"So you pushed me to kill *myself*. How does that make you any different than them?"

"I am *not* one of them." His eyes flashed a violet swirl of anger and sorrow before he closed them. When he blinked them open again, they'd faded back to a resigned cornflower. "On the beach, the night you met me, what were you doing, Eden?"

"I was . . ." She looked away at the dark memory of the days before she'd met him. He crossed the room, squeezed her hands.

"You know you would have killed yourself if we hadn't found each other. I kept you alive as much as you kept me from Falling. But keeping you happy kept you mortal. I just wanted us to have a chance to be together."

She met his eyes, let him see what his loss had done to her. What it was still doing to her.

"I fucked up. I should have told you everything." He cursed under his breath, running his finger over her thumb. "We can fix this, right?"

"I don't think we can. If you'd come to Kristen's—" She dropped her gaze, couldn't stand to see the regret in his eyes. "Why couldn't you have just trusted me?"

"What's burning?" Gabe stood in the doorway to the kitchen, his hair tousled. He stepped into the room, scrunching his nose, yesterday's broken ankle healed. Eden snatched her hands from Az. Behind him, the pan gave off plumes of fresh smoke, blooming against the ceiling.

"Damn it!" He pulled the pan from the burner.

"Az trying to cook breakfast." Gabe smiled, rubbing an eye. "The bane of overworked chickens everywhere."

He flopped into the chair next to Eden, yawning as he watched Az poke at the charred remains. "Those are not edible, so don't even try to pass them off. He tell you about the time he almost burned down our apartment over a few pizza rolls?" Gabe snickered.

Az scraped his second failed attempt into the trash. "We got to talking. I was just distracted," he said, his voice genial as he pointed the spatula at Eden. She followed his lead, trying to smile. Just talking. She almost managed it, but Az's words ricocheted through her mind. *We can fix this, right?*

"Talking, eh?" Gabe raised an eyebrow. "Then why does she look like you two just got busted?"

Eden's grin faded. Az cast an embarrassed glance her way.

"Gabe," he said, his voice low. "We were just talking."

"Just like old times." He shrugged off the flicker of warning in Az's eyes. "Minus her boy on the side, of course," he added.

"You're such an ass, Gabe," she mumbled, rising so fast the chair fell back, clattering against the wall.

She heard Az, his bitter, "Damn it, Gabe," followed by the rush of his feet. He caught her arm in the living room.

"Eden," he said as she tried to pull free of his grasp.

"Why are you doing this to me!" she yelled, loud

enough that she was sure the door she stood in front of would open, and Adam would come charging out. "Why can't you just leave me alone?"

He still held her wrist, but his fingers were loose, the thumb making delicate circles as he waited for her to finish.

"I'm with Adam now," she insisted. "There's nothing left to fix." She wanted to go on, wanted to say so much more. But she couldn't pull her attention away from the tender way he held her arm. It would be easier if he screamed, argued, if he'd let her pick a fight. Anything.

"Let's just stop, start over," he whispered. "We were great together. We can be like that again."

"Like it's that easy?" she argued. Her hand was starting to shake. She slid a ring over her knuckle, driving it back against the web of her fingers, letting the motion soothe her.

"It could be. I did everything I could to help you."

"You're honestly gonna try to lie your way out of this, too? You didn't do anything for me."

"How'd you get this apartment, Eden? Panhandling?" he grimaced, shaking his head. "No, that's not it. Maybe a rumor started after you left Kristen's? One that benefited you?" He fell silent, waiting for her to make the connection.

Her mouth dropped open at the revelation. "You . . .

you sent them. You told the Siders that I could free them?"

"Fifty bucks seemed more than fair."

"Do you have any idea what you did?" She shook her head, her chest tight. "Az, I was supposed to keep a low profile."

"I only told a few Siders. Just enough to get you a hotel until you figured out an apartment. I figured it would die out pretty quick once you stopped." He glanced up, his voice unsure. "Why didn't you stop?"

"What does it matter?"

"Eden." All he had to do was say her name. A gentle breath of letters. There was so much there that only she understood, layers calling her out. He wrapped his arms around her when she didn't answer. "What's going on?"

She'd wanted so much to be held by him for so long and now it felt tainted. "Forget about all that other stuff, okay?" He paused, running a hand down her cheek, his eyes full of pain. "Why didn't you stop?"

"I . . ." She hesitated, pulling away to meet his eyes. "I couldn't," she whispered. "They need me. You wouldn't understand." She dropped his hand and sat down on the armrest of the couch. His head leaned forward, his long black bangs hiding his face.

"You come here, after everything that's happened and . . . I've spent the last months trying to get *over* you!"

Eden stopped, starting over. "What right do you have to do this to me?"

Az looked up in surprise. "Every right." He lowered his voice until she had to close her eyes and concentrate to make out the words. His hands rose to her shoulders. "I'm gonna fix it. I don't care how long it takes. We'll figure it out, okay?"

She took a deep breath. "You're not forgiven yet. You know that, right?" she said, wishing she'd just kept quiet. It had been the eyes. And the fingers on her skin. And the . . . *Shut up*, she told herself. "How the hell do you think you're going to fix things?"

He smiled. "Let's start small. Something that I'm sure will make you happy," he said quietly, standing and taking a hesitant step toward her.

"And just what would that be?" She stepped away from him, compensating, but he walked past her, heading for the front door. He winked as he opened it.

"Breakfast. I'll be back in a few."

She stood there for a moment, watching the closed door and wondering what the hell had just happened. Memories rose, rippling like pebbles tossed into the lies she'd told herself to try to forget about him. Before they could wash over her, she headed back to the kitchen.

Eden didn't say a word to Gabe as she passed him on her way to the sink. Instead, she cranked on the hot water, squeezing too much soap onto the sponge. She pulled the pan Az had used from where he'd left it on the stove and scrubbed at the charred crust on the bottom.

"You know," she said finally, slopping the sponge back into the water, "I really didn't appreciate that." She slid a glance over her shoulder and was surprised to find Gabe smiling.

"Yeah, that was kinda bad form," he said.

"So do you have some kind of problem with Adam all of a sudden? I don't get it, Gabe. You knew about him and it didn't seem to bother you much before." She gave up on the pan, leaving it to soak, and dried her hands on a paper towel.

"Because I was sure with Az back in the picture the choice would be clear. You belong with him, Eden."

"Why?"

"Because he belongs with you," he said, shrugging his shoulders.

Eden scoffed. "A bit dramatic, Gabe."

"Do what you need to do, but you know what they say, right?" he asked smiling. "Once you go celestial . . ." He paused before laughing. "Yeah, I got nothin'." He reached out his hand and took hers, his face going serious. "You do realize, if you and him don't make it, he won't last."

"That's not fair," she whispered.

"But it's the truth." He squeezed her hand. "He'll Fall. We'll lose him."

Adam rounded the corner as Gabe was dropping her hand. Eden blushed as he passed by, opening the fridge and pouring himself a glass of juice. He wrapped an arm around her from behind, kissing her cheek.

"How long have you been awake?" he asked. "You weren't there when I woke up."

She held Gabe's gaze as she lowered her hand to stroke Adam's arm. "But you were there when I did," she said. She felt him smile against her skin.

Adam stood behind her, resting his head on her shoulder. "Where's the other one?" he asked.

She couldn't see Adam's face, but Gabe's went hard.

"The *other* one went to get everyone breakfast."

"How'd the floor work for you? Sleep well?" His voice was pleasant enough, but there was an undercurrent to it.

"I actually had the pleasure of the couch," Gabe said through gritted teeth and a plastic smile. Then she felt Adam's arm tighten, his free hand sweeping her hair back as he kissed her behind her ear. She tilted her head away reflexively, lifting up her shoulder.

"You're tickling," she said, but Gabe had raised his eyebrows, his face a mask of barely concealed amusement. Adam didn't move his arm away.

# CHAPTER 38

The tension hadn't cleared since the first night Gabe and Az had come. Though it'd been a week, every time Az so much as walked by, Adam's fingers snatched hers, claiming her. It'd gotten so bad that even his hand on her knee was enough to set her teeth grinding.

With Gabe and Az staying with them, Eden felt safer, but each day that nothing happened, their constant presence irked her more.

She'd spent the last two days holed up in her room aside from her few minutes in the alley each morning. So far she'd read four paperbacks cover to cover and listened to the entire playlist on her iPod twice through. Boredom had settled in.

Sighing, she ripped her headphones from her ears.

She stretched, killing a few minutes before she stood up and threw on an outfit for the day. She didn't bother with makeup. Opening her door, she crept out, hoping to avoid interaction long enough to grab a muffin.

No one was in the living room. The television was silent, the computer humming to the walls. Az had folded his blankets and added them to Gabe's pile at the end of the couch, but Az and Gabe themselves were gone. The apartment was silent.

Eden opened the refrigerator, scanning the shelves, snagged an apple and a Mountain Dew. When she closed the door Libby was rounding the corner into the kitchen.

"If I watch one more surprise paternity test result I think I'm gonna puke." She slid past Eden, grabbing her own apple and taking a bite. "Please tell me again why we're just sitting here doing nothing?"

"We're not. We're lying low. Gabe and Az are trying to figure out what the Fallen know. Who killed James."

"Jarrod said they were headed to the Bronx."

Eden nodded. "Kristen's there. Maybe she got a lead."

Libby took another bite of the apple, wiping her chin. "So do you think something's really going on?"

Eden pulled out a chair and sat. "What do you mean?"

"Well, I mean, obviously something happened with James. But they seem so sure it wasn't a Sider. Which, yeah, but they went all conspiracy theory. I just think it's a bit ridiculous that they're keeping you locked up in here. I mean, something could just as easily go after Jarrod or

Adam, right? They're both out and we're stuck here. It just seems a little . . ."

"Sexist." Eden shot her a smile, rolling her eyes.

"I mean, give me chivalry. I'm all about having doors opened for me, but this whole fragile girls thing is turning out to be really boring." Libby dropped into the chair beside her. "How about we plan a girls' night out?"

Eden bit into her apple, chewing slowly. A night out could be fun. Something different. *No. I need to stay inside. Just until we figure things out.* Eden sighed. "The guys aren't going to let me out of their sight." Libby cocked her head, raising an eyebrow at the weak excuse. They weren't exactly locked in. *I can take care of myself, anyway.*

"You underestimate me, my dear," Libby said, putting up a finger. "Now, don't judge until you've heard me out, but I've kinda been chatting to Adam the last few days about the whole Az situation. I told him I was on his side, and that usually a girl just needs a good second opinion," she gushed, and pointed at herself.

Jarrod and Adam had taken Libby out, helping her spread what built each day, keeping her stable. And now she was the only one keeping Eden sane. She seemed to know exactly when Eden was about to snap, suddenly showing up to steal Adam away in a whirlwind of questions that she needed to be answered. More than once, Eden had mouthed *thank you* and gotten a wink in return, so she knew Libby was doing it on purpose.

"Libby," Eden started. "It's not gonna happen."

"Meanwhile, in another movie," Libby cut her off, "Az seems to know the rules of the game and is trying to get on the BFF's good side. So *that's* taken care of."

Eden gave her an incredulous look. Since when were they best friends? Also, Libby had overlooked a key element. "But you forgot—"

"Gabe. Who I happened to overhear, telling Az that he had something to do tonight." Libby was positively beaming.

"I don't know." A night out, though. No Siders or dosing or drama. Just a normal night out. She couldn't deny the temptation. "I mean, where would we go?"

"We?" Libby's grin was contagious. "So you're in?"

# CHAPTER 39

Az stood near the door, leaning against it as if he wasn't entirely sure whether he was going to let them leave or not.

"You're sure you have your cell phone?" he asked for the third time. Eden pulled it out of her pocket, again, and flipped open the screen.

"See? Fully charged. We'll be fine, Az. Just a movie, maybe something to eat after if we feel up to it." She smiled, hoping it was passable. Butterflies wreaked havoc on her stomach. He was going to decide it was too dangerous.

Under her jeans, the skirt she wore was bunching up. She fought the urge to smooth the rippled material, knowing it would only draw attention.

Libby came out of the bathroom, grabbing her clutch off the couch. She'd changed into a sweatshirt and baggy jeans. *He's going to know*, Eden thought, panicking. Libby could get away with the casual look, but Eden never dressed like this. She wasn't even sure she'd *worn* the jeans before tonight.

"Ready, hon?" Libby asked innocently.

Eden glanced back at Az. He tapped his hand against the doorframe before dropping it.

"Ugh. Just the movie and back," he said as he finally stepped aside. "And you have to promise you'll call me if you so much as get a funny feeling."

Libby squealed, hooking Eden's arm in hers. Eden smiled back; the girl's enthusiasm was almost too much.

"Gabe's gonna kick my ass," Az mumbled. "He wants one of us with you at all times."

Libby raised three fingers. "He'll never know. Scout's honor, 'kay?" She patted his cheek playfully. "Don't worry, babe. I've got your back." Eden caught the wink Libby gave him, his face going red.

*Clever*, Eden thought. Libby had probably said the same thing to Adam that she'd played up to Az. It wasn't like the guys were likely to get together and compare notes or anything.

They pounded down the stairs without looking back. Eden heard Az's footsteps on the landing above them, pausing at the railing, but he didn't follow.

Eden hesitated at the security door. She glanced back over her shoulder, up the stairwell. A rush of guilt hit her. *No*, she thought. *It'll be fine. I deserve this.* She took a deep breath. The door opened and the stairs were empty. Eden ignored the disappointment tempering her relief. Libby pulled a plastic bag from her pocket once they'd gotten to the alley.

"Best I could do without it looking all wonky," she said.

From their apartment the only window view on that side was in Eden's room, and she'd been careful to lock her door before leaving.

With no threat of prying eyes from above, she unbuttoned her jeans, handing them off to Libby, who'd already shed her extra layer. She rolled them tight, tossing both pairs into the bag before adding the sweatshirts on top. She tied the bag, then lifted an overturned soggy cardboard box and set the bag underneath.

Libby twisted her hips, flaring out the bottom of her skirt.

"I can't believe we're doing this." Eden wrapped her arms around herself, glad she'd gone with long sleeves. Even though the material was thin, it still offered her a little protection. Libby insisted on forgoing coats. If they were supposed to be taking a cab to the movies, they really weren't necessary. Another little detail to give Az reason to believe her.

"I can't believe we *have* to do this. Confession?" she said, turning to Eden. "I was absolutely terrified of you that first night. You were so in control. Why are you suddenly letting them tell you what to do?"

Eden slowed her footsteps. "Can we not talk about it, Libby? I just want . . . this," she said, twirling her hand around. "A normal night out without fucking drama." Her voice grew frustrated, the tension creeping back into her shoulders.

"Ya know what?" Libby stopped, peeking out to case either side of the street before leading the way out of the alley. "I'm sorry I brought it up. Let's just forget about all that for now and have fun. Sound like a plan?" she asked, her eyes trying to pry a smile from Eden.

"Yeah." Eden forced a grin. "Sounds like a great plan."

"Freedom!" Libby sighed as they headed out of the alley, waving down a cab. Eden laughed as they slipped into the backseat. "Ready for your surprise?" she asked before turning to the driver. "Aerie, please." The driver nodded absently, starting the meter.

"Aerie?" Eden asked.

"Yeah . . ." Her face glowed as she undid the snap on the clutch, pulling out two tickets and handing them to Eden. "Have you heard of Dawn's Supernova? There was a video up on FreePlay and it's already gotten like a million hits in five days. Totally went viral. So they've gotta be good, right?"

Eden's mouth dropped open. "Libby, I can't go there."

"What's wrong?"

"The first night, when Az brought me home and Gabe got all messed up. We were coming from Aerie."

"Okay," Libby said slowly, her voice full of disappointment. She glanced down at the tickets. "Well, what did the guy look like?"

Eden hesitated. "I didn't see him."

She still remembered the fear on Gabe's face when they'd been chased out. Alone, she didn't know who to run from.

Libby scoffed. "So let me get this straight. You have an invisible enemy who you've never yourself seen and you can't go out because the boys don't think it's safe?"

"It's just . . ." The memory of the music sent a shiver of anticipation through her. "Maybe just . . . maybe just for a few songs."

"Are you sure? We don't have to go *there*. This is supposed to be fun. If you're gonna be uncomfortable, we can do something else."

"Like what? Go home?" Eden shook her head. "No. We're out. You've already got the tickets. We'll just stay for a few songs." It was a flimsy excuse, but she couldn't help it. She deserved a fucking night out.

Twenty minutes later, the cab pulled up to the curb. The crowd spilled over the sidewalk. As Eden opened the door, she was rushed by half a dozen teenagers.

"You got tickets? How many?"

"I'll buy them off you!"

"Whatever he'll pay, I'll double it."

She shook her head, making a rush for the door. The show had started half an hour ago, but the crowd gathered outside showed no signs of weakening.

"This is insane!" Libby yelled, gripping Eden's waistband so she didn't lose her in the crowd.

The same bouncer was at the door. Eden looked down the street, unsure why she hid her face as she held out her arm for the wristband.

As the door swung open, Eden forced herself to concentrate on the throbbing strobe lights. She wandered past a few teenagers clustered around the door, stopped dead in their tracks. Libby caught her hand as the last of the keyboard notes faded, pulling her along behind her through the crowd, toward the stage. They didn't make it, only midway across the floor when the drums, too, went silent. Eden glanced around. The place was packed. They'd be anonymous enough.

The room stopped gradually. The flailing arms around her settled, falling calmly as every head turned up to the single spotlight streaming down on center stage.

Eden kept her own eyes to the floor. Without the chaotic movement, she tugged Libby's arm, easily winding forward. No one else was taking advantage of the stillness.

At an earsplitting wail, her eyes flicked up to the stage.

It was him, the same singer. He screamed, dragging his hand over the strings of the guitar slung across his chest. Before she could wince, his fingers raced across the frets.

*No one should be able to play that fast*, she thought. He shredded up and down the neck of the instrument, the motion enough to make her lightheaded. Some kind of classical riff spilled through the amp, but she couldn't place it.

"Do you know what that is?" Eden asked.

Libby shook her head, rapt. "I've never heard anything played like that."

Eden's eyes swung back to the stage as the notes surged and died, the fingers holding the final chord in a diminished fifth. His head hung, loose curls spiraling down to his collarbones. His shoulders rose and fell with every breath.

No one clapped. The last time she'd watched him play, cheers and screams had drowned out the last notes of every song. This time the audience was too spellbound and dumbstruck to believe it had ended.

She was close enough to see a smile twitch the corners of his lips before he touched the strings again. The smile; it was like a secret they shared, and Eden's cheeks stretched with the wide grin plastered across them. It didn't matter that he hadn't even been looking at the audience; she was sure the smile was meant for her.

When he reached for the microphone, a sigh broke from her. She needed to hear that voice again. Eden strained closer, leaning against the sweaty back of the girl standing in front of her. She felt Libby fill the space behind her.

"This is for . . ." He stopped, adjusting the guitar, and raised his head. The light hit his face and Eden got her first clear view of him, cheekbones highlighted as he squinted his eyes, shading them with one of his hands. He started from the left side of the crowd, sweeping his brooding dark eyes over them. When he paused in the middle, Eden was almost sure he was looking at her, but then they moved on. "Anyway, she's supposed to be here, so . . ."

He slipped his hand across his shoulder, pulling the strap, and stepped up to the mic as he sung the first line. "These lies that permeate my life, I saw you standing there." He strummed a delicate melody, humming softly, shifting the song into a lullaby. "Words fall like pebbles to the floor, my mouth is filling up with stone. I fell the longest drop of all. Oh God, don't you take her away."

"Jesus, it's like Az could have written that. He's singing about us. Me and Az." Eden spun around to Libby, unsure of what to do, but sure she had to do something. She compromised by pushing her sleeves up. A second later, she pulled them down again. "Doesn't it sound like he was? Am I crazy?"

"Actually, I thought it was about me." Libby gazed up at the stage. "Maybe it's like a horoscope? Everyone thinks it's just for them, because they want it to be. That's gotta be it, right?"

"Right," Eden agreed absently. Libby gave her a strange look.

"You don't know him," she said. "I mean, there's no way it could actually *be* about you."

"I guess not." Eden took in his face again, studying the perfect cheekbones, the full lips. Knew the features. Even the curls seemed familiar. "Maybe he looks like Az?" she asked. "Just a little?"

Libby considered it for a moment before shaking her head. "I don't see it." She pulled her cell phone from her pocket, checking the time. "We've got about an hour and a half before we should be back. A little more if we're going to dinner," she said, throwing her fingers up in air quotes at the last word and smiling. "I need water."

"I'll be here," Eden said, turning back to the music, but Libby grabbed her hand, pulling her along. She tried to jerk away, but Libby only squeezed tighter.

"I promised I wouldn't let you out of my sight. And I'll never be able to make it this close again," she yelled, leaning in to Eden's ear as the band struck up, launching into a fast song at top volume.

Libby dragged her, shoving through the first rows of

people packed in behind them before they were able to just dodge around them.

Eden felt shoulders bumping into hers and closed her eyes, trusting Libby to guide her away from where he screamed out lyrics. Without him to distract her, she slowly became aware of the bare skin around her. Her fingers itched.

She glanced back, but his eyes had rolled up into his head as his body crashed against the mic stand, thrashing as the drums pounded. He wasn't even really singing words anymore; it sounded like he was speaking in tongues. The connection she'd felt to him was lost in the noise, but the crowd was the opposite. They'd come to life again. Mad seizures of dance erupted in her wake. Something slammed against the top of her hand, strong fingers gripping her wrist as she curled her fingers into a fist. She spun to face a bouncer, a dark block cupped in his hand.

"What the hell is that?" she demanded, yanking her hand back. There was a cold spot, liquid drying on her skin.

"He wants to meet you. Head backstage after the set," he said, winding his way through the crowd.

Libby turned to her, face radiant. Eden didn't return the smile.

# CHAPTER 40

Eden didn't have a chance to buy a bottle of water before the song ended. Libby didn't release her hand, even when they'd been standing still at the bar. There were black-lights running throughout the club, the stamp the bouncer had placed on her hand alternating between bright white and invisible. They crept closer to the door separating the club from the backstage area. Every few seconds, Libby glanced back, eyes shining with excitement. Eden couldn't help the nervous stirring in her stomach.

"Can you believe it?" Libby screamed, grabbing Eden's arm. "Are you excited?"

"He's just a singer," Eden said, more to herself than Libby. "Don't go all fangirl over him." At least there would be less people backstage. Eden checked her phone. Still more than an hour until they were supposed to be on their way home.

The bouncer guarding the door ignored them, watching

the stage. The jukebox drivel pumping through the speakers did nothing for her, and she wondered if she'd ever be able to listen to anything else again. The crowd milled listlessly as if counting down the minutes until the band returned.

The bouncer held a finger to his earpiece, and nodded almost imperceptibly to whatever instructions had been given. He stood suddenly, swinging his bulk to the left and pushed the door from its frame, but only an inch. Red light streamed out from behind, sending sharp lines through the last remnants of smoke from the show.

"Hold your hand up," he said. He studied their marks in the cool light from the recessed blue bulb. Under the blacklight, the stamp glowed, a thick circle with three curves emanating from it. Satisfied, he moved aside to grant them access. Eden looked back once at the empty stage she could see through the speakers and passed over the threshold. The door closed solidly behind her.

Red bulbs flickered, driving them down the narrow hall. Eden tried trailing her fingers on the black-painted plywood as they walked, but splinters scraped into them. Without the distraction, the nervous energy built in her.

"I don't know about this." The sudden lack of people was oddly unsettling. Libby's footsteps echoed through the tight space.

"Do you want to go back?"

"No," Eden answered as she tried to stay close, somewhere between walking and running. "But could you at least slow down, Libby!"

A trickle of fear puddled in her stomach, but she managed to fight it off until they rounded the corner into a room.

The light from a wide circle of dozens of candles fought to cancel out the purple hazy glow from blacklights. The walls were painted in fading Day-Glo, neon mushrooms and ripped posters advertising shows from months ago. The musicians she'd seen on the stage occupied black beanbag chairs randomly thrown about the room.

One of the backup singers had tilted each of the candles near her, the different colors of wax splattering in front of her like a Jackson Pollock painting. Now she ran her fingers through it, smearing little peaks and valleys into the mess. *Definitely in her own little world*, Eden thought, wondering what the girl was on. The room looked like some kind of circus on an acid trip.

Eden's eyes stopped short at the head of the circle. The singer. His head snapped up.

"I wondered if you'd make it back here!" he said, smiling as he rose to his feet. His tone was one part surprise, one part pride, like they'd just conquered some kind of labyrinth instead of a straight hallway. Beside her, she saw Libby shudder. "It's a pleasure."

He kept his eyes on Eden. "Now, she's Libby, but I didn't catch . . ."

"How did you know her name?" Eden asked, but he waved off the question with a flurry of his fingers.

"Sound carries in the hall. What's your name?" he asked again, taking a step closer.

"And who are you?" she asked, denying him. The thought occurred to her too late to make something up.

"Me? I'm just a singer in a rock and roll band." He laughed then, a sound like static feedback.

Eden couldn't choke back her own snort at the melodrama. "This is all a bit . . . ridiculous, no?"

"Eden!" Libby mumbled. "Don't be a bitch." The singer gave her a smile, and then turned back to Eden, his face full of apology.

"You'll just have to forgive me, Eden. If you can find it in your heart." His voice was different than it had been the night she had first heard him or earlier, when he'd been onstage. The heavy smoothness had gone, leaving it sarcastic and pitchy. *Condescending*, Eden realized. *He's playing with me*.

"Well, honestly, I don't know what I was expecting, but I'm let down," she said. "Let's go." She reached for Libby's arm, but the singer slid between them, grabbing Eden's wrist. She splayed her fingers away from him, yanking back.

"Eden doesn't like games," he said loudly.

It was a command; a cease and desist order.

The drummer set down his sticks and picked up a book that had been lying next to him. Wax girl scraped the last of her art from her fingers, looking embarrassed. Someone else turned on the lights, and suddenly the room lost its strange feel and became only a dingy backstage hideaway.

"Better?" The velvet undercurrent had flowed back into his words. "So no games?" He didn't wait for her to answer before he released his grip. Eden's cell phone trilled in her pocket.

"Silence is golden," he said as she pulled it out.

"What's that supposed to mean?" In her hand the last notes of her ring tone played out. She glanced at the caller ID. Fucking Adam.

"I think he means put it on silent," Libby whispered. Eden shrugged, thumbing the volume down.

"Meanwhile," he said, turning to Libby, "my drummer has taken a special interest in you, my dear."

"Drummer?" Libby's smile faltered. A flash of impatience clouded his dark eyes and then dispelled.

"He insisted on the chance to meet you." He leaned in, close enough to not be overheard by the drummer, but Eden could still hear the exchange. "I'd consider it a personal favor," he said, with an emphasis on the "personal" that nixed any chance Libby had to deny the request.

"Let's give them some privacy?" the singer suggested, as Libby plopped down next to the drummer's beanbag. He led Eden through a back door she hadn't noticed before, grabbing a bottle of water on their way out.

Not until the door closed behind them did she realize how ludicrous his line had been. A half dozen other people were in the room with Libby. But Eden was alone. With him. *I still don't know his name*, she realized.

She took a quick survey of the back lot, weighing her escape options. A tall wooden fence cut off the street. A green recycling Dumpster with GLASS scrawled across the front in fading permanent marker and another labeled CARDBOARD were too far from the fence to climb and use to jump over it.

He leaned against the door, the only way in or out, casually running a hand through his long curls before letting out a heavy sigh.

"God, that club gets hot as Hell," he said, twisting the cap off the water bottle and taking a long drink. Eden licked her lips. He held it out to her, but she shook her head. The last thing she needed was to pass him Touch. "You have to be thirsty."

"No thanks," Eden said thickly, but it took every ounce of her resolve not to reach for his offering. He rolled his eyes.

"It's just water. Look," he said, taking another drink.

The bottle was half empty now. Her lips stuck together when she parted them. He adjusted his grip, holding it by the neck, offering her the base.

"Thanks," she said, taking the bottle. She took a swig and tossed it back. He raised an eyebrow as he caught it. "Is this your attempt at luring me in with your 'bad-ass rocker boy' act?" she asked, leaning against the Dumpster. "Because I'm afraid it's hopeless."

"You think I'm after some groupie blow job?" Looking down, he wore a coy grin as he kicked the toe of his boot absently against the concrete. "Well, at least I know you swallow. Come off it, Eden. I know the crowd you hang with." He spit out the sentence with disdain. The ball of tension in her chest bloomed into fear.

"Who are you?" she demanded.

He moved slowly, hands spread wide and low, the heels of his combat boots scraping across the asphalt with each step. When he reached for her hand, she pulled back instinctively, but he caught her, fingers tightening around her shirtsleeve. A cloud of breath hissed through her teeth.

"Easy," he whispered gently, raising her struggling hand to his cheek. Eden froze as he laid her palm against his skin.

There was no glow.

"You're one of the Fallen." She whispered it. Somehow

saying it out loud only made it more unsettling.

"I sure as Hell don't have your boyfriend's pretty wings." His eyes danced playfully as she tensed. He leaned back against the door, pulling out a cigarette, lighting it with the Zippo he flicked across his hip. "So it's true then. The rebellious Az is shacking up with the Rogue!" He sounded delighted.

"He is *not* my boyfriend," she said, through gritted teeth.

"Even better," he interrupted. "No loyalties."

"I didn't say I didn't have loyalties. I only said I wasn't with him." She risked a glance at him. "What do you want? If you were going to kill me, you would have done it already."

"Obviously, Az and Gabriel haven't told you about my style." He breathed, the end of the cigarette glowing red, then slowly fading to gray in the silence. A reminiscent smile crossed his lips. "Your boyfriend's heartstrings make such a lovely melody when they snap."

She flashed back to Az on the balcony. The girl, the reason he'd been cast out. Dead, he'd said. *They'll hurt you, Eden.* There'd been so much fear in his eyes. What had they done to her? "Az and I are barely even friends," she whispered.

The door opened suddenly, slamming into his back. The drummer leaned his head out.

"Luke, three minutes," he said before the door fell closed again.

*Luke. Lucifer.* "Jesus Christ." She slid back a step.

"Hardly." He cocked his head, his smile twisting to a smirk. "Oh, come now. Don't get judgmental. Tales of war are always told by the victors. Add a few translation errors and suddenly I have this horrible reputation. I mean, I'm Dawn's Supernova. Where's the darkness in that?"

Eden raised an eyebrow, trying to keep her terror hidden as she leaned against the cold metal of the Dumpster. "*You're* Dawn's Supernova? Bit of an ego. What about the rest of them?"

"Lesser demons. I'd love to get into it, but unfortunately, I've got a show to do. Perhaps we should get to it." He hit the cigarette, blew out a quick exhale. "Holy wars have become so cliché these days. I approached Gabriel about a truce, hoping he'd be able to put aside our differences to figure out what's going on with you Siders. I'd get my answers, he'd save you and Kristen. He was less than enthusiastic."

"You know Kristen?" Eden's stomach dropped.

He smirked. "Of course I do. I know quite a few Siders. Unfortunately, Kristen isn't exactly my number one fan. She made it clear she's a harps and hymns girl." At his back the door opened an inch, but Luke knocked his shoulder back, shutting it. "Coming!" he yelled.

"Look. The Siders will get noticed by the Bound. And when they do, you'll be their first victim. If I were you, I wouldn't make any declarations of loyalty just yet." He reached a hand behind him, feeling for the knob. "I was hoping we could work together? That you'd at least consider it." He twisted the knob, but didn't open the door. "Before we head back in . . ."

*Here's the trap*, she thought.

He tapped a finger against his cheek as if considering something. "I'm wondering if I could ask a favor. In the spirit of future friendship and all."

The door was right there, her escape blocked only by his broad shoulders. Eden nodded absently, stepping closer.

"Rumor is you're on lockdown. If an opportunity presents itself, I'd like to be able to continue this conversation. There's no reason for Gabriel to know we've spoken. Any objections?"

"I'll have to think about it," she said.

"My second request." He pulled the metal door and held it open, his arm high, so that she'd have to duck under to go through. Eden waited for him to speak, but when he didn't she moved forward, her last few steps a dash for the backstage room. He caught her shoulder as she went through, freezing her at the threshold. Eden kept her eyes ahead.

Inside, the lights were still on. Libby was on a beanbag chair, her hands moving in some conversation Eden was too far away to catch.

"I want you to be careful around Az," he said. Eden's attention snapped to him.

"Az? Why?"

"You of all people should know, Eden," he said, his voice low and guttural. "Because he's only half Fallen. Struggling constantly with violent urges." He dropped his arm so she could pass. "How *did* you die?"

# CHAPTER 41

Snowflakes melted on the window of the cab, headlights flicked kaleidoscopes of shadows and glare, but Eden didn't see any of it.

She heard Libby's voice change, but only as a distant hum of confusion.

For a block, she leaned against the window, but the cold leeched through the glass. She dropped back onto the worn vinyl, tried to push Luke's last line out of her mind.

*How* did *you die?* The cocky insistence in it. Her mind drifted back to the night in the hotel. Luke had been implying something. *What if I didn't do it?* she thought. *What if Az did?* He'd faked the fall or faked being hurt. But how would Az have known she'd run to the beach? If he wanted her dead, why didn't he just do it in the room? It couldn't be true. Only manipulation. Az had gone through with his elaborate plan because she had to do it *herself.* Suicide was her fate.

He was scared, though. Worried about the Fallen hurting her.

When the cab stopped she exited, then moved up the stairs. She didn't wait for Libby to pay the driver.

A voice called as she slid her key into the door, and she fell out of the trance enough to know to wait.

"Jesus, Eden. You almost blew it!" Libby hissed. Eden stared at her blankly. "Clothes?" she reminded her, sweeping a hand over the short skirt she most certainly hadn't been seen leaving the apartment in. "What happened? What's wrong with you?" Libby asked when they'd made their way to the alley. Eden blinked slowly, sliding her jeans over the skirt, tucking it into the legs so it didn't bunch.

"Nothing," Eden said quickly, leading the way around the corner and through the entrance. In the stairwell their footfalls echoed, collapsing over one another, complicating with each flight.

At the apartment door, Libby slid her hand over the keyhole before Eden had a chance to unlock it. Eden didn't speak, just stared at the door. Her fingers held the key, waiting.

Eden forced herself to look at her.

"God, you're like a zombie." Libby searched her face. "You better at least fake *something*. If you go in like this . . . What's going on, Eden?"

“I’m fine,” she said. Libby hesitated and then finally stepped back toward the door.

Eden twisted the key and opened it.

Adam sat stiffly at one end of the couch. On the other end, as far from him as possible, Az turned, a bowl of popcorn balanced on his knees. Even she could feel the tension between the two.

“You’re back,” Adam sighed in relief, getting to his feet. “How was the movie?”

There was a second of silence before Libby covered for her, bubbling out some current box office plot she’d Googled earlier. Hours ago she’d made Eden memorize the details. Now there was nothing.

“Eden?” Adam asked, waving a hand in front of her face.

“Yeah?” she said, trying to force herself to smile.

“So you had a good time, then?” Adam asked. The way he said it, she knew it hadn’t been the first time. Maybe not even the second.

“Was the movie any good?” The voice was calm and strong, reassuring, until she realized Adam’s lips hadn’t moved. *He* was talking to her.

She looked around the room. Az was on the couch, and the light burning under Jarrod’s door gave away his location. “Is Gabe here?” she asked.

Az laughed. “No, we’re totally in the clear. No worries.”

He smiled at her. Eden cringed before she could flick the veil of a smile back into place.

"No worries," she echoed. The two words hummed darkly. She could taste them, coppery and bitter, when she opened her mouth to speak.

She hesitated, trying not to look at him, knowing it made her look guilty. He'd twisted to face her, the bowl of popcorn settling in a tilt on his thigh. A few of the kernels drifted into the crack between the cushions. Az letting her go through with her death, doing what would happen anyway. . . . It was wrong, but it wasn't murder. When she'd woken up at Kristen's, her clothes had been damp. *He lied, screwed up*, Eden thought. *He wouldn't kill me. I drowned.* She imagined Az, holding her under the water, swallowed hard at the thought of his hands around her throat. In her mind, he laughed as she fought underneath him. Enjoyed it. *No,* Eden demanded, forcing the image away.

"Thanks, Libby. I really needed it," she said, keeping her tone light and grateful. "But I'm gonna let her fill you guys in. I'm beat." She pulled her hands into the sleeves of her sweatshirt. Her imagination clicked into overdrive, visions of Az pummeling her in a rage. *He's never been violent with me. Never. Luke was just trying to fuck with my head.*

The girl was babbling before Eden had even closed her bedroom door. The heavy wood cut her voice off mid-tangent, something about pasta and chocolate cake.

Her blood hissed against her temples, empty static. The room was too quiet. She opened the window just a crack to let the far-off sounds of the traffic in, but it hardly helped.

Standing in front of her nightstand, she opened the drawer. Inside, the portrait of her and Az sat on top of receipts and loose change. She thought about throwing it out the window, even craved the sound the shattering glass would make as it hit the asphalt. Instead, she tossed it into the closet, telling herself she hadn't deliberately aimed for the pile of clothes in the corner, and stretched out on top of the covers.

*Could it have been him?* She stared up at the canopy above her, counting the holes in the lacy material. *Think it through. Prove it to yourself.* What happened that night? *Me and Az were on the balcony. He went over. Hit.* Even now, knowing it was an act, she felt sick. *And then what?* Running down the stairwell. Lobby. Boardwalk. Everything after was hazy, darker the further past sunset her mind reached. *I was on the beach. I told Gabe to leave. I was alone on the beach.*

Cold air drafted through the screen and past her. She held her muscles taut, not allowing herself to shiver. She made each inhale a sharp sip, let the air out far too slow.

Her temples ached from the concentration. *I was alone*

*on the beach. And then . . .* Eden gasped. Her eyes shot open. *The sound of a footstep. Muffled by the sand, but loud enough to be heard, loud enough that she'd turned.* Someone had been there.

Stars prickled her vision. She sucked a shaky breath, looped the memory, and played it over again in her head. The footstep—she started to turn and then, nothing. Had it been Gabe coming back to check on her?

*No.* Her heart ached. *Please be wrong*, she thought. *Az couldn't hurt me like that.*

Another image fought its way up. Az here, in the kitchen. She remembered the way he'd gripped the spatula, his knuckles white. *Sometimes your brain shuts out the bad stuff.* She'd thought he was talking about her nightmare.

Luke's words shimmered behind her closed eyelids. *Violent tendencies. You of all people would know that, Eden.*

# CHAPTER 42

Hours later, but before the black sky had begun to brighten to its normal grimy yellow, Eden slipped out of her room. Creeping into the living room, she passed a shrouded body under a blanket on the couch and the crown of Gabe's curls snuggled into the pillow on the floor. She concentrated on her feet, avoiding every creak in the floorboards. A movement near the door startled her and she misstepped. Beneath her socks, the wood gave an angry pop.

"You're up early." Jarrod balanced on one foot, his hand thrown against the door as he slid a sneaker on.

"I'm not. I never slept."

He tilted his head. "You okay?"

Eden shrugged. "Lot on my mind. I'm fine."

Jarrod seemed to take her at her word. "I was gonna go for a walk. Get some air," he whispered. He thrust his chin out toward the two sleeping forms. "They make it smell weird in here. Gives me a headache."

She nodded. "Like snow or something."

He stopped, staring at her. "Kind of, actually."

She tucked her hands into the pocket at the front of her hoodie. Jarrod considered her for a second as he grabbed his jacket up from the floor.

"Wanna come?"

Once they were outside, Eden noticed the subtle difference. She took in the city air, the scents of exhaust and crisp steps and rushed caffeine. Jarrod had been right about the apartment. Outside, though, even beneath the city air, she could still smell Az on her. Eden shivered.

Jarrod kept his eyes down, kicked a tattered shred of newspaper. It caught on his shoe, slid and hung on the laces as if it wasn't quite ready to let go yet. He used his other foot to scrape it free.

"So, you're kinda screwed with the whole Adam and Az thing, huh?" There wasn't a hint of hesitation in his voice. *Count on Jarrod to cut through*, she thought. "You and Az have some pretty thick history." It wasn't a question.

"You could say that."

"So where's that leave Adam?"

Eden slowed her steps, but Jarrod matched them. Finally she said, "Better off than you'd think." Jarrod nodded, as if her answer had made perfect sense.

"He's my friend. But you need to do what's right for you." He stopped, his eyes drawing her in. "You know I've got your back no matter what happens with that, right?"

Eden didn't answer.

Instead of heading toward Milton's they took a left. Her eyes strayed to the doorway where they'd found James as they passed.

Empty. No crime scene tape, no flowers. Not for a death that hadn't registered to the mortals.

They should have done something. Marked the spot. Later, maybe, they could come back. Put up some flowers or something. She glanced at Jarrod, wondering if he felt the same, but his face was twisted away. He couldn't even look.

Eden toed at the frozen ground. She wished they had gone the other way, toward Milton's. They walked on in silence.

She thought of things she should have been asking him, like what was going on with him and Libby, and if he was holding up against the Touch. For a second she even considered telling him what she suspected about Az. But that would require telling him how she'd found out.

"You're quiet," he said finally. She didn't answer, because she wasn't about to deny it. "How long are they staying? Until they think you're safe, right?"

She nodded.

"They don't think we can do the job, huh?" There was a heavy silence before he spoke. "What do you think?" he asked.

She was tempted to just shrug again, but forced herself to answer, to actually think about it herself. "I don't know. The bad guys searching me out. The good guys swooping in to the rescue." She flexed her bare fingers and thrust them into her pockets, twisted her hands against the lining. "Something doesn't sit right with me."

He waited, scratching a fingernail across his zipper. "You think Az and Gabe aren't telling you everything?"

"Jarrod, every Sider who's made it to our stairs had our address. You can't tell me the Fallen wouldn't have been able to find it out."

Jarrod stopped. "Jesus. I never thought about that."

She nodded, lost in thought. "I think the Fallen knew where I was the whole time. I don't think they want me dead." Jarrod's eyes widened but she went on. "What if I didn't kill myself? What if that's why I'm different?"

"Are you asking me, or telling me?" He tucked his arms into the space next to his chest to keep them warm. They were almost around the block, heading back through the alley.

"I don't know. I just have a feeling."

Jarrod stopped at the base of their stairs. "Eden, you

wouldn't have said anything if it was just a feeling. And that came out of nowhere. What's going on? Adam said you don't remember what happened when you died."

"I remember some." Eden sighed, zipping her jacket tight against her neck. She had only climbed one stair, barely opened her mouth when her ring tone sounded. The number didn't look familiar, but she snapped it open anyway.

"Told any good stories lately?" the caller asked.

Eden gripped the phone tight enough that she heard the chime of the speakerphone come on.

"Hang on a sec," she told Luke, pressing the Speaker button again to shut it off. Jarrod dropped down two stairs. "It'll be a minute," she told him.

Jarrod was already shaking his head. "Not leaving you alone out here. I'll wait up by the door if you need privacy or something."

"Go!" she said. He stepped backward once, raising a few inches.

"Eden."

"We're not done talking, I promise. But I need to take this."

She descended to the sidewalk and crossed the street. Behind her, the door slammed.

"I figured it would take you quite a bit longer to shake him," Luke said.

"Where are you?" Her eyes ricocheted across the parked cars, sidewalks. "What do you want?" she asked.

"Through your alley. I'll meet you on the other side, doorway of the cabaret. Walk my way, but don't stop. I'll follow you." He hung up before she could answer.

# CHAPTER 43

She stared into the alley, her heart thumping wildly. For all she knew it was a trap, Luke waiting for her behind the Dumpster. But what other choice was there?

She cursed under her breath, taking a tentative few steps. When nothing happened, she hurried through. As she passed the doorway to the cabaret, she caught his shadow in her peripheral vision.

He fell into step beside her two blocks later.

"How did you get my number?" she asked, trying to keep her voice from shaking.

Luke regarded her for a moment. "I applaud the effort, but you'll have to forgive me if I keep my secrets for now. I'm here to finish our conversation. I feel a bit of sympathy for you, I think. I want to offer you my protection."

Eden leaned against the brick face of a bakery, throwing a sole up on the wall behind her. "Protection from what, exactly?"

He dragged his Zippo from his pocket, flipping the lighter across his knuckles before snapping out the flame with the lid. "The Bound," he said.

She scoffed. "Gabe would never put me in danger."

"Honestly, Eden, I'm surprised he's held out this long. He must care for you very deeply."

"What do you mean 'held out'?"

Luke smiled as he stretched.

"Eventually all good boys tattle to Daddy. Gabriel will have to tell Upstairs about the Siders. About you. It's encoded into his makeup. He's not bad for a Bound, but you don't know the others like I do."

She gave him a once-over. "Just why would I need protecting from them again?"

A hiss escaped through his teeth. "Big mistake, underestimating the Bound. They've flooded the world on a whim, killed off an entire generation of children in Egypt because someone called in a favor." He sighed, the sound soft and sad. "Eden, how do you think they'll react to the Siders, the way you undo their perfect little paths with your Touch? They will smite your ass without a second thought. Not to mention what will befall your poor Gabriel for leaving them out of the loop."

Her eyes flicked to his, that same self-satisfied grin stretched across his face, dancing in his dark eyes. They caught the morning light, only an impossibly deep brown, not the black she had suspected last night. "I just want you to consider that maybe there's a better option than waiting to see what happens. Waiting until maybe another of your friends is stolen away. Where was Gabriel when you needed him then?"

She gave him a second to believe she was considering it, another to convince herself she wasn't.

"He didn't know about that," she said defensively. "He only came to me after."

"Eden, he's been watching you for months now." Luke laid his hands on her shoulders. Her muscles twitched as if to avoid his fingers. "The Bound might already know about the Siders. Which means you're running out of time."

Eden met his eyes. What would Gabe do if the Bound came after her? Would he help, go against his own side? The Fallen didn't have rules to follow; they were free to do whatever they wanted. Whatever they had to. It was a freedom Gabe didn't have. Luke slid his hands from her shoulders, but didn't break eye contact.

"I think," he whispered, "you should consider my offer." Her head bobbed slightly, her thoughts feeling far away. A memory of Az floated through her mind. They used to be so happy. Why had he been so eager to throw it away? A candle of rage flared to life. He'd never answered that question. Luke at least was giving her answers. *No*, she thought. *Concentrate. Luke is not the good guy.*

*Blink*, something deep whispered.

She forced her eyelids down, the lashes crushing together. "Don't . . . don't look at me like that." Her throat oozed the words out.

"You're a strong-willed little thing, aren't you? Is that why Az is so captivated? Why Gabe risks everything for you?" She heard him biting back the anger in his tone. The smooth carefree voice was back when he spoke again. "I just want you in the right frame of mind, Eden. Doing nothing will not end well for you."

"Are we done here?" When she opened her eyes she had to squint against the brightening morning. It had to be at least eight by now. The rest of them would be waking up soon. She wondered how long Jarrod would be able to hold Gabe off before he launched a search party.

Luke smashed a fist against the bricks beside them. She stepped back, his sudden rage catching her off guard. An elderly couple making their way toward them startled, before turning into the bakery. "You can do something no one else can do. Do you realize the power you have?"

"Yes. I send them Upstairs."

Luke cupped his hand, the bloodied knuckles smearing against his other palm. "Really now. Who told you that fairy tale?"

"Gabriel," she hissed, his proper name tripping on

her tongue. "And the Bound can't lie." She spun, heading back through the alley.

She didn't stop until she was through her security door, pressing her back against it, her breath coming in gasps. She swallowed hard, tried to force herself to control her breathing.

Her fear faded enough for anger to ease in. Now, apparently Downstairs *and* Up were after her.

And it all led back to Az. She clenched her hands into fists at her sides. He'd ruined her life, and now he was fucking with her afterlife.

Eden stomped up the stairs, her toes screaming as she slammed them against each step. The weak pink rubber of her shoes did nothing to absorb the shock.

She flung the door open, skirting her eyes across the room until she found Az on the couch. Jarrod was slouched in a chair with Libby next to him on the floor. She ignored them.

"You," she said, pointing to Az. "We need to talk. Now." She turned to Jarrod. "Where's Adam?"

"Sleeping. Your room," he stuttered, eyes wide.

"Then we're borrowing yours," she said, yanking Az from his seat.

She snapped the light on in the boys' room, the smell of gym socks and body spray overpowering. They couldn't even clean. Az closed the door behind him.

"What got you all twisted?" he asked. She reared her palm back, sent it forward with every ounce of hatred she could muster, fingers curling at the last second. The pad of her hand cracked against his cheek, nails gouging the skin there.

She reared again, but he ducked his head and caught her hand. A pang shot up her arm as her finger jammed, the pain tripling when he crumpled her fist in his.

"You prick," she growled, yanking her hand away. "You fucking prick." Az took a step, old wrappers crunching underfoot. He crouched, hands spread, as if she were going to charge. Her skin hummed for her to do it, attack him, beat the shit out of him.

She panted, trying to slow her breathing, steadied herself on the dresser. The knobs dug into her back.

He straightened, taking a chance that she was done, and drew his fingers along the oozing claw marks. "Jesus, Eden! What the hell's wrong with you!"

*I hit him*, she thought in disbelief. The energy in the room seemed to crackle and sputter. Everything went still, silent.

"Did you kill me?" she whispered.

The change in his face caught her off guard. He parted his lips, but closed them without a word. She couldn't place the emotion in the muted muddy color of his eyes.

Az slumped to the floor, crumpling onto a pile of dirty shirts and jeans left against the wall. He dropped his head, his face out of view.

Her arms were sticky against the lining of her coat as she slipped it off. She let it fall, heat escaping from the sleeves. She dropped slowly, leaning her back against the dresser in defeat.

"Aren't you going to say anything?" she asked.

He raised his head, meeting her eyes. "Who told you that?" he asked weakly.

Her vision blurred. She didn't bother to blink, just let the moisture build against the dam of her eyelashes. It reached the tipping point, spilling over. "I want the *truth*, Az."

He cupped a hand under her jaw, his fingers against her cheek. "Do you realize what you're asking me to do?"

She heard a commotion through the door, coming from the living room. The muted voices of Jarrod and Adam arguing and Gabe chiming in. Gabe, who'd told her in Milton's that sins couldn't be spoken out loud.

She met his eyes, saw the pleading in them. "Do you know how hard it is to keep these things in?" he asked. "The risks taken for you?"

"You think just because you took some tiny risks that I'm going to be okay with this?" Az closed his eyes, wincing at her words, and she realized he'd risked Falling.

Risked everything. He scooted across the floor until his knees touched hers.

Everything stopped except the pounding rush in her ears. She shook her head. The emptiness there spread, filling her arms, her legs, everything going dead inside.

"Don't make it for nothing." He pulled her hand suddenly, the momentum raising her onto her knees, tumbling her toward him. Her breath stalled as she caught herself inches from his lips.

He kissed her, a soft hesitant flutter asking permission.

"I hate you," she whispered. Her hand caught his neck, her fingers twisting into the curls there, and she almost believed she had the strength to pull away. "I hated you." But then she tipped forward, just enough, and his mouth met hers hard, desperate and hungry.

She kissed him back, her body remembering his, anticipating, moving into his arms as they came up to pull her closer. A thousand complications sprang to her mind. She pushed them back down. All that mattered was Az, there and in her arms and kissing her.

He broke away, his breath rushing across her lips. His eyes met hers, the pupils dilated. Pain, she realized. His eyes were full of pain. And fear.

"Az?" His head pitched, his hand wrapping across his gut as he doubled over. A moan swelled from his throat as he curled tight. Her brain tried to make sense of it, the sudden change, but all she could think of were the roly-poly bugs behind the stones in her backyard when she'd been little. The way they'd balled up at her touch. His lips peeled in a grimace as his head jerked back to his spine.

She'd already brought her hand down, almost brushing against him, and the hand hovered there, frozen. Her lips tingled. Touch.

"Oh God," she murmured, terror springing tears to her eyes. "Gabe!" Her throat ripped out the name, cracking and choking her off mid-scream.

The door burst open and Gabe fell down next to them.

"What's going on?" Gabe asked, pulling at Az's arm. Az was shivering now, his skin slick and gray. "Eden?"

"Touch. I passed him Touch." She heard a thumping that she thought was her heart before she realized it was the rest of them running to the threshold.

"But . . ." Gabe grew quiet. "Oh!" he whispered, his mouth a surprised oval. He looked down to Az, then back at her. "Oh."

Az's head rolled on his shoulders. "It burns," he said weakly.

"I'm sorry." She would have cried if there'd been time to think about it.

"Why would you do this?" he whispered before he lolled forward again.

"Get him up," she said, uncoiling one of his arms,

yanking his deadweight. "We've got to get him downstairs. He has to spread it."

Gabe looked sick. "He can't."

"What are you talking about?" She strained, trying to lift Az's shoulders.

"He's not a Sider, Eden. He *can't* spread it."

Misery coiled inside her, mirroring his body. *What have I done?* Az shuddered, his breath coming in sharp, shallow gasps.

"This is just the start, Eden." Gabe crouched next to her. "He's constantly fighting the need to complete his Fall. Battling his darkest thoughts." He closed his eyes, lowering his voice. "You know what Touch does."

Az's eyes fluttered open.

They weren't blue anymore. Or the angry red they'd been minutes ago in the bedroom. She could see the vessels, the cord of his optic nerve, the muscles concaving around the back of the orb. He blinked and they flashed obsidian black.

# CHAPTER 44

She grabbed Az's hand. "I'm so sorry. I didn't mean to." Her face crumbled.

He tried to whisper, the words too low to make out. She leaned closer. "You said you hate me. It was all for nothing. Nothing worth staying for."

"No, Az. Please . . ."

"Eden, leave." Gabe pulled her shoulder. "Go!" he yelled. On the bed, Az quaked.

She broke into a sob, his fingers slipping out of hers as she staggered back toward the door.

"Az, look at me." Gabe grabbed his jaw, forced him to make contact, though he couldn't calm him down unless Az was open to it, allowed it. Az blinked hard and stared into Gabe's eyes.

Eden turned, closed the door behind her. She ground her tears away with her palm before she made her way to the kitchen. Jarrod sat at the table by himself.

"He okay?" Jarrod asked.

She shook her head, blinking hard.

"Should be about ten hours until we're out of the woods, right?"

"It's not the same as it is with the mortals. He's fighting against Falling." Her voice broke. She looked around, stepping closer to where Jarrod sat. "Where are Adam and Libby?"

Jarrod was suddenly very interested in the can he was holding. "Adam left right after . . ."

Eden closed her eyes. He knew what she'd done. They all did.

"Did he say anything?" she asked. Jarrod wouldn't look at her.

"Nothing you want to hear."

She flicked her tongue across her lips, rapping her knuckles against the tabletop as she tried to fight a breakdown. "Nothing I don't deserve."

Jarrod glanced up for a second before he went back to the can.

"And Libby?" Eden asked quietly.

"She left a few minutes ago. Didn't say anything. Think she needed air."

She covered her mouth in an attempt to stifle the sob and leaped up, grabbing her coat. She couldn't be there when the door opened again. Couldn't see him that way, broken because she'd given in, wanted to love him again.

Jarrod called her name, but she was already halfway down the second flight of stairs. By the time she'd hit the security door, her phone was going off. She ignored his call, thumbing it to silent.

She stopped short on the stairs. Not a single Sider in sight. *There haven't been any in days*, she realized. What if Luke was right? The Bound knew about them, were taking out the Siders a few at a time. Libby had just left.

Adam.

She had to find them.

Her feet numbed as an hour passed, then another, the cold cutting through her as she wandered the streets. She'd checked Milton's, the alley, and then taken the train aimlessly, getting off at random stops to search. Tried to keep her mind on Adam, but it staggered back to Az every time.

*I'm going to lose him. All over again.* She stopped, leaning against a building, everything inside her raw, ripped open. Hollow. She closed her eyes, but when she did, all she saw was Az's face as he'd gone over the balcony. The emptiness after, swept away and drowning in her grief. What wouldn't she have given in those days for even another minute with him.

*I can't watch him Fall.* But what if he needed her now and she wasn't there? She threaded through the streets toward home, broke into a jog as she turned up the alley. It wasn't empty.

Her brain skipped right over relief and splashed into denial. Libby stood in front of a boy no taller than her. She took his hands. A breeze whipped her hair into corn silk twists as she leaned into his lips. The boy shuddered. And fell.

"That's impossible," Eden said, but her voice betrayed her, shaking. Libby turned toward the sound and smiled. Her toe twirled in some kind of ballet move. What had been left of the Sider crumbled into a swirl of ash. She lifted her arms.

"Ta-da! God, I've been dying to tell you! Especially when you were so upset that you were the only one!" she said, smiling as she dropped her arms back to her sides. "I'm *fairly* positive it's just us, though."

Eden's eyes widened.

"But when I dosed you," Eden said suddenly, clinging to the only evidence of denial she could. "If you were like me, saving it wouldn't . . ." She stopped when she saw Libby's eyes dancing in amusement. "You were so bad."

"I was pretty amazing, wasn't I? Acting classes," she said. "Since I was seven. Lead in the school play three years running. After graduation I was going to make a go of it in Hollywood, but I got a better offer." She flexed her fingers, rolling her wrist with a grimace. "I'd already racked up quite a list of sins by last summer. Then I met Boyfriend and added a few more. I bet you thought you were the only one who could snag an angel, huh?"

"Luke," Eden said. Her brain seemed a dozen steps behind, too slow to keep up. "You didn't have a suicide pact. You're with Luke." She felt sick.

"Turned out I was dating the ultimate bad boy. He was a bit surprised when he checked my path." Libby smiled. "Luke told me everything. Luckily, I decided to let him speed things up." Her eyes were far off, wistful. "My death was so beautiful." She seemed to come back suddenly, pity creeping into her face. "What Az did to you, though? Lying. Manipulating you. Letting you wake up *alone*? I can't even imagine."

"He did it to save me," Eden choked out.

"From the Basement?" Libby's voice brimmed with sympathy. "They're not so bad. Not compared to Az."

Eden shook her head, her eyes tightening into a glower as she tried to stare Libby down. Libby didn't return the glare, but didn't break it either. "I got in with the side that will help us, Eden. The Bound will try to wipe us out. Can't you at least consider changing your mind?"

"Never going to happen."

Libby sighed. "I didn't think so. I'm supposed to pass along a message." She glanced away. "First, Az loves you.

At least, I think he would want me to say so. But I'm supposed to give you—"

"Az?" The name came from Eden's lips, hard and strong.

Libby paused, awkwardly. "Oh God, Eden, I thought you knew. Az is with Luke now."

"He Fell?" The words were barely audible, but loud enough that they brought an uncomfortable giggle from Libby.

"Of course not! No, he's *with* Luke."

"You're bluffing," Eden whispered, swallowing hard. "Az is . . ."

"Struggling to keep from Falling because of what you did?" Libby said gently. "That's where he was when you left. But that was hours ago. It's possible someone rushed into the apartment. Someone who told him he had to come right away. That you were in trouble." Libby fell silent, waiting for Eden to make the connection.

"You," she whispered.

Libby shook her head, dropping her voice. "There's no way I had time. Try again."

Eden's brain ricocheted through the list. Kristen. Jarrod. Adam. She snapped her eyes up to Libby. "Adam?" she said.

Libby reached into the pocket of her white hoodie. "And what a twist *that* was! I didn't think he'd answer my phone call. He was so furious when he left. But once I told him how angel eyes have a tendency to influence and explained Luke's offer to him, he was all for it."

"Adam would never betray me," Eden said, her tongue flicking across her lips.

"He thinks he's protecting you from Az. Blames everything on the eyes." Libby pulled something out of the pocket and held her fist out to Eden. "Right now you're playing it through: would Az have been strong enough to make it out of the apartment, down the stairs? Would Adam have been able to get him out before Gabe noticed? Luke figured you'd find it a bit hard to swallow."

Eden didn't take her eyes off Libby's fist. "What is that," she demanded.

Libby twisted her hand palm up and opened it. A feather twirled between her fingers, matted with maroon.

"It's amazing how much damage a pair of gardening shears can do," Libby whispered, brushing it away and rubbing her hands on her jeans.

Eden's resolve finally crumbled, a stubborn tear tracing down her cheek.

"It doesn't matter. He can heal."

"True, but how much pain can he take before Falling seems like a better option? Especially after you dosed him?" Her eyes drifted down to the feather, swirling in the channeled wind hissing through the alley.

Eden straightened. Her jaw went hard. "Obviously you want something, and you came here, so you want it from me," she said.

"We want you to listen to reason. Luke tried to get you to see. If you had, it would have saved everyone a lot of unpleasantness."

"Okay," she said. "Take me to him. I'll listen this time." She couldn't keep the note of desperation out of her voice.

"No," Libby said. Eden raised her head, surprised. Libby leaned forward, reaching a hand out. Eden flinched as the girl pulled a stray thread from her shoulder.

"Listen, just between us, I think it would be better if you gave him some time to calm down. He's been a little . . . violent . . . lately." She turned, walking down the sidewalk. "Eden, if you're really going to fight us on this, bring whoever you have left to round up. Alone, you have no chance and, well, it won't be pleasant."

"Adam!" Eden called out. "Where is he?"

Libby stopped, waiting for a car to pass before she could cross the street. "Keep your cell handy. We'll be in touch soon."

Somewhere near, the feather would be drifting on the drafts from passing cars, catching in the sludge. She didn't want to find it.

# CHAPTER 45

Gabe jumped from the couch as Eden burst through the front door, relief nearly stopping his heart as he caught her in his arms. "Where were you? Az is gone, Eden! I've been calling you for—"

"They've got him!" A thick warbling sob choked her off. "They have Az!"

He pulled away from her. She swallowed hard, pressing her palms against her eyes. Gabe yanked her hands down, forcing her to look at him. "Who has Az?"

"Luke!" she screamed.

Gabe froze. "How do you know that name?"

"He's Libby's boyfriend! They're both with the Basement!" she said through chattering teeth, her whole body shaking. "I saw her in the alley. Gabe, she can kill Siders!"

"What did she *say*, Eden?" he asked, gripping her shoulders. "Everything. Maybe she gave something away that you didn't catch? Where they are?" He was almost frantic, struggling to keep his words from tangling together.

"It's bad." Her voice broke. "Gabe, it's really bad."

His hands drifted from her shoulders, falling to his sides. The rest of his body crumbled down with them, until he was on one knee, head bowed. *Tell. Tell it all. I've already lost.* He forced the thought away, steadied himself with a shaking hand as he took a deep breath. "Did she say that he'd Fallen?"

She shook her head.

*At least I have her with me*, he thought. *As long as Az knows Luke doesn't have her, he'll hang on.* At least, he would have if he hadn't been dosed. "There's still time," Gabe said. He tried to make his voice strong, sure. "But we have to get to him. Luke will do whatever it takes to break him."

Her eyes darted past him, to the bedroom door. "Jarrod!" she screamed.

"Jarrod left, Eden," he whispered. "He got a call and took off."

Her hands folded against her forehead, hiding her face, the fingers tangling in her hair. "I . . . I lost them."

"What do you mean you lost them?"

"I mean they're"—she hesitated—"they're with Luke now."

"What?" Gabe's rage lifted him, until he was bearing down on her from above.

"It was Adam," she added in a rush. "Adam gave them Az. That's what she said. I'm supposed to wait for her to call," she said, swallowing thickly.

"Oh, fuck that," Gabe seethed. "She expects us to just sit around and wait while they . . ." He didn't finish the thought. "No. We have to do something. We have to find him." He tried to hide the glimmer of maroon he knew flooded his eyes, the anger a quicksilver of colors that would be glistening like an oily sheen.

"How?" He could hear the desolation in her question, the acceptance. They'd lost him. *Az is going to Fall.* He caught the thought as it drifted through her mind. *He's going to Fall because of me.* "I don't know what to do," she said, her voice breaking.

*It's over*, he thought. His throat burned with confessions as he looked at her.

"Your eyes," she said. "They're yellow."

He stepped toward her; for a second he was sure he was going to fall and held his arms out to her. Her hands were enough to steady him.

"There's still time," he said. "We just need a plan."

# CHAPTER 46

"She won't help," Eden repeated yet again. Gabe still hadn't said anything, staring past her out the window of the subway door. They'd sat as close to the door as they could, Eden sandwiched against the bars that kept her on the bench, with Gabe beside her. The car was packed and stifling, bodies in every seat and filling every space. Eden pulled her leg in, twisting it away from the people, closer to Gabe.

If she hadn't heard it from Libby's lips she wouldn't have believed it, would have died defending them, because of loyalty. If anyone had told her a week ago that this was a possibility, she would have laughed. Because of their loyalty to her.

*All lies*, she thought. The memory of Jarrod's words on their walk slithered inside her. She felt like she needed to throw up; anything to get them out of her.

"Gabe," she tried again. "I know her. She won't help."

"You know her," he said. "Now." He smiled at her as if everything should have been clear, and Eden wondered if maybe he'd lost it a little.

Eden shifted in her seat under his gaze. "Exactly," she said. "If there's no incentive for Kristen to get involved, she isn't going to bother."

Gabe sighed and went back to the window, his arm behind her on the back of the plastic bench.

"So we're wasting our time," Eden pressed. She was hoping he'd agree, tell her it was stupid and that they could get off the train at the next stop.

The air was toxic, cologne and perfume and office stink, not nearly enough oxygen. *I'm going to suffocate in here*, she thought again. She gulped in the stale air, trying to slow down her breathing. Her fingers wrapped a death grip around the steel pole. The train lurched and a hand slid over hers. It pulled away near instantly, but it was too late.

Touch slipped out, sending a shudder through her, a long moan humming from her lips. Days. Almost a week without taking a Sider but as soon as their fingers had connected, she felt the power of it, all that poison, all that Touch built up inside her. *I can get rid of it*, she found herself thinking. *Here, now. I can just . . .* Her fingers uncurled like spider legs, inching closer to skin, any skin.

Fingers twined into hers and she dropped her head

back in anticipation, waiting for the release, clenching her teeth, the air that escaped screaming like a steam valve.

But it didn't come. Someone had a tight hold of the hand in her lap now, too.

She looked down. Gabe had a vise grip on her hands, her fingers gone white. She tried to focus.

"Better?" he asked cautiously, as if she would lash out any second and tear through the car. She nodded slowly. "Sure?" he asked.

"I'm sorry," she said automatically. He shook his head, releasing her hands. She rubbed them together, the fingertips still tingling and eager for more.

"I saw. Wasn't your fault. But you need to save it for later." He wrapped an arm around her, pulling her closer to him. She wasn't sure if he wanted to give her some kind of comfort, or just wanted her further from the temptation.

"Can I ask you something?" She waited for his nod before she went on. "What will happen to Az? If he's Fallen?"

Gabe looked away, his words coming slowly. "Are you sure you want to know?"

"I need to." She squeezed his hand, prodding him on.

"His impulses will take over the first few weeks. He'll live off anger, hate. It will be all he knows. He'll cause pain just for the sake of watching another in agony. He'll glory in it. The Az you know will be dead, Eden."

He didn't look back, didn't see the tear slip down her cheek. "Will he remember me?"

"He'll be confused. It's likely he won't remember you at first, but he'll remember me. He'll see me as an enemy. Eden, if Az does Fall, it would be better if he forgot you." Gabe took a deep breath. He finally turned to face her. "But we're not going to let it get to that. We're going to get Kristen's help."

"Gabe," she said, trying to make her voice gentle. "Kristen's heartless."

"Trust me, she's never quite been that. She'll help us if we make it worth her while. Kristen can be an amazing asset when she chooses." His face clouded over. "We need her, Eden."

"She told me she owed you." He nodded. "But she said you were even, because she took me in."

"So I'll owe her. She'll love that," he said, giving her a weak smile. "Kristen hates the Fallen. If it means keeping Az from them, she'll help. And if that's not enough . . ." His expression darkened. "Just trust me. I'll convince her, Eden."

# CHAPTER 47

"Are you out of your fucking minds?" Kristen gripped the dark walnut railing, her face twisted by shadows the roaring fireplace cast. Eden tensed, sure Kristen would go over. Instead she yanked back and came down the stairs like a wash of fluid, the red taffeta of her dress blooming around her.

She pointed to Sebastian, who had ushered Eden and Gabe into the foyer. "You. Go!"

"Kristen," he started, his eyes venturing among the three of them.

"Now!" she demanded. He hesitated, backing away slowly as if waiting for her to suddenly change her mind, decide she wanted him there. Finally, he retreated through the door to the kitchen.

"Hey, Kristen." Gabe smiled apologetically. "Sorry to just drop by unannounced, but I know how much you've missed all your girl time with Eden."

"Don't think I don't know what you want. You asked for an alliance and I specifically told you no. Did. I. Not." She drilled her finger closer to Eden with each sentence. Each word twisted into a hook, barbed to yank Eden out of any hope she had of Kristen making this easy.

"We need you. We need your help," Eden said. "We need your . . ."

"You need my numbers. You need an army and you can't have mine! Did she tell you the Fallen are able to kill Siders?" she spat, her eyes once again on Gabe. "Or was it the Bound, Gabriel? You *knew* she needed to be prepared for this. You knew her abilities would bring them out and yet you did nothing! You said we were immortal!"

"Kristen," he said, his voice calm, as if there was some chance of talking lucidity into her. "You don't know what's . . ."

"Oh, go to Hell, Gabriel," she hissed. "You think I'm so cut off that I don't hear? The Fallen want her and now you just expect me to jump in and protect her? I did my part. She's going to get us exterminated."

"It wasn't an angel!" he yelled. "It was a Sider. She has the same talents as Eden. But this one is loyal to the Fallen."

Kristen scoffed, trying to cover her alarm. "Another one? Wonderful. You gonna send this one my way too?

Though if she's with the Fallen, maybe you can pass her on to Madeline."

"Kristen." His voice was calm, demanding her attention. "'Darest thou now O soul, / Walk out with me toward the unknown region / Where neither ground is for the feet, nor any path to follow?'"

"Whitman? Honestly, Bukowski says it so much better." Kristen took half a dozen steps back, the eyelets of her antique leather boots squeaking against the laces. "'Beware of them; for one of their key words is "love" and beware those who only take instructions from *their* God.'"

Gabe moved toward her, almost too quick to see. Kristen didn't flinch at the hand he laid gently on her cheek. "They have Az, Kristen," he said softly. "They've taken Az."

A look of surprise washed over her face; Eden actually watched her pale as the anger streamed off, her lips falling closed. She opened them again as if she was going to speak, but no sound came out. Instead, the finger that had jabbed angrily at them now dropped in a slow arc.

"He Fell," she said. Eden watched as Gabe ran a hand across Kristen's forehead, smoothing away her brown hair. She'd never seen anyone touch Kristen. Not like that.

"Not yet. But there were complications." He didn't look at Eden, but she felt shame redden her cheeks. "We need to get him back as quickly as possible, Kristen. We need your help."

"Lucifer?" she asked hesitantly. Gabe nodded, and she dropped her head against his shoulder for a second. "Damn him."

Gabe pulled her away from his shoulder. "Kristen. Please." She winced. "Please," he said again.

She closed her eyes, drawing a deep breath. "I won't tolerate your losing Az to the Fallen. Not while I have the chance to steal away that little joy from Luke." She turned away from Gabe to Eden.

"We have to find him." Eden barely recognized her own voice, laced with the dark end that would come to anyone who kept her from Az. She dropped her eyes, couldn't let Kristen see the telltale shine that would reflect the candlelight.

"Anything, Gabriel," Kristen said, finally giving them the answer they'd hoped for. "What do you need to stop Luke?"

# CHAPTER 48

The fire burned. Logs popped as they dissolved into ash. Eden was studying the room, much as she had been for the past two hours. Nothing had changed since the last time she'd been there, the same trinkets collected from who knew where.

Kristen lounged in an overstuffed chair, her head resting on one of the armrests, legs hanging over the other. One of her feet pendulumed, the heel drilling into the crushed velvet upholstery, the momentum carrying the toe of her boot en pointe before it fell again.

Stretched out away from the warmth of the fireplace, Gabe rested his head on his hands.

"Gabe, there's something you should know," Eden said, breaking the silence. "I met with Luke."

Gabe shot ramrod straight on the floor. "What do you mean you 'met with him'?"

She lowered her head. "Libby convinced Adam and Az

to let us have a girls' night. We were supposed to go to the movies and grab something to eat, but we didn't. She took me to Aerie and he was playing. He talked to me."

Gabe shook his head, unbelieving. "Eden, what were you thinking?"

"The second time . . ." she whispered.

"The second time?" he yelled as he stood, throwing his arms down. "How could you *not* tell me this?"

"Like there aren't things you didn't tell me!" she yelled back, her cheeks burning. The fire popped, sending a flurry of sparks up the flue. "Luke said you weren't trying to protect me from him, that you were more worried about the Bound. He said you would be the one to *tell* the Bound. That if you don't you'll be punished." She'd only intended to find out the truth, but he looked absolutely shattered. Only he wasn't looking at her. He was staring at Kristen.

"Gabriel?" Kristen's legs swung slowly to the floor. "What is she talking about?"

"I'm the Messenger, Kristen. You know that. It's my job to go between the worlds, report back."

"Exactly. So what the Hell does she mean you haven't told Upstairs about us?" Kristen said, her voice uncertain. "Az told me you said they'd decided to leave us alone if we behaved, didn't upset the balance." She froze. "Az. You had Az lie because you couldn't."

His eyes flashed to Eden, before going back to Kristen. Gabe sat up with a pained smile. "Perhaps we could change the subject, Kristen?"

"No! I blathered on to Eden about keeping a low profile, staying safe. I thought if she did, they wouldn't see she was different. But we've been in danger of being discovered the whole time? You've told me stories of how the Bound can be when they're crossed! Gabriel, if they find out you knew about the Siders and said nothing." Kristen looked ready to weep. "And then the new information, what Eden can do. You've been resisting this whole time? How?"

"Resolve." He smiled. "I've had a good teacher."

Eden watched, confused at the range of emotions flooding over Kristen's face. "But if you get wings, can't you just go back and explain?" Eden asked.

"It's not that easy, Eden," Kristen answered for him. "He could be banned from here." Gabe climbed off the floor, sat down on the armrest of the chair, and took Kristen's hand.

Kristen squeezed. "You did this for me, didn't you?"

"You will never get as bad as you were when we met you. I promised you, Kristen. I'm trying so hard to keep it." Gabe put his fingers to Kristen's temple.

Eden opened her mouth just as her phone rang.

She pulled the phone from her pocket, forcing herself to let her ring tone nearly finish before connecting the call.

She racked her brain for something to give her the edge, but finally seethed, "Where is he?"

"Easy," Gabe whispered behind her.

"First things first. Most importantly? Az is still alive *and* he's not Fallen," Libby said.

Eden closed her eyes, stifling her moan of relief. "Fair enough. If he hasn't Fallen, I owe you." She could practically hear Libby's smile.

"I'm hoping we can still be friends after this, Eden. I'm *really* hoping we'll be on the same side. Which brings us down to business. We're going to meet at your place. Luke's not in the mood for trouble. The easier the exchange is made, the better. You for Az. If he Falls before then, the deal still stands. Two o'clock tomorrow."

"Two o'clock," Eden repeated. *Fourteen hours?* Her eyes went back to the clock. *Why would they want to wait so long?* Libby spoke again, breaking her thought.

"Oh, and Eden? Silence is golden. Understand?"

A chill ran through her. "I understand," she said, though the phone had already gone dim in her palm. She didn't close it as she spun to Gabe and Kristen.

"Tomorrow?" Gabe asked.

"Do you think he'll last that long?" Kristen adjusted in the chair, turning to face them. The phone was at Eden's hip. She ran her finger down the side, thumbing the Volume button until she was positive it was on silent.

Snapping it shut, she slipped it into her pocket.

"If he makes it through the night," Gabe answered. "Where do they want to meet?"

"At the apartment. I'm not sure if they think we're still there. But that's going to cut down on how many of yours we can bring," she said, turning to Kristen.

They'd hammered out a loose plan by two in the morning, when Kristen insisted Eden and Gabe try to get some sleep. Eden finally looked up at Gabe. What she saw of his eyes between long blinks had faded to pale amber.

Kristen turned to her. "You can take the room at the top of the stairs. I'd offer your old room, but it's . . . occupied at the moment."

"Not a chance. I'm taking the couch." Eden let her come to the conclusion she knew Kristen would, but Eden wasn't thinking about the Screamers. Or the locked doors lining the upstairs hall. Only of how close the couch was to the front door. "Gabe can have the bedroom."

Gabe gave his head a halfhearted shake. "I'm staying with you. I'll sleep fine on the floor." Eden opened her mouth to argue but Gabe cut her off. "Don't. Please?"

She nodded, hoping he was exhausted enough that he'd sleep like the dead.

With the lights out, she concentrated on the sound of Gabe's breathing from the floor until it grew steady. She clutched the warm phone in her fist, under the pillow.

She was trying to make out the hands on the tiny clock on the mantle when numbed vibration hummed against her ear. Slipping the covers over her head to dull the glow, she flipped the phone open. One new text message. With a shaking hand, she hit the OK button.

*Change in plans. Roof. Just you. 10 minutes.*

A second message popped up. It was an address, not far from the apartment.

*Not at home.* She typed out. *Be there in 40 minutes.*

She waited for a reply, the soft tick from the clock on the mantel counting off the seconds. When a full two minutes had passed, she decided to go. Either they had gotten the message and accepted, or she was wasting time.

Eden slid her foot to the hardwood floor, easing across it to keep down the creaks and groans of the boards. Every move seemed to take an eternity. She was almost to the front door when she heard a swish of fabric behind her. She turned.

Kristen arched an eyebrow as Eden's shoulders dropped.

*What are you doing?* Kristen mouthed. Eden pointed to the door, put a finger to her lips, and stepped out onto the porch. Kristen followed.

"They want me there now. Don't tell Gabe?" Eden

whispered, casting a glance through the tiny window to the still sleeping form next to the couch.

"It's too dangerous, Eden."

"They want me alone. We don't have time to come up with something better." Kristen closed her eyes. "Kristen, I'm going."

"Where are you meeting them?"

Eden hesitated. "They gave me an address." She pulled her phone from her pocket, flipped it open, and showed her the text. Kristen stared at the screen until Eden slipped the phone back into her pocket, pivoting to head down the porch stairs.

She startled as Kristen wrapped her arms around her, twisting her back around and pulling her to her lips.

Eden's stomach careened, the Touch Kristen passed into her rocking her onto her toes. She would have fallen if it wasn't for the grip on her wrist.

Every movement shimmered with pain. Eden clutched her stomach with her free hand, trying to find her equilibrium again.

"Focus. Take it in," Kristen said, her voice trembling as she pulled away. "I've been storing, having the Screamers dose me. That's everything I have."

The yard looked sharper, everything different. Eden took a long breath.

"Better now?"

Eden nodded slowly, and the world wobbled. Kristen slumped, her knees giving out, caught herself on the doorframe before she fell. Eden moved to help her, but she shook her head, leaning heavily against the wall.

"Luke doesn't make deals out of the kindness of his heart, Eden. Do not trust him," Kristen whispered.

Eden took a careful step down, still dizzy. "Thank you," she said.

Kristen looked over her shoulder, to the floor beside the empty couch. "I'll have to tell him where you went. The best I can offer you is a head start."

Eden turned, ready to head down the darkened street when Kristen's voice cut through the silence.

"'Hope' is the thing with feathers—/That perches in the soul—/And sings the tune without the words—/And never stops—at all."

# CHAPTER 49

Eden's mind fluttered through the subway ride, up the stairs, guts writhing in agony. She'd never carried so much Touch.

She flashed back to the rave as her feet dragged across the asphalt, how she'd lost control in the crowd. She'd felt fine before that first brush of skin, and then everything had to spill out. Clutching her hands tighter into her pockets, she whimpered every time someone passed within reach. She repeated Az's name, a hushed soundtrack to close the world out.

Her eyes wouldn't stay down, scrambling across the bare flesh peeking out from behind scarves. Ungloved hands sent a shiver through her. Though it wasn't yet six, the more popular parts of the city would be bustling. Luckily, Libby hadn't sent her to Times Square or anything. The weaker her resistance to passing Touch got, the louder his name left her lips. The louder she was, the crazier she seemed to the few passersby. She must have looked more wrecked than she felt if New Yorkers were avoiding her.

Soon there was no one. The buildings were decrepit shells, windows and doors boarded shut. There weren't addresses, but she knew she had to be getting close. Her pace slowed. Around her, the silence of dawn had settled in. The lack of noise sent her hackles up. It was never quiet, not even in these parts of the city.

The streets were clear. Eden peered warily down the spaces between the buildings, each one cluttered with windblown trash.

Against the rust of a fire escape ladder, a flash of white caught her eye. She took a last look around and stepped closer.

Scotch taped to the last rung, a row of feathers dangled by their quills. Each one had been chopped, sheared apart. The two largest, almost as long as her arm, had been sliced in half vertically. The tips were shorn off others, leaving the feather shaft a skeletal spine. She lifted her hand, cringing as they etched across her palm. From above came a scream.

*I can't do this*, she thought, but her hands were already grasping the rung, her feet digging into the wall for purchase as she hoisted herself up.

The scream came again, louder. It was Az. She

quickened her climb, the rusting metal flaking onto her fingers. When she reached the roof, she threw herself over the lip and onto the wrinkled tar paper.

Adam, Jarrod, and Luke were in a line thirty feet away, their eyes already on her. In front of them, Az was tied to a chair, shirtless, head bowed. His back was to her. Libby stood next to him, her hand hidden where he'd doubled over. A moan rose out of him before he fell silent again.

Eden stumbled forward, fists curled tight as she took him in. Whip marks gaped where they intersected, weeping down his pale skin. His mangled wings clung tight into the hollow that housed them, the scant traces of the feathers left broken and tattered.

"Stop," Luke commanded. "She's here."

Libby pulled away. In her fist, the gardening shears reflected wetly in the first strains of sunrise.

Az's shoulders strained, his head bobbing as he struggled to lift it.

"No," he moaned. Luke made his way to the chair, rocked it onto its back legs, and turned Az to face her. She couldn't stop her feet, couldn't take her eyes from his broken face. Every step brought his wounds into sharper clarity. An eyebrow jutted in a broken line, the cut forcing the eye closed. A distorted patch of dark purple bruised from cheekbone to temple, yellow green at the edges where it had tried to heal. The marks from her own fingernails, where she'd slapped him, stood out unhealed.

"Az." Her voice broke on the syllable, cracking in her throat. A single, desperate word slid through his split lips.

"Run."

*Never*, she thought.

Libby lifted his head, giving Eden a better view. "She's not going anywhere," she said consolingly. "Eden's here now. We can stop."

For the first time Eden's attention went to the others lined up behind the chair. Only two of them mattered. Jarrod had turned away, but Adam was staring back at her, his eyes full of fire.

"You came for him," he said. A shadow crossed his face, a mixture of the hurt and pain he was trying to conceal. "It wasn't just the eye trick, was it?" Eden felt no pity. Libby left Az's side and threw an arm around Adam's shoulders.

"You fucking traitor," Eden seethed.

"Me? I wasn't making out with my ex behind your back! You . . ."

Libby plinked her finger against his nose. Adam turned to her in surprise.

"You," she picked up, "have served your purpose. Spare us your little Emo speech."

Libby gripped his collar. He was already off balance when she gave it a yank.

As Libby's lips neared his, his eyes met Eden's. She saw him take the breath in. Saw his brown irises flare, fall gray as he stumbled backward, his arms and legs dimming to spent ash. By the time he should have hit the ground, there was nothing left.

Jarrod took a step, faltered, his hand held out as if he could strain Adam out of the breeze. The ashes twirled, a blurred whirlwind.

"I warned you that you'd lose more of your friends, didn't I?" Luke's voice was tender. "If you'd only listened, none of this would have had to happen. Such a shame." He brushed back Libby's hair to kiss her cheek.

"You did so well," he whispered in her ear. Libby blushed.

"Where's Gabriel, Eden?" Luke asked, giving a chummy grin that made her skin crawl.

She kept her eyes down. "I came alone. I did what you said."

"I thought you'd at least have some plan." Luke almost seemed disappointed. "See, Eden, you and my girl have a talent in common. Both so cunning." His face lit up with pride. "With you being so closely watched, I was concerned about Libby. Honestly, we planned on pulling her out of there much sooner. But she spoke so highly of you. Said you two were friends. You have to admire anyone who can crack that shell of yours, right? I mean, poor

Adam there . . ." He pointed to his left, confusion on his face when the space proved empty. "Well, there . . ." he said, his finger twirling lazily through the air.

"Anywho . . . Even Adam never really had a chance." He strolled slowly toward Az. "Because of this one." He ruffled Az's soaked curls. She wasn't naïve enough to believe it was sweat twisting his hair into tight spirals.

"Eden, go." Az racked out a cough, a glob of pink phlegm hitting the ground at his feet.

"Aw. She would never leave you!" Luke said cheerily, giving Az's jaw a rough squeeze. He spun to Eden, his features sharpened with the potential of untapped cruelty. "Would you, Eden?"

She froze.

Az coughed weakly. They all turned to him, though Eden was the only one who wore a look of concern. Luke waited for him to stop before he went on.

"I tracked the Siders Libby killed. The fact that I was *able* to track them should tell you enough, being as I only have access to one set of records."

"Mine aren't going Downstairs," Eden said. The hard edge in her voice startled her, but she didn't let it show.

"I assumed the Siders were going Downstairs because they were damned, pathless. But it's dangerous, relying on assumptions. Almost a sin." Luke took a step toward Eden. "Did you ever get around to asking your boy here about how you came to be?" The look on Eden's face gave him the answer he needed.

Az shook his head, too tired to lift it or speak.

At his side, Libby's hand twitched, ready and eager.

"Az won't tell me what happened on the beach." Luke held out his hands. "Perhaps you can enlighten us?" Luke's head dipped in a subtle nod. "Libby, convince Eden to tell the truth."

Eden went rigid as the blades flashed closer to Az. "You harm a single hair on his head and I swear . . ."

Libby ran her free hand through his dark curls, revulsion and terror swarming in Az's eyes at her touch.

Libby squeezed the handles together as she yanked up a handful of hair. With a dull snip, the curls fell from Libby's fingers, scattering. "It wasn't even painful. You should just tell the truth, Eden. It's only going to get worse for Az. Don't make me hurt him."

Luke ran a finger over the broken skin of a wing and Az winced. "If you'd feel more comfortable, Eden, you can always convince him to Fall. There's room for both of you on my team."

"No." Eden kept her eyes on the shears in Libby's hand, the tips grazing Az's scalp. "You said it would be a fair trade. Let him go."

"You haven't convinced me of your loyalty yet, Eden," Luke said sadly. "I just don't feel like I can trust you."

"What do you want from me?" She looked from him to Libby.

"I want you to answer my question, Eden," Luke said. "You were with Az in the hotel. I watched you walk in. An hour later I found you on the beach, dead. What happened in between?"

"I don't remember," she insisted. She hesitated, shot a desperate glance at Az, and moved on to Jarrod. He met her gaze, his eyes intense. *Lie*, Jarrod mouthed. Eden froze.

"What was that?" Luke strode across the roof. He caught Jarrod by the throat. "What did you tell her?" he asked.

"Nothing!" Jarrod forced out.

"I don't believe you," Luke said.

Eden's mind flashed back to the park and his pledge of loyalty. But what had he been doing with Adam? Spying? What was she supposed to lie about if she really couldn't remember?

"Let them go, Luke!" The voice materialized behind Eden.

"Gabriel," he said, adjusting his grip, twisting Jarrod against him as he spun toward the fire escape Gabe had climbed. "Finally!"

"You okay, sweetheart?" he asked Eden. She nodded, but kept her eyes on Libby.

"Your timing is perfect. Eden and I were just having a chat while we waited for you," Luke said.

*Waited?* Eden thought.

Behind her, Eden heard a soft cry from Az. Fire in Gabe's eyes.

"Libby, shears," Luke yelled. She threw them high over Eden's shoulder, and Luke snagged them from the air. "How did you die, Eden?" Luke asked. He shifted his grip on Jarrod, drawing the blade across his shirt. The fabric split with a gush of red. Jarrod screamed. "Tell us how you died."

She saw Gabe flinch, her eyes darting between him and Luke. Eden shook her head. Luke yanked Jarrod's hand, catching it between the blades, squeezing the handle to keep it there.

"Don't! Please! Okay," she croaked, tears filling her eyes, her hand held out. "Someone killed me." She blinked, sending the tears coursing down her cheeks.

"And who do you think did it, Eden?"

She hesitated, shot a glance at Gabe before going back to Jarrod. Blood streamed from his hand.

"Answer, or I help myself to his fingers." Jarrod's eyes bulged in fear, found Eden.

Eden swallowed hard. "Az," she moaned. "Az killed me."

Gabe didn't move. She waited for him to react, but his features stayed hard and drawn tight, only the sudden sadness of his eyes giving away that he'd heard at all.

"Eden, I'm feeling generous. Would you like to save your friend?" Luke smiled, his eyes cruel. She nodded dumbly. "Even if it means taking his place?"

"No!" Gabe shouted.

Eden's stomach churned. She nodded, walking slowly toward Luke. With so much Touch, Luke could do his worst. It didn't matter. She'd take the pain. Heal. She could free Jarrod.

Eden edged closer. Luke spun, tossing Jarrod aside and ripping her into his arms. She screamed at the sudden movement. The shears against her throat cut off the sound, the blades leaving shallow cuts as she trembled. Luke turned his attention to Gabe, tightened his arm around Eden. "She lets her friends suffer before she spills her secrets. How much will you make her suffer before you spill yours?"

Gabe's foot crunched against the buckled tar as he took a step forward. "Az killed her, Luke. Is that all you need to hear?"

The words stung. Hearing Gabe say them was even worse, knowing there was no chance of them being untrue. She shook as the blade moved from her neck, up her cheek. The point stopped beside her eye. Eden froze.

"Luke, don't." Gabe sounded desperate.

"Gabriel!" Luke chided. "I don't want to hear Az's

secrets." He leaned his head against Eden's. She gasped as the blade sunk into the skin beside her eye socket. "I want to hear yours."

Eden tried to keep her head still, flicked her eyes to Gabe.

"I don't have any."

Luke tsked. "See, Gabriel, that's the problem with lying. It's a skill. Doing it well takes practice." He twirled the tip of the shears closer to Eden's eye, digging. She winced as the trickle of blood thickened, coursing over her cheek, dripping from her chin in double time. "Spill it, or I carve out her eyes." Gabe hesitated, his eyes shifting from maroon to gold and back. "If you'd like," Luke added, "I'll save them for you in a jar."

"No, you've had your fun. Let her go," Gabe whispered, looking sick. He snapped his hand back, hooking the back of his shirt and yanking it off in a single motion. Eden gasped. A rush of feathers surrounded him as his wings expanded.

# CHAPTER 50

Gabe staggered, the weight of the ungainly things throwing him off balance. He'd had them almost an hour and still had no idea how Az made them look so graceful. He swallowed, trying to catch his breath. It'd taken him forever to run the last few blocks and climb the damn fire escape. Already he missed the easy instantaneous travel of the Bound. Clearly, there was a lot to learn. Not that he would. The wings wouldn't be there long.

Az had talked about how it felt, the pull of both worlds while he was between them, the constant pressure of making a choice. Gabe felt none of it, the skin of his back yanking tight as his left wing dipped. Instead there was only the ease of words, the intrinsic knowledge of how simple it would be to speak them aloud, to come clean. To be free of it. He straightened the wing, this time using the correct muscles without a second thought.

"Like the new look?" Gabe stepped back, taking a

deep breath. "I told the Bound. Now let her go or we can add wrath to my list." The violence seemed to fill him, strengthen him. He felt strange, free. Threats bubbled into his head, the horrible things he could do if he chose. Everything about Upstairs, it all felt far away. Foreign. On the rooftop, everything felt…consequenceless. "I said let her go, Luke."

He glanced to Eden again. Her mouth hung open, Luke's arm around her, the shears near her cheek now. Gabe cast up a useless prayer that she would be strong enough to seize the moment, use the distraction to make a move. Az was still tied to the chair. Eden hadn't moved. Everything rested on her. He could only buy so much time.

"Is that all, Gabe?" Luke smiled. Gabe hesitated, unsure for the first time. Luke's eyes were locked on him, prey caught but not yet devoured. "Libby's Siders are Downstairs when she finishes them. She's *tied* to me, Gabriel. But if Eden's tied to Az, why couldn't I find hers?"

Luke stepped closer.

"You know," Gabe whispered.

Az yanked up on the bindings, his face pale but for the crimson leaking from his eyebrow, sliding down across the gouge marks on his cheek. "Gabe, no! Don't say anything!"

Gabe silenced himself. Why was it so easy to say these things?

But it would be so easy. It made sense. The power was there for the taking; all he had to do was come clean. Such a little detail. A shiver thrilled its way down his spine, the wings quivering as if they were a separate entity, a parasite feeding off the dark admissions under the surface, begging to be spoken. The wings were a flaw, a sign that things were incomplete. That there was more to be done. He wanted them off. Gone.

"What did you do, Gabe?" he heard Eden gasp.

"She's tied to me, Luke," he said, his voice drowsy, his head full of cotton. He could feel Eden's eyes on him, heavy with uncertainty. He met them.

"Gabriel," Az yelled, sudden strength in his voice, drawn out by sheer desperation. "Please, listen to me! Fight it! Don't say it!"

But the desire burned too strong. *Confess*, it whispered. *Fall. Be glorious.* His voice came out strong, the truth behind it undeniable. "I murdered Eden."

The confession sent a rush of hot shame across his tongue. He stopped, swallowing hard.

"It's not true! Gabe's just trying to protect me!" Az yanked up on his bound arms. "He's lying!"

"I did it for Az," Gabe said, lifting a shaking hand. "I couldn't let him lose the wings. If you'd gotten a hold of Eden, he would have."

Luke's head tilted, a smile playing at his lips. "I thought

so. As soon as Eden said she was sending them Upstairs. After that, it was only a matter of getting you to admit it aloud." He loosened his arm, setting Eden down gently before turning his attention back to Gabe. She curled, rolling onto her knees, crawling away. Luke made no move to follow.

Gabe's mouth felt like it was on fire. He'd failed. It'd all gone wrong. "I meant no harm," he whispered, turning to Eden. She'd made it a few yards across the roof to Jarrod, sat looking back at Gabe in shock.

His lungs burned. He choked out a breath, sure he heard the crackle of fire in his chest.

Great plumes of rippled steam rushed from him and the taste of disappointment slid out across the enamel of his teeth. His met Az's eyes, terror widening them until they were almost comical. They both knew what was happening. It had taken centuries for Az's fire to burn out, for him to go cold, but for Gabe it was happening all at once. *So, this is what it feels like when Heaven leaves you.*

Fallen. *Now*, he thought frantically, eyes darting to Eden. *Do something.*

*Forgive me.* It was his last thought before the shudder ripped through him, a slosh of frozen spray sliding across his insides, filling him.

*It doesn't even hurt*, he marveled just before the first spasm of pain ripped through his shoulders, dropping him to his knees. The root of each feather, like a barbed hook, shredded his flesh as it pulled free. They scattered across the rippled tar and plummeted over the edge. His skin burned as the puckered leftovers of the wings collapsed. The bones disintegrated, digging their way into his back, the flesh ripping and stitching itself back together. His scream broke the air.

# CHAPTER 51

It *wasn't Az.*

Gabe. The whole time it had been Gabe.

Her eyes went first to Az, still in the chair, crossed over Libby and Jarrod, and finally settled on Gabe. His shoulders twitched, the skin there still rippling beneath the surface. But the sudden terror she felt had nothing to do with Gabe. Luke was looking at him. His eyes blazed.

He moved, cast a hand down toward Gabe's shoulder. Gabe hadn't noticed. His fingers dug into the black goo on the roof. She wanted to scream, to warn him, but nothing came. A frantic search of the roof and she saw no one had moved. Jarrod was the first to attack.

He wasn't going for Luke.

Jarrod's dive caught Libby around the shoulders, the momentum dragging her down practically onto Eden's lap. Libby grunted in surprise as she crashed hard against the tar paper. A snap cut through the air, the arm she'd raised too late to catch herself bent unnaturally between wrist and elbow. Her scream was piercing, but not loud enough to blot out Jarrod's shout.

"Do it, Eden!" he roared as he landed on top of Libby, rolling until he was behind her and yanking her arms back. He cringed as the slice on his chest pulled open, but he jutted his knee into her spine, thrusting her face out toward Eden. Libby's eyes went wild as she tried to twist free. She knew exactly what Jarrod wanted done.

"Eden! Now!" Jarrod screamed.

Eden's hand drew back, then rushed forward with more strength than she should have had. Her palm crushed into the base of Libby's nose. A wet, disintegrating crunch let it carry further.

A shocked spurt of red choked out of Libby. Now she had no choice but to breathe through her mouth. Eden pounded another punch into Libby's face for the hell of it. Her fingers dug into Libby's flushed cheeks, sliding and tangling into her hair.

Catching hold, Eden squeezed her hands into fists, ignored the pop of detaching follicles as she dragged Libby's face to hers. Jarrod glanced over her shoulder. He jerked in surprise.

"Eden, quick-like?" he pressed. A growl of rage that could only belong to Luke lanced through the air. He'd spotted them.

Concentrating, Eden held down Libby's hands as Libby struggled against Jarrod's grip. A breath out. Libby's chin lifted with the next respiration. A cloud of condensation burst from Eden's lips in the cold, swirling between them before the vapors were dragged down Libby's throat.

Gray fringes veined across Libby's forehead, wound up her neck to cloak her chin.

"Get away from her!" Luke screamed, his weight slamming Eden to the ground, crushing her shoulder into her collarbone. He scrambled off, her vision swimming before the world snapped back into focus.

From where she lay she could see Gabe, bloodied but rallying. All that was left of Libby was a greasy smear of gray. Luke tumbled into it, rolling onto Jarrod, clamoring over him in a scuttling half run across the roof. Eden's brain spit out the first answer—They'd won! He was running away!—before her eyes jumped the ten feet ahead to where he was running.

Still in the chair, Az yanked against the ropes that tied his wrists, his palms pulling up. They made a rather pathetic shield as Luke hammered into him.

The chair had been rickety and half rotted, a last minute addition dragged up from one of the abandoned buildings nearby. It splintered under the weight of them when it hit the ground. Az's arms flailed, the broken stakes that used to be the chair's arms bound to his wrists.

Eden took off at a dead run, but Luke had Az in a choke hold. By the time she got close, he'd backed them near enough to the edge that Eden faltered and slowed. Loose gravel skittered as Gabe and Jarrod flanked her from behind.

Her breath caught, choking off, every muscle in her body cramping at once. Libby's Touch was working its way into her.

Luke's eyes burned crimson, intense enough to cauterize, darting between the three of them. Yanking Az with him, Luke slid back six inches until his boot heel ground against the concrete lip running around the roof. Only a foot high, it would be easy to stumble over. Or throw someone over.

"No," Eden whispered. The memory of the fight on the balcony, of all the seconds she'd wasted as he'd gone over. The taste of bile slicked the inside of her cheeks. He was injured already. He wasn't healing. She stared at Az, willing him to open his eyes as pain tore up her arms, across her chest. It was nothing compared to what Az must have felt. He made no effort to break free, didn't claw at the crooked elbow at his neck. His eyes stayed closed. Eden wondered if he'd given up. *Don't Fall*, she thought, desperately.

She'd tensed to take the first step toward them but paused when Gabe spoke.

"Why does he have Az?" Gabe whispered from behind her. She paused, confused before she focused again on Luke.

"How much more pain do you think he can take?" Luke asked. "And falls are painful, aren't they, *Gabe*." He tightened his hold on Az.

Az was finally trying to stand, his knees still half bent but holding him up, his head just below Luke's chin. He gave his hands a weak shake. Below the cord, his fingers had purpled. The broken arms of the chair still dug into the flesh of his arms. He curled his fingers behind the curved balls, jutting out past his wrists like an extra appendage. Az opened his eyes, searching Eden out.

"Why are you fighting this, Eden?" Luke asked, but Eden couldn't take her eyes from Az, his lips. They were moving, forming soundless words. "If Az Falls, you two can be together. I give you my word." It almost looked as if Az was mimicking Luke, but the words didn't quite match. She squinted.

Unconsciously, she took a step forward.

Luke shot a pointed finger up as she moved. "Don't come any . . . !"

Az's hand flashed, the balled end of the broken chair arm smashing Luke on the chin, his head flying back. Az raised his other arm and dropped through the loop of Luke's loosened grip. He hit the ground with a hard *oof,* already crawling, even before his knees made contact.

Luke gave his head a rough shake, but there wasn't enough time to recover before Jarrod crashed into him. They teetered on the ledge, a whirl of arms before Jarrod pushed his hands into Luke's chest—the last momentum needed to topple them both over the edge.

"No!" Eden yelled. She leaped for Jarrod's arm, barely caught it in time. His head snapped up, eyes panicked as his body hit the building. Her fingernails scraped his skin, his other hand whipping up, trying to catch her hand as her grip slipped down to his wrist. "Jarrod!" For a second she thought she had him, but his fingers slid through hers.

She tipped over the edge, one hand stretching into the empty air as he dropped. The other desperately swatted away the hands grasping her waist. A tangle of arms wrapped around it, pulling her back.

Ten stories below, the two bodies laid on the debris in a shattered heap.

"He's moving," Az said from beside her. Luke wriggled out from under Jarrod's legs, flopping them off to the side.

"We gotta get down there. I gotta dose Jarrod. He'll need more Touch to heal." She winced, spasms cramping her abdomen. "I have to get rid of some too."

Luke's face snapped up. He reached for Jarrod's face, yanking the jaw back and forth before Luke dropped his hand. The deadweight of Jarrod's head smacked back against the ground.

Even from the roof she could make out the smile twisting Luke's mouth.

"It's a start," he yelled up, his voice ricocheting between the buildings, the threat echoing in doubles. He rose slowly as if testing his limbs to make sure they still worked, then lifted Jarrod over his shoulder. "We're not done, love," he promised before he winced, an arm slung tight across his ribs. He only made it a few steps before he fell to his knees.

"You're fucking right we're not done," Eden yelled, her hands curled over the edge. She clambered to her feet. "Gabe! Come on! He's headed out of the alley!" Gabe stared at her blankly, like she spoke something close to, but not quite, English.

"What are you waiting for! If he takes Jarrod, he'll torture him!"

Gabe moved toward her. The look in his eyes shifted something inside her, her blood running cold. His head tipped to the left, the angle strange, almost avian.

Az stepped closer to her. "Careful. He's not himself right now."

"I don't care what he did, Az." She moved forward, shaking her hand free when Az grabbed for it. "Gabe, I forgive you. It doesn't matter anymore. But we need to go get Jarrod now." Eden bolted across the roof, down the rusted ladder, not waiting for Az with his wounded limp.

Luke hadn't made it far. He kneeled half a dozen paces from where Jarrod leaned up against a wall. Eden kept an eye on Luke as she dropped down, leaned in to dose Jarrod with Touch.

"That should help. Give it a minute." She squeezed his shoulders. "You okay?"

"Okay is a bit of a stretch. Not so tight." She pulled back enough to catch his pained smile and settled for a death grip on his hands. "I was so right," he said.

"About what?" Eden asked, confused.

"Skin and concrete. So don't mix." Jarrod grimaced.

"Don't come any closer." At Az's voice, she looked up, her smile faltering. Luke swayed on his feet.

"What're you gonna do?" he challenged, a bubble of blood popping from his mouth to coat his chin red.

"He couldn't carry me," Jarrod said. "He's bluffing."

Eden's eyes flicked to Az. He hesitated. "You can barely stand. It's over, Luke."

Luke smeared his hand across his lips, fresh blood coloring the skin even as he wiped it clean. He gave a resigned nod.

"For now. Two out of three isn't so bad." He started to stumble away, holding himself up on the wall.

"Eden isn't yours," Az called after him.

Luke looked back. "Gabe made her. Her Siders go Downstairs now."

Then he turned the corner. Eden shuddered. It was over. She felt Az's arm at her waist, turned into his arms.

"I thought I was going to lose you," she said, tucking her head onto his shoulder. He rubbed a hand down her back, ran the fingers of his other through her hair.

"Never." He pulled back, gazing into her eyes. "I love you."

She ached to kiss him, knew she couldn't. "I love you too."

He leaned forward, pressing his lips against her forehead. She closed her eyes. *Is this all we'll be able to have?*

"Az," she said quietly. "Was Luke right? About my Siders going Downstairs."

She wasn't sure he would answer, but he whispered, "I don't know. I think he might be." He wrapped his arms around her again. "We'll make sure before you take any more Siders, okay?" Eden thought about Libby, crumbling into nothing. *Too late*, she thought.

Jarrod let out a long moan. She pulled out of Az's arms, dropping down to him. "You all right?"

"Everything hurts," he mumbled, his breaths sharp, erratic pulls for air. His skin was pale.

"Jarrod needs rest. Help me get him up." Eden glanced past Az as they struggled to get Jarrod to his feet. "Where's Gabriel?"

"He Fell, Eden."

"I know that. But where is he now?"

Az wouldn't look at her, shrugged a shoulder under Jarrod's arm to take on more of his weight. When Az spoke, his voice came out quiet and broken.

"There is no Gabriel anymore."

# EPILOGUE

Hovering behind them, Gabe let his gaze wander to Az. Az he knew.

Az he could count on, even if he was only half Fallen. Gabe stepped forward. The black-haired girl, pink strands twisting wild. The boy who'd swan dived off the roof.

The girl was next to Az. Did she belong to him? He held a hand out, but stopped when he caught the look of caged fear in Az's wary glance back, the way he moved to put himself between Gabe and the girl.

Gabe tensed. Something was wrong. Why was Az protecting a mortal? They were such dispensable, delicate toys.

Gabe stepped back from them slowly.

The girl was . . . Vague, foggy memories rose like bubbles in a tar pit, never quite reaching the surface, caught under a layer of sticky darkness. The memory of her was trapped in there somewhere. She felt safe, harmless but . . . not. He inhaled, searching the air for clues, thoughts. An old habit? Either way it didn't work.

But the girl? His head pounded as he tried to put it together. Eden. Her name. It had to be. Whenever she spoke, it rang through him like a melody. She, Eden, was sitting up now, getting to her feet. Az reached out, grabbed her hand. There was kindness on her face when she glanced at Az, a blatant weakness that dulled the curves of cheekbones with such potential for cruelty. So wasteful.

Gabe stood back from their little group. He had no reason to stay any longer.

The others didn't notice his absence. They were not his kind. He wandered off toward the street. He could sense wicked beings, dark like him, huddled in the dim recesses of the dilapidated buildings flanking the blacktop. The possibility of wicked things was crisp on his tongue, begging to be tasted.

Squinting through the dim shades of morning, Gabe followed the cracked sidewalk alone.

# ACKNOWLEDGMENTS

Thanks go out to my made-of-awesome agent, Rosemary Stimola, who believed in this book even when it was missing rather important pieces (like . . . the first hundred or so pages) and for finding it the perfect home at Greenwillow. And to my editor, Martha Mihalick, and her mighty Editorial Pencil of Doom for pushing me harder and farther than I ever thought I could go. Both my book and I thank you for it.

Thanks to my mom and dad, my sister Marley, and my brother John, who've shown me crazy amounts of support, and to Heather Aslaksen who (somehow) kept me sane(-ish) by knowing the exact moment to smile and to nod when I started talking about plot holes. To Erin, Anna, and Devyn, for always being up for adventure, and to Jacinda, for giving Luke a song to sing. To Tracy Corso, who kept my secrets in the vault and who I'm sure is the only boss to let an employee stay home and write if the words were flowing. To the whole crew at QueryTracker, especially Patrick, Jason, Mary, and Jess, who kept me going, and to Chris McDonald for being one of my first readers. To the YA Rebels, past, present, and future, for being awesome.

And to Scott Tracey, who uttered the words, "At least he made an impact" to start our friendship, the line "Skin and concrete do not mix" to start this book, and who more times than I can count has picked up my pieces and set me back on the ledge. Thanks.